"You've been avoiding me all day."

"I'm doing the job you hired me for," Kendra reminded Levi.

"You know very well that we left yesterday's conversation unfinished."

"But what's left to say, Levi? That there was a misunderstanding? That your intentions weren't as nefarious as I imagined?"

"Yes. Exactly. Do you realize how much that changes things between us?"

"It changes nothing. No matter what our intentions were, they don't alter the fact that you bought out my father and sent him on a gambling binge. Good intentions don't change what happened."

"They might change how you feel about me. About us."

"There is no us."

Testing the theory, he stepped closer to her. "Are you sure about that?"

She opened her mouth to speak. To argue?

Then, Kendra shocked the hell out of him by closing the inch separating them to seal her lips to his.

An excerpt from *Stranded with a Cowboy* by Stacey Kennedy

"What do you need, Nora?"

"The pleasure those eyes promised me the second I met you," Nora answered.

"What happens after I give you the pleasure you're looking for?" Beau asked.

"I go to Paris."

"So, you want a fling?"

"I want to be with a man where it doesn't end in disaster. I want to feel good."

"Why?"

"Because I've always been a romantic at heart. But I want to feel a man's touch where it doesn't end with me brokenhearted."

"Who says I won't break your heart?"

"Because you're not looking for love. You've already found the love of your life. Besides, Adeline told me that you haven't been in a serious relationship since Annie. I mean, if a relationship is what you're looking for, then obviously, this can't happen."

"I can handle just sex, Nora."

"Well, good. So, that's a yes, then?"

USA TODAY BESTSELLING AUTHORS

JOANNE ROCK
&
STACEY KENNEDY

———

THE RANCHER'S PLUS-ONE
&
STRANDED WITH A COWBOY

HARLEQUIN
DESIRE

Recycling programs
for this product may
not exist in your area.

ISBN-13: 978-1-335-45759-2

The Rancher's Plus-One & Stranded with a Cowboy

Copyright © 2023 by Harlequin Enterprises ULC

The Rancher's Plus-One
Copyright © 2023 by Joanne Rock

Stranded with a Cowboy
Copyright © 2023 by Stacey Kennedy

For questions and comments about the quality of this book,
please contact us at CustomerService@Harlequin.com.

Harlequin Enterprises ULC
22 Adelaide St. West, 41st Floor
Toronto, Ontario M5H 4E3, Canada
www.Harlequin.com

Printed in U.S.A.

CONTENTS

USA TODAY bestselling author **Joanne Rock** credits her decision to write romance to a book she picked up during a flight delay that engrossed her so thoroughly, she didn't mind at all when her flight was delayed two more times. Giving her readers the chance to escape into another world has motivated her to write over one hundred books for a variety of Harlequin series.

Books by Joanne Rock

Harlequin Desire

Kingsland Ranch

Rodeo Rebel
The Rancher's Plus-One

Texas Cattleman's Club

The Rancher's Reckoning
Make Believe Match

Return to Catamount

Rocky Mountain Rivals
One Colorado Night
A Colorado Claim

Visit the Author Profile page
at Harlequin.com for more titles.

You can also find Joanne Rock on Facebook,
along with other Harlequin Desire authors,
at Facebook.com/HarlequinDesireAuthors!

Dear Reader,

One of my favorite parts of writing a series is getting to return to the same setting and group of characters. When I love a place and the people, I don't want to leave them!

This month, I'm back in Silent Spring, Montana, to check in with the Kingsley family at Kingsland Ranch. Levi Kingsley, the oldest of the clan, is in a tough situation as he tries to hold the family together in the wake of some seriously bad PR. Luckily, he knows a PR-crisis expert. Not so lucky? Their one-night stand didn't end well! So when he asks Kendra Davies for help, she sets some important terms before she'll consider taking the job.

I hope you enjoy this return to Kingsland Ranch as much as I have! Remember, you can visit me at my website, www.joannerock.com, to learn more about my upcoming series.

Happy reading,

Joanne Rock

THE RANCHER'S
PLUS-ONE

Joanne Rock

For my oldest son, Taylor,
trailblazer and natural-born leader.
Thank you for inspiring me to try new things.

One

Across his desk in the Kingsland Ranch office, Levi Kingsley's brother Quinton glared at him over black boots he'd propped on one corner of the mahogany.

"If you don't contact her, I will," Quint threatened, pointing at Levi with his cell.

Her. Just thinking about the woman ratcheted Levi's stress level along with his pulse. But he refused to borrow trouble yet.

Of Levi's three brothers, Quinton was the least likely to argue with him. Quint did his own thing, pulling his weight at Kingsland Ranch while quietly starting a tech company on the side. He never complained about the workload and he performed his duties with care, even though Levi happened to know

Quint had been itching to move on from Kingsland for all of his adult life.

So it was a surprise when the guy dug in his heels about anything, let alone decided to oppose him. Levi sure as hell hoped he came around because Quinton Kingsley took a long time to rile, but when he was adamant about something, there was no changing his mind.

"No one is contacting her," Levi told his brother evenly before turning his attention back to the screen of his desktop computer. "At least not yet."

The *her* in question being public relations crisis manager Kendra Davies. She was exceedingly skilled at her job. No doubt she would be a tremendous asset to them now that the Kingsley family businesses were in the grip of a publicity nightmare.

If it weren't for the fact that Levi had slept with her in the hottest encounter of his life, he would already be dialing Kendra's number.

He continued to scroll through another day's worth of incendiary comments on social media about their family's businesses, Kingsland Ranch being the largest and most lucrative.

Or at least, it *had been* the most lucrative before their dad's divisive will tore apart the family and started a scandal. Duke Kingsley's final directive had ignored two of Duke's four biological sons, leaving the clan's considerable assets solely to Levi and Quinton, the sons by his first wife. Initially, the story had been barely a blip in social media, causing gossip around the Montana ranching community but not much more.

Then secrets of Duke's life began to leak out, which led to one story after another about the former patriarch's misdeeds. With the newest allegations that he'd accepted a payoff to allow a local electric supplier to dump coal ash on a piece of Kingsley-owned property, the outcry against the family companies had reached a fever pitch. Influencers from around the country had been quick to call for boycotting Levi's Gargoyle King liquor brand, as well as his brother Quinton's tech company and security software.

Now, in today's latest post from an environmental photographer, images of land ruined by coal ash deposits had culminated in a call to sanction Kingsland Ranch.

Since it was social media, the grievances were made in the most inflammatory way possible.

#KancelKingsley had been trending all day.

So while Levi remained as furious as anyone about his father's sabotage of an ecosystem, he and his brothers were being held accountable for the damage done. He resented being painted with the same brush as his dad, but since his name was on the deed to the property, Levi needed to take ownership of the problem.

More importantly? He needed to get the land cleaned up and figure out how to mimimize long term damage.

"It isn't like you to be this unreasonable," Quinton mused a moment later, voice speculative as he dropped his boot heels back onto the floor. "Especially when it comes to protecting the family."

Levi ground his teeth together, reminding himself to be patient.

"There is nothing I wouldn't do to safeguard the Kingsley name and help the ranch thrive." Those had been his missions for as long as he could remember. His father had been more concerned with power and manipulation. Or, if the latest allegations could be believed, with selling out Mother Nature for a buck. So it had been up to Levi, as the oldest of his siblings, to shoulder responsibility at an early age.

Had his father really been as shady as these pseudo-news stories made him seem? Levi had yet to find evidence beyond conjecture and hearsay amped up by the fact that Duke Kingsley had become this week's big shot that people loved to hate. But it didn't matter if the allegations weren't true when the public still believed them. The negative publicity could tank all of the Kingsley businesses. Something Levi refused to allow.

"Nothing except call Kendra Davies and admit that you need her help because we're in over our heads with the public outcry against Kingsley brands." Quinton rose to his feet and snagged his black Stetson off the back of a hideous, custom-made leather chair with a network of elk antlers interlocked over top of the high back.

The thing had been crafted to their father's specifications and looked like a Gothic-meets-Western nightmare, but all the antlers meant no one ever lacked a place to hang their hat in the Kingsland Ranch office.

"We are not in over our heads." Levi turned off his tablet and left it on the desk while he rose to walk his brother out. "Just because Dad was greedy doesn't mean he was corrupt. None of his accusers have proof of wrongdoing."

He walked out of the office and into the foyer a step behind his sibling, the cavernous house where they'd grown up quiet and unmoving in the late afternoon. Levi still lived in the main house, maintaining the business from the ranch office that had belonged to their father.

Quinton had a place in Sunnyvale, California, close to the base operations for his tech business, but he maintained a residence on Kingsland property as well. He'd been living on the family's Montana spread since their father's death three months ago. Now, as Levi stepped out of doors and followed his brother toward his silver truck in the driveway, he whistled for his border collie, Gunner.

"How much do you want to bet someone will find proof, sooner rather than later?" Quinton asked while the dog came racing toward them in a black and white blur.

The question halted Levi in his tracks.

"You really believe Dad did those things everyone is saying about him?" Bending to stroke Gunner's silky ears, Levi tried to imagine patriarch Duke Kingsley collecting bribes for activity that would taint the soil and groundwater for decades to come.

Granted, the site of the contamination wasn't anywhere near where they worked cattle or horses. But still. His dad would understand better than most the implications of that kind of environmental crime. And Levi had worked closely with his dad for years to manage the ranch. Long enough to be aware of his work habits. Long enough to have kept an eye on the accounting ledgers for their business.

"I think our father showed one face to the world and a very different one in private." Quint hesitated at the door of his pickup, looking like he wanted to say more.

"What is it?" Levi pressed his brother, wondering what he was missing. "If you know something I don't about Dad's activities, I sure as hell wish you'd give me a heads-up."

Quint shook his head, scowling down at the ground as he swiped his boot through a patch of stones that had spilled from one of the landscaping beds onto the brickwork driveway. "I don't know anything about him taking bribes. But I could tell just from occasional use of Dad's computer that he was a career cheater on every personal relationship he ever had."

Straightening from where he'd been petting the dog, Levi peered at his brother with new eyes. Quinton was a tech wizard, after all. It made sense he would pay attention to a digital data trail. But how long had Quint been paying attention to their father's activities online? Of course, it was public knowledge that Duke had cheated on Quint and Levi's mother no matter how much he claimed to adore his first wife. The existence of their illegitimate brother Clayton was proof of that much. But Duke's second wife had come into their lives when they were young. Isla Mitchell had been their nanny before she'd married their father after their mom had died in a ranching accident. Levi had been nine years old and Quinton had been eight at the time. Had Quinton been peering into Duke's digital past even then?

"So if he cheats on women, he's more likely to cheat in other areas of his life." Levi finished the idea that his brother had left unsaid. It was starting to sink in that his dad's recklessness truly could have put the whole ranch at risk. Losing the family land was not an option.

Quint shrugged as he glanced up at the Madison mountain range looming over the ranch to the east, beyond the grazing fields. "Make of it what you will. But he wasn't a faithful husband. And since his death, we now know he was the kind of guy who wouldn't even recognize two of his own sons. That's all I need to know about his character right there."

Huffing out a frustrated breath, Levi thumped a fist against the pickup's truck bed, hating that he couldn't resolve this old argument with his stubborn sibling.

"You think Dad screwed over Clayton and Gavin, and you don't want any part of that. I get it. But Kingsland Ranch doesn't have to reflect Dad's values anymore because it's no longer his. It's *ours*. We can turn it into something all four of us can be proud of. But we need to do it together. As a family."

Tugging open the door of his truck, Quinton stepped up the running board and slid into the driver's seat. "I've built something different for myself. Something that isn't tainted with Dad's bullshit and games."

He didn't mention the other thing that had chased him out of Silent Spring. The memories of their mother's death that were all the more unhappy for Quinton since he'd been there when it had happened. He'd dealt with the trauma, yes, but Levi had long known the ranch hadn't been the same for Quint since they'd lost her.

Now, the resigned look in his brother's eye made Levi wary that Quint would be leaving before they'd settled the inheritance mess. "All I'm asking is that you wait to make any decisions about your share of the ranch until after we find Clayton. Until after all four of us can sit down and hash out what we want to happen to this place. Okay?"

Their brother Clay Reynolds had been out of touch for three years, ever since a big falling out with Duke. Levi had hired a private investigator to find him, and Quinton had made numerous calls about Clay's last known whereabouts for himself. But so far, they had no concrete leads.

From the seat of his truck cab, Quint snapped his phone into a holder on his dash, not making eye contact. "I can't promise you that. Not when Clay could be gone for good."

Levi wanted to argue more, but both their phones chimed at the same time. Quinton's screen lit up. Levi's pocket buzzed. A weather warning? The blue sky in all directions sure didn't give any indication of a storm. By the time Levi had his device in hand and he'd unlocked his screen, however, Quinton was already reading the news aloud.

"'Witness comes forward in the Duke Kingsley allegations,'" he said dryly before switching on the engine of his truck.

Levi cursed when he saw the headline in his alerts a moment later. They'd both set up alerts for family news since the publicity crisis had begun. "Maybe it's just someone with an axe to grind and not anyone credible."

He scrolled through the short news snippet, searching for details.

"Credible or not, our problems with the Kingsland brand just multiplied," Quinton said over the hum of the engine.

Tension cranked Levi's shoulders like a vise. "I'm reading more now," he muttered, scanning the brief details issued from a Bozeman news source. "They're saying it's a source from inside the power plant."

Quinton remained silent. He didn't seem surprised

by the news. Whereas Levi's stomach sank. His skin went cold as the prospect of his father committing criminal activity became a whole lot more real.

But the news made one thing crystal clear. He'd have to give in and take the next step that Quinton had already requested.

Clearing up this mess was too important to trust to anyone but the best. Even if it made things tricky on a personal level.

"I'll get in touch with Kendra. Today," he vowed as he shoved his phone back in his pocket.

Things hadn't ended well between them, but she wouldn't turn away business just because of that. She was ambitious. Driven. Sexy as hell.

And she just happened to hate him.

Standing outside her childhood home, Kendra Davies juggled bags of groceries to find the key that would let her into the house where her father still lived alone. The house where she stayed whenever she returned to her hometown of Silent Spring, Montana.

Which was more often than she would have preferred, but considering her father's mental health and gambling addiction, her frequent visits were necessary. Spending two and a half years on her own in Denver had been rewarding, financially and professionally, but there'd been a toll on her dad. One she hadn't fully appreciated until she returned home for a Christmas visit to discover the place almost bare of furnishings and artwork.

Sold to pay gambling debts.

Now, setting one of her canvas bags on the top step of the simple log cabin home, Kendra found the correct key on her heavy Tiffany & Co. key ring and opened the lock.

"Dad? Are you home?" She hesitated at the threshold, listening.

Unwilling to surprise her bachelor father with a guest. She still shuddered to think about the one time she'd visited unannounced, only to find him entertaining on the floor in front of the fireplace. Not that she begrudged him company. Far from it. If her dad started a steady relationship with someone, it might alleviate some of the depression that was still strongly connected to her mother's defection a decade ago.

But there was no answer to her call. Her father wasn't home.

Stepping deeper into the house, Kendra deposited the groceries on the kitchen island. The log home had a split floor plan with a bedroom on either side of the common areas. There'd been a time when it had felt cozy to the point of cramped with custommade couches and heavy wooden end tables, and with thick Turkish rugs in brightly colored patterns covering most of the planked floor. All of those were gone now, so that the only piece of furniture in the living room was a secondhand leather sofa Kendra had picked up at a consignment shop so there was at least somewhere to sit.

Kendra's mother had loved kitchen gadgets too, and all of the high-end appliances were gone as well, leaving the quartz countertops bare except for a cheap, drip coffee maker. Her gaze went to it now as she debated making herself a pot for an afternoon pick-me-up. Her day had been a flat-out sprint since sunup when she'd awoken to a work call from one of her regular clients—a well-known fashion and beauty influencer who was perpetually convinced she needed crisis intervention. Today, the woman was positive her dip in social media followers must mean there was some catastrophic news about her brand.

After hunting all morning and into the afternoon, Kendra had traced the data blip to a small organic farm business that had done a blog post about waste in the food industry, citing lavish A-lister parties as a repeat offender in this department. The comments section had then referenced one of the beauty influencer's parties and called for a "mass unfollow" that still made only the barest fractional dent in her client's following.

First world problems.

But Kendra didn't knock it since she was good at her job. Little did the world know that problem solving came as second nature to a woman born into the chaos that had been her life.

Crossing the kitchen to fill the carafe at the sink, Kendra was calculating how long she should stay in Silent Spring this time when the doorbell chimed.

Had her father forgotten his key?

Shutting off the water, she spied a tall shadow through the leaded glass.

A debt collector? Repo man? Her stomach clenched at the possibilities. Her father had so little left to take. Grip tightening on the empty coffee carafe still in hand, she tugged open the door.

To find Levi Kingsley on her front step in all of his gorgeous, six-foot-two glory. Her heart stuttered and she could only hope her face hadn't betrayed her. With his dark brown hair and piercing blue eyes, he was a man who turned women's heads. In his jeans and boots, and a Stetson the color of desert sand, he was downright crush-worthy.

But in spite of his outward appeal, Kendra knew damned well she would have been better off with the debt collector.

Her lips pursed as she bit back one sarcastic greeting after another. Ah, the hell with it.

"To what do I owe this unexpected pleasure?" she finally said by way of greeting, remaining on the threshold of the door so he wouldn't get the idea he could enter the house.

She knew better than to give an inch to the newly anointed patriarch of the powerful Kingsley clan. Levi had already taken too much from her family.

"A public image crisis." Levi's words were brusque. Clipped. Sounding as if they didn't come any easier to him than hers did.

Good. He *should* be uncomfortable around her

after the way he'd swooped in to take her father's fledgling liquor business from him. From her too, since she'd been helping her dad with the business plan. Working on the ideas for Gargoyle King was the last time her dad had shown any hint of his old zest for life. The gambling and depression had only grown worse since then.

"I'm not sure how that affects me." She backed up a step, fully ready to shut the door on him. If he wanted something with her, he'd have to spell it out.

"I want to hire you." His jaw flexed as that penetrating gaze met hers.

And *argh*. Had she really just thought in terms of *penetration* with Levi Kingsley in reach? She cursed herself … and him.

"You can't possibly be serious." Shaking her head, she tried to clear her brain of the wayward thoughts about this man. Not to mention the boatload of resentments. "Have you forgotten we slept together?"

She wanted to call back the words as soon as she'd uttered them. But really? How could he ask her to work for him?

One dark eyebrow lifted a fraction as he seemed to consider her question.

In the weighty silence that followed her question, his gaze collided with hers. Held hers. Communicated things that made her face heat.

Or maybe it was her recollection of that night that made her whole body flush.

"I assure you," he said finally, his voice deepening. "I remember. Vividly."

If she thought her face felt hot before, it had to be flaming now. Not that she was embarrassed about a single thing she'd done. To the contrary, she'd never reached the sexual peaks he'd driven her to that night. Over and over.

But it was tough not to regret being with him when he'd followed up that night by stabbing her in the back. He'd dangled a check under her father's nose a few days later, making Seth Davies an offer he couldn't refuse for the liquor business that Kendra had pinned so many hopes on.

"In that case, it should be obvious why it wouldn't be appropriate for us to work together." Kendra gripped the door, preparing to close it for the second time since Levi had arrived.

"Kendra, please." Sweeping his Stetson off his head, he tapped the brim against his thigh. "I know how you feel about me. I promise you I wouldn't be here if Kingsland wasn't facing a publicity disaster."

The sincerity in his tone gave her pause even before his words sank in. Even then, the first thing her brain fixated on was his presumption that he knew how she felt.

Not a chance.

She'd stuffed her resentment down deep, refusing to let him see a fraction of her anger at his treachery.

Slowly, however, the deeper import of his visit became clearer to her.

"You want me to manage a PR crisis?" She mused on that, her fingernails lightly drumming the edge of the door where she maintained a grip on the wood.

The Kingsley family owned an impressive—and lucrative—array of companies. From the Gargoyle King liquor brand that Levi had turned into a household name, to a technology company, the ranch and many smaller businesses including a local bar. A publicity problem for a holding company that big would mean a profitable contract for the expert who could guide them through it. Kendra could use that kind of contract to demand a partnership in her company. Hell, she could use it to start her own firm, if she chose.

All of which meant she couldn't close the door on Levi Kingsley. No matter how much she'd rather deal with a repo man.

"Maybe you'd better come in," she said finally, stepping aside to open the door wider.

Welcoming trouble back into her life.

Two

After outlining his publicity problem for Kendra to consider, Levi took a sip of the coffee she'd offered him. She'd brewed a pot while she listened, moving easily around her father's small kitchen as she had measured the grounds and poured the water into the machine, releasing the scent of java into the air.

Was she keeping busy to maintain distance from him? From the attraction that still crackled between them?

Now, she sat at a counter stool beside him, their elbows almost touching at the narrow breakfast bar in Seth Davies's log cabin home. Levi couldn't help but notice how barren the place was, with no furniture besides a couch in the living area and no artwork on the walls. Had the older man always lived this way? Kendra had grown up in Silent Spring, but they hadn't moved in the same circles so he'd never been in her home when they'd been kids. She hadn't even lived with her old man full time, spending part of each year with her mother and a stepfather in Las Vegas.

The one night he and Kendra had shared had been at his place after a rodeo where his brother Gavin had been competing. They'd found themselves at the same after party, each avoiding former romantic interests. Conversation had flowed easily, as did the drinks.

The next thing he knew, they'd left the party together and were tearing one another's clothes off in an overheated make out session in his truck. Something he hadn't done since he'd been a teen. But the charged kisses were only the beginning of one of the best nights of his life.

Then he'd woken up to a note saying she'd call after she returned from a work trip. When she hadn't, he'd contacted her a week later.

Only to have her explain why the whole thing had been a mistake and she wouldn't be seeing him again. To really seal the deal, she'd moved out of town and had spent the last three years in Denver other than the occasional weekend home to see her father.

"What do you think?" Kendra was asking him a moment later, making him realize he hadn't been paying attention.

Too busy reminiscing and rehashing their one-night stand gone wrong.

"About?" Setting his cup down, he swiveled on the wooden counter stool to face her. "Sorry. I've got a lot on my mind since the news broke regarding Dad's potential involvement in that environmental mess."

Kendra straightened in her seat. Unlike the last time he'd seen her at his bar, the Stockyard, with a couple of her girlfriends, she was dressed down today. Faded jeans hugged generous curves, while she hooked heeled suede boots on a rung of her seat. An ivory colored sweater slid to the edge of her shoulder, displaying an enticing amount of kissable skin at the base of her neck. Her blond waves were tied in a loose brown ribbon. She studied him with speculative hazel eyes.

Eyes that he still saw in his dreams, except that gaze was loaded with passion.

"I want to know that you're personally committed to this, Levi. If I take on the project, I'm going to need the face of Kingsland to be in the spotlight, setting the record straight about your companies."

"There is no higher priority for me than Kingsland." He'd poured everything into the family businesses. "But as for putting myself in the spotlight?" He shook his head, lifting his mug. "That's what I'm hiring you for."

"That's not how this works." She swung her stool around to face him and folded her arms as she gave him a level stare. "I can help you navigate the fallout from this mess, but I can't be the face of Kingsland."

Frustration fired through him and he gripped the

cup tighter. "So write it into your contract, Kendra. I'm willing to pay you well—"

"And you will, assuming I agree to represent you. But no paycheck is going to magically transform me into a Kingsley who is qualified to speak about the Kingsley brands."

He wanted to argue the point, but something about her ramrod straight posture told him she wasn't backing down on this. The only sound in the log cabin was the ticking of a utilitarian white clock hanging above the kitchen window.

"Maybe I can talk Quinton into taking on the role," he mused aloud, knowing as soon as he said it that he had even less chance of convincing laid-back Quint to be in the spotlight than he had of persuading Kendra to relax her "must be a Kingsley" requirement.

Furthermore? Quint had questioned their father's activities even before the public had started looking askance at Duke Kingsley. And he wanted to walk away from Kingsland anyhow.

"So we'll talk more about this once someone in your family is committed to putting a good face on your companies. Until then, there's not a thing I can do to help." Rotating her stool back to the counter, Kendra lifted her white coffee mug to take another sip of her drink.

Damn it.

She had him over a barrel.

Was it his imagination, or did she seem sort of pleased about that fact? Her seeming lack of empathy for his situation—hell, she'd barely let him set foot in the house—had him wondering what he'd done three years ago to tick her off to this degree. He'd been so certain at the time that she'd been as onboard with sleeping with him as he'd been with her.

Something had fallen apart between them somewhere and he didn't have a clue how it had gone wrong. At the time, he'd been embroiled in getting Gargoyle King on the market and hadn't explored the reason for her cool withdrawal since he hadn't been in the market for a deeper relationship anyhow. Then, or now.

But he'd wondered about her sudden retreat over the years.

"Let's say for a second that I take this on myself." A weary sigh shuddered through him as he focused on the more important matter at hand—securing her help. How many times had he borne the weight of his name and been the responsible one? He'd done his damnedest over the years to protect his younger brothers from the upheaval and unhappiness that had gone hand in hand with being raised by their self-centered, mercurial father. That didn't mean he enjoyed the job. "What would being 'in the spotlight' entail?"

He'd always been a better behind-the-scenes guy, monitoring his bar from the backroom and his ranch from the office. The secret to his success had been hiring good people and letting them do their jobs. Most of the time, that meant staying the hell out of the way and not pretending like he had all the answers.

"To minimize the damage your father has done, you would undertake a goodwill campaign to replace the negative narrative with a positive one." Sliding out of her seat, Kendra rose and walked her coffee cup over to the kitchen sink.

She rinsed the cup with her back to him, making him wonder if their meeting was over. Irritation flared. He'd come here for her help, and it hadn't been easy. He didn't appreciate her cold shoulder when he'd maintained a professional approach.

"In layman's terms?" he pressed, reminding himself he couldn't afford to alienate her when he needed her expertise. "What would I be doing?"

After drying her hands on a dish towel, Kendra pivoted on her booted heel to face him. She didn't rejoin him at the counter, however. Leaning against the apron sink, she watched him from the opposite side of the small kitchen.

"I would set up a goodwill tour for you, and you would spend the next few weeks attending high profile charity events."

He scrubbed a hand over his face. A muttered curse escaped before he could call it back.

"And how exactly would wasting my time at a bunch of black-tie parties help the Kingsland cause?"

She gave him a brittle smile. "You would make generous, publicly visible donations, and I would ensure your contributions received extensive media coverage. You'd then make yourself available for photos and interviews to discuss your new charitable mission for Kingsland."

His head throbbed at the thought of leaving his businesses for weeks on end. How much could go wrong in the day-to-day operations of the ranch? The bar? His liquor brand that was on the verge of expansion?

And yet, what were the consequences for those companies if he didn't get on top of the negative publicity? Not just for him, but for Quint's tech company? Gavin's new breeding operation?

The stakes were high for all of them.

Foreboding rippled through him. But he couldn't say no.

"I'll do it," he agreed finally, shoving his empty mug across the counter toward her before he rose to his feet. "But you're going to have to accompany me on this goodwill tour—every step of the way—so I don't botch the whole thing."

She frowned. "I can provide your itinerary and talking points after I set everything up, but there's no need for me to be on-site—"

"There absolutely *is* a need." He wasn't ready to question why this was a point he was willing to dig his heels in about. "I want you close by as backup if I get into a dicey publicity situation." He felt certain she'd be a welcome asset if someone put him on the spot with questions he didn't know how to handle. "You'll be my plus-one at each and every one of these events."

* * *

A rogue flare of attraction heated her skin at the fiery look in Levi's blue eyes as he strode closer to her.

She had no business responding to him that way. Especially when he was trying to call the shots in this surprising negotiation. When she rolled out of bed this morning, she never would have guessed her former lover would show up on her doorstep asking for her professional help.

In a perfect world, she would have been thrilled to slam the door in his handsome face. But she couldn't afford to act on the old resentments when this job he offered could catapult her career into making partner in her firm.

Would that level of success prove to the world she was nothing like her mother, who defined herself in relationship to the men in her life? More importantly, would she convince herself of the same thing? She'd been aiming for the goal even before her disastrous one-night stand with Levi. But afterward, looking back at her impulsive decision to sleep with a wealthy and powerful man, she'd been all the more determined not to be the kind of woman who needed men's validation.

Levi's deep voice intruded on her musing. "Do we have a deal?"

He stood near her at the kitchen sink. Not crowding her, but close enough to make her very aware of him. His cedar and musk scent. His clear blue eyes that she could see all the better since he'd left his Stetson on the hat rack near the door.

"No." She shook her head, willing away thoughts of her history with this man to focus strictly on the business at hand. "What you're suggesting is not only unorthodox, it's inappropriate in a professional relationship. My workplace would never approve time off for me to be glorified arm candy for a client."

That wasn't entirely true. Her boss would be over the moon about this contract and would gladly accommodate whatever travel schedule Kendra dictated.

But she had her own reservations about spending that much time in close contact with Levi. Look at what standing next to him in her father's kitchen did to her peace of mind. Her pulse sped. Her skin heated. And she didn't even like the man.

"Arm candy? Kendra, I'm not interested in the fact that you're an attractive date. I'm asking for access to your professional training during a PR crisis."

She weighed the idea of pushing back on his dictate, but she feared he'd walk out the door. And some corner of her brain didn't want that to happen after they had opened a dialogue again. Plus, now that he'd dangled the prospect of this job in front of her, she couldn't deny that she wanted it.

Levi spoke up while she considered her options.

"What if I offered you a personal incentive to make it work?"

Her throat went dry at the thought of what he might propose. She swallowed.

"What did you have in mind?"

The clock on the wall over her head ticked a noisy rhythm, the sound reminding her of the few cheap furnishings her dad had bought to replace the things he'd lost to his gambling debts.

One more reason she wanted this job. She loved her dad despite his faults, and she wished to see him comfortable and happy again.

"What if I provided your father a spot on the Gargoyle King's board?" He studied her in the weak sunlight filtering through the kitchen window as the day outside turned overcast.

She tried not to let her jaw unhinge, even though he'd just shocked the hell out of her. Did Levi know how devastated she'd been when he'd bought out her father's rights to the company?

All these years that she'd nursed her grudge against Levi, she hadn't known for certain if the wealthy Kingsley heir understood how much he'd taken from her and her dad. Seth Davies had agreed to the sale for the sake of a short-term buck—cash that had only fueled a three-day gambling binge. But he hadn't really considered how much selling the company would rob him of a productive purpose in life.

Not to mention how far it would set him back in curing his gambling problem.

But if Levi would offer her dad this spot in the company, maybe he understood perfectly well how much he'd hurt her family.

"You could arrange that?" She glanced away from

Levi's too-perceptive gaze to fiddle with the strap of one of the reusable grocery bags still sitting on the kitchen counter. She hadn't finished stocking her dad's cabinets with the things she'd brought from her apartment in Denver when Levi had shown up.

"Absolutely. I can make that happen. We're not a publicly traded company. The board consists mostly of people I've appointed to be there. People whose opinions I trust."

Her stomach knotted at the complicated proposal. Not to mention all the moving parts of it. She'd have to travel with Levi and be his plus-one at events for weeks, a scenario that would test their attraction as much as her long-standing bitterness toward him. Yet she couldn't deny that she wanted to be the person who brought in a lucrative contract like this so she could secure that partnership in her company.

Plus, her father might gain some purpose in life once more if he could apply his sharp mind and creative abilities to something constructive. Once upon a time, her dad had written a bestselling work of fiction and had been hailed as a literary rising star. He'd met Kendra's mother at a book signing, where then twenty-two year old Jennifer Leonard had sensed an opportunity to rise above her humble origins and leave the Kansas town where she'd grown up. Jennifer sank her hooks in deep. But eleven years later, when Seth's money ran out and he'd failed to produce a follow-up book, Kendra's mom moved on to a husband with more discretionary income, leaving Kendra's dad heartbroken and directionless. Therapy hadn't helped, but Kendra truly believed a new project might.

"And you would listen to my father's input?" she asked, pacing away from the man whose presence had a way of derailing her ability to think rationally. "This wouldn't just be a figurehead position? I know my father has made mistakes, but he has valuable insights and experience."

When she reached the mostly empty living room, her boot heels echoing on the hardwood floors, Kendra pivoted to see Levi frowning at her, a thoughtful expression scrawled on his handsome features.

"Why would I fill a spot on the board with someone who didn't have anything to offer me?" He spread his arms in a questioning gesture. "Of course I'd listen to his input. It was your dad's business sense that generated the core concept for Gargoyle King."

The answer mollified just a little of her longstanding anger at Levi for buying out the company. At least he recognized her father's contributions had been substantial.

A sigh huffed from her chest.

"I'd still have to consult my company before I share a final cost estimate for a job like this," she cautioned, giving him every opportunity to walk away from this deal.

A deal she feared would be unwise but couldn't possibly refuse.

"Of course. I would hope to see a contract as soon as possible, however, since every hour the Kingsley name is dragged through the mud is damaging to my family's ranch as well as other businesses."

Some of the tension seemed to have left his shoulders as he walked toward her, pausing in front of the hat rack to lift his Stetson from a brass hook.

Her heart thudded against her rib cage in a way she did not appreciate. How could she consider spending more time with him when she still reacted to him in this inconvenient way? More importantly, was she even capable of hiding it? She held herself very still as they locked gazes, her body remembering his touch.

Craving it, even after all this time.

"I'll do what I can." She forced herself to stand tall. To resist the urge to hug her arms around her body in a poor substitute for his. This man had dealt a grave insult to her family. A damaging betrayal that both she and her father were still reeling from. The reminder helped cool her heated skin. "Best case scenario, you'll see a fee estimate and contract in your inbox by the end of business today. Typically, we ask for half up front."

"Not a problem. And I appreciate your willingness to work with me in spite of—" he allowed the sentence to dangle unfinished for a moment while he settled his hat on his head and cast his blue eyes in shadow "—everything."

Had she thought the temperature of her skin was under control? That pregnant pause of his had her remembering in full, vivid detail the past they shared.

Not the betrayal.

But the no-holds-barred sex that had come before that and the night that turned them from mere acquaintances to lovers who knew intimate details about how to pleasure one another. How to wring moans and sighs of pleasure from each other. How to set one another on fire.

With an effort, she said coolly, "I think it would be best if we forget the past and focus strictly on the professional nature of this new arrangement."

She knew it wouldn't be easy.

Especially when his gaze dipped to her neck, bared by her off-the-shoulder sweater. Could he see her pulse jumping there? She could certainly feel it. But she would be damned before she let him know how much he still affected her.

Levi's mouth flattened into a grim line before he spoke. "I'm happy to focus on business. But as for forgetting what we shared, Kendra?" He reached for the door handle to let himself out, though he never took his eyes from hers. "Not going to happen."

She didn't realize she was holding her breath until the door closed before him. Then, the air expelled from her lungs so hard that she slumped against the couch in the middle of the living room.

What had she just gotten herself into?

Three

"Can you test your microphone for us, Mr. Kingsley?"

Hearing his name, Levi glanced up from a note card with his talking points as he sat at a table on a raised dais inside the Kingsland Ranch show arena. One of Kendra's production assistants—an athletic brunette whose prosthetic leg covers were designed to look like chain mail, complete with fire-breathing dragons—gestured for him to use the microphone she'd pinned to his jacket lapel a few minutes earlier.

Levi spoke the first few words of his carefully crafted press release until the petite brunette nodded her satisfaction and hurried off to consult with the guy taping off spots on the temporary staging laid over the show ring's dirt floor for over two dozen designated media guests. Kendra was busy briefing Gavin and Quinton—both seated with him at the table—on their roles in the upcoming meeting with the media.

The arena had been chosen by Kendra as the location for a press conference two days after he'd requested her help in managing the Kingsland publicity crisis. Her first line of defense was to meet with the press in order to take ownership of the problems associated with the Kingsley family businesses and outline their response to the accusations of Duke Kingsley's alleged environmental crimes.

Things had moved quickly after he'd read and approved the contract that put Kendra in charge of publicity damage control. He'd assumed she would start putting together the goodwill tour she'd mentioned. And she had done that, as well. But her very first order of business was for Levi to respond publicly to the claims against his father with a scripted statement, followed by a brief question and answer period. Now, the venue was full of the team she'd assembled for ensuring the press event ran just the way she'd planned. Metal folding chairs were being set up below the table where Gavin and his brothers were seated, a trick that Kendra had said would make the Kingsley family appear authoritative and in control of the situation.

Quinton leaned over toward Levi now as Kendra turned her focus to Gavin's microphone.

"So did you patch things up with Kendra?" Quinton asked, voice low as his gaze went from Levi to the woman in charge of today's press event.

"There was nothing to patch up." Levi covered his microphone with one hand. "And try to remember that if you're mic'd up, someone's probably listening."

Quinton unclipped the device from his gray suit jacket and set it on the industrial style metal table while the production crew continued to work out lighting and sound issues.

"There. That's one concern alleviated." He waved his hand over the removed equipment. "Now, please don't bullshit me, as it's been obvious to all of Silent Spring that you and Kendra have been in a standoff for the last few years."

Levi's gaze darted to Kendra. Dressed in a minimalistic navy blue suit with a cream colored silk shell beneath it, she was the epitome of understated elegance. High heeled taupe pumps did exquisite things to her calves as she leaned forward to adjust Gavin's microphone.

Pulling off his own device to let it drop on the table, Levi scowled at Quint. "If that was true, and I'm not saying it is, then it would be a private matter between the two of us."

"A private matter?" Quinton gripped his temples between his thumb and forefinger. "When she's got the power to make or break all of our businesses? Are you kidding me right now?"

"I hired her the way you asked me to." He pointed a finger in his brother's face, fed up with the pressure of the social media nightmare, the backlash against the ranch and the fallout with Kendra for reasons he didn't fully understand. "Don't push your luck by prying into my personal life."

His brother studied him while metal chair legs clanged against the platform floor and the sound team tested speakers at the back of the arena.

After a long moment, he shook his head slowly, seeming unperturbed by his brother's outburst. "I can't believe you didn't smooth things over with her before you brought her onboard. Who are you and what did you do with Levi, the responsible diplomat in the family?"

Grinding his teeth against the urge to break down for Quinton the precise meaning of "mind your own business," Levi was losing the battle when Kendra walked toward them, coming to a halt between their chairs.

"Everything okay over here?" she asked, glancing back and forth between them, her lips pursing with concern as she took in Levi's face. "Levi, you look ready to burst a vein. Do you need a breather before we begin? We're almost ready to open the doors to the media."

"I'm fine." He bit the words out, ignoring his brother's quickly stifled smirk to return his attention to the note cards on the table in front of him. He scraped them together in a pile and straightened them to go through the talk one more time. "We'll be ready when it's time to start."

But Kendra didn't move on. She frowned down at him as her hazel gaze fell on the microphone he'd displaced.

Their hands met as they both reached for it at the same time. Her pale skin and short red nails lay briefly on his wrist, a delicate opal flashing from a silver filigree band on her middle finger. For a moment, he had the briefest impression of her cool, soft skin on his while he caught a hint of her jasmine fragrance.

The scent alone triggered a hundred memories of their night together when he'd teased kisses along her neck, finding the places where the fragrance was strongest.

Now, her breath caught audibly as she took the microphone from him.

"Let me get it." With brusque fingers, she re-clipped the device to his jacket lapel before adjusting the angle. "Everything needs to run smoothly today, okay? There is no more important facet of crisis management than our initial response."

Levi agreed wholeheartedly. Even as he sincerely tried not to notice that her breasts were at eye level, her blond waves spilling over his sleeve where he still gripped his notes.

The card stock wrinkled as his hold tightened.

"We'll be ready," he assured her, grateful that she was at the helm. "Thank you for organizing this."

"Just remember, our main objective is to take

ownership of the situation. Demonstrate honesty and integrity." Straightening, she shifted her attention to Quinton, who had already replaced his microphone. Then, she gave Levi a tight smile that looked like it cost her a mighty effort. "And no need to thank me. This is what you're paying me for."

As she walked away, head held high while announcing to the room at large that the doors were about to open to the media, Quinton whistled low under his breath.

"Damn, Levi. With all due respect to your private life, that woman does *not* like you." Quint straightened his shoulders as the first batch of journalists entered the building in a buzzy wave of cameras and sound equipment. "Since we're being honest today."

Tamping down his irritation, Levi maintained a neutral expression with an effort. "Then it's a good thing she doesn't have to like me to do her job."

"Maybe not. But it sure makes me wonder why you dug your heels in about bringing her on the media tour when she can't even fake a smile for you." Quint bent his head, and it sounded like he was stifling a chuckle.

"And that amuses you?" He kept his voice low, still mindful that they could have an audience.

The folding chairs in front of the conference table began filling as journalists and camera crews set up their taped-off spaces with equipment.

"A little bit, yeah it does. You're the Kingsley most apt to be liked, you know. So I find it entertaining that the woman most capable of saving our asses doesn't find you even mildly charming." Quinton's expression cleared as he looked up from the table to take in the gathering crowd who could very well hold the future of the Kingsley businesses in their hands today. "And given that everything we've worked hard for is currently crumbling down around our ears, you can hardly fault me for finding a momentary diversion from the mess our father left us."

With the weight of their futures in the balance, Levi felt the full impact of the sinking Kingsland brands. And for the first time all day, he couldn't agree with his brother more.

Standing at the floor microphone on the raised dais that she'd had constructed for the press conference, Kendra listened as Gavin Kingsley addressed a reporter's question about his horse breeding business, ready to step in to redirect if Gavin required a bailout.

But Gavin was succinct and to the point, his answer delivered with smooth competence. She couldn't have scripted it any better herself. In fact, all three of the Kingsley brothers in attendance had been model clients during a tense meeting with the media. She had to admire how effectively they came together as a family to support one another, a quality sorely lacking in the household where she'd been raised.

Levi had delivered his opening notes with conviction ringing through every word as he assured the public he would finance and personally oversee the cleanup of the environmental mess, whether or not his father had been at fault for it.

Then, his brothers had taken turns answering questions to give Levi a breather, each offering heartfelt, brief responses, precisely as she'd coached them. Still, she was bracing herself for the difficult questions that she knew would come. As chair of the event, she'd been in charge of calling on members of the media who had questions, and so far Kendra had picked reporters who didn't have mercenary reputations.

But the time had come to give at least one of those attendees a chance to speak. She stepped closer to the mic to call on the next journalist.

"Mr. Daniels of American Economy." She spoke his name clearly as she met the older man's gaze.

Kevin Daniels shot to his feet, his salt and pepper haircut just above the collar of his tweed jacket.

"This one is for Levi," the business columnist began, consulting an old-fashioned yellow legal pad full of notes. "What will your response be to environmentalists who say that cleaning up the physical damage of the coal ash won't address the long-term effects to the groundwater and health of local citizens? Are you aware of the cancer rates linked to illegal coal ash dumping?"

A murmur traveled through the crowd. Kendra debated censuring the writer for piling on a second question when each attendee had been briefed to ask only one.

But Levi was already answering.

"The health and well-being of local citizens is our number one priority." He sat forward in his seat, his strong shoulders squared toward the speaker to demonstrate his full attention on the issue. His deep voice held a grave note, yet he spoke with confidence. "We will accept all recommendations from the environmental agency monitoring the cleanup to ensure a full ecological recovery."

Kendra watched him carefully to best gauge when he'd finished his remarks. When she suspected he'd finished, she intervened before anyone else could ask a question.

"And that wraps our press conference," she said into the floor microphone, allowing her gaze to sweep over the assembled attendees. "As you've learned today, our speakers all have urgent claims on their time, as they turn their attention to taking the next steps on the issues we've discussed."

She could hear a few mutters of disappointment, but for the most part, the press members moved to start gathering their gear.

Until, from the audience, someone ignored protocol to shout, "Are you calling a goodwill publicity tour an urgent claim on Levi's time?"

Heads swiveled toward the stage again as everyone waited to see if the question would be answered. Kendra swallowed back her annoyance, hoping that addressing the question head-on would soothe some of the discontent directed toward the Kingsley family.

"I take full responsibility for the publicity tour, so I'd like to respond." She directed her remarks to Levi as much as the assembled group. He'd invited her on the goodwill tour because he'd wanted her to run interference on issues like this, hadn't he? At his subtle nod giving her the floor, she continued speaking, this time directing her full attention to the members of the media.

"It was my idea to divert some of the Kingsland charitable funds toward environmental causes at a time when this family wants to show their support for clean air and groundwater." She'd already lined up appearances at the biggest benefits for nature conservancies and environmental defense groups taking place around the country throughout the month. "So while Gavin and Quinton oversee the cleanup operation on-site, Levi will use this opportunity to bring more attention to sustainability best practices."

At her final words, her production team supported her efforts to end the event by opening all of the exit doors and turning up the lights. Mia Barton, her primary assistant for the conference, waved the Kingsley brothers off the stage, gesturing for them to exit.

Kendra followed a step behind, which put her in close proximity to Levi as they descended the dais steps and headed toward the arena main office.

Or at least, everyone else filed into the main office as planned for the post-conference debrief. At the threshold, Levi pivoted on his boot heel, his lapel microphone already gone.

She spied the cord leading into his jacket pocket.

"Do you really think we're doing the right thing based on that last question?" The urgent tone in his voice surprised her, coming from a notoriously even-keeled man. "Should I be in town through the cleanup to show support for it? To show empathy?"

Her gaze darted up to meet his. Concern etched his features. Worry, even.

She felt some of her old anger at him soften. It was clear to her, whatever other faults he might have, Levi was deeply distressed about Duke Kingsley's misdeeds. While the press corps filed out of the room, overseen by three security members of her team acting as ushers for the event, Kendra stepped to the far side of the office entrance—tucked under the scaffolding of the arena seating—so they could speak privately.

"I guarantee this is the right play." She'd been at her job long enough to feel certain on this point. "You're fortunate you have brothers who can be on-site in your absence, but even if you didn't, I would urge you to circulate in public now and use the awareness of your issues to call attention to how you are making a difference."

Frowning, Levi raked his fingers through his dark hair. "Seems so damn self-serving."

His disgust at the idea of doing something that

would benefit him made her wonder how he'd justi-
fied buying out her father. She thrust the unhappy
subject from her mind, needing to focus on the important job he'd hired her to do. A job that would
catapult her career to the next level.

"But it isn't. Consider how much money you would
be pouring into all of these good works if this situation hadn't occurred." She shifted on her heels, the
shoes less comfortable after she'd been walking on
the arena's unforgiving floors for hours to set up and
execute the event.

"None," he admitted grudgingly. "That's not to
say we don't support charitable causes already."

"I'm sure you do. But not to this extent. And the
spate of publicity you're hating today is going to ul-
timately drive a lot of attention—and therefore outside donations—from the media." She understood the
dynamics of how these operations worked. Of how
she could make them work for her clients.

As they stood in the shadows of the scaffolding
that held up the arena seating, Levi's expression
eased. Something like respect glinted in the depths
of his blue eyes for a moment.

"I hope you're right about that. It would be a small
consolation for finding out my father wasn't half the
man I believed him to be."

Curiosity about his family tugged at her. Normally, she didn't allow herself to ask personal questions of a client. But she and Levi had sped through

that stop sign long before they began working together.

"Do you think he's guilty of the crimes he's been accused of?" She hadn't been able to read him about that issue. And in that long ago evening that they'd spent getting to know one another after the rodeo, she'd had the impression that he really respected his dad.

"My brothers all do," he hedged, shoving his hands in the pockets of the jeans he'd worn with his jacket. As Montana ranchers went, Levi tended to dress more formally than most. Yet today, he'd wisely chosen jeans and boots with the gray jacket and white shirt, a look that improved his relatability. "And they may have seen a more realistic side of my father than what he showed me. His antics with the will—cutting off two of his sons—went a long way toward showing me his character."

Empathy for his disillusionment with a parent resonated inside her. How often had she been forced to revise her opinions of both her mom and dad over the years?

"I'm sure it's not easy for parents to admit they are not the people their children hope they are," she conceded.

She would have said more since the topic touched a nerve for her because of her father, but Mia approached them then, her quick, distinctive steps signaling her arrival before Kendra spotted her in her peripheral vision.

"We should begin the debrief," her assistant urged, a tablet in one hand illuminating her tense expression. "You've got an office full of stressed folks eager to be set free."

"I'm right behind you," she promised the woman, pivoting away from Levi to take care of business.

Her client was right on her heels.

"Kendra, wait a moment." Levi had his phone in his hand, his thumbs tapping the screen. "I'm sending you the details for our flight to New York tomorrow. It makes sense to use the jet this month so we can have more flexibility with our travel."

Her phone vibrated in her jacket pocket like a phantom touch from him. She cleared her throat and her thoughts. "I appreciate you arranging that portion of the tour."

Even if the thought of the seclusion a private plane afforded made her throat go dry.

"Not a problem." He pocketed his phone. "Would you like a ride to the airfield in the morning?"

Her belly did a flip and she hoped it was because she hadn't eaten since breakfast. Hoped. But knew the cause was standing right here in front of her.

"I'll meet you there," she insisted, knowing full well she'd need as much time as possible to get used to the idea of spending the next three weeks with Levi.

Turning away from him, she strode toward the arena's office. Concentrating on the job she did well made her feel in control. That grounded her. Settled her nerves.

Whereas time spent alone with Levi?

The shiver that ran through her at just the thought of being near him told her how much he affected her.

She needed a game plan for the next few weeks. One that didn't have anything to do with publicity, and everything to do with self-preservation.

Four

A few hours later, Kendra steered her sedan down the gravel driveway alongside the Madison River that divided Kingsland Ranch from Gavin Kingsley's holding, the Broken Spur. One of Kendra's closest friends, Lauryn Hamilton, had moved in with Gavin just a few weeks before and convinced Kendra to stop by the house so she could share a few dresses to supplement Kendra's travel wardrobe. Considering Kendra would be attending one black-tie event after another, she'd been in no position to refuse.

And yeah, after all the turmoil with Levi, maybe she needed some good old-fashioned girl talk.

So after finishing the press conference debrief, she'd supervised the breakdown of the staging in the arena, then made follow up phone calls to so- lidify the next stops on Levi's goodwill tour. Now, it was nearing the dinner hour when she parked her Lexus in front of the main house at the Broken Spur, a two-story red cedar home in an L-shape around a brick driveway.

Lauryn, who ran a horse rescue operation nearby, sat on the front steps in a pink tank top with her jeans and boots, her arm slung around an adorable black dog with tan points. The pup looked like a Rottwei- ler, but his snout was longer, and he had a full tail with some extra fluff. An all-American, cute-as-can- be mutt.

The two of them rose at the same time to greet Kendra while she stepped from her sedan.

"Hello lovely," Lauryn greeted her, holding her arms wide to give her a hug. "I took some time off from the horse rescue to be at the press conference supporting Gavin today, but you were so deep in work mode I thought I'd give you space to do your thing." She squeezed Kendra tight, her chestnut hair smelling like orange blossoms. "It seemed like it went really well."

"As well as could have been expected considering what the Kingsleys are up against with allegations that their dad took money to allow illegal dump- ing on family land." Stepping away from her friend, Kendra took in the grounds and the dog who looked up at her hopefully. "And who is this handsome fel- low? Can I pet him?"

"By all means. Please say hello to Rocco, my new best friend." Lauryn laughed as the dog nodded his head as if he was urging Kendra to get on with the petting already.

"Hello, Rocco, you very good boy." Kendra scratched him behind his ears. "He looks like a Rottweiler, but he must have something else in the mix. He's super cute."

"He's definitely got some husky in him." Lauryn waved her toward the front door. "But come inside and see what I have for dresses. I've had to pick up a few more formal things since Gavin and I got together."

"I really appreciate it," Kendra answered as she followed her friend across the threshold into the foyer, the scent of roast chicken wafting from a kitchen deeper in the house. Rocco panted alongside her, clearly as at ease inside the house as outdoors. "I only brought enough clothes for a weekend with my dad, and I don't have time to return to my place in Denver before Levi's first few galas."

She would order some new things, but in the meantime, she greatly appreciated her friend's generosity so that she didn't arrive at her first event in travel-weary outfits.

"Frankly, I'm glad to see black-tie clothes get used. It always seems sad to buy a dress that you only wear a handful of times." Lauryn jogged up a split-log staircase and turned into a room at the top of the steps. Rocco hurried to catch up to her. "But tell me how Levi talked you into being his plus-one for the duration of this campaign. Is it just me or is that… um…more personalized service than you normally offer?"

Following Lauryn into a pristine cream-colored bedroom with a pale yellow duvet on the queen bed, Kendra paused to admire a bouquet of white ranunculus on a small nightstand. The lack of personal items suggested it might be a guest room. Lauryn strode to the back corner where she entered an archway that led into a connected bathroom and walk-in closet with racks on one wall and floor-to-ceiling shelving on the other. Understated industrial pendant lights were shown at intervals and a love seat rested in the middle of the closet.

"Wow." Kendra spared a moment to admire the organization of her friend's clothing. "This space is beautiful."

Rocco seemed to sense they'd reached their destination because he circled around in front of the love seat a few times before dropping to lay beside it with a doggy huff, his big head resting on his paws.

"I thought it was a little over the top when I first saw it, but I will admit it's fun having my own dressing room. I could share Gavin's closet in the main suite, but I like coming up here to get ready for the day." Lauryn paused in front of the rack with floor-length dresses in red, green, ivory and black. "Here are the gowns I was thinking of. But first I need the scoop on you and Levi."

"There is no scoop." Kendra tried not to bristle at

the thought of her friends and family assuming she had a relationship with Levi because of their business agreement. Hadn't she worked hard to distance herself from the kind of self-serving flirtations her mother had leveraged? And yet, she knew that's not what Lauryn implied, so Kendra tried not to bring her own baggage to the question. Instead, she ran her fingers over the black silk of a strapless number with a high slit up one thigh. "He wanted me to attend the events with him in case he needs backup when members of the media put him on the spot."

"And you agreed," Lauryn continued, busying herself with taking a green minidress with a long crepe bow from the rack. "Which I wondered about since you and Levi seem to have some history?" She thrust the dress at Kendra and rushed to add, "Hope and I noticed it when we all went to the Stockyard last time. You made comments about Levi that made me think there was bad blood between you two."

"Ugh. Are you really holding me accountable for things said while under the influence?" She held the gown up to her and admired the way the emerald color looked against her hair. "This is a definite if you don't mind parting with it."

"You are supposed to take all of these," Lauryn insisted, reaching for a garment bag from a wooden drawer under another set of racks. "And I'm not sure one beer counts as under the influence."

"Says the sheriff's daughter?" Laughing, Kendra

shook her head. "I'm pretty sure your dad wouldn't agree."

"If I'm being too nosy, you know I'll back off." Lauryn tucked a brown wave behind one ear, her hazel eyes more green than gold. "But I won't pretend I'm not dying of curiosity."

As much as Kendra hadn't wanted to spill the mistakes she'd made with Levi in the past, she couldn't deny that her friend's input might help. If nothing else, she might feel less burdened to share the truth with Lauryn.

Giving up on shopping her pal's closet for a moment, she walked over to the pale yellow wingback chair in the center of the room and perched on one arm.

"Three years ago, Levi and I went home together after a local rodeo," Kendra confided, her mind scrolling with memories, her heart racing faster now, as it had then. "You were out of town that week and it was just before I moved to Denver."

She'd been planning to relocate anyway for better career opportunities, but the incident with Levi had fast-forwarded the plans.

Lauryn's eyebrows shot up as she rehung the dress she'd been holding. "You and Levi?"

Kendra nodded, for once allowing her brain to remember an evening she usually tried to forget. For a moment, she would savor the power of their encounter.

"I'd known him from around town, obviously, but

I'd never really spent time with him until that night
and we just…clicked." They'd talked about everything. He'd shared his frustrations with his father's
business decisions. She'd confided about her dad's
gambling addiction and depression. They'd both been
raised without a mother in their lives since Levi's had
died in a riding accident when he'd been a kid and
Kendra's had walked out on the family.

There'd been a connection right away.

"You had good chemistry," Lauryn observed with
a knowing glance as she settled on the opposite chair
arm from her.

"Without a doubt." She couldn't afford to dwell
on that part of the equation though, because that part
had been beyond amazing, and she hadn't found a
man since who could turn her inside out the way
Levi had. "But I really believed it was more than
just chemistry because we had a lot of other things
in common. Or so I thought."

"What happened?" Lauryn bent low to stroke a
hand over Rocco's head where the dog lay nearby.

The Rottweiler mix thumped his tail against the
soft carpet.

"Levi used what I'd told him about my father's
business to go behind my back and purchase the
company from Dad without my knowledge." Looking back, she still couldn't believe how fast the deal
had come together. One day, she'd been working on
ideas for the logo with her father. Seemingly the next,

Seth Davies had been gambling with the money from the sale of the company. "I was devastated."

Straightening from where she'd been petting the dog, Lauryn shook her head in disbelief. "Levi did that? He always seems so responsible and honorable. I can't imagine how—"

"I assure you, he did it." Kendra remembered how it had felt when she learned her dad had a small fortune to lose on horses at the racetrack, all thanks to Levi. She'd been shattered. Like the rug had been pulled out from under her feet. "He would have never even known about Gargoyle King if I hadn't told him—"

"Your dad came up with Gargoyle King?" A smile lit Lauryn's face briefly before she recalled the context of the story and her face fell again. "How awful that he doesn't get credit for the company when it's been a runaway success."

Kendra shrugged as if it didn't matter, even though deep down, the hurt still lingered over the feeling of betrayal. "I realize that much of the success is due to Levi's business savvy. He took Dad's vision and ran with it, plus he had the resources to put behind the company in a way my father never could have done. Still, it hurt to have him take what I'd confided and turn it into personal profit while Dad—"

She broke off, her emotions getting the better of her as she thought about the downturn in her father's life after he'd returned to gambling. And lost nearly all of the money he'd made on the sale of the business.

"Honey, I'm sorry I brought this up—" Lauryn began, circling Kendra's shoulders with one arm.

"I'm glad you did," Kendra assured her, then dragged in a deep breath to steady herself. "I didn't realize how much I needed to share the story, but the resentment toward Levi all came to a head when he showed up on my doorstep to ask for my help."

They sat in silence for a moment, soaking in the comfort of friendship. Would it have helped her navigate the explosion with Levi if she'd confided in her friend long ago?

"How are you going to get through the next few weeks?" Lauryn asked afterward, her arm sliding away. "Won't it be tough to be around him nonstop for weeks?"

Tough? Now that was an understatement.

Kendra rose to her feet and returned to Lauryn's dress rack, determined to choose some outfits so she could start packing. "I'm just going to keep my eye on the prize with my big commission from this job, and the certainty that my boss will have to bring me onboard as a partner after I complete it." She hung the red dress near the others she was taking with her and then lifted the garment bag to zip them inside. "That will make the time I spend with Levi all worth it."

Hopping to her feet to help her, Lauryn lifted all the hangers from the rack to thread them through the top of the garment bag. "Or maybe this trip will help the two of you reconnect," she ventured lightly before catching Kendra's skeptical glance. "There's a chance that you weren't wrong about him when the two of you met. Maybe he had other reasons for buying out your dad. Reasons you don't know about."

Kendra chewed her lip, trying to be fair to Levi, but failing to see any alternative answer that equaled something besides treachery. "I appreciate the dose of optimism, but I have to be realistic. Levi betrayed my trust after I let him get close to me the first time. I won't make the same mistake twice."

Grateful for the listening ear as much as the dresses, she gave her friend another hug and then bent to scratch the dog before she headed for the door.

She had bags to pack for her trip with Levi, and even if she had zero intention of repeating the mistakes of her past with him, she still wanted to look like a million bucks every second they spent together.

Pacing in front of the open Jetway stairs leading into his compact HondaJet, Levi double-checked his watch after reassuring the pilot they would depart on time.

In just ten minutes from now.

Where was Kendra?

He'd told her to be here twenty minutes ago. But just when he was about to text her again, he spied her tall figure dressed in a short black wrap dress and a pair of oversized sunglasses perched on her nose. She towed a rolling suitcase behind her, with a second bag strapped to it. A buff colored handbag rested on her forearm while her shiny platinum waves caught the late morning sunlight. Sky-high beige heels arched her feet in a way that flexed her calves and gave her legs that would stop traffic.

Her bright red lips parted as she smiled at him. "Good morning, Levi."

He scrounged to recall his annoyance with her and put a damper on the heated attraction her sexy appearance had stirred.

"You're late," he informed her, more harshly than he'd intended. He reached to take her luggage from her. "I'll stow this for you."

"I thought I was nearly—" she paused to check her watch near the Jetway stairs "—eight minutes early."

Levi waved her up the steps ahead of him and raised his voice so she could hear him over the plane engine that was already running. "I asked you to arrive half an hour before takeoff because the pilot needs time to load and taxi."

"Sorry. I assumed you were just building an extra half hour into the schedule in case I was the kind of person who ran late. Which I don't." She climbed the stairs in front of him, giving him an incredible rear view of those luscious legs. "In the future, I'll know better."

He forced himself to wait a moment before he

followed her, even though the scent of her fragrance made him want to sniff in her wake. Once she'd cleared the threshold of the jet and he saw her lower herself into a seat through one of the cabin's round windows, Levi ascended the stairs.

He stowed her bags next to his and then pulled the door to the aircraft closed. Moments later, after seating himself in the leather chair across the aisle from her, he texted the pilot that they were ready for takeoff.

Or at least, he thought darkly as he glanced over at her, they were as ready as they'd ever be. Was Kendra's waltzing in at the last minute an indication of her unhappiness at working with him in the first place? He really didn't want to begin this mission on the wrong foot.

"Look, Kendra—" he began at the same moment she tapped on her watch face and held it out for him to see.

"Ready for takeoff precisely at ten thirty," she pointed out, her red manicured nail underscoring the digit on the rose gold face. Her sunglasses were now perched on her head, holding her hair away from her face.

"Point taken," he acknowledged wearily, hating everything about flying from the enclosed space to the lack of control. "I just want to be sure we're on the same page as we begin this thing."

He stopped speaking when he saw her looking at him. Frowning.

"Do you have a problem with flying?" Her hazel gaze studied his face while she tugged her sunglasses off her head and tucked them into the handbag at her feet. "I see you have a patch behind your ear. I didn't realize—"

"It's nothing." He waved away her concern, not ready to share the issues he had with not being at the helm himself. "I'm a simple Montana cowboy at heart, so I'd always rather have my boots close to the ground. But I fly frequently for business."

She nodded, seeming to accept his answer, though her gaze remained speculative.

And why did it matter what she thought of him? Or even that she expressed concern? Frustrated with himself for giving this woman way too much mental real estate, he pulled out his tablet and began scrolling through open tabs for his digital planner.

"Can we go over the schedule now? I noticed you added a few events and I want to make sure we've got enough time between them for travel and regrouping." He tapped on the dates for the following weekend. "It looks like there is no breathing room in here."

She shifted in her chair and peered over at his screen. When she lifted her long hair away from her neck to rest the silky mass on one shoulder, he caught a hint of her jasmine perfume.

The stuff was an aphrodisiac, reminding him of their night together and the subtle scent that had clung to his sheets afterward.

"It will be tight, but there is a major Earth fair taking place in Long Island next weekend and I booked you a booth. The media coverage will be excellent." Kendra straightened in her seat and withdrew her phone. "I'm working with some of the interns on the coal ash cleanup team to come up with an informative and interactive display. You can scroll through the photos to see what they've done so far."

She passed her device to him while he tried to catch up to everything she'd just said. Instead of asking the ten different questions her words had generated in his mind, he looked at the screen instead.

A brightly colored board depicted an electric power plant and described the process that generated coal ash. Scrolling to the next image, he saw more information about responsible disposal of coal ash and ways it could be used in manufacturing. He'd only just begun researching this stuff himself and had learned that it could be repurposed into the making of Portland cement and gypsum board—uses that were addressed on a third board in another photo.

"When do you sleep?" he finally asked her, beginning to recognize the level of value her service had provided his company. He would have never thought of the kinds of initiatives she was pushing for his company to make. "I mean, I saw how the team you hired helped with the press conference. But you must have had a whole other crew to work on things like this. Not to mention coordinating media coverage for the events we will attend."

Passing the phone back to her, the last of his annoyance over her late arrival faded. While he'd been packing a couple of tuxedos, she'd been arranging for him to participate in highly focused environmental events around the country. And not just arranging. Hell, she'd been designing the support materials he'd need to do an effective job.

"I'm good at what I do, Levi. The same way you're good at what you do." She slid the phone in her bag before tipping to rest her head on the seat back. "Which, I happen to know, is more than a simple Montana cowboy's work, no matter what you'd have me believe."

There was an edge to her words. As if she didn't appreciate that he ran a big business or somehow resented that he was good at what he did. But that didn't make any sense.

One day, he would discover what it was that had caused her about-face from being a woman who gladly lost herself to passion in his arms, to someone who wanted nothing to do with him. But today, as they set out on a professional venture that he desperately needed to succeed, he wasn't about to rock the boat.

Five

"I don't think this is the way to the hotel." Frowning, Kendra checked her phone for her trip notes as their chauffeured luxury SUV accelerated through a green light in Midtown Manhattan. "I'm sure the place I booked was right around the corner from the venue."

She'd sent the address to the car service ahead of time, so when their driver picked them up at the airfield, she'd relied on the woman having the correct information. Now, as they drove farther up Madison Avenue, she sat forward on the buttery leather seat to press the call button for their driver.

Levi's hand fell over hers before she could push the lever. "We're going the right way. I asked your travel administrator to upgrade some of the lodging choices on the itinerary."

"You did?" She bristled, miffed she hadn't been notified. And yes, a little insulted that he didn't approve of her choices. "I would have taken care of that if I'd known—"

"I am sure you would have." His hand slid away, but her skin remained warm where they'd touched. "But I knew you had a lot on your plate, so I asked my assistant to contact yours. And in Midtown, I've had good experiences with the Plaza."

She tried to remind herself that with any other client, she would be deferential. Accepting. He would be footing the bill for the luxury accommodations, after all. Yet with the history between her and Levi, Kendra couldn't help but feel maneuvered.

Was his high-end choice a way of setting a scene for romance between them? She hadn't gotten any vibes from him like he was trying to re-create the past. Maybe she just felt prickly because stepping into a world of affluence reminded her of her mother. Mom would eat up the private jet and the Plaza Hotel and never think twice about the cost, let alone the environmental impact.

Levi's voice interrupted her spiraling thoughts.

"I trust that's not a problem?" The deep resonance of his tone vibrated through her, reminding her how close they sat next to one another in the back of the SUV.

His palm rested on the seat between them, just inches from her thigh.

"Of course not," she rushed to answer when she managed to tear her thoughts from his hands and her thighs. She really needed to get herself together. "I just want to make sure we're on track to keep our schedule."

A slow smile spread across his features. "Just like I felt when you were late for the plane today. We're not all that different, you and me. We like things done a certain way."

"Didn't we already establish I wasn't late since I didn't delay takeoff by so much as a second?" she shot back, unable to rein herself in when his words had hit a little too close to home. They were *very* different, damn it. She didn't backstab people. "And I don't think we're all that alike when you prefer things done your way, and I want them done mine."

His grin only widened, making him even more roguishly handsome. "My point exactly."

She opened her mouth to argue, only to realize the absurdity of the conversation. Plus, it wasn't easy to argue with him when he was being charming. And the memory of his touch still tingled over her skin.

Settling back against the seat, she told herself that this would be a long few weeks if she needed to win every point. If she kept her focus on their professional relationship—remembering Levi's preferences as her client would have to guide their journey—she would get through this publicity campaign with her temper in check.

"I'm sure this will serve the purpose," she conceded as the SUV pulled up to the Plaza Hotel perched on a part of 57th Street known as Billionaire's Row.

Already, a liveried bellman approached the vehicle as it rolled to a stop in front of the iconic entrance.

"Let's hope so." Levi unbuckled his lap belt, his knee brushing hers as he shifted in his seat. "I got us a suite with a terrace overlooking Central Park. I thought it would be a nice lowkey spot for dinner before the gala tonight."

The thought of sharing an intimate meal with a man who attracted her like no other flustered her. Robbed her of speech for a moment.

She was saved from responding by the bellhop opening her door.

"Welcome to the Plaza Hotel." He greeted her with a smile as she stepped down from the SUV.

"Thank you," she murmured, taking in the sights and sounds of the city as pedestrians crowded toward the entrance to Central Park across the street. The exhaust of idling traffic mingled with the scents from a falafel food truck parked at a corner nearby.

"Are you ready to head inside?" Levi's voice sounded close to her ear, his fingers briefly brushing the small of her back as he joined her near the entrance.

Was she?

They were on day one of this venture and she already feared she was losing control of the trip. Not just the itinerary, but with her attempts to keep him at arm's length. While the hotel staff unloaded their bags and brought them inside the building, Kendra kept her focus on the reward at the end of the journey.

She'd be a partner in her public relations firm and she didn't need to stay in Silent Spring other than the visits to see her dad. She could do this.

"More than ready." Tightening her grip on her handbag, she headed toward the glass doors. "I'm looking forward to attending our first event so we can start turning the tide of public opinion about Kingsland."

"So am I. But Kendra?" Levi held the door open for her, a blast of cool air-conditioning welcoming her.

"Mmm?" she answered distractedly, taking in the opulence of the marble-clad hotel lobby from the pattern of the inlaid floor to the huge columns framing the entrance to a bar area.

"I hope we can take a break from talking about the tour over dinner."

His request caught her off guard and she turned to gauge his expression. Blue eyes stared back at her, sincerity in his gaze.

"If that's what you'd like," she began, hesitating a bit since she hadn't been prepared to talk about anything but work.

Keeping things professional was her best defense against Levi's masculine appeal that lingered no matter how often she reminded herself of his betrayal.

"I definitely need time to decompress between engagements. That's part of the impetus for the upgraded hotels. We can't work 24/7."

Her mouth went dry at the thought of veering away from the professional realm. But she wasn't about to argue with him anymore this afternoon. For now, she simply nodded.

"Of course. I understand."

Levi, seeming satisfied with her answer, went to the front desk to check them into their suite.

Kendra lingered in the center of the gleaming marble floor as she banked on a couple of hours to retreat to her own room. She needed to come up with a plan for a private dinner on a terrace overlooking Central Park with a gorgeous man who still had the power to charm her. She would be surrounded by luxury and probably plied with decadent foods.

Oh, and by the way, she couldn't hide behind work or use that as a shield against the attraction simmering every time she turned around.

For a moment, the evening seemed hopeless.

Until she recalled her father living in a near-empty house because Levi's money had propelled Seth Davies to new gambling extremes. Withdrawing her cell phone from her bag, she figured now was the perfect time to check on him.

Remind herself of the kinds of consequences that came from acting on something as fleeting as sensual chemistry.

Adjusting his black bow tie as he moved through the two-bedroom suite, Levi laid his tuxedo jacket over the back of an armchair in the living area before tugging open the door.

Two members of the room service team stood in the hallway with food carts to set up the meal he had ordered.

"Come on in." He waved them into the suite so they could prepare for dinner on the terrace. A meal he wanted so he could decompress before the gala.

He hadn't really wanted any part of being on this tour in the first place since the spotlight was his worst nightmare, so he planned to do whatever he could to make the next three weeks more bearable for himself and for Kendra too.

He recalled all too well that she hadn't wished to join him on the publicity tour, a fact that still nettled considering the scorching night they'd once shared. No matter how many times he told himself that he shouldn't concern himself with what happened in the past, every second he spent with her was like iron trying to resist the draw of a magnet. Earlier, he'd heard the tub running in the bathroom and had been plagued with visions of her naked body surrounded by bubbles.

Now, as he texted the manager in charge of the Stockyard while he was out of town, he heard the door to Kendra's suite open. Anticipation vibrated through him.

His reaction to her got tougher to ignore every single time he saw her.

Hell, he *hadn't* set eyes on her yet, and just knowing that he soon would had him wound tight and unable to concentrate. Setting aside his phone on a mahogany secretary desk, he spun to face her.

And his jaw honest to God fell open.

With her hair pinned up in a bun like a ballerina, she looked like something out of a high fashion magazine, in a gown of black silk and tulle. A strapless, body-skimming silk sheathe covered her from breast to mid-thigh. Flowing over the barely-there dress, however, was a layer of sheer tulle with a lacy pattern stitched into the fabric. The cut of the overdress was almost demure in its puffed sleeves and collar that went to her throat. But the effect of the dress beneath it? Racy. Siren-like.

So sexy that he wanted to...

He scrubbed a hand over his face, wishing he could block out those thoughts. Because the dress had him wanting to do things he had no business doing with her.

"You look incredible," he said finally, realizing that she was looking at him with something close to worry in her eyes.

"Maybe it's too much for a charity gala?" she mused, glancing down at the fabric to assess her legs through the silky screen of black tulle. "I borrowed it from Lauryn and I almost fell over when I read the designer label. I can't believe she loaned me a Valentino without warning me."

"It suits you," he assured her honestly, regretting that his moment of gawking had made her second-guess herself. "I'll be the envy of every man in the room."

A wry smile curved her lips, painted in a pale shade of coral as she glanced back to him. "I'm not sure that's what I should be going for. But thank you." Her hazel eyes traveled over him. Lingering? She cleared her throat. "You cleaned up well yourself."

Recognizing that even if she was still drawn to him, she planned to fight it tooth and nail, Levi shut down the visions of her legs wrapped in nothing but delicate lace.

"I do my best." Pointing toward the terrace visible through the French doors, he reached for the closest handle. "Are you ready to eat? It looks like they've finished setting up outside."

Soon, they were seated on cushioned patio chairs around a tile-topped wrought iron table. He'd texted in their orders ahead of time, so their meals were waiting under silver-domed trays. After ensuring they had everything necessary to enjoy their meal, the waitstaff departed with their serving carts, leaving Levi alone with Kendra and a million-dollar view of Central Park and the Hudson River in the distance. At over thirty stories high, they could see one iconic building after another over the short cedar hedge lining the balcony rail.

While Kendra picked at an heirloom tomato salad and pan-seared chicken, Levi dug into the lobster pappardelle. He hoped that if he allowed her some space to enjoy her meal, she'd eventually come around to conversation that wasn't business. He'd tried to make it clear that he'd booked the better hotels in an effort to find some breathing room from the publicity tour—he couldn't afford the stress of thinking about the mess his father had left behind every hour of the day.

But when long minutes had passed without a word from her, Levi searched his brain for a neutral topic. One without emotional baggage attached.

"What did you think of the new Gargoyle King IPA?" he asked, remembering her visit to the Stockyard a few weeks before. He'd sent a bucket of assorted Gargoyle King beers to the table where she'd been seated with Lauryn Hamilton and Hope Alvarez, so he knew she'd seen his brewery's latest offering.

Kendra's fork clattered to her plate. "I can't believe you would bring that up."

"I'm not sure why. Is it a lost cause to think we can talk about anything outside of the professional realm?" He tried to make sense of her response and failed.

"Gargoyle King is your business," she reminded him coolly, regathering her utensil to stab at her chicken. "That is the very definition of work."

Frowning, Levi struggled to figure out what had upset her. He reached for the crystal water pitcher and refilled both their glasses.

"I understand your point, but it was the publicity tour that I needed a conversational break from, not any of the Kingsland businesses." Resettling the pitcher on the far side of the table so it wasn't in the way, he tried to get a read on her expression. "I enjoy my work tremendously. Especially the bar and brewery, which has been a welcome respite from the headaches of the ranch since my dad's passing."

"I'm sorry about your dad," she replied slowly, leaning back in her chair as the setting sun painted the terrace behind her in shades of pink and gold. Her blond hair glowed brighter in the light. "Despite the difficulties of his will, I know losing him must have been hard."

The understanding in her gaze called to mind all the ways they'd connected with one another that first night they'd met. Their complicated relationships with their fathers made for an immediate bond. Kendra had understood loving a parent whose actions had often been hurtful.

"Thank you," he said, clearing his throat. He shifted aside his empty plate. "It's hard coming to terms with him slighting my half brothers in his final wishes. I want him to be here so I can tell him what a mistake he's making by cutting them out of the legacy that is rightfully theirs. But I'll never know why he did it, and I'll never be able to change his mind." It hurt that he hadn't known his father nearly as well as he'd thought. "For that matter, I'll never know if I *could have* changed his mind."

She reached across the table and gave his hand a quick squeeze, compassion in her eyes. He returned the gesture, pressing her palm lightly with his fingers, before her hand slid from his.

The silence between them grew.

After a moment, Kendra lifted her water and took a long sip. He watched her throat close as she swallowed and felt his hunger for her stir. His thoughts drifting to the way her skin would taste if his lips grazed the hollow at the base of her neck. When she finished, she replaced the crystal glass on the table and said in a flat voice, "I've been meaning to tell you that the Gargoyle King's new IPA is excellent. Citrusy with just the right hint of bitterness."

"You liked it?" Her approval surprised and pleased him, begrudging though it might be.

He shoved aside thoughts of what her neck tasted like to focus on her words.

"I did." She glanced away, staring out over the shadows lengthening on the trees in Central Park. Her jaw flexed as she seemed to sit in thought. "My father has tried the IPA as well, and he thinks it's one of the standouts for the label."

"I'm really glad to hear that," he confessed, relieved to know Seth Davies thought Levi had contributed something positive to the business. "It makes me happy to know your dad sees some merit in how I've steered the company."

Kendra's brow furrowed. Her pretty coral lips pursed.

Something in her eyes appeared censorious. Reproachful.

"What's wrong?" Concerned, he lifted his napkin from his lap and folded the linen onto the table. His hand so close to hers it wouldn't take but a simple unfurling of his fist for their fingers to touch. "Is there some other part of the business that your father finds fault with? I really do look forward to his input when he begins his stint on the board of directors. I've already sent him the information on the next meeting."

He'd considered extending the position to the older man before but hadn't been certain if Seth was in a good emotional and mental place to take on the extra responsibilities. Kendra had confided that he struggled with addiction issues and the last thing Levi wanted was to exacerbate a problem for her or her dad.

But before Kendra answered, she pushed back from the table and rose hurriedly to her feet, black tulle swishing tantalizingly around her legs.

"We really need to get under way if we want to be on time for tonight's gala." She picked up her phone from where she'd laid it on the table earlier. "I'll text the driver that we're heading down and to bring around the car."

The conversational shift gave him whiplash.

He hadn't wanted to talk about work. But he definitely needed to revisit whatever it was they'd been circling around during this meal. Something about Kendra's reactions were all off, making him wonder what he was missing.

They'd been discussing the night at the Stockyard. Now that he thought back, he recalled that he'd sent the round of drinks to her and her girlfriends because some guy had been hassling them. Gavin had eventually encouraged the guy to leave the bar, and Levi had figured that had been an end of it, sending over the beers as a way to make it up to the women for a pushy dude inserting himself into their girls' night out.

But had there been more to it than that?

"Wait a minute." Rising from his chair, he reached for her, his hand settling on her arm as he stepped closer. "Kendra, is everything all right? Did something happen that night at the bar?"

Concern for her tensed his shoulders. He didn't like the idea of anyone hassling a woman. But the thought of someone hassling *this* woman triggered all kinds of Neanderthal instincts. Knowing as much, he let go of her arm, unwilling for her to see how much she affected him.

Still.

"Nothing happened at the bar." Shaking her head, she looked up into his eyes, making him realize how close he'd stood. "And everything is fine."

Her pulse jumped in her neck just above the delicate lace collar of her dress. Because she was fibbing about everything being "fine"?

Or was it because she felt a fraction of the heat currently setting him on fire?

He hoped like hell it was the latter. Especially

because his hands itched to touch her. To drag her against him and hold her there, until her body remembered all the ways he could bring her pleasure.

When her eyelids drooped to half-mast, he felt the surge of impending victory at that small sign of her desire for him.

"Kendra." Her name left his lips in a sound that was half whisper, half growl. But still he didn't touch her.

He needed her to want this as much as he did.

At the sound of his voice, she lifted her hand as if to touch his chest. Her fingers hovered there, just above his heart, as if she could sense it hammering for her.

Before she could lower her palm, however, her cell phone chimed on the table, the simultaneous vibration making it jump.

Kendra fairly jumped along with it, springing back from him as if the near-touch had never happened. Her hands were unsteady as she plucked the device from the tiles and read the screen.

"Our car is waiting for us downstairs," she informed him, her voice chilly, professional.

Then, without a backward glance, she swished past him in a brush of black tulle. Levi remained on the terrace for another minute, willing himself back to calm.

To the coolness she seemed to adopt so easily.

One way or another, he'd find out what this thing was that kept her apart from him. Tonight, he'd uncovered a hint of the old passion for him. Next he would puzzle out why she was so hell-bent on not acting on it.

Because time hadn't done a damned thing to ease his hunger for her. If anything, Levi realized that he wanted her more than ever.

Six

Tipping her chin to catch a spring breeze from a landscaped terrace overlooking Fifth Avenue, Kendra allowed herself a moment of much-needed personal space while a black-tie charity gala remained in full swing behind her.

She gripped the carved stone railing as she watched the lights from traffic at a crosswalk below. The venue for the gala took place on two floors, including the upper level terrace that featured a retractable roof so it could be used in all four seasons. After the frustrating conversation with Levi back at their hotel earlier, she'd been in need of some alone time to gather her thoughts.

Now, as the delicate tulle of her designer gown

blew gently against her calves, Kendra allowed the polite chatter of small talk and the music of a chamber ensemble to soothe her frayed nerves. If only the cool air could chill the mixture of frustration and attraction that heated her every encounter with her compelling client.

"May I join you?" a familiar voice asked from over her right shoulder, the deep tone of Levi's words affecting her like a finger trailing down her naked spine.

She hid her shiver as she turned to face the man who had never been far from her thoughts, even when they'd circulated the party separately. Levi extended a glass of water toward her while he held his own in the other hand.

"You are more than welcome," she assured him, donning the mask of politeness the event required while she accepted the drink. Checking the small face of a jeweled watch, she added, "I think we could safely leave in another half hour. You've done a great job connecting with the movers and shakers at this event."

When they'd arrived, Kendra had introduced him to the chairperson for the Environmental Defense Society and two well-respected members of the media. Levi had charmed each of them in turn, discussing sustainable grazing methods at Kingsland Ranch and asking for guidance on how he could play a bigger role in safeguarding the land.

He'd been an ideal client, keeping his remarks

upbeat and positive. He moved easily from one con-versational group to the next, and she hadn't even been able to enjoy the success due to her lingering frustration.

"It's easy when I have you pointing out who's who for me." He settled his glass on the railing and looked out over the city, his gaze sweeping from the Flatiron Building on their left to the Empire State Building on the right. "I appreciate you being here tonight."

She took a sip of her water as she tried to gauge his angle. Why did he bother being kind to her when he'd never offered anything close to an apology or an acknowledgement that he'd wronged her or her father? "You don't have to thank me when you're paying for my help."

"I disagree. I do need to thank you, because we both know you would have preferred to refuse me." Picking up his glass, he tilted it to shift the ice around before taking a long drink.

Somehow, despite the sip she'd just had, her throat felt dry watching his move on a long swallow. His Adam's apple lowered and raised above his black bow tie.

Watching him now, dressed in a tuxedo and ex-changing confidences with her in a quiet corner of the party, made her remember the night they'd met. The night they'd been at a rodeo after party and she'd been so caught up in the hot chemistry that she'd let her guard down.

When she remained silent, he spoke again, turning away from the railing to face her. "What I don't understand is why you wanted to refuse me. Or why you shut down on me over dinner tonight."

Did he really not know? Was there a chance he truly didn't understand how his purchase of Gargoyle King had devastated her?

Behind them, the chamber musicians shifted from a classical piece to a string rendition of a modern love ballad and the faux torchlights illuminating the terrace dimmed.

"As long as we get the job done, does it really matter?" she asked, handing off her empty glass to a passing server.

"It very much matters." His blue eyes locked on hers as he reached for her hand. "Dance with me, and I'll explain why."

Once more, she wanted to refuse him. Or at least, she knew she *should*. But between the warmth of his fingers wrapped around hers and the hypnotic gleam in his seductive gaze, she couldn't find the will to walk away.

"Just one dance," she agreed, her body already leaning toward his as if drawn by an irresistible force.

His jaw flexed as he gave a satisfied nod. Then, keeping hold of her hand, he guided her through the well-heeled crowd to the dance floor under the stars.

Less than a dozen couples joined them, giving them plenty of room to move. Plenty of privacy to talk. Yet, as Levi pulled her toward him, wrapping one arm around her waist to secure her against him,

Kendra couldn't work up much interest in conversation.

She was too busy cataloging the onslaught of sensations inspired by his touch. The almost-brush of his hip against hers as they moved together. The glide of her sheer dress around her legs, fabric tickling already sensitized skin. She breathed in the notes of cedar and musk that must be from his aftershave, the scent only detectable around his jaw. His neck.

Both right at nose level for her as they swayed and shuffled around the dance floor.

She was so lost in the way he made her feel, she almost forgot what they'd been discussing. But when his voice rumbled close to her ear, she remembered that he wanted to know why she'd been so adamant about not accompanying him on this trip.

"It matters to me," he began in a low tone. "Because I thought we really connected that one night we shared. Yet you've pushed me away ever since, and you've never told me why." He eased back to peer down at her in the moonlight. "If we're going to have a successful trip, I think it would help to put the past to rest. Something I can only do if I understand your reasons for the about-face three years ago."

While the string rendition of the love song swelled to the chorus, her stomach clenched around emptiness, reminding her she hadn't finished the meal he'd tried to get her to eat before the charity gala.

Recalling the lavish room at the Plaza Hotel and the thoughtful meal he'd ordered for them, Kendra struggled to hold on to the old grudge. But if he didn't know why she'd pulled away back then, she was more than happy to explain.

"You bought out my father's company when it was the only thing holding him together during a vulnerable time in his life," she explained, her hand flexing against his shoulder where it rested for their dance. The strength and warmth of him steadied her as she picked at an old wound. "He has struggled with depression and addiction ever since my mother left him, but especially then, when she'd just remarried for a second time."

Levi's expression clouded, his brow furrowing. "You told me about his gambling problem. You also mentioned the possibility of addiction replacement with him starting a liquor business."

Surprised at the accuracy of his memory—since she'd all but forgotten that worry—Kendra missed a step.

Light on his feet, Levi adjusted so that he didn't step on her. With strong hands, he guided her hips to catch up.

"I remember," she admitted haltingly, her brain casting back in time to the conversation she and Levi had. They'd been in his kitchen, making a late night snack after their first—or was it second?—time making love. "His doctor warned him that some people replace one addiction with another. So even though starting the liquor company was helping him recover from the gambling problem, Dad could have been setting himself up for an unhealthy relationship with alcohol."

An older couple waltzed past in perfect harmony, their eyes locked on one another. Kendra wondered if she would ever feel so in sync with someone. She'd only been with one other man since that memorable night with Levi, and that eight-month long relationship had ended when her boyfriend accepted a job on the west coast and she realized she had no wish to follow him.

After Levi's betrayal and her live-in lover's sudden exit from her life, Kendra had been content to pour everything into her work.

"That's exactly what I remember," Levi agreed, his arm shifting higher to rest on her waist, his palm on the small of her back. "You expressed a lot of anxiety about your father's new company. I bought it so that would be one less worry for you."

Kendra's feet stopped moving all together. Her world tilted sideways.

"Excuse me?"

Levi gave up the dance, his hands sliding away from her as they fell to his sides.

"I was under the impression I was doing you a favor when I bought Gargoyle King from your father." His eyes appeared troubled.

He looked ready to say more, but the chairperson for the event—a tall, lanky man in a navy blue tuxedo—paused at the edge of the dance floor and waved them over.

"Excuse me, Levi." The man, Bruno Delacorte, had a tablet in one hand and a glass of champagne in the other. "We're trying to coordinate a photo with a few of our other key donors. Would you mind joining us at the information table near the entry on the loft level?"

"I'd be happy to," he assured the other man, though his eyes lingered on Kendra as he lowered his voice to speak only to her. "Would you come with us? We need to discuss this more."

But she was already backing away from him.

She needed air to process what she'd just learned. And, perhaps, a call to her dad to refresh her memory on a few details. Had she misjudged Levi? If so, how did that affect her perceptions of other conversations they'd had lately?

"I need to get back to the hotel," she murmured, confusion tying her stomach in knots. "We can talk more in the morning."

"Kendra—" Levi began, his hand reaching for her arm.

But she didn't remain to hear the rest, nor did she allow him to stop her retreat. Because if Levi was telling her the truth, he'd just upended every single thing she thought she knew about him.

Levi strolled the seashore along Long Island's Great South Bay next afternoon, breathing in the salty air off the waterway that was technically a lagoon. After a packed day's schedule of events that included Kendra skillfully avoiding any downtime for a conversation, he was ready for a few moments of solitude, to feel the moist breeze on his face.

He'd worn cargo pants and a pair of boat shoes for the environmental festival held at a National Wildlife Refuge in Islip, on Long Island's south shore. The grounds of the sanctuary hosted a wealth of exhibits, games and demonstrations on environmentally-safe practices, while the shoreline remained open for visitors to take in the natural beauty of the protected space. Upbeat folk music from a guitar-playing duo harmonized with the muted sound of the waves lapping the shore at Levi's feet while a couple of shrieking teenage girls ran past him in the water, flip-flops in hand as they splashed their way by.

Kendra hadn't had time to give Kingsland a booth at this fair, but she'd insisted their attendance would give them ideas for future events. She'd booked him into two other festivals over the next few weeks. Today, he was only responsible for gathering ideas to connect with fairgoers and, of course, making a large donation to the wildlife refuge sponsoring this event. He'd already given the organizers an oversized check suitable for photo opportunities so his work for the day was complete.

All that remained was finding Kendra.

He wouldn't be accepting any more excuses for why they couldn't finish last night's conversation.

Turning from the water, Levi studied the line of exhibit tents, searching for a glimpse of Kendra's tall, slim form. His phone vibrated in his pants pocket before he could find her.

Hoping to see her name on the screen, he knew a moment's disappointment when his brother Quinton's name flashed instead. Brushing aside the feeling, he connected the call, eager for news from the ranch.

"Hey, Quint. What's up?"

"Sorry to bother you on the road." Quinton's words were clipped. He sounded agitated. "I know you've got a lot on your plate with the PR tour, but I thought you should know there was an...incident... at the Stockyard last night."

"You were there?" Levi was accustomed to his brother Gavin dropping by the bar on occasion, but Quinton rarely made time in his life for anything other than work.

"I dropped by to see for myself how business was faring in the wake of the revelations about our father." The edge in his voice was even more pronounced at the mention of Duke Kingsley.

"It's been dismal." Levi ran a frustrated hand through his windblown hair, hating that his bar business had taken a nosedive with the news of his father's alleged criminal activity.

Actually, business had dropped off right after Duke's games with his legacy had been made public knowledge. He paced along the water's edge, his boat shoes squishing into wet sand.

"And it continues to be," Quint confirmed. "But

I thought it was noteworthy that Seth Davies was at the bar."

Levi quit pacing, curiosity roused along with concern.

"Kendra's father was in my bar last night?" He'd never spotted the older man there before. "Maybe he wants to check out my businesses since I'm giving him a seat on Gargoyle King's board."

"I'm pretty sure professional reasons didn't have a damn thing to do with why he was there," Quint observed dryly. "Seth was three sheets to the wind and telling everyone who would listen that Gargoyle King was his business, not yours."

Levi felt his eyebrows shoot up. Shocked. Concerned. "He was drunk?"

"Totally sloshed. The bartender called a ride for him." In the background of the call, Quinton rattled ice cubes in the glass of whatever he was drinking.

Levi could picture his brother in the Kingsland Ranch office, stopping by to take care of ranch business as a favor to Levi even though Quinton never spent more time in Silent Spring than strictly necessary.

"And was anyone else around to hear the claims he made?" Levi turned on his heel as he reached the end of the beach, mentally running through the list of regulars who still showed up at the establishment even when business was bad. A few local ranchers. A couple of old-timers who met up for a weekly game of darts.

"Three or four folks I didn't recognize. But Sheriff Hamilton was there with his wife." More agitated ice rattling.

"Damn it." Levi pinched the bridge of his nose where a stress headache was starting to tighten.

Their brother Gavin had a long-standing feud with the local sheriff, although Levi hoped it was on the mend now that Gavin had started dating the lawman's daughter, Lauryn.

"My thought exactly. I'm going to call Gav next and see if he can convince Lauryn to talk to her father, make sure that Seth's ravings don't get around via the sheriff."

"But that doesn't mean the rest of last night's patrons aren't already spreading the word," Levi grumbled.

Had Kendra spoken to her father last night about the conversation she'd had with Levi? All the more reason he needed to speak to her.

"At least you can ask Kendra what gives with her old man," Quinton suggested, sounding more optimistic about that tactic. "Maybe she can talk to him?"

If only Quinton knew how little pull Levi had with Kendra Davies.

"I'll see what I can do," he assured his brother as he headed away from the beach toward the exhibition tents to find his publicity campaign manager. "Thanks for the heads-up."

Disconnecting the call, he pocketed his phone and

hastened his step, determined to shake answers free from his tight-lipped plus-one on this trip.

Of course, that image called to mind the more pleasurable ways to loosen her lips. Memories from their night together blasted across his brain, more vivid than any of the fair activity in swing all around him.

Their dance last night had reminded him how perfectly she fit against him. How fast her light jasmine fragrance could fire his neurons and make him want her. Most of all, that dance had showed him that she wasn't immune to him either. He'd felt the way she sighed into him when he'd pulled her closer.

Heard the way her breath caught when his hands moved over her hips to steer her through the dance.

By the time he spotted her bright blond hair two booths away, the hunger for her was like a fever in his blood. He pointed his feet toward where she stood with two other women in front of a colorful display detailing native bird species.

She wore a fitted blue sundress with white buttons down the front and matching blue sandals. Her hair was loose today, the waving strands swirling around her shoulders as if they wanted to wrap her up the same way he did.

When he was a few yards away, she turned as if she'd felt his eyes on her. Their gazes met. Held. The air around them crackled.

And, almost as if she could read the hot intention

in his expression, she excused herself from her companions before heading toward him.

"Is everything all right?" she asked, hazel eyes roaming his face.

"We need to talk." Taking her hand, he drew her through the crowd that had multiplied in the last hour as the dinner hour approached. A nearby food tent overflowed with strollers and young families, the scent of barbecue and other spices wafting from the hot grills sponsored by local restaurants.

"We should speak to a few more organizations before we leave the event—" Kendra began, fidgeting with a slim gold hoop earring with her free hand.

Halting on the walkway surrounding the environmental center building—an impressive repurposed French chateau—Levi turned to face her.

"You've been avoiding me all day," he reminded her, still holding onto one hand. He stroked his thumb along her knuckles, not sure if he was trying to soothe her or himself. "I'm not having a conversation with one more stranger until I have one with you."

She glanced down to their connected palms as if surprised to see him touching her. Or, maybe she was surprised to see that she was allowing the touch. He distracted her by reaching for her other hand.

They were in sight of the festivalgoers here, but with the main attractions on the beach and in the exhibition tents, the elegant stone building that housed the educational center remained quiet. The stone walkway where they stood was empty except for them.

"I'm doing the job that you hired me for," she reminded him, her voice unexpectedly husky. "It's your choice if you want to ignore the contacts I'm making to benefit the standing of your business."

His gaze dipped to her mouth where only a hint of her pink lipstick remained. The natural color of her lips bled through the hints of pink gloss, calling to him to lick away the remnants. With an effort, he dragged his focus back to her eyes.

"I can't work every minute of every day. And you know very well that we left yesterday's conversation unfinished."

She huffed out a breath. "But what's left to say, Levi?" She sounded exasperated as she tugged her hands away. "That there was a misunderstanding? That my worries about my father were never significant enough to warrant you swooping in and taking his company? That your intentions weren't as nefarious as I imagined?"

"Yes. That's exactly what needs discussion." His eyes narrowed. "Do you realize how much that changes things between us?"

She shook her head. "It changes nothing. No matter what our intentions were three years ago, they don't alter the bigger picture. That you bought out my father and sent him on a gambling binge to end all gambling binges." Shrugging, she folded her arms around herself. "Good intentions don't change what happened."

"They might change how you feel about me. About us."

"There is no us," she shot back, anger flashing in her eyes.

Or was it some other heated emotion?

Testing the theory, he stepped closer to her. Saw the way her pupils dilated. The way she nipped her lip between her teeth.

"Are you sure about that?" He couldn't help the way his voice lowered as his head dipped.

His mouth hovering over hers so that they breathed one another in.

She opened her mouth to speak. To argue?

But then, Kendra shocked the hell out of him by closing the inch that separated them to seal her lips to his.

Seven

What are you thinking?

A critical voice inside Kendra's head was already sounding off about her impulsive move to kiss Levi.

But the seductive sweep of his tongue along her lower lip was sending a whole other round of messages to her brain. Overruling her good sense.

Echoes of the environmental fair faded into the background. Laughter and conversation from the food tent barely registered. Giggling children and the folk music from two guitars swirled on the breeze, but none of it distracted her from savoring the sensation of Levi's hands cupping her hips to pull her closer.

Or the feel of his broad chest when her curves molded to the hard muscles.

Her heart galloped faster, knocking into her ribs. Memories of being with him three years ago wound through her, urging her for a repeat of that unforgettable night, until she clenched her fingers into fists to keep from tunneling under his shirt and splaying over his chest.

Instead, she simply focused on the way his lips teased along hers, nipping and licking. They were out of sight of the festivalgoers behind the corner of the building. No one would see her indiscretion. For a moment, she went boneless against him, her whole body settling deeper into his.

A quiet groan rumbled through him. His fingers tightened on her hips where he touched her. An electric current seemed to zip from that point of contact right to the heart of her, making her ache for more.

But he eased away from her a moment later, breaking the kiss to tip his forehead to hers. They breathed together, chests rising and falling too fast as she tried to collect herself.

"I never meant to bring trouble to your family," he said finally, stroking a thumb along her jaw as he straightened to look into her eyes. "I should have checked with you before I made your father that offer."

Some of the lingering heat inside her cooled at the reminder of their old standoff. And yet, Levi finally seemed to be giving her a fraction of what she'd long wanted from him.

An explanation. An expression of regret.

"Yes, you should have." She flipped her hair behind her shoulder as she stepped away from him, wishing she could just let it go. It would be better for their professional relationship. Yet, from a personal standpoint, she couldn't forget that Levi had tried to buy his way into her good graces by taking her father's business off his hands, never considering how it might upend their lives. "But it's done and over. At least I know your heart was in the right place at the time. So thank you for telling me."

Levi's eyes tracked her as she paced a few steps from him. She could sense his stare even when her back was turned, as if there was an invisible string connecting them ever since they'd kissed. Dragging in a deep breath of sea air, she rounded the corner of the building so she could refocus her attention on the festival.

Behind her, she heard Levi's footsteps following.

"Are we going to talk about what just happened?" he asked, his deep voice sending a shiver through her despite the warm day.

Fumbling for her phone, she withdrew it from her dress pocket to give her something else to think about besides what had just happened.

"It might be better to take a breath before we revisit today's events." As they neared the festival tents, she tried to keep her voice offhanded. Calm. But she was twisted up inside. Uncertain about her motives.

What had made her throw caution to the wind

and kiss him when she'd been trying so hard to keep her distance?

"Don't you think our work will suffer for it?" he asked in all seriousness. "It's bound to make things awkward having a kiss hanging over our heads."

She ground her teeth together for a moment, mindlessly tapping buttons on her phone screen to avoid looking at him.

"It took you three years to discuss the mistake you made the last time we were together." Pausing just outside the food tent, she saw a text from her father in her messages. She knew she'd need to speak to him sooner or later. "Shouldn't I be entitled to a few hours to get my thoughts in order before you grill me about this?"

Pocketing her phone, she glanced back at Levi.

Her companion studied her thoughtfully, his blue eyes stirring the embers still hot from that kiss.

"Fair enough," he agreed finally, pulling up alongside her. "I'm sure we both have work to do before the Los Angeles leg of the trip." Shoving his hands in the pockets of his jacket, he rocked back on his heels. "We'll revisit the kiss then."

She felt some of the tension in her shoulders ease a fraction at the reprieve. She really did need to get her head together before she did something crazy like throw herself at him again.

"Fine. Are you ready to head back to the hotel? We should start packing if we're going to stop in Milwaukee to pick up the booth displays." She'd been grateful to Levi for offering to hand-deliver the exhibit materials she'd had custom-made for their first environmental fair in Chicago. But in order to transport them by his private plane, they'd need to make an extra stop tonight.

"You're right. We should be underway." He slid an arm around her to guide her through some pedestrian traffic crowding into the fair. "But I got so distracted by that kiss, I forgot to tell you something important."

Kendra's breath quickened at his touch, though he released her once they reached an open area of walkway leading back to the parking lot.

"I'm listening." She kept pace with his long strides, ready to get back to work.

"I spoke to Quinton earlier and he told me your father was at the Stockyard last night."

His halting tone made her turn to look at him.

"What aren't you telling me?" She could tell by his expression that there was more to the story.

As always, when it came to her father, she feared the worst. But Levi's establishment was a bar, not a casino. How much trouble could he get in?

"He'd been drinking a lot, apparently." Levi raised his arm to signal their driver who waited farther down the curb in front of the environmental center. "Quinton thought he was fairly intoxicated."

Fear for her dad clutched her insides. "Did he get home all right? Did anyone make sure he's safe?"

"Our bartender is good about that," he rushed to

assure her while the luxury black SUV rolled to a stop in front of them. A driver jumped out to open the rear door. "Quint said he called a car for your dad."

Kendra climbed inside the air-conditioned coolness of the leather-trimmed interior, her thoughts tumbling over one another as she tried to make sense of her father's outing. Was it a one-time thing? Or was the drinking something to be concerned about.

"I tried to reach Dad last night," she murmured, remembering the message she'd left as she buckled into her seat. "He hasn't answered my text yet today, so I'll try him again soon."

She still wanted to ask her father about his experience with Levi and the sale of Gargoyle King. At the time, she'd been so furious about the gambling binge that had cost him all of his money, she hadn't cared about the details of the sale. But now, after talking to Levi, she wondered.

Levi settled into the seat beside her, one long leg brushing hers as he shifted into a comfortable position. The contact zinged through her, reminding her of the kiss she'd initiated. Her skin heated at the thought of it.

"I brought it up as I know you were worried about the possibility of replacement addiction three years ago," Levi reminded her as he clicked the seat belt into place and the SUV moved forward. "I wanted to be sure the drinking wasn't a new habit."

He tugged his tablet from the seat pocket of the

SUV where he'd left it earlier and, true to his word, seemed to turn his attention to work.

But even though Kendra followed his example, opening her email on her phone to check the status of their next few stops on the tour, she couldn't get Levi's words out of her head.

Was it possible her father was drinking to excess on a regular basis?

She hadn't heard about any incidents before this, but she spent most of her time in Denver. Unease made her stomach roll with a reminder to keep her focus firmly on protecting her father, whatever form that took—business or personal.

As soon as they were back at the hotel, she'd call her dad and have a heart-to-heart.

At a small airport in Milwaukee later that evening, Kendra walked around the jet Levi had hired for the duration of the publicity campaign. Their pilot had landed the vessel half an hour before, but they'd had to wait for the arrival of the truck with the custom-designed booth displays for the Kingsland Ranch sponsored booth at the Chicago environmental fair.

Under the glare of a few nearby runway lights, Levi stood with the pilot and, now that the truck had finally arrived, oversaw workers who loaded the displays into the cargo area of the aircraft. The scent of jet fuel and truck exhaust mingled in an early evening haze, the nearby runway empty at the small field on the west side of the city. Kendra remained out of the way, stationing herself on the opposite side of the folding stairs leading up to the plane as she scrolled through her phone messages.

A few involved work-related issues that she sorted out simply by connecting colleagues or delegating an issue to a team member that was helping with the Kingsland Ranch job.

One came from her mother saying how much she loved Kendra's Valentino gown in a post she spotted on social media. Her mom then went on to urge Kendra to "go after" the gorgeous man who'd been on her arm in the same picture. Levi Kingsley, in other words. That message Kendra deleted, without even listening to the rest of her mother's inevitable rant.

The harangues about marriage and dating always ran the same course. Beginning with the reasons Kendra needed to start thinking more about a family and less about her career. As if she couldn't have both whenever she was ready. Then ending with specific suggestions for potential partners, ranging from the offspring of Jennifer's friends to random men she met through her work on her latest charity event.

All of whom had only one thing in common. Money to burn.

As if that was Kendra's motive for being with someone.

Freshly perturbed by her mom's newest insistence that Kendra chase Levi for the sake of a comfortable future, she jabbed at her phone screen to close the voice mail window.

Just as one more message began to play.

"Sweetheart, it's Dad—" her father's gravelly voice began.

Then quickly stopped again once Kendra's device caught up to her scrambling efforts to close the screen.

"Oh shoot," she grumbled to herself, levering away from the railing along the plane's fold-down stairs.

Her father had finally gotten back to her and she'd missed the call while they'd been airborne.

Instead of listening to whatever message he'd left, Kendra pushed the button to phone him directly. Once more, she listened to the phone ring a few times. Finally, he picked up.

"Hello, baby girl," Seth Davies greeted Kendra with the same fatherly affection that had comforted her since childhood. No matter what his personal troubles might be, her dad had always made an effort to show he loved her. "To what do I owe the pleasure of all those messages you left me?"

Refusing to quibble about whether or not two texts and a phone call over the past couple of days was overkill when her dad had addiction and mental health issues, Kendra paced the tarmac around the private plane as workers slid the final display board into the cargo area under the passenger cabin.

He sounded well enough. But she knew distance

could hide his real feelings. She'd become adept over the years at reading between the lines while living apart from him.

"I wanted to make sure you're all right, Dad," she reminded him gently—the same way she had in her messages. "I heard you were at the Stockyard two nights ago."

She left her comment at that, wondering if he would level with her about drinking to excess.

"So I did," he admitted, voice jovial. "A man has to find something to keep him amused when I don't have any family in town."

Kendra waited. Silent.

She didn't plan to make it any easier for him to keep uncomfortable truths from her. Still, she needed to tread warily.

A moment later, her father's explanation continued.

"The sheriff and his wife were there." In the background of the phone call, she could hear the beeping of the coffeepot, the sound signaling that a fresh brew was ready. "He sent me over a drink as a thank you for my book. Have I told you he's a big fan?"

She'd heard that before. Her dad's larger fame may have faded in the decade-plus since he'd had his last bestselling novel, but he still relived the high points of his career on occasion. Sheriff Hamilton had been at a long ago book signing, cementing her father's favor forever.

"I remember that." Her gaze lifted to the people

from the delivery company shaking hands with Levi before striding back to their truck. The pilot was busy buttoning up the cargo hold while she got to the point with her father. "Dad, you needed someone to call a ride for you to return home. Don't you think that means you've been drinking too much?"

His wry chuckle did nothing to ease her anxiety for him. Around her, the wind down the runway blew so hard she had to turn sideways to keep her dress from lifting like a parachute.

"I thought my gambling was the problem I needed to fix?" he asked, an edge in his voice beneath the facade of agreeability. She could hear the familiar squeak of the screen door in the back of the house, and she could picture him taking his coffee outside. "Let a man have at least one of his vices. I was celebrating a new book idea that came to me."

"Really? You thought of something new to write?" Even knowing that he was probably trying to distract her with tales of a book concept—something she'd been hoping he'd find for years—she couldn't help a wary leap of hope in her chest.

"Just the germ of something," he cautioned her, his words a shorthand for communicating that he wouldn't share anything with her. "I need to turn it over some more in my brain before it's ready to write. But yeah, I've got something juicy this time, Kendra. Something that will shut up the critics."

Nearby, Levi waved her toward the plane's stairs, indicating it was time to take off again. Her eyes flicked to the pilot's window where she could see that the man at the controls had already taken his seat in the cockpit again.

She hated to cut short this phone call, but she also didn't want to interrupt her dad if he genuinely had the book idea he'd struggled to come up with for so long. Turning her feet in the direction of the aircraft door, she wound up the conversation as Levi waited for her to precede him.

Hastening her step, she lowered her voice.

"So having too much to drink in the bar a few nights ago was just a one-time thing?" She hadn't noticed any other signs of the replacement addiction issues she'd worried about.

"Of course it was," he said rather distractedly, as if his thoughts had already fled the conversation. "Have you heard from your mother lately? How is Jenny doing?"

Kendra hesitated at the foot of the plane stairs, steeling herself against the automatic draw of her body toward Levi's as they stood in close proximity. She still couldn't believe she'd responded to that tension earlier by *kissing* him.

Even though it had felt amazing for those brief moments that she'd indulged herself. Every bit as tantalizing as she'd remembered, and then some.

Recalling the conversation with her dad as an afterthought, she rushed to wrap things up.

"Mom is fine," she reminded her father, wishing he could see his ex-wife as clearly as Kendra did.

Seth Davies was the perfect example of what could happen when someone indulged their longing for the wrong person. An example Kendra refused to follow. "I've got to go now, Dad. Please devote some time to working today, okay? You know as well as I do that writing always brings out the best in you."

"Sure, baby girl. Take good care."

She disconnected the call and slid the phone into her pocket.

"Is everything okay?" Levi asked as they ascended the steps together, his warm voice rumbling though her back.

A shiver tripped through her even as she told herself to lock down all those feelings that had no place in their relationship.

"I hope so. My father said the incident at the bar was a one-time thing. And since I haven't had any other reports of him drinking too much, I'm inclined to believe him." But she also knew that addicts were notorious liars about their problem. Reaching the main aisle between the seats of the small aircraft, Kendra slid into the leather seat she'd come to think of as hers on the right-hand side of the plane. "He said he was celebrating a new book idea."

Levi finished securing the plane door behind them, alerted the pilot they were ready, then dropped into his spot across the aisle from her.

"Plenty of people overindulge once in a while without it becoming an issue." Tugging his lap belt into place, he turned thoughtful blue eyes her way.

"Did you ask him about the day I made my pitch to buy Gargoyle King from him?"

Her heart sank as she remembered the other reason she'd wanted to touch base with him.

"I forgot, actually. I was too worried about the new possibility of alcoholism." She gripped the armrests on her seat as the small jet rolled forward in a tight turn to get back on the correct runway.

But now that she thought back to that conversation with Levi about him buying out her father's business as a favor to her, she realized she already believed him. She didn't need to check out his story. Levi Kingsley might have an overabundance of confidence in his own opinions that pushed him to do what he saw as fit for others, but he wasn't a liar.

"Maybe next time you can ask him." Levi reclined his seat as if to sleep. Then, he tipped his Stetson so it shaded his eyes from the overhead lights in the cabin. "Don't work too long," he cautioned her. "We've got a busy couple of weeks ahead of us."

Right. They'd be landing in Chicago shortly. And there would be a rush to set up the Kingsland Ranch booth at the World Wildlife Improvement Fair in the morning, where Levi would spend an hour before a team of representatives took over for him.

An afternoon meeting with the media. Then a charity gala where Levi would give a short speech and make a large donation. The schedule was packed.

But all of it felt doable to Kendra since Levi had told her he would give her some space before he asked her about that kiss she'd laid on him earlier. Managing work was never a problem. Managing her complicated feelings where Levi was concerned?

Not as easy. Especially not now that she'd had a taste of his lips on hers again.

Her stomach knotted at the memory, even as silky ribbons of pleasure teased her elsewhere if she allowed herself to relive those heated moments. What did she want to happen next with him?

The question was a loaded one, since what she wanted was definitely something she shouldn't have.

Eight

With the Beverly Hills' sun warming his shoulders on the back terrace of a rented villa, Levi adjusted the flame on a high tech outdoor grill. He and Kendra had checked in the day before and would stay for just two nights, but the exclusive property only leased in two-week stays, so Levi would have use of the place well after he needed it.

But he refused to skimp on the accommodations when he'd asked his brothers to join them for the next event on Kendra's promotion campaign. Gavin and Quinton would be arriving shortly for a briefing from Kendra on what to expect at the Greener Planet event the next evening. Then, they'd spend the weekend in the villa's guest quarters before flying back to Silent Spring, Montana, while Levi and Kendra continued on to stops in Denver and Seattle.

Closing the hinged lid on the heavy grill, Levi rechecked his preparations for a dinner by the pool while Kendra emerged from the huge, multi-slide glass doors that opened the villa's kitchen and living areas to the fresh air. Dressed in a white silk sundress printed with a purple orchid, she wore her hair in a loose topknot and carried a covered white platter toward the grill.

The thin fabric of her dress blew lightly against her curves, outlining her frame in a way that made him ache for her. But then, that was the nature of being around this woman. He never stopped craving her. It didn't matter that he'd witnessed the toll that messy relationships could take on a family after his father's failures. Levi's gaze sought out Kendra anytime they were in the same room.

Even so, he'd given her space after their talk in New York. She'd seemed genuinely surprised to learn about his motives for buying the Gargoyle King business from her dad. Levi didn't know if she needed to fact-check his story, or if she'd simply wanted some breathing room to reconfigure her idea of him after the false perceptions of the past. Either way, he'd done all he could to give her time after the unexpected kiss they'd shared. He'd focused solely on work in their communications since then, but the grace period for not talking about their chemistry expired tonight. And somehow, the heat that had simmered on the back burner these last days already seemed to flame higher.

With her high heels clicking on the tiled floor surrounding the pool area, Kendra walked toward him, setting down the platter on a butcher block countertop in the outdoor kitchen. "The security system just chimed with your brother's arrival at the gate out front," she informed him as she rinsed and dried her hands at the sink near the grill, two thin silver bangles jingling. "I thought you might want to put the steaks on soon."

"Thank you for bringing them out." Standing at the head of the patio table, set with gray stoneware plates for the meal, he eyed the vase of flowers on the white linen runner—the decor another contribution she'd made to the meal. "And thank you for everything you've done to make the place feel welcoming for Quint and Gavin. I realize having something catered would have been easier tonight but—"

She took a step toward him to gently squeeze his forearm, just above the place where the sleeves of his button-down were rolled. The touch was brief, but considering how much he'd been thinking about having her hands on him, it felt electric at the same time.

"It's a pleasure, honestly," she assured him with a warm smile even as she hastened back a step.

Had she felt that pulsing leap in her bloodstream too?

"Stopping by the grocery store on the way to our accommodations so I could deliberate over cuts of beef for twenty minutes was a pleasure?" He raised an eyebrow, remembering how long he'd taken to choose a handful of ingredients at the farmers' market afterward. "I know that's hardly what you signed on for this trip."

"Yet I stand by what I said." She gave a small shrug as she straightened the table runner where an errant breeze had flipped it up. "It was fun watching you pour time and thought into making your brothers' stay more comfortable. I have no siblings. And my parents split up when I was still a kid. So I consider it sort of fun to have a front row seat to someone else's family."

For a moment, Levi could see the better aspects of the Kingsley family through her eyes. While he resented the ways his father's games played Levi and his brothers against one another, he could also appreciate that at least he had those brothers. Even Clayton, whom he hadn't seen in three years, held an irreplaceable spot in his heart.

Grateful for that bond, he was about to thank her for reminding him of it when voices called from the other side of the gated side yard.

"Paging Levi Kingsley," one of them said at an outdoor volume. It was tough to even distinguish which of them was speaking as Gavin and Quinton sounded a lot alike. "Is there a Kingsley in the house?"

The call came from behind the outdoor kitchen, where a gate led to the side yard and the driveway out front. Levi caught Kendra's eye and they shared a smile at the arrival of more Kingsleys.

"Yes, I'll be there in a second," Levi returned as he moved toward the gate.

"I'll give you all a few moments to catch up," Kendra offered, backing away toward the house as if to retreat.

"That's not necessary." Pausing midstride, Levi turned to pin her with his gaze so she could see his sincerity. "They'll need you to explain their roles at tomorrow's charity event."

"We can talk business later." She made a dismissive gesture with her hand. "Enjoy some family time first. I know you stressed how much you wanted a chance for personal recharging on this trip."

Bitten by his own words.

He wasn't relenting on this, however. He needed to remind her of the bargain they'd made back in New York. "Yesterday, that would have been fine when I was giving you space. But we agreed once we arrived in LA, we would revisit out personal relationship."

The kiss they'd shared wasn't overtly referenced, yet the memory of it filled the air between them so tangibly she even took a faltering step toward him. The heated stillness was broken by another shout from the side yard.

"Levi, my brother," one of his brothers called again above the sound of stirring branches and twigs breaking. "If you're not here, I'm getting on the plane straight back to Silent Spring. I've got a horse breeding business to run."

Levi didn't move until Kendra gave a quick nod, her loose topknot wobbling with the gesture.

"All right then. I'll stay." She stepped toward the bamboo patio table, planting her hands on the back of one of the matching, slatted chairs. Chin held high, she appeared more prepared for a battle than a family reunion, but he understood she wasn't looking forward to the other conversation they would have.

Later.

When he planned to rehash the episode of The Kiss. In full, glorious detail. Preferably complete with reenactment.

Just the thought of it had him wanting to speed through this meal to get to the end of the next evening. Because Levi would wait to talk to Kendra about the heated embrace until after the gala tomorrow night, when they would have plenty of time to figure out what they wanted to happen between them next.

As he reached the side gate and tugged it open to admit his siblings, he already knew exactly what he wished for. And it involved Kendra Davies in his bed for at least the rest of this trip.

Retreating to the villa's kitchen to retrieve the dessert after a delicious meal prepared by Levi, Kendra glanced back at the patio table and its occupants.

Quinton. Gavin. And, of course, Levi.

All three of them with the tall, proud bearing she recalled in their father, Duke. But whereas Quinton and Levi shared their French Creole mother's darker hair and skin tone, Gavin's coloring was lighter, his medium brown dark hair longer. Levi was the sole Kingsley son to inherit his father's blue eyes, but that wasn't what drew Kendra's attention to him at the head of the table again and again.

Levi commanded the gathering with the easy air of someone who'd been in charge for a lifetime. His manner was milder than either of his more outwardly passionate brothers. Yet they both looked to him like the rudder sure to steer true.

And yes, she couldn't deny that quality in him drew her as well. She'd wearied of being the only person in her family to make careful, considered choices. While Levi had definitely overstepped with his decision to purchase Gargoyle King to "help" her family, she'd had time to reflect on his motives and she could see the situation from his perspective—understand that he hadn't intended the act as a betrayal of her trust. He really thought that he was helping at the time.

How many people in her life had ever done something with the main purpose of helping her? She'd been stunned to realize that Levi had bought out her dad for her sake. Even as she'd been angry that he would make an offer like that without consulting her, another part of her had been touched at the effort he'd made to alleviate her worries.

Which was why she'd ended up in a lip-lock that replayed at length in her dreams at night. Fortunately, she knew better than to act on those feelings these days. Even if Levi had meant well when he'd turned her life upside down, he'd still charged in without consulting her first, deciding what was in her best interest without her. And that all seemed a little too close to what her mother sought in a man for Kendra's comfort. She refused to be a decorative accessory in a rich man's life.

Tearing her eyes from where Levi sat outside, Kendra opened the refrigerator and slid out the covered tray she'd prepared earlier. The dessert board had been her sole contribution to the meal. Strawberries and blueberries fresh from the farmers' market, alongside cheeses and chocolates.

She popped a blueberry in her mouth as she carried the treat-laden silver platter out of the house and onto the patio overlooking the pool. Levi passed her as he headed into the kitchen, his arms full of the dishes he'd cleared from the table. Quinton was opening a bottle of port with a corkscrew while Gavin paired his phone to an outdoor speaker. As the soft strains of a jazz tune filled the patio, the outdoor lights strung around the deck flickered on from some unseen timer system. The golden glow reflected in the pool water as Kendra took her seat across from Levi's vacated chair.

She could hear him loading the dishwasher inside the house and took the moment to address his brothers.

"I hope you both know that I'm grateful for any feedback on our efforts to manage the PR crisis at any time," she began, unsure what either of them thought of the strategy she'd devised. "I don't expect to see a tangible rebound for the Kingsland businesses yet, but I would hope you're encouraged to see some other small signs that we're making a difference."

Quinton filled fresh wine glasses all around the table. "Such as?"

He wore a white button-down with his black jeans and boots, his clothing the halfway point between Levi's more formal jacket and Gavin's laid-back, faded denim and long-sleeved gray Henley.

"A decline in negative social media posts?" she suggested, not surprised to hear some skepticism in Quinton's voice. "An uptick in positive press coverage for Kingsland's environmental awareness?"

Levi strode back out onto the patio to rejoin them, then slid into his seat opposite her. Her heartbeat did something close to a flutter.

Something it had no business doing. Reaching for a square of dark chocolate and a couple of strawberries, Kendra hoped she could distract herself with sweets.

"We're talking business again?" Levi asked, an eyebrow raised as he glanced around the table.

"That's why we're here," Gavin reminded him as he sliced off a hunk of Brie for himself. "And I can't say that I've seen any measurable difference in my business, but I read up enough on crisis PR to know we're following an appropriate course of action. I'm going to trust the process and hope for the best."

"Agreed," Quinton said quietly, lifting his glass of port in Gavin's direction before taking a sip. "Although, I still think the next best remedy is to find Clayton and divvy up the shares of the ranch."

Confused, Kendra leaned forward in her seat to meet Quinton's eyes around the sunflower arrangement she'd bought at the market. "I don't understand. How would that help the PR problem?"

She remembered hearing the local gossip about Clayton Reynolds' departure from Silent Spring three years ago. He'd had an argument with his father and vowed never to return. Or so she'd heard.

Levi cleared his throat. "Even before Dad's worse misdeeds became a news item, Quinton and I both saw a drop in our respective businesses once the terms of Duke's will were made public. A lot of customers of my bar and Quint's cybersecurity company didn't like the idea that we were the sons of privilege, viewed as not sharing the family legacy with our half brothers."

Scowling, Quinton leaned back in his chair. "I've tried like hell to turn over my shares of the ranch to Clay, just so I can be out from under the family name and all the crap that comes with it." The heel of his hand hit the table, a gentle rap of frustrated emphasis. "But I'll be damned if we can find him."

"We're going to locate him." Levi's tone was calm. Certain. His eyes met his brother's briefly, then flicked to Gavin's. Then hers. "It's just a matter of time. Until then, we stay the course to minimize the fallout from the negative publicity."

As deftly as any public relations expert, Levi navigated the troubled family waters as though he'd been keeping the peace his whole life—a trait her family had been sorely lacking. Kendra watched him turn the conversation around to something more fun— an update on the progress of some calves and then an anecdote about the Chicago environmental fair when he'd run out of promotional T-shirts in kid sizes and promised to send a whole third grade class their choice of bull, lamb or horse shirts with the ranch logo.

Even Kendra smiled to remember him painstakingly taking down the correct sizes for each child's chosen animal T-shirt, then confirming an address for the school with the teacher's name. She was pretty sure the teacher had been swooning a little as he wrote it down.

And who could blame her?

Levi Kingsley wasn't just a rich rancher and successful entrepreneur. He was charming when he chose to be and jaw-droppingly good looking. People wanted to follow a natural born leader.

And all of those warm thoughts about him made her realize two things. First, that she probably shouldn't have had that last glass of port because that had to be the reason for her thoughts veering into a sexy direction. Second, she'd almost certainly been staring at him.

Again.

"It's getting late," she murmured to herself, getting to her feet.

Then, seeing all three masculine heads swivel in her direction, she realized she probably hadn't spoken as quietly as she'd thought. All three Kingsley brothers stood.

Her cheeks warmed as she rushed to add, "That is, it's late for me. I still have a few things to confirm before tomorrow's event." She picked up her dessert plate and empty port glass. "Don't let me interrupt your evening."

Levi rounded the table and tugged her chair back to give her more room. "I'll walk in with you."

She wanted to argue for him to remain with his brothers, but she noticed Gavin and Quinton had already left the table to take in the view of Beverly Hills from the railing of the terraced patio. Besides, Levi's strong, warm presence so close to her was having a far more intoxicating effect on her than any wine.

"That's really not necessary," she protested weakly when they were already halfway to the kitchen. "I genuinely have some calls to make about the last leg of the goodwill campaign."

Although they could wait until tomorrow.

"It is necessary." As he contradicted her, he took

the dishes from her hands and, as they reached the kitchen, set them on the countertop before he pivoted to face her once more. "Because I've been wanting a moment alone with you all evening."

Her mouth went dry at the heated look in his blue eyes.

They stood too close together, concealed from anyone outside by the kitchen wall. The ticking of the clock from over the fireplace in the dining room sounded suddenly noisy in the otherwise quiet space.

"I thought we were going to wait to talk about... *that*." She felt like a teenager stumbling over her words when a cute boy was nearby. Except Levi Kingsley was all man staring down at her right now. And her heart rattled her ribcage so hard she couldn't hear anything else. "Until after the gala. Right?"

"Just to be clear, you mean the kiss we shared?" He reached for her shoulder and skimmed his hand lightly along the bare skin covered only by a thin spaghetti strap from her silk dress. "Or do you mean the way the air is so charged between us that I can't think straight when we're this close?"

A shiver rolled through her.

He couldn't have possibly missed it.

When his fingers halted at the curve of her neck, he stroked her collarbone with his thumb. Back and forth.

Stoking the fire inside her.

"I mean all of it." She edged the words past dry lips even as she swayed toward him. "The kiss. The charged air. The brain fog exacerbated by proximity. We ought to table the discussion about any of it until after the most important stop on this tour."

His gaze dipped to her mouth. Lingering there.

"That's tomorrow." His thumb never stopped stroking her skin.

He had to feel the way her heartbeat galloped with his touch. Her breathing quickened.

"*After* the gala," she specified, knowing she was treading into dangerous waters with this interlude in the darkened kitchen, but unwilling to pull away.

Her fingers reached toward his jaw of their own volition. She trailed them along the light growth of beard that shadowed his cheek.

"Excellent. Tomorrow night is for talking." He shifted closer still, his feet sliding to either side of hers, backing her up until her spine met the cool marble countertop. "Tonight is for this."

His arms slid around her waist before he pressed her against him, giving her plenty of time to protest. But she answered the unspoken question by tunneling her fingers into his dark hair.

His growl of male satisfaction made her toes curl even before he brushed his mouth over hers. Testing. Tasting.

And, at last, feasting.

Nine

One kiss ignited an inferno.

Heat blasted up Levi's spine, flames licking higher over his skin just as her tongue stroked along his. Searing.

He swore he heard the roar of the blaze in his ears, the sound filling his head until he couldn't hear anything else. Because here, at last, Kendra's hands clutched his shoulders. Her body seeking his with every arch and sigh, every needy whimper.

How could he do anything but answer that call?

His arms banded tighter around her, pressing her to him so she couldn't miss his hunger for her, an urgency stoked by every look she'd slanted his way that night. By every seductive smile. Every throaty laugh. Every soft curve pressed against him.

Even now, her thighs shifted between his, her hips rocking in a rhythm that could only mean one thing.

He was debating the logistics of lifting her up onto the kitchen counter when a man's voice outside cut through his thoughts. Nudging aside passion.

Reality returned, chilling his insides as he recognized how close he'd just been to forgetting everything else but Kendra. A dangerous reaction for a man like him, who prided himself on being in control of his feelings.

He broke the kiss. Her eyes searched his, questioning.

Almost as if she'd been as lost in the moment as him.

"Tomorrow," he promised her, his voice a harsh rasp as he tilted her face up to his. "After the gala ends, we'll finish this."

"We will," she agreed, her voice as breathless as his had been.

Technically, they'd only agreed to a conversation.

But when Kendra gave him a solemn nod, her hazel eyes almost gold in the dim light from over the range, Levi couldn't help but wonder if they'd promised one another a whole lot more than just words.

He remained indoors for long moments after Kendra had retreated to her room. He needed the extra time spent cleaning up the kitchen to cool off and pull himself together.

Finally, his thoughts mastered once more, he strode across the patio to a strip of lawn near the balcony railing where his brothers had tossed a few logs into a copper fire pit and lit a flame. Quinton sprawled lengthwise on a patio couch, a pillow propped under his back while he scrolled through his phone. Gavin sat on the end of a lounger on the opposite side of the fire, having a video call with Lauryn, his significant other.

Circling around to give Gavin some privacy, Levi dropped down to sit on the cushioned chair near Quinton. He needed to address something his brother had said earlier in Kendra's presence. It rattled Levi that Quint was so eager to give up his claim to the family lands once they found their missing sibling.

Keeping his voice low, he asked, "Do you think it's wise to talk about more negative family business in front of the woman we hope will convince the world that we're trustworthy, accountable people?"

Slowly, Quint lowered his phone, the bright screen fading before it landed on the cushion next to him. "If she's good at her job, she already knows everything about the Kingsley family."

Irritation flared.

"Kendra is excellent at her job, as I believe you pointed out to me when you wanted me to hire her. That doesn't mean she is familiar with every quibble and source of infighting among us." He scrubbed his hand through his hair, stress squeezing his temples from the frustration of being away from his ranch and the real work he enjoyed. It hadn't been a full two weeks yet and he already felt claustrophobic from too much time in cities and small spaces. He needed blue sky. Mountains. Endless fields dotted with cattle.

He needed to finish the kiss with Kendra.

"What are you saying, Levi? I destroyed her illusions of us as one big happy family?" Quinton tugged himself to a sitting position and faced him squarely, boots thudding to the ground. "I'm pretty sure the whole world knows that's not the case if they read any business news."

In the background, Levi could hear Gavin's voice still talking low to his girlfriend. He wanted it to stay that way since Gavin wasn't the root of this problem. The fire between him and Quinton crackled as more of the sticks caught flame.

"The public may know about Dad's will—" he conceded, fuming anew over Quint's rush to leave the family "—however, no one but the three of us was aware of your desire to shrug off the legacy and hand it over to Clay once we find him."

"And that ticks you off why, exactly?" Quint folded his arms as he leaned deeper into the seat cushions. "Does it come as any surprise to you that I've never wanted to be a part of the ranch?"

The question was a sharp arrow that hit home at a time when Levi's nerves were already ragged. Quinton had traumatic memories of their mother's death at Kingsland. She'd saved Quint when a horse had charged him. But in doing so, she'd put herself between her son and the pawing hooves.

Levi had always tried to be respectful of what his brother had gone through, but he also knew he didn't understand the depth of Quinton's dislike of the place where they'd been raised.

"I've never expected you to stay there—" Levi began, shifting his seat to avoid the smoke from the fire as it turned in a new direction.

Then, seeing Quint's raised eyebrow, Levi amended the claim. Because Quinton had been on-site at Kingsland for weeks, overseeing the ranch so that Levi could do the goodwill publicity, and before that, Quinton been around to sort through the paperwork involved in transferring their father's assets.

Trying again, Levi said, "This situation since Dad's death has been an exception. Before that, I've always supported your wish to do other things. I invested in the tech business. I never complained about you relocating to Silicon Valley—"

"You've been supportive sometimes, yes. But you won't accept that I can still be a Kingsley and not have my name on Kingsland Ranch." Standing, Quinton lifted a long stick that lay near the fire pit and used it to move around the logs.

Sparks flew, the orange glow spreading for a moment until Quinton dropped a fresh log into place.

Levi couldn't argue that last point since it was true. He wanted all of his brothers' names on the deed. He wanted the satisfaction of building a family for them despite their father.

Besides, their mother had loved that ranch. She

didn't risk her life for one of her sons just so he could walk away from the legacy that was every bit as much hers as their father's. But this wasn't the time for that conversation.

"I will admit I'm struggling with that part." Levi saw a light switch on upstairs in the home they'd rented. Kendra's bedroom. And just like that, the memories of kissing her in the kitchen roared back into his brain, dragging his thoughts from his brother.

"Sooner or later, you'll have to accept it." Quint dropped back down into his seat. "But until we find Clayton to sort out the shares, I'll be sticking around."

A tall shadow fell over them as Gavin joined them. He must have finished his phone call as Levi saw no sign of the device.

"What'd I miss?" Gavin asked, his eyes darting between his half brothers as the bonfire crackled sparks into the night air. "You two look just the same as when you were both ticked off that Ruby-Marie Reed liked me better than either of you."

Levi exchanged a quick look with Quinton before they both burst out laughing. The conversation effectively turned to Gavin's days of hell-raising on the rodeo circuit. It had been a time all three of them had used to gain some breathing room from Duke Kingsley's expectations. While Gavin had been an out-and-out rebel with good cause, Levi had appreciated the excuse to drive around the surrounding states to see his bull riding competitions. Quinton had joined them more often than not, flying in from whatever city he'd been working in to expand his tech business so he could spend time with his brothers.

As talk grew quieter and the fire started to dim, Levi wondered if maybe Quinton had a point about their family. They had a bond that went beyond the ranch where they'd grown up.

But no matter how much he enjoyed the evening reminiscing with them, his gaze returning often to the window where Kendra lay, he still felt the emptiness of missing their other sibling. Until he found Clay and convinced him to return home, they were in a holding pattern. Waiting. For all they knew, he would contest their father's will when he returned. He had every right to do so.

For now, Levi could only search for him while he tried to hold the family and the businesses together. And if he spent some of that time convincing Kendra that resurrecting the old flame between them—temporarily, at least—was a good idea?

All the better.

By the time Kendra's driver pulled up to the Greener Planet fundraiser at a private home in the Pacific Palisades, the party was well underway. Light spilled from every window of the European-style stone mansion as the SUV from a hired car service pulled around the horseshoe-shaped driveway. Ahead of them, a valet was taking the keys to a low-slung silver McLaren while another attendant slid into the driver's seat of a convertible Bentley.

Kendra was grateful for the additional time they had to wait in a line of vehicles, since it gave her a moment to check her lipstick in the mirror of her compact and give herself a pep talk where her client was concerned.

Twisting the cap off her makeup brush, she added some color to replace the cherry red layer she'd worried away on the trip over without Levi. She'd left the Beverly Hills rental house early that morning— before Levi could protest—and taken her gown with her so she could dress for the party while out doing errands. It hadn't been as glamorous to step into the gown in the women's lounge area of an upscale Los Angeles department store, but it had bought her some space to air out her thoughts following the heated encounter in the kitchen the night before.

She'd hardly slept for thinking about that kiss. About how close she'd been to forgetting everything else but being with Levi again.

After the gala ends, we'll finish this.

His words had echoed around and around in her head, mingling with hers. *We will.*

By the time the morning sun had risen, Kendra knew she would never be able to concentrate while under the same roof as Levi all day. Hormones and hunger were still scrambling her thoughts when she needed to be sharp, because no matter how attracted she was to Levi, she couldn't afford to forget that this was the biggest account she'd ever brought into her small public relations agency. The campaign *had* to be a success. Since she had a laundry list a mile long of tasks that needed completing before the evening gala, she'd called for a car and left him a note on the kitchen counter of the villa, explaining to Levi that she would meet him and his brothers at the event venue.

Finishing the touch-up of color around the Cupid's bow of her mouth, Kendra retracted the lip brush into its case and tucked it and the compact back into her silver-beaded evening bag as the SUV rolled slowly forward. She had just unbuckled her seat belt when a valet opened the door and welcomed her to the Greener Planet fundraiser.

The salty tang in the air told her they were close to the ocean. She wondered if she might hear the waves if it wasn't for the music of a live band belting out a fifties rock tune from somewhere around the house.

A warm breeze gently lifted her hair from her shoulders as she stepped out onto the driveway.

"Ms. Davies?" the young valet asked as he took her hand to help her to cross the stone pavers in her fitted white satin gown.

Surprised, she glanced over at the man who assisted her, not recognizing him. He looked college-aged with earnest brown eyes and a kind smile. His name tag read "Freddy."

"Yes, I am." She returned his friendly expression as he released her arm. "Have we met?"

"No." The valet shook his head while Kendra's SUV drove away. He withdrew his phone from the pocket of the vest he wore over a white collared shirt, then tapped something into the screen. "But Mr. Kingsley asked the valets to keep an eye out for your arrival and to let him know when you were on-site."

"I see." Idly, Kendra wondered how Levi had spread the word to all of them, let alone described her well enough that her companion had known her right away. But it didn't matter.

He'd effectively ensured he'd be alerted.

Freddy pointed toward a red carpet leading to the front door of the elegant stone mansion where the festivities were already underway. "Mr. Kingsley said he'll meet you inside."

Her stomach flipped at the thought of seeing him after the kiss they'd shared the night before. Part of the reason she'd avoided him was a fear that she might take one look at him today and spontaneously combust.

She hoped that wasn't possible.

But last night's interlude had told her that she was deceiving herself to think she could work this closely with Levi and resist the magnetic pull between them. Boundaries would have to be redrawn after the publicity tour.

While they were on the road together, however?

She could devote one night to excising this insane attraction. One night to purge the tangled feelings that had festered for years after the last time they'd been together.

Now, stepping inside the foyer of the huge mansion and giving her name to a woman with a clipboard, Kendra paused to get her bearings. A huge stone staircase wound in front of her, the baroque banister painted black and gold while a tapestry of a medieval banquet feast covered another wall. Guests milled around a bar that was visible through the archway beneath the stairs, in a room with dark mahogany walls and parquet floors. The whole mansion was a nod to another era. From here, Kendra could see the room's French doors were open to the terrace where the band played outside. The group had swapped to an upbeat Beatles song that had the guests singing along, their raised voices audible over the sea of cocktail conversations closer to the entryway.

"Welcome, Ms. Davies." The greeter checked Kendra's name off her list before handing her two blue poker chips. As Kendra took them, she saw Levi appear in the doorway to the next room. "Enjoy our casino tables with your first game on us—"

The woman continued to explain the party layout and the whereabouts of the silent auction items, but Kendra's attention had shifted to Levi. She was captivated by the sight of him dressed in a classic tuxedo, custom-tailored to his athletic frame. He could have been a Hollywood native with his piercing blue eyes and sharp jaw, his dark hair waving in the humid air.

And speaking of air—his presence seemed to suck all of it from the room. Kendra dragged in a breath and still felt light-headed at the knowledge of what would happen between them tonight. Unless she called it off, of course.

Which she would not.

Could not.

"Thank you," she murmured absently to the party ambassador who'd been trying to tell her when— or maybe where—the silent auction items would be announced.

Kendra's heart pounded too loudly for her to hear much beyond that insistent rhythm anyhow. So, tucking her poker chips into her bag, she walked across the foyer to where Levi's eyes followed her every movement. Waiting.

Had she been worried she might spontaneously combust when she saw him? The concern seemed well founded. Her temperature spiked the closer she walked to him. Especially with the way his gaze traveled over her with slow thoroughness as she drew nearer.

Stopping in front of him, she wondered how they'd navigated all their other encounters before now. Because tonight, some buffer had been stripped away between them, leaving behind a raw, primal need.

"Are you looking for me?" She hadn't meant to flirt with him. And yet here she was. Shamelessly engaging in a dance as old as time.

He lowered his head to speak close to her ear, one hand palming the center of her back to pull her to him. "Looking for you doesn't begin to cover all the ways I'm craving you right now, Kendra. You're beautiful tonight."

Briefly, his fingers flexed against the smooth fabric of her dress before he released her, the dark hunger in his eyes tamped down as he took her arm to escort her around the party. He led her through the gaming tables where guests played with purchased chips to win donated prizes. Blackjack tables took up half of the room, while a roulette wheel, craps and baccarat tables composed the other half.

Servers in white uniforms passed hors d'oeuvres and trays of champagne while the band from outside filtered in through three sets of open French doors leading to a terrace and—Kendra guessed—the sea beyond. Even here, the air was salty and damp.

"Thank you." Kendra smoothed a hand over the white satin of her fitted, halter-neck dress. "I was fortunate that Lauryn and I are the same size so I could borrow some things. I've never attended so many events in a three-week span, let alone been photographed as much as I am when I'm with you."

Levi frowned, his polished black leather shoes halting on the parquet floor as he turned her to face him.

"It never occurred to me there would be an additional financial burden on you for a wardrobe. I hope you added that to the bill—"

Shaking her head, she interrupted him there. "Certainly not. Dressing myself appropriately for client events is a part of the job."

He appeared prepared to debate the point, so she redirected him toward the Greener Planet event chairperson, very ready to begin their rounds of handshaking in order to get on with the evening.

Turning, she searched the outdoor terrace for a glimpse of Gavin or Quinton in order to make sure they met the right people as well. But before she could find either of them, a tall, stick-thin vision from her past stepped in front of her.

"Hello, darling." Jennifer Leonard Davies St. Simon stood before her, dressed in a floor-length, strapless gown of blue silk with a thigh slit cut to the edge of decency.

Her brown hair had been cut in a new look, spiky and modern. It was flattering of her delicate features, even if she bore little resemblance to the last time Kendra had seen her.

"Mom?" Surprise knocked her sideways. She hadn't mentally prepared herself for a run in with the woman who'd abandoned her and her dad, and frankly, it always took some girding of her emotional defenses. But her mother lived in Los Angeles, and dating wealthy men was her mom's main occupation, so she shouldn't be too surprised to see her mother here, on the arm of a much older man.

Between the push-up bra that hiked her mom's assets to sky-high heights and the leather choker decorated with a pendant that she was pretty sure doubled as a nipple ring, it wasn't easy not to gape.

Not that Kendra had any issue with nipple rings.

But why did her mom have to reinvent herself for every man she met? This latest incarnation was definitely new. And about as different as possible from the earth mother phase Jennifer had gone through when she'd dated a chiropractor in Sedona and taken classes in alternative healing.

"It's so good to see you." Jennifer wrapped her in an anemic hug that was mostly for show. "And with a very promising specimen too."

Her mother's eyes cut to where Levi still stood, talking to the Greener Planet event chairperson.

It took all of Kendra's restraint not to explode at being reduced to someone's date as her mom went on to introduce her new boyfriend and inquire about Kendra and Levi's "status."

"I'm working, Mom," she protested finally, scrambling to put some boundaries up. She hated that they couldn't have a better relationship, but after many efforts, tears and more than a few therapy sessions, Kendra had learned that allowing her mother to get close to her only hurt more in the long run. "But it was really great to see you. And so nice to meet you as well," she added for the benefit of the burly older man sweating profusely around the collar of his tuxedo.

"Good luck with the new catch!" Her mother called after her as Kendra hurried away through the crowd.

Past the blackjack tables. Past the roulette wheel. Straight through the French doors leading outside to the terrace overlooking the sea.

Breathing deep, she clenched her fingers into the stone railing, grateful for the strong breeze blowing off the Pacific. It teased through her hair and riffled her dress around her legs while she tried to shake the tension from the unexpected meeting with her mom. The band played on the opposite end of the terrace, the oldies rock still upbeat and fun, but the dancing crowd was well away from her here.

Her heart still beat too quickly, reminding her that she needed to take her commitment to her emotional health seriously. She'd seen the way ignoring physical cues had taken a toll on her father's health over the years, and she refused to follow in his footsteps. So she renewed her effort to inhale slowly until she felt her pulse slow down again.

"Is everything okay?" The deep voice behind her made a shiver trip down her spine.

Especially when Levi's strong hand landed on her hip.

It was all she could do not to lean into his strength as she felt the warmth of him behind her. But they hadn't finished their work at the party yet.

"Not really," she confided, turning in the circle of his arms to face him. "But I will be as soon as we're done here."

His eyebrows lifted at the urgency he surely heard in her tone. "Then we're on the same page, since I've been ready to fast-forward to the end of this evening all day long."

The words stoked the fire inside her again, and for once, she didn't ignore it or try to suppress it. She welcomed the heat to burn away all the negative energy the encounter with her mom had stirred.

"Good. I think we can stage a couple of quick photo ops and be out within the hour." Over Levi's shoulder, she could already see two people she needed for a picture. "Maybe your brothers would remain a bit longer to shake some hands and be a Kingsley presence."

Levi's hand curled possessively around her waist. "I discussed that with them earlier in the evening. They know we're leaving here separately tonight."

Kendra relaxed a bit more, glad that Levi had been looking forward to their night together as much as she had. "That's excellent planning by you." She swayed closer to him, appreciating the way the dark corner of the terrace hid them from view. "If only we didn't have an hour-long drive back to the villa."

Levi's smile was feral, white teeth flashing in the flicking torch light. "Then it's a good thing I made arrangements for us to stay in the guesthouse tonight."

"Guesthouse? I don't follow."

He placed his hands on her shoulders and turned her toward the beach view on the far side of the terrace railing, waves crashing on the shore. "You see that building beyond the pool?"

Thanks to the landscaping lights, she spied a small stone cottage near the infinity pool. Anticipation fired through her as she nodded.

Levi leaned closer, his muscular chest pressed to her back as he whispered in her ear. "That's where I'm taking you as soon as we finish here."

Ten

Tonight, Levi left nothing to chance.

His fingers tightened around the key to the guest-house in the pocket of his jacket, anticipating his time with Kendra tonight. Time that seemed long overdue considering their first encounter three years ago had been hot enough to singe its way into his memories forever. He'd planned the date to the last detail, from renting the guesthouse—just steps away from the party venue—to having his brothers on standby to cover for them when they departed the event early. He wanted to make this evening perfect for her.

So special their time together would be seared into their memories forever. Because even though he wanted no part of a permanent relationship, he could still enjoy the chemistry between them for as long as possible.

Now, as they finished the last of the photo opportunities Kendra had arranged for him, he excused them from the group they were speaking with and guided her toward a private exit on a lower level of the mansion their host had shared with him at the beginning of the evening.

"This feels very *Phantom of the Opera*," Kendra observed as they descended narrow stone steps. "I wasn't expecting to approach the guesthouse via an underground labyrinth."

The sounds of the party—the band, the laughter, even the ocean waves—faded to nothing as they walked toward the guesthouse. The world shrunk to the two of them.

Pausing on the steps, he reached back to take her hand and steady her. "Our host suggested this way since the outdoor stairs leading to the cottage can grow slick when the waves are high." He gave her high heels a dubious glance. "Especially in those shoes."

At the bottom of the stairs, they reached a long marble hallway with wrought iron sconces at equal intervals to light the way. Ahead of them, an arched blue door awaited.

Kendra's mouth quirked in a half-smile as she peered down at her feet in the echoing subterranean corridor leading them away from the main house. "Stilettos are for making an entrance, not hiking."

Admiring her toned legs through the high slit in her white satin gown, Levi battled the urge to simply lift her into his arms and carry her the rest of the way. But he was a gentleman and not a beast carting her off to a lair, no matter the old world setting of the hidden stone passageway.

"You turn heads no matter what you're wearing," he told her honestly, withdrawing the key from his jacket pocket while he modulated his pace to match hers. "In fact, I still have very explicit dreams about you in those red boots you were wearing the day of the rodeo when we first connected."

"Do you?" The pleasure in her voice matched the high color in her cheeks as they moved closer to the blue entrance flanked by two flickering sconces. Not candlelight, but bulbs designed to mimic the effect. "Perhaps I should have resurrected them for tonight. I wouldn't want our time together now to fall short of the memory."

He stopped in his tracks to step in front of her, needing to halt that line of thinking. "There's not a chance of that happening," he assured her, still holding her hand. With his other he caressed her cheek, enjoying the way her hazel eyes dilated at his touch. "I guarantee it."

She exhaled a slow, stuttering breath that warmed the heel of his hand where he cradled her face. In the warm light bathing the corridor, her skin glowed bronze while a soft echo of her words bounced off the marble walls. She looked radiant in the white satin gown, so sexy and feminine that he'd been fantasizing about ways to undress her from the moment she'd stepped into the party.

"That's good to know." Her voice was a barely-there whisper between them. Her pulse leapt in a rapid tattoo that he could feel in her neck. "I've been looking forward to this. I don't want anything to spoil our night."

His heart pounded hard, demanding he spell out that he craved more than a single evening with her. But he refused to let her feel pressured. He wouldn't burden this time with too many expectations. Not when he was just grateful for this moment.

Leaning closer to kiss her temple, he breathed in the jasmine scent of her skin. "That would be impossible," he murmured, savoring the unique fragrance of her beneath the perfume.

His body stirred, ready for her to the point of pain.

Her eyelids fell to half-mast as her fingertips landed on his chest. Circling lightly over his silk jacket. She peered up at him with passion-dazed eyes.

"Then let's open that door before this dress sizzles right off me," she urged, the words smoking over his senses while her fingers clenched the fabric of his jacket.

It took all of his willpower to turn away from her and open the door, when all he wanted was to drag her against him and see how fast he could peel away that white satin from her skin. Still, he forced himself through the motions of inserting the key in the lock and twisting the handle. Then, he pushed the entry open for her to precede him up another stairwell, this one winding into the small turret that graced one side of the cottage.

"The next door leads into the guesthouse kitchen," he called to her as he followed her up the steps, the outdoors visible again through narrow, arched windows meant to look like old-fashioned arrow slits.

Through one of the windows, he could see the main house all lit up, the party still in full swing on the terrace. He couldn't be more grateful to be away from the crowd. Trying to carry on normal conversation when all he could think of was the woman in front of him had been torturous.

Pausing behind her, he waited as she pushed her way inside another blue painted entrance. Light spilled onto the steps from the simple, farmhouse-style kitchen where reclaimed wood floors and cabinets gave the new building an aged patina. He'd requested a fire to be laid in the hearth to take the chill out of air damp from the proximity to the ocean, and it burned brightly now. Thanks to a two-sided fireplace, the blaze would also be visible in the primary suite.

His current destination.

Closing and locking the door behind them, he wrenched off his jacket and laid it on a sturdy wooden chair while Kendra turned in a slow circle on her narrow stiletto heels, observing their surroundings.

Heat surged through him hotter than anything laid by a match.

Especially when she faced him again and reached behind her neck to unfasten the halter of her dress. White satin slithered down her body in blatant invitation as the semi-sheer cups of a strapless lace bra were revealed.

He forgot words for a moment, his brain too stunned to do more than stare.

Kendra hadn't been kidding about being ready to sizzle out of her clothes. The looks Levi had been sending her way all night were hot, blatant invitations. And she'd gone too long without his touch to resist a second longer.

Still, she knew a moment's pause when her partial striptease froze him in his tracks in the middle of the farmhouse-style kitchen. They stood beside a rough wooden island, a teak bowl of fresh lemons infusing the air with their citrusy scent.

She watched Levi as his pupils dilated so far his blue eyes turned nearly black, and she could hardly think he was unmoved by her display. Encouraged, she felt for the zipper sewn into the side of her gown and lowered it inch by inch, teasing them both with the slow reveal of skin ending in a tiny white thong.

The guttural sound he made when that hint of lace became visible gave her new courage. Wriggling out of the dress, she let it fall to the dark wood floor around her high heels while the warm air from the fieldstone fireplace teased her bare skin.

Without a word, he reached for his bow tie and tucked his finger beneath it to loosen the black silk. A moment later. the ends of the material slid apart, exposing his collar beneath it. Mesmerized by his movements, Kendra watched while he unfastened button after button, exposing more of his chest and abs, his body illuminated by the golden glow of the fire in the hearth. His upper body rippled with the sculpted muscles of a man who had known hard physical labor.

Muscles she desperately needed to touch. To taste. To feel against her skin.

Reaching for him, she slid her hands into the half open shirt and splayed her palms over the warmth and strength of him. She teetered on her heels and stepped out of them, canting closer to Levi and all the pleasure his touch promised.

"I've waited a long time for this," he reminded her, a gruff edge in his voice as his hands glided up her hips to her waist before cruising still higher. "But it's going to be so worth it to have you in my bed again."

Shivers danced along her skin while his breath warmed her neck. Shivers from his words and from his caress, because she liked knowing that he'd thought about this. Thought about her. He cupped her breasts in his palms, thumbs circling the sensitive peaks of her nipples where they strained the sheer lace of her bra.

"Then let's not wait any longer." Arching forward, she pressed herself into his hands, molding her body to him. "I'm ready for you now."

She'd been ready for hours, her body on a knife's edge of wanting all evening. By this time, she felt like she would come out of her skin if she had to delay another minute. She unbuttoned the last of his shirt and dragged it off his arms.

"Sometimes waiting makes the payoff all the sweeter." He kissed beneath her ear, his tongue stroking her in a way that made her hyperaware of everywhere he hadn't kissed yet.

The ache inside her sharpened.

"When it comes to this particular kind of reward—" she rolled her hips against his to underscore the point "—I choose quantity over quality."

"Never let it be said I don't deliver." His arms banded around her waist, lifting her against him as he walked her backward through an arched stone doorway and into a whitewashed bedroom with no furniture, save a huge white bed and a dark wooden nightstand. A sleeve of foil packets glinted in the firelight, the presence of condoms on the nightstand assuring her that Levi had been here earlier. A hurricane lamp sat in a deep windowsill, the small flame a counterpoint to the blaze in the two-sided fireplace. A rough wood plank served as a mantel, mirroring the exposed beams of the raftered ceiling.

The cottage had an otherworldly feel, like they'd stepped into another century. Timeless.

How fitting for this one night with Levi that couldn't be repeated. For a moment, it seemed surreal.

But then, his hands roamed her hips, fitting her tighter against him, and she forgot everything but how good it felt to be with him. Working the fastenings on his tuxedo pants, she helped remove the last of his clothes, until the only barrier between them were her underthings.

She worked the clasp of her bra and let if fall to the floor. Hooking a finger into the lace strap of the thong, she would have lowered that too, but Levi's hand wrapped around hers.

"Leave them. The first payoff is going to happen before you even remove them," Levi promised as he nudged her backward until her calves hit the mattress.

Excitement stole her breath. She opened her mouth to protest—mildly—and thought the better of it when he tipped her back to lie on the thick white duvet.

"If you insist." She drew him down on top of her, but he planted an elbow onto the mattress beside her, keeping his weight off of her while his hand slid between her thighs.

Pleasure rushed through her with dizzying speed.

"Oh, I insist." The deep tone of his voice vibrated up her spine while his fingers worked her through the damp lace of her thong. "If it's quantity you want…"

A whimper escaped her lips as her legs began to quake.

The hunger for him that had been building all

day—even before today, if she was being honest—
had her body begging for release at just the slightest
touch. Combined with that smoky quality in his voice
and the dark knowing in his blue eyes, it was all Kendra could do to last a minute of that sweet torment.

Her orgasm burst through her so fast and so fiercely
that she writhed with it, her hands both clutching his
wrist to keep his touch right where she needed it. Not
that he seemed inclined to leave her anytime soon. He
stroked through every last pulse of her finish, teasing
out one sweet shudder after another.

Only when she was wrung out and panting in the
aftermath did he drag the lace panties off her hips.

"That's just the first one," he informed her as he
reached over to the nightstand for a condom packet.
"There are more where that came from."

She didn't doubt it for a moment. But, taking the
foil package from him, she wanted to make something very clear.

"When I suggested we go for quantity, I wasn't re-
ferring solely to me." Ripping into the foil, she tugged
the condom out and rolled it slowly into place. "I plan
to deliver for you too."

The tendons in his neck stood out as she stroked
him, the firelight casting shadows on his face as his
jaw flexed.

"I forgot your competitive streak runs as strong
as mine." He bracketed her shoulders with his hands
on either side of her, his body poised over hers for
a long moment before he edged his way inside her.

Pleasure blindsided her. Moments ago she'd felt so sated, and now she craved him all over again.

"But in this, we can both win," she reminded him even as their union threatened to steal her breath.

She fisted her hands in his hair, clinging to him as his hips worked deeper. Deeper.

A primal scream built in her throat, but she swallowed it down, unwilling to let herself go over the precipice of bliss again until Levi had found that same peak. Gritting her teeth against the sensations threatening to overwhelm her once more, she pressed his chest in an effort to reverse their positions and rolled with him until she sat over him.

Kissing him deeply, she worked her hips in a slow undulation. Again. And again.

Watching his face, she searched for clues as to what made him feel the best—speeding up sometimes, grinding her hips against him other times. When his fingers sank into her curves, holding her steady, she remained exactly where he'd positioned her, wanting to see pleasure take over his features.

A moment later, his finish rocked them both, his shout mingling with her cry as he drove deeper inside her. His powerful muscles shook, his face wracked with the tension of intense pleasure. A pleasure she'd given him.

The knowledge filled her with as much joy as the orgasm he'd given her. More, perhaps, as she didn't think controlled Levi Kingsley let himself go so fully very often in life.

His eyes flicked open a moment later, catching her staring. The moment felt intimate. Intense, even. She was tempted to simply close her eyes again and curl up against his still-heaving chest, but something in his expression wouldn't allow her to look away.

Her heart skipped a beat, then squeezed tight in her chest.

And in that moment, she feared for her emotions.

Swallowing back the confusing tangle of feelings, she mustered a half-smile. "At least the score is even now."

His blue eyes narrowed in the moment before he flipped her to her back. "Now you're just asking for trouble."

Laughing, she wrapped an arm around him, grateful for the moment of levity. "No, I'm really not."

"Yes, you really are." He fluffed a pillow behind her head and hauled the goose down duvet over them both, cocooning them together while tucking her against him. "But since I need five minutes to catch my breath, you have a brief reprieve before I wreak sensual retribution."

His fingers stroked through her tangled hair while they stared into the flames in the hearth at the foot of the bed. One of the windows must have been cracked because fresh sea air blew through the bedroom, keeping it cool despite the lively fire. Slatted storm shutters still gave them privacy from anyone on the rocky shore outside.

For long moments, she simply breathed in the contentment of hearing his heartbeat beneath her ear, his exhales ruffling her hair while he combed through the strands. She slid her leg over his, nestling closer. In five minutes she would remember that this night was about sex and hunger and need. But until then, she couldn't help but think about what might have been if Levi hadn't been the one to upend her life three years ago.

If he wasn't the kind of wealthy and powerful man who would insist on always calling the shots in a relationship. The kind of man who charged ahead assuming he knew best. Logically, Kendra knew she wouldn't fare well with someone like that. Especially when she'd spent a lifetime distancing herself from her mother's manhunting ways.

Yet, in moments like this, when Levi made her laugh and reminded her how fast they'd felt a connection three years ago, she could almost wish things were different.

Almost.

Thoughts of her father drinking himself into a stupor at the Stockyard rattled through her, reminding her why she wouldn't lower her guard.

Levering up on her elbow, she peered down at him in the golden glow from the fire. "I should fly back to Silent Spring sometime this week on one of the days when the schedule is clear. To check on my father."

"All right," he agreed after a moment, studying her closely. "I'll go with you."

She shook her head, skirting her gaze away. "That's really not necessary—"

"It is." He touched a finger to her jaw and gently guided her face until their eyes met again. "And I'd be glad to touch base with my office for a few hours while you spend some time with your dad."

Biting her lip, she weighed whether or not to accept the offer. But considering how much easier it would make the travel plans, she finally nodded. "If you insist. Thank you."

"Are we still okay?" he asked, his warm palm circling the back of her shoulder.

Comforting. Caressing.

Taking a deep breath, she reminded herself that nothing had changed between her and Levi. She could enjoy great sex without getting tangled up in her feelings.

And she would enjoy it to the fullest.

"Absolutely," she said finally, then kissed her way down his chest. Lower. And lower. Much better than looking into his magnetic gaze that searched hers too astutely. "But your five minutes are up."

Eleven

Somewhere in the recesses of his brain, Levi recognized that Kendra was trying to distract him.

But it was tough to follow the thread of any thought when her lips moved over his hip bone and her tongue traced circles on his skin in a way that about drove him out of his mind.

He would return to the subject, he promised himself a moment before her mouth closed around him. After that, he had no choice but to give himself up to the slick heat of her ministrations.

"Kendra." His fingers twined through her hair, his restraint slipping.

What was it about this woman that made him forget everything else? His duty to the family name and legacy, his mission in Los Angeles. Three years hadn't been enough to make him forget her. Now that he had her by his side again, he couldn't stop thinking about ways to keep her there for a little while longer.

Her hair fell forward and tickled his stomach, his senses on overload. And suddenly, the need for her wouldn't be denied.

Sitting up on the bed, he grasped her shoulders and lifted her until they were face-to-face. Her hazel eyes flashed with golden streaks in the firelight, her breath huffing over him as he reached for another condom.

Rolling it into place, he positioned her on his lap, her legs straddling his so she could ride him. And damn, but she was so beautiful in the firelight, looking like his every fantasy come to life when she wrapped her arms around his neck and worked her hips to take all of him.

She felt incredible.

But he wasn't about to lose himself in the sweet give of her body yet. Not when he'd made her pleasure his priority. Banding one arm around her waist to steady her, he reached between them to stroke her the way she liked best.

Her body rocked with the first twitchy wave of sensation, and he knew she was already close to coming. He circled her clit slowly at first, then gained speed as she began to tense. Soon, he took one nipple in his mouth, and drew hard on the stiff peak.

And then her back arched, her whole body quaking with her release. He buried himself deeper inside her, needing to feel every lush contraction for himself. Gripping her hips, he slid her back and forth on his lap, taking what he needed while she savored the last waves of her orgasm. Just seeing her that way— lost to the pleasure—could have sent him over the edge. But combined with the way her body squeezed his, he didn't stand a chance of holding back another second.

Shouting her name, he wrapped her tight in his arms while his finish pummeled him. For long moments, she felt like a lifeline through the storm of sensation. In the aftermath, he could only draw her against him as they fell back onto the pillows.

Heartbeats syncing as their breathing slowed.

Contentment threatened to steal some of the night from him, the urge to rest his eyes and sleep too strong to ignore. He would wake again soon, he told himself. And then he would return to making this time special for Kendra. He would also find out why she'd been cagey in their conversation about her father.

Something had seemed off with her at the party, but he hadn't put his finger on why exactly. She'd been only too glad to put the evening behind them to spend time in the guesthouse, which had worked out well for him, but he didn't want to overlook something that was bothering her either.

But first, he needed more than five minutes to recover this time. With Kendra's breathing long and even, her silky hair pooling against his chest where he held her, Levi had no choice but to slip into sleep.

A cell phone vibrating woke him.

Confused to awaken in bed alone, Levi jackknifed to a sitting position, trying to orient himself. The fire had gone out in the whitewashed bedroom at the guesthouse, and Kendra's side of the mattress was cold. Her pillow still held the indent from where she'd lain.

His phone vibrated on the nightstand again, the screen lighting up the still-dark room. Reaching for the device, he saw Quinton's name on the screen. He also saw the time—four in the morning.

Clearing his throat, he answered the call.

"I'm here. What's wrong?" Standing, he dragged on his boxers, wondering where Kendra went.

"Sorry to wake you." Quinton's voice was terse. "But I figured you'd want as much time as possible to respond to the latest PR problem."

Relieved that the middle-of-the-night call wasn't any kind of personal emergency, Levi tried to bring his brain online to deal with a work issue while he pushed open the bedroom door. "What happened?"

Peering around the guesthouse kitchen and living area, he saw no sign of Kendra anywhere. Her dress was gone from the floor where she'd stepped out of it the night before. Anxiety tightened his gut at the thought of her leaving. Her shoes were still there, however. He hoped that meant she hadn't gone far.

"Check your messages," Quinton suggested as an electronic beep sounded on Levi's end of the call. "I've sent you screenshots."

"Hold on a sec." Levi juggled the phone to his other hand so he could scroll through texts and use the speakerphone feature.

The first attachment from his brother was a photograph of Levi and Kendra dancing at the Greener Planet fundraiser party. His gaze stuck on Kendra for a long moment as she stared into his eyes, a sweet, happy expression on her face. When he managed to tear his attention from her, he read the caption that accompanied it, posted by Kendra's mother:

Looks like we may not have to wait long for an engagement! Congrats, Kendra and Levi. Wishing you the same happiness Doug and I have found. #KingslandHappyEverAfter #KingslandForever #EngagedMomandDaughter #DoubleWedding?!

There were about ten other hashtags related to Kingsland used in the post, most of which were specifically generated by Kendra as part of her efforts to turn around the Kingsland image. Levi's heart sank since he could only imagine Kendra's reaction. Was that why she'd left? Had someone alerted her to her mother's post in the middle of the night?

"It's not true," Levi said carefully, even though a part of him admitted he and Kendra surely looked like a couple in that photo. "But why is it a publicity problem?"

Quinton's dry laugh held no humor. "You haven't read the comments yet. Look at some of the other attachments I sent you."

Dropping into one of the heavy wooden kitchen chairs, Levi scrolled to the next photo from his brother. This one was a screenshot of comments on one of the Kingsland Ranch social media pages. There was an outcry about "spoiled rotten" Kingsland heirs buying their way out of their problems with money. Or in this case, buying good publicity with a sham engagement to a PR crisis manager.

Levi guessed there were far uglier words and accusations on those message boards. He knew his brother had probably searched for the milder remarks to share with him out of kindness to Kendra and him. Levi wasn't sure he wanted to read anything more critical for himself either, so he appreciated his brother's tact.

Cursing, he turned off the speaker feature and returned the phone to his ear so he didn't have to look at any more negative posts.

Quinton hefted a gusty sigh on the other end. "It doesn't help that she used all the hashtags Kendra allotted for her publicity tour. We're getting some ugly flak from one of the environmental groups you're supposed to visit next week."

"All before sunrise," Levi remarked, frustrated his time with Kendra had to end this way, but more concerned about her. "I'll ask Kendra what our next steps should be and get back to you."

When he found her.

Disconnecting the call, Levi located his overnight bag and slid on a clean T-shirt and jeans. On a hunch, he exited the cottage through the main door that led out to the beach instead of using the kitchen passage where they'd entered the night before.

And, peering down toward the rocky shore, he saw a figure in white illuminated by a half-moon and the phone in her hand. Waves crashed around her feet, the hem of her gown soaked as she stood in the surf.

Kendra.

Relief rocked through him, letting him know exactly how worried he'd been that she'd left altogether. Not wishing to startle her, he ambled closer across the sand before calling her name.

Selfishly, he hoped she was only upset about that photo in the paper and not that she had regrets about their night together.

"Kendra?" he spoke her name softly into the ocean breeze.

He'd been prepared for her to be upset. But not for the cold fury in her eyes as she turned to face him.

"Have you seen this?" Holding up her phone, Kendra waved her mother's insipid social media post in front of Levi.

Judging by the concerned expression on his face,

she suspected she gave the appearance of someone who was overreacting to a maternal mistake. No doubt Kendra looked a fright in her party dress and bare feet as she clambered over the rocky beach in the middle of the night. But she'd been so angry when she'd awakened to the repeated buzzing of her phone with alerts that her hashtags were producing well over the anticipated usage.

She'd been sleeping so deeply at Levi's side, her body thoroughly sated by his repeated attentions. Once she'd pulled herself out of the lovemaking haze, however, she'd been rattled to her core to see her mom's presumptuous online machinations. Slipping into her dress, she'd left the cottage for some fresh air to try to cool her temper, but she'd been out of doors for half an hour and still felt riled. Now, knowing that Levi had seen the post, she tensed with new embarrassment. What if he thought—even for a moment—she shared her mom's marriage-minded schemes?

"I did see them. My brother called and shared screenshots." Crossing a patch of sea grass visible on the moonlit shore, he reached for her. "And I understand that you must be upset, but please come inside before you cut your feet."

His arms were around her a moment later, and it was all she could do not to simply close her eyes and allow his strength and compassion to absorb some of the emotional tumult stewing inside her. She did take a moment to breathe in the scent of his freshly-laundered shirt and the hints of cedar that she associated with his aftershave. But she stopped herself before she could bury her head against his chest.

Their night together had ended. Cut short by the reminder that she could not afford to be the kind of woman who allowed every paramour to shape her path like her mother did.

Straightening from the shelter of his arms, she nodded. "All right. I wasn't thinking straight when I came out here." Lifting the sodden hem of the gown so she wouldn't trip on it, Kendra chose her steps carefully to return to the cottage. "My mother and I have a difficult relationship to say the least. She's been content to stay out of my life for the most part since she deserted my father and me. But I should have guessed she'd want to insert herself back into my world when she saw the two of us together."

Hadn't Jennifer referred to Levi as a "promising specimen?" Kendra knew her mom had a weakness for wealthy men. Even as potential sons-in-law, apparently.

"You couldn't have possibly foreseen something like this," Levi reassured her, as they walked over the damp sand to the flagstone path circling the cottage.

"Oh, but I should have. She left my father when the money ran out, and she's been chasing bigger meal tickets ever since." She ground her teeth together, trying to stop the angry words bubbling up from inside. But she hurt too much to be calm about this. It had been a mistake to be lulled into enjoying herself with Levi tonight when she should have been on guard after the run-in with her mom. "For some reason, she seems to think I'll follow in her footsteps."

"You couldn't be more different from her," Levi observed, sounding so certain of himself.

Just hours ago, she'd entered the charming beach guesthouse under the influence of searing chemistry, ready to let the attraction burn all night long. Instead, their time together had singed them both. Potentially derailing all her hard work to turn around the negative Kingsland publicity. She should have known they would be photographed. It was her job to know. She wouldn't be so reckless again.

"Either way, my mother's ridiculous speculation might have cost us all our good PR momentum." She'd read the posts that called the Kingsleys entitled, suggesting they bought their way out of their father's crimes.

Suggesting they'd bought *her*.

Arriving at the front door, Levi pushed it open and guided her into a kitchen chair before disappearing into the bathroom. He returned with antiseptic and bandages for her feet, plus a throw blanket for her shoulders.

She hadn't realized until he laid it around her shoulders that she'd been shaking. Whether with emotion or a chill though, she couldn't say for certain.

"Is it ridiculous though?"

Levi's question hung in the quiet kitchen while he bent to wrap a kitchen towel around her feet.

His kindness to her at a time when he had every

right to be furious about her mother's antics slid past her defenses. Touched her.

"What do you mean?" She tried to make sense of his question. To rewind the conversation and understand what he was asking.

"You called your mother's speculation ridiculous," he explained while he examined her feet in the kitchen light, searching for cuts beneath the small pebbles still clinging to her skin. "And while it might have been presumptuous, I think she had good reason to believe we look like a couple who were completely wrapped up in one another in that photo."

Blinking, she tugged the blanket tighter around her shoulders. "You can't possibly condone her behavior."

Levi sat back on his heels, briefly studying her face in the too-bright kitchen before he grabbed a bottle of antiseptic. "I don't pretend to understand your relationship." He carefully cleaned an abrasion on her toe before blotting it dry and ripping open a bandage packet. "All I'm saying is that she wouldn't be the first parent to harbor hopes to see their offspring marry, so I can't hold it against her."

With slow precision, he pressed the bandage in place.

Biting her lip against the urge to argue—to explain that her mother's sudden interest in Kendra's life was rooted in something more selfish than maternal love—she recalled that Levi had lost his mother when he was just a child. Three years ago, they'd bonded over the mom-shaped holes left in their lives—he by Adele Boudreaux Kingsley's death, her by Jennifer's defection.

Softening, she sighed back into the chair. Why did it have to be even harder to keep some boundaries around this man when he was this thoughtful? "That's kind of you. And I promise I'll figure out something to stem the tide of negative publicity."

"I already have." Rising to his feet, he recapped the antiseptic. "We do nothing. Let the world believe we're in love and not worry about the speculation."

The word tripped so smoothly from his tongue.

Yet just hearing it made her feel light-headed. Her stomach knotted. Both reactions seemed over the top. But maybe that was just because he didn't understand how crisis PR worked.

Yes. That had to be it.

Because she was not the sort of person to get emotional over a frank discussion of publicity logistics. And that's all this was.

"I don't think that's a good approach," she said finally, realizing she'd been quiet a beat too long. "Better to get out in front of it with a clear statement that we're not together—"

Levi shook his head. "I disagree. People enjoy a love story. If we fail to react to the negative comments, I think the public will come around in time. Who doesn't want to believe that love conquers all?"

Her heart clutched at the words in some leftover reflex from her girlhood. Ruthlessly, she ignored the reaction as she got to her feet. She needed to put some distance between them. To put this night behind her. Before the chemistry stole her reason.

Locating her shoes, she slid into them, needing to move on.

"I believe that would be a mistake. But you're the one in charge of the Kingsland campaign, so it's your call to make." Her heart beat too fast. Her whole body warm from Levi's blue gaze that saw her too well. She clutched her phone tighter in one hand. "While you consider next steps, I'd like to use the time to fly home and check on my father. He will be upset if he sees that post and the intimation that my mother is engaged again."

"I already told you I'd return to Silent Spring with you." Levi glanced toward the open bedroom door where the bed they'd spent hours pleasuring one another was still visible. "We could catch a few hours of sleep before we travel—"

"I'd like to leave as soon as possible, but I don't want to inconvenience you." If she returned to that bed, she suspected they'd wind up tearing one another's clothes off all over again.

Simply sleeping wasn't an option. And she knew herself too well to pretend otherwise. Besides, if her father was upset about her mother's engagement, it greatly increased the chance that he could turn to his addiction for comfort.

"It's no inconvenience." After withdrawing his phone, Levi pressed a few buttons, a new coolness in his tone. "I'll notify the pilot we'll fly at first light and request a ride to the airfield."

He was already tapping commands into the device. A shiver rippled her skin as a chill set in.

Their night was over.

And she'd pushed away his efforts to extend it.

"Thank you." She owed him more than just her thanks. He'd been considerate of her feelings. Forgiving of her mother's behavior. Maybe that was part of the reason why she felt the urge to see her father. Because no matter how much she saw a kind side of Levi now, she couldn't forget that his high-handed decision to buy out her father without consulting her had plunged her dad into the worse spiral of his addiction. "I just need to pick up my things at the villa."

"Of course." He never glanced up from his phone, his behavior returning to all-business mode. "I'll have the driver stop there on the way."

She'd set the tone for these renewed boundaries, and yet she couldn't help but mourn the loss of his closeness. His warmth.

"What about your brothers? Will they be joining us?" She didn't know Gavin or Quinton's plans, but they'd both made it clear that Levi was the point person for the publicity campaign. She didn't expect them to remain on the goodwill tour indefinitely.

"Not if I can help it." Pocketing his phone, Levi faced her without touching her. "We want to leave as soon as possible anyhow, and they can cover for us on the next stop if necessary."

With nothing more to say, Kendra simply nodded rather than risk upsetting this new relationship territory she and Levi seemed to be treading. She retrieved her discarded jewelry and purse without a word, her worries about her job, her mother's machinations and her father's addictions converging in a knot of anxiety.

Yet, even with all of those concerns to occupy her mind, the thought that kept returning to her brain over and over was Levi asking, *Who doesn't want to believe that love conquers all?*

The words circled her mind.

Too bad she already knew that he didn't believe in that any more than she did.

Twelve

Parking his pickup truck in front of Seth Davies's house back in Silent Spring that afternoon, Levi had a sinking feeling about this visit.

Although some of that bad mojo might have stemmed from how quiet Kendra had been during the entire trip from the cottage. They'd shared an incredible night together, and yet it was like a switch had been flipped ever since they'd awoken to Jennifer's post speculating about a union between him and Kendra. He understood that Kendra had a difficult relationship with her mom. But she seemed to particularly resent any intimation that she would consider marriage to him.

Was she anti-marriage overall? Or just to him?

And why did that matter so much to him—more than he would have expected?

He'd been trying his damnedest not to allow that to bother him. Yet how could he help being just a little offended, especially in light of what they'd shared? Not that he wanted any part of love and marriage either. Levi would spend the better part of this year administering damage control after his father's messy love relationships. He had no plans to subject his own heirs to that brand of hell.

That didn't mean he and Kendra couldn't have an affair though.

Now, Kendra paused as she unbuckled her seat belt and prepared to exit the truck. "You really don't need to stay."

Irritation nettled.

"You've made that more than clear. But I'd like to at least say hello to your father. Welcome him to the Gargoyle King's board of directors in person." He heard the terseness in his voice.

But it was only a response to the coolness in hers.

How had things deteriorated this quickly?

Exiting the vehicle, he followed her to the front door of the log cabin home, overgrown with weeds and devoid of any decoration. He reminded himself she had every reason to be worried about her dad. Three years ago, she'd been concerned about him too. But Levi had misread the cues, and in his efforts to help, had done exactly the opposite. He couldn't fix what had happened in the past, but he wouldn't make the same mistake again.

He just hoped it wasn't too late to salvage his relationship with Kendra. They were good together. Smart enough to avoid the pitfalls that had led to the unhappiness his father's marriages had wrought for the family.

"I'm sure Dad would appreciate that," Kendra agreed after a long hesitation. Then, she knocked twice on the warped screen door, and she used her key to let herself inside.

"Dad?" she called into the house as she opened the door partway. Then, when there was no answer, she pushed it open more fully.

The interior was dim. The blinds were all drawn against the afternoon sun. Open pizza boxes littered the kitchen counter along with empty wine bottles. Beer bottles. Booze bottles. A stale, musty odor mingled with something more pungent.

It took Levi's eyes a moment to adjust to the deeper gloom in the next room. To see what Kendra must have spotted an instant before him. She was already rushing to the worn sectional sofa in the living area when Levi saw her dad slumped there. Dressed in jogging pants and a T-shirt, Seth Davies clutched a bottle of Gargoyle King whiskey in one arm. In the other, a broken picture frame.

He could tell it was broken because shards of glass fell from the older man's lap as he straightened, blinking owlishly at them. His thinning hair stood on end. The picture he held looked like an old wedding photo.

"Kendra?" Her dad's voice rasped as though it hadn't been used in days. Still slumping to one side on the couch, he lifted the whiskey bottle to display the label. The very one he'd designed before selling the company to Levi. "It looks like I shouldn't have sold the business after all," he remarked, squinting at the wording on the bottle as if he couldn't read it clearly. "Then you wouldn't have had to get engaged just to land your old man a job."

Levi's heart sank at the remark that had the sound of deep regret, no matter how influenced it might be by alcohol. The words called to mind how often Kendra must have heard similar remorse over the years.

"Dad, I'm not engaged," Kendra corrected him softly. She plucked a throw blanket off the back of the sofa and wrapped it around the broken picture frame, minimizing the chance of either of them getting cut. "You got the job on your own merit, because Gargoyle King was your brainchild."

Her words and actions both employed a tenderness Levi had never been privy to in her before. Her love for her father was obvious, no matter how personally devastated she must feel at the moment.

Levi moved closer to take the broken glass from her.

"How can I help?" he asked as he withdrew the blanket from her arms. He was unsure what her next steps might be, but he wanted to lend assistance.

"I'd like to transport him to a rehab facility," she said quietly, still picking shards of glass from the arm of the sofa and laying them aside on the floor. "If you can help me get him to the truck."

"Of course." Grateful to be of use, he rounded the sofa to take Seth's other arm to assist the man to his feet.

Her father didn't seem to notice their efforts, however. He stared down at the bottle, tracing the outline of the silver, crowned gargoyle seated on top of the bottle. "Your design was a clever one, Kendra," Seth mused aloud. "I hope your fellow knows how much of his success he owes to you."

Levi stilled, absorbing the words. Information that Kendra had never shared with him before. Just how much ownership of the Gargoyle King brand could Kendra have rightfully claimed?

He wanted to ask her about it, to find out how much personal effort she'd put into the fledgling liquor company before Levi had bought it from her father. All along, he'd been under the impression that Seth Davies had been the sole creative driving force of the ideas and the business plan. Had Kendra been far more involved than she'd let on? But when he opened his mouth to confront her, she shook her head.

"Leave it for now. Please." The look in her eyes was a warning he couldn't ignore.

Returning to the task at hand, Levi levered a supporting arm around Seth's shoulders to help haul the man to his feet. He would set aside the topic of the liquor company for now because she'd asked him to.

But he would not forget about it.

Because if what he feared was true, and Kendra had a far bigger role in the liquor brand than Levi had previously understood, he'd wronged her all the more by not consulting her in the deal he'd made with her dad. A deal that had resulted in Seth gambling away the full amount of the purchase price, leaving Kendra with no recognition of her contributions.

And while Kendra's father might have been comfortable about robbing his daughter of her lawful share of that income, Levi was not. He just needed to figure out how he could make it right.

The dinner hour came and went by the time Kendra had her dad settled in at a rehabilitation facility. As Levi drove away from the recovery center, she shuffled through the brochures she'd been given, none of which guaranteed "recovery." Only access to the tools to make it happen.

Would her father do his part to stop drinking?

Her head tipped against the passenger side window as she peered out at the late-day sun spilling golden light over the green Montana hillsides, the views of grazing cattle pastoral and serene. Inside, she felt anything but calm.

"What can I get you for dinner?" Levi asked from the driver's seat. "You must be starving after spending all afternoon at the clinic." He was headed toward the airfield and the plane that would take them to their next stop on the goodwill campaign.

Little did he know that she wouldn't be joining him for the last leg of it. How could she when her father was dealing with so much?

Levi hadn't been inside the office of the intake counselor at the rehab center to hear Kendra's explanation about possible "inciting incidents" for her dad's most recent episode. Levi couldn't possibly understand how deeply responsible she felt for the series of events that had led to this latest downward spiral.

"I'm not hungry." With her fingernail, she flicked a corner of the pamphlet about family support. The one filled with advice she had known but hadn't implemented well enough. She hadn't been here in Silent Spring when her father needed her. "And I really need to return to my dad's house now."

"Are you sure about that?" Frowning, Levi tapped his thumbs restlessly against the steering wheel of the pickup truck, but he turned on his signal light to turn off the highway. Toward her father's empty home.

"I'm certain. I need to clean up the place." She remembered the shock of walking into the house where she'd been raised to the rancid smell of alcohol and sickness.

She'd understood immediately what it had meant. That her dad had been hiding a growing problem from her for months. He couldn't have consumed that much alcohol in a couple of weeks unless he'd been increasing his tolerance level for a long time.

As the pickup bumped over a speed hump near the local elementary school, Levi spoke again. "A cleaning crew could take care of that—"

"Not as well as I can," she cut him off sharply. Agitated and on edge. "I've been turning a blind eye to his problems for long enough."

She'd known addiction replacement was a common way of relapsing, and yet she'd chosen to be Levi's plus-one for the sake of her job. Or maybe worse, she'd chosen to go on the tour with him because of the attraction to him.

Now she'd reaped what she'd sown, and it was her father who was paying the price as he faced a night of delirium tremors and all the violent illness that they would bring as he dried out.

"Have you?" Levi asked gently as he turned off the main avenue through Silent Spring to the ranch access road where her father's house had been built on a former cattle spread. "Or have you been giving him a chance to take ownership of his problems and make his own decisions?"

"I see you've been reading the family support literature too," she observed wryly, recognizing the advice for the loved ones of addicts. "Maybe you missed the part about being a presence in an addict's life to provide in-person recovery help."

She didn't appreciate suggestions from the very person who had orchestrated her dad's biggest setback three years ago. Especially at a time when her nerves were still ragged from her mother's stunt.

"I read that too," Levi continued, despite her growing frustration. "But caregivers need to care for themselves first and foremost, or you can't be any help to others."

Anger rushed through her before she could quell the red-hot burst.

"I recall." Shifting in her seat, she pivoted to face him. "But do you think having me as your plus-one at every Kingsland event is something that takes care of *me*? Or is it all for you and the benefit of your business?" She recognized that her nerves were wound tight. That she might be being unfair. But she didn't care. Levi hadn't been fair to her and her father either. "Which, by the way, is the same one you wheedled away from Dad without ever talking to me about."

Her heart pounded furiously. She should have confronted Levi about this—really confronted him—before she'd accepted the crisis management work for him. But she'd told herself she was a professional and she could move past it.

She'd never expected the issues or her father's addiction to rebound on her to this degree.

"I understand you're upset," Levi began as he steered the truck past the detached garage to park in front of her dad's home. "And with good reason. I had no idea that you were so involved in the Gargoyle King business when I approached your father with a buyout offer."

"I worked on the ideas with my father because I enjoyed the time being with him. Enjoyed seeing him flourish creatively again after the frustrating years when he was trying to write a follow up book." She didn't move to exit the truck once they stopped. She knew they needed to have this conversation now, before things went any further between them.

Across the truck console from her, Levi stared at the darkened cabin home for a long minute, his jaw working while he seemed to weigh her words. When he turned to meet her gaze, his blue eyes were wary.

"But you do remember telling me you were worried about the potential problems with your dad in a liquor business, don't you? The possibility of addiction replacement?" He reached to lay a hand on her forearm.

The touch was a comfort she wouldn't allow herself, no matter how much she wanted to lean into it. She needed to hold herself together for her dad. And yes, to protect herself as well. She lifted the stack of brochures and drummed them into a tidy pile on the dashboard.

"Of course. For as long as I've been aware of my father's problems, I've had worries for him. It's part of loving him." Stuffing the pamphlets into her purse, she lifted the handbag and laid it on her lap. "But you have to understand, I was worried about a far-off future. And now, the potential of a crisis has developed into an actual one."

"I shouldn't have approached him about that sale without talking to you."

She shook her head, anger at herself building. "This is my fault. I should have been here with him. If I'd stuck closer to home, maybe I would have had time to see what was unfolding before it got to this point."

She should have been in Silent Spring.

Instead, she'd been at one extravagant party after another while her loved one suffered alone. Just like her mother.

"You're saying you regret the time we've spent together these last weeks?" There was a wealth of words unspoken in that question.

Scenes from their time together spun through her brain, reminding her of the way their connection had been so red-hot and demanding that it had blinded her to everything else in her life. To how easily she could lose herself in this man.

"How can I not regret it when my dad is locked away for the next six weeks, sick and alone?" That she'd put him there for his own good didn't comfort her in the least.

Especially when she felt responsible for driving him to drink. Even knowing that her dad had to be responsible for his own sobriety, she still couldn't shake the sense that she should have kept a closer watch over him. She would have seen the warning signs and nudged him toward help sooner. If she hadn't been on that tour with Levi, she wouldn't have attracted the photographer's attention. Her mother wouldn't have been compelled to write a social media post speculating about a wedding.

And her dad wouldn't have been devastated by mistaken thoughts of his daughter seeking out Levi just to give her father a spot on Gargoyle King's board.

"That's not your fault. And I feel certain that when you reflect on this later, you'll agree it's not my fault either." Once more, Levi reached for her. His warm palm cupping her shoulder through the thin silk of her blouse. "Take a few days away from the campaign if you want, but don't just walk away from the good work we're doing together."

Work?

Her brain stuck on the word while her body tensed beneath his touch.

"Is that all you think we've been doing together?" she asked, knowing she didn't want to hear the answer.

Then again, perhaps she needed to hear it. Needed a tangible reminder that Levi wasn't interested in anything more than an affair with someone he viewed as little more than a colleague.

His hand fell away from her.

"Of course there's more between us than work." His gaze darted around the truck, as if looking for an answer he couldn't find. "But you can't deny we're also accomplishing good things as a team—"

She didn't need to hear any more.

Seeing herself at his teammate was more than

enough to convince her she'd been a fool all over again for this man.

"I'm glad you're pleased with my efforts on behalf of Kingsland," she said woodenly, trying to maintain what dignity she could after revealing far too much of her heart and her vulnerabilities to him. "But I think going forward, your account will be better served by one of the other partners in my firm."

"Kendra, that's not what I meant," he began, his brow furrowing. His expression troubled. "Why don't we go inside? I can make you something to eat and we can talk about this."

As if the problem was just a simple matter of a misunderstanding. As if they could resolve it with a conversation.

"Talking about it won't change the fact that I've fallen for you." She gripped the door handle on his truck and wrenched the door wide. Something inside her prevented her from stepping down to the driveway though. Some perverse hopeful instinct that made her turn back to him. "Unless, of course, you've developed feelings for me too?"

She could tell by his hesitation—his sudden stillness—that he wasn't prepared for the question. Worse, he didn't reciprocate those tender emotions. The gulf between them widened at the same time her last hope deflated.

Of all the ways this day had pained her, this latest blow was the worst.

"Never mind." She held up a hand to stop him just as he'd opened his mouth to reply. She couldn't bear to hear another speech about what a good team they made. "I have my answer. And I would appreciate it, Levi, if you would leave me and my father alone. I'll make sure you receive the contact details for your new account representative within the hour. Now, if you'll excuse me, I've got a lot to do."

Heart hurting, she didn't look back when Levi called her name.

Because she understood, even if he didn't, that there was truly nothing left to say.

Thirteen

One week later, Levi returned home to Kingsland Ranch after the goodwill publicity tour officially ended.

Alone.

The same as he'd been ever since he and Kendra had parted ways. Parking in the darkened three-bay garage, he tugged his overnight bag from the passenger seat of his truck and headed toward the steps leading into the mudroom. Quiet dogged his steps.

A quiet that had grown louder since he'd left this place the last time. Now, he knew the fulfillment that came not only from spending his days with someone who was sharp and business savvy—every inch his professional equal—but from spending his nights with someone sexy and giving. A person who shared pleasure and tenderness. Someone caring.

As he toed off his shoes and dropped his bag on the antique deacon's bench in the hallway, Levi thought of all the times he'd almost called Kendra this week. But what more could he say to a woman who'd made it clear she needed more from him than he knew how to give? A woman who deserved far better than his inadequate assertions that they made a good team.

Too bad he didn't have a clue how to be more than a supportive teammate.

Yanking open the refrigerator door, he stared into the emptiness, a single expired carton of milk chastising him for not ordering groceries before returning home. He'd been distracted for days, unable to focus on the mind-numbing charity events he'd attended, one after another. All without Kendra.

All while knowing he'd hurt her.

The wounded look in her pretty hazel eyes when she'd asked if he'd developed feelings for her would haunt him forever. She wouldn't have understood the way he'd carefully avoided anything of the sort. Being raised under Duke Kingsley's demanding roof hadn't allowed for emotions. Levi's father had only respected work and effort.

He slammed the refrigerator door closed as headlights flashed across the kitchen window. An engine sounded in the driveway.

For the briefest moment, he wondered if it might be Kendra, stopping by to see how the publicity tour had gone. He hadn't spoken to her once, not even so much as an exchanged text, since she'd passed off his account to one of her colleagues in the publicity firm. Wasn't she curious how the Kingsland brand had rebounded?

But he knew better than that. He'd recognized the finality of her retreating shoulders when she'd walked away from him the last time. And considering how invested she was in her business, she'd probably already taken note that the Kingsland brands were resurging. The negative publicity had quieted. Cleanup was underway on the illegal dumping site, and Levi had made sure to provide all the support he could for the crew working the site. A few positive social media pieces about the Kingsley environmental efforts had generated good press.

Now, as Levi walked to the front door to see who was out front, he spied Gavin striding toward him, a takeout box of pizza in one hand.

"Welcome home," Gavin called, boots striking the flagstones as he grinned at him. "I brought an offering in my new efforts to be a better brother."

Despite the dark mood that had dogged Levi all week, he felt his lips curve in a begrudging smile. After his days as the prodigal son and rodeo rebel, Gavin was making an effort to be a part of the family again. Now, if only Levi could convince Quinton to get onboard, they could start working on a plan to find Clayton so they could divide the ranch shares fairly among them.

"Considering I just got home and was staring into

an empty fridge, I appreciate that." Levi held the door wide for his youngest sibling.

Hanging his Stetson near the door, Gavin wiped his boots before continuing into the kitchen. "I will confess, I saw your flight schedule on the Kingsland calendar and had a question to ask."

Curious, Levi followed him and took down plates from the open shelving in a kitchen Isla Mitchell Kingsley—Gavin's mom—had redesigned in the brief time she'd been married to Duke.

Those five years had been happy, a miracle really, since Levi and Quint had lost their own mother in the ranching accident the year before. But Isla had been kind to them and her baby—Gav—had distracted the boys from the hurt of their mother's death. Odd to think about Isla now, as he laid out the plates she'd chosen on the island countertop. They were white china decorated with subtle pink bitterroot blooms— the humble wildflower that was the state flower of Montana. Isla, his nanny before his stepmother, had been the last recipient of Levi's unadulterated affection. Love, even. What would she think of Levi's response to Kendra when she asked about his feelings?

One of the plates dropped heavily onto the counter, clanking discordantly and making him recall Gavin had just said he had a question for him.

"What did you want to ask?" Sinking onto one of the counter-height leather stools at the island, Levi would be all too glad of a distraction from the dark thoughts that had hounded him this past week.

"I saw the photo of you and Kendra at the Greener Planet event," Gavin began as he lowered himself into another leather bar stool. He pried open the lid on the pizza box and slid it closer to Levi. "The one speculating about an engagement."

His chest burned at the memory of that picture. Of the unforgettable night that had followed it. Before their tentative new relationship crumbled to dust. His appetite vanished.

Still, he forced himself to take a slice of Gavin's dinner offering out of politeness. And because he didn't want to be alone.

"What about it?"

Sliding the box back toward himself, Gavin loaded his plate with two slices. "Is it true? Do you plan to ask Kendra to marry you?"

The vision that created in his head—one of him and Kendra together for real—made him ache.

"I lost any chance of that," he admitted slowly, forcing the words past the hollowness in his chest. "Even if I could have been the kind of person she deserved."

"What are you talking about?" Gavin's pizza hovered halfway to his mouth. "What did you do?"

He shrugged, not knowing where to start. He spun his plate absently. "It's more what I didn't do. What I can't do. I don't have a clue how to navigate feelings and relationships successfully. And she deserves someone who can. Someone who's—"

The thought of her with anyone else delivered another blow to his gut. And the sentence remained unfinished since he refused to think about the kind of person she should be with.

"Since when do you suck at relationships?" Gavin gave up eating, letting the slice fall back to the plate. "You're the only thing keeping this family together. In my book you're the only one of us who has a clue how to navigate the emotional stuff."

Levi shook his head, not believing it. "Please. I learned to be unfeeling from the same Duke Kingsley School for Mental Toughness that you did."

Gavin frowned. "And yet, when I was reeling with how to figure things out with Lauryn, who was there for me, telling me to get my head on straight before I lost her?"

"Just because I recognize a good woman when I see one doesn't mean I'd be any more successful than Dad was when it came to keeping them." Levi recalled Duke cheating on his first wife and divorcing his second without making any provisions for his youngest son.

"Levi, you're nothing like him. You're like the polar opposite of our father." Gavin's voice raised, jabbing his finger to make his point. "When he sent me and my mom packing, do you remember who slipped all the best toys into the moving boxes so I wouldn't feel as slighted?"

That shared memory warmed him a little. He'd tried his damnedest to make things easier for Gav and his mom when they'd left. Levi had only gotten to visit with his younger brother at holidays after that. But as for Isla? Duke made sure she didn't come around Kingsland at all.

She'd relocated to Florida while Levi was in college and he regretted not visiting her once he was old enough to do as he pleased.

"You deserved a hell of a lot better than Dad gave you," Levi reminded him, glad to change the direction of the conversation. "But I'm curious, what made you ask about Kendra and me? There haven't been any more social media posts about that, have there?"

Something shifted in his brother's expression. A happier light came into his brown eyes. "I didn't want to step on your toes if there was going to be an engagement announcement for you two, because I'd like to ask Lauryn to marry me."

Happiness for his brother shoved aside his own pain. He clapped Gavin on the shoulders. "I couldn't be more pleased for you, Gav. Good for you."

For a few minutes, Gavin discussed the ring that he was having specially designed for her. He returned to his food, and Levi forced himself to finish his slice of pizza too. But all the while, he wondered about what Gavin had said.

That Levi was nothing like his father.

That he was better at navigating relationships than he realized. And, for that matter, the sight of those optimistic bitterroot flowers on the edge of his plate made him recall that he hadn't grown up with only Duke Kingsley for a role model. He'd witnessed the way others loved.

Even if it hadn't ended happily for his mom or for Isla, they'd shown him how to be selfless. Giving.

Gavin's words a moment later called him from those memories.

"So that won't be any problem?" his brother asked, peering over at him expectantly as he stood from the leather bar stool to gather their plates.

"The engagement?" Levi asked, thinking they'd already covered that. "Of course not."

"No, brother." Gavin shook his head as he rinsed the plates. "An engagement party here. Assuming Lauryn says yes, I'd like to have our friends over to the ranch to celebrate. We haven't had a big shindig at Kingsland since Lauryn's bachelor auction."

"Right. I'm glad you're committed to Kingsland. Of course you should have the party here." If only he could convince Quinton the Kingsley businesses were all worth keeping too.

"And it won't be awkward for you if Kendra is there? She's one of Lauryn's best friends, so—"

"Don't think twice about it," Levi assured him, actually all in as hopefulness surged at the thought of seeing her. He got to his feet as he boxed up the leftovers to put into the refrigerator. "Kendra is always welcome here. We owe the resurgence of our business to her."

As for Levi, he owed her far more than that.

He needed to explain his inability to answer her that day she'd asked him about his feeling for her.

The engagement party might be his only chance to make her listen.

His only window of time to tell her how wrong he'd been.

Because even if she wanted no part of Levi in her life again, she deserved to know the truth. That he loved her with every flawed part of his heart.

Lights gleamed from every window of the Kingsland Ranch main house the night of Lauryn's engagement party. Kendra tried to smile at a small throng of guests she didn't know as she walked around the perimeter of the infinity pool, her short green silk dress blowing lightly around her thighs as a welcome spring breeze tickled over her skin. Southern rock music played on the outdoor speakers hidden discreetly around the pool and back patio area where a crowd of about seventy-five people had gathered to celebrate the future bride and groom. Sheriff Caleb Hamilton, Lauryn's father and the former nemesis of Gavin Kingsley, held court on the far end of the patio near the pool house, his arm slung around his future son-in-law as he retold a story of Gavin's drag racing.

Apparently they'd put their tense past behind them for the sake of Lauryn. It warmed Kendra's bruised heart to see. Still, she checked her watch as she moved toward the punch bowl table on the patio to refill her glass. As Lauryn's future bridesmaid along with their friend Hope Alvarez, Kendra knew she needed to remain at the party for at least a little while longer.

While she was thrilled for Lauryn and Gavin, she found it painful in the extreme to fake a smile when the source of her broken heart remained in plain view. She was exhausted from the sleepless nights she'd spent thinking about Levi and the hurt of losing something that he refused to recognize between them. As if there was nothing there at all. Currently, he stood under a wisteria covered pergola, deep in conversation with Ellen and Chip Crawford, Lauryn's former foster parents who owned a nursery in Twin Bridges, the next town over.

Ten different times she'd debated approaching Levi tonight to congratulate him on the successful completion of the publicity goodwill tour, only to lose her nerve. She'd tracked the Kingsland social media accounts even after she'd reassigned the client to a coworker, and she'd seen for herself the signs of improving public opinion. Of course, it helped that Levi wasn't at all the same man as his father. He was doing everything right to clean up the environmental mess his dad had created. And he seemed to be doing an equally good job at healing the rifts in his family.

At least as far as his brother Gavin was concerned.

She'd noticed that Quinton hadn't stayed at the party for long. Kendra had debated following him out when he'd left, but her loyalty to her friend had won out over her personal hurt.

Either way, in each instance where she thought about talking to Levi and brazening her way through a conversation as if she wasn't walking wounded, her courage failed her. She feared a single look in those impossibly blue eyes might send her right back to the day he hadn't been able to answer her when she asked if he'd had any feelings for her.

Downing most of her newly poured punch in one gulp, Kendra turned back to the bowl to ladle herself another splash of the nonalcoholic option, telling herself she could get away without talking to anybody if she kept walking and sipping.

"Hello, Kendra."

She shivered at the sound of that deep, sexy voice over her right shoulder. Her punch glass slid in her hand and she might have managed to spill it if Levi hadn't reached for it at the same moment.

"Whoa." He righted the glass in her hand and his warm fingers brushed the back of her knuckles as he settled it in her grip. "I didn't mean to startle you."

Her breath hitched in her throat. Around them, the southern rock song switched to a country anthem and a few people cheered as someone turned up the volume on the speaker system.

The pool lights made a watery, shifting glow on Levi's handsome face as he stared down at her. His white long-sleeved shirt was crisply pressed, the sleeves folded halfway up his forearms, the top button unfastened. Olive colored trousers and leather loafers were more casual clothes than he'd worn throughout their trip. But tonight was about family, not work. He looked good. Excellent, actually.

With half an arm's length between them, she

could still feel the warmth of his body near hers. Still remember how it felt to be much, much closer.

Her heart hurt with remembering.

"You didn't. I'm just—" She huffed out a sigh as she shook her head, unable to fake anything close to normalcy with him. "Okay, I'm fresh out of excuses. I'm on edge tonight because I don't want things to be awkward between us for Gavin and Lauryn's sake. And yet—" She shrugged helplessly. "Of course they are."

Levi glanced around them, where friends and family held happy conversations and laughter abounded. Then his attention returned to her. "Have you heard from your father? Any update on how he's doing?"

Disappointment sank inside her at the realization he only wished to make polite inquiries of her dad. That was kind of him. But considering everything else that had taken place between them, she'd hoped he'd wanted to discuss something else.

"I can't visit him until next week, but I've heard from his counselor that he's doing really well. It sounds like he's thoroughly committed to recovery." Kendra hoped the woman was right, because the counselor had been upbeat and seemed to connect with her dad. "I'm hopeful."

"I'm really glad to hear that." The relief in his voice sounded genuine. "Can we talk privately for a minute about that?" He nodded toward a gazebo with a few seats underneath it that weren't in use. "Over there, maybe, where we can hear one another better?"

Nerves twisted at the request. Yet wouldn't it be

best to put this awkwardness behind them as much as possible if they were going to be seeing one another at more events leading up to the wedding? For Lauryn's sake, she nodded and set down her punch glass to accompany him.

At least, she told herself she was joining him for the bride's sake. That was easier on her conscience than admitting she would be glad for just a few more minutes of time alone with Levi. To have his full attention on her, his blue eyes focused solely on her.

When they reached the gazebo, just outside the glow of the landscape lighting illuminating the pool area, Levi gestured for her to take a seat on the gray cushioned patio sectional.

Smoothing the thin fabric of her green silk dress around her legs, she took the offered seat and was surprised when Levi took the cushion beside her. Closer than she would have expected.

Her pulse notched into a higher gear, and she told herself to ignore it even as she fastened her eyes on his.

Waiting.

"I want to apologize for what happened the last time we spoke," he began, his voice sincere. Warm.

Her cheeks heated, embarrassment seizing her at the memory of how she'd practically flung herself at him and he'd been…unmoved. Silent.

"There's no need," she rushed to explain, folding her arms protectively around her midsection. "I'd prefer not to revisit that actually. Ever."

"For me, there's definitely a need," he contin-

ued, seemingly undaunted by her words as his gaze
turned earnest. "Because I can't live with the idea
that I left you with such a wrongheaded impression
of how I feel."

"On the contrary—"

"Kendra, please." His palm rested on her bare
knee. Briefly. Warmly. "Let me just get this out. If
you'll listen to me for five minutes, I promise I won't
ever bring it up again if you don't want me to."

His blue eyes were beseeching. Between the raw
look in his eyes and that fleeting touch still tingling
the skin over her knee, she couldn't have possibly
refused him. She forced herself to relax her grip on
her midsection as she nodded for him to continue.
Curious, yes, but warily so.

"All right, I'm listening." She laced her fingers
together and rested them over one knee. Trying not
to think about how much better it had felt when he'd
been touching her there.

"I won't bore you with all the reasons that I have
long equated being a Kingsley with being dispassion-
ate. Remote, even. I don't think I ever viewed it as a
problem before because I thought it helped me avoid
the pitfalls of my father's life." Levi leaned closer to
lay his hand on her forearm. Gently. "Until I met you."

His fingers brushed a light caress over her arm,
reminding her of all the other times he'd touched her.
All the other times she'd craved having his hands
on her body.

The clamor in her brain for more of his touching

almost distracted her from the words he was saying. But her mind seized on that last part. "Why until me?"

"Because suddenly I didn't have the tools I needed to be in a relationship, something I craved even as I told myself I could fulfill that hunger with an affair." His brow furrowed. Worry clouded his gaze. "And yet you deserved so much more than that, Kendra. It hurts now to think that I tried to cheapen what we had by relegating it to the realms of work or sex when what I really wanted was so much deeper."

She swallowed hard. Tried to digest the words even as she struggled to make them fit in the context of that last conversation when he seemed to push her away.

"You wanted something more?" Her fingers slid on top of his, holding his hand in place where it rested on her arm.

She was suddenly very, very invested in this conversation that had taken an unexpected—incredible—turn.

What was he saying?

Her heart pounded harder. Faster. The sound of it knocking around her rib cage drowned out the music from the party and the noise of the conversations and laughter.

All that mattered in this moment was Levi.

"I wanted so much more." He lifted both of her hands and took them in his. "More than anything, what I craved was to love you. To maybe even be loved by you one day."

Everything inside her stilled. Hope filled her.

Yet she needed to be sure.

"But when I asked you if you had feelings for me—" she began, trying to piece together all of what he was explaining.

"At the time, I didn't trust that I could be the kind of man you deserve." His voice sounded pained, eyes echoing that emotion. Windows to his soul. "Logically, I know that loving relationships work. But I saw my father destroy one good thing after another and I had it in my head—as his heir—that I somehow would follow in his footsteps that way too."

Her heart hurt for him and the feelings he may have missed out on in his past. Yet how could she not rejoice at the same time, when maybe that had paved the way for him to love her?

"You're nothing like your father." She tipped her forehead to his, needing him to understand that in no uncertain terms. "I didn't know him well, but he left a very public legacy that bears no resemblance to the good and honorable man I know you to be."

Behind them at the party, the music changed to a country love song, and there were wolf whistles and shouts for Gavin and Lauryn to share a dance. But Kendra's spot in the shadowed gazebo with Levi felt a world away from the engagement party. Here, the scent of night-blooming jasmine rode the breeze, and the hope curled her toes in her sandals as Levi brushed a soft kiss over her lips.

Once. Twice.

"Thank you for saying that," he breathed against her mouth as he eased back. "Something Gavin said to me a couple of days ago helped me see it. Ever since, I've been counting the hours until I saw you here so I could tell you that if you'd ever consent to give me another chance, I would be sure you never, ever regretted it."

Kendra's heart swelled and she let herself dive into the emotion, to trust in the earnestness of his vow. Love for this man filled her with new hope and so much more.

A smile pulled at her lips.

"I can't imagine you ever failing at something you promised." She tunneled her fingers through his dark hair, tilting his face so she could see his expression clearly in the moonlight. "I believe in you, Levi Kingsley. And I love you."

"I love you more than I ever thought I was capable of loving anyone," he vowed, wrapping her in his arms and kissing her until they were both breathless.

When he released her, he edged back enough to pull a folded paper from his pocket. "I should have given you this earlier, but I was so nervous that you might not hear me out, I forgot my carefully planned speech."

Confused, she took the paper from him and unfolded it. "You had a speech ready?"

"I'd been rehearsing for days, but when you looked like you were going to bolt at the mention of our last conversation, I fast-forwarded to the most important part." His sheepish smile was endearing. "But go ahead and read it."

Glancing down at the paper, she read a few lines. "It's a bill of sale. For Gargoyle King?"

"It's a transfer of ownership since there is no money involved," he explained as he pointed to her name on the form, followed by a blank line. "I wasn't sure if I should be transferring the company solely to you or if you'd like your father's name on it too. But I won't maintain ownership of Gargoyle King any longer. By rights, it's yours and your father's as much as mine."

Stunned, she passed him back the paper, blown away by the beauty of his gesture. "You already paid my father for it. And you've invested all your own capital—"

Levi wouldn't take the form. He held both hands up. "This is happening, Kendra. At the very least, you and your father can be my equal partners if you wish, but I refuse to run the company in my name alone. Either it's yours outright, or we're partners."

Glancing down at the paper again, she felt three years' worth of old resentment melt away. How could she have thought poorly of Levi?

Furthermore, was it possible that she and her dad could take creative roles in the business they'd once dreamed up together? She'd helped him because it was a labor of love for him, but she'd enjoyed every minute of working with her dad.

"I'm not sure what his counselor will say." She pressed the paper to her chest, touched beyond measure as tears stung behind her eyes. "But this is incredibly kind of you, Levi."

He kissed her forehead and stroked her hair while the music ended at the engagement party.

"It's no more than you and your dad deserve. I've got a ranch and a bar to run, so I'd be glad for help with the liquor business. Especially if it brought you to Silent Spring more often." His look was so hopeful that she had to smile.

"I've already told my publicity firm that I need to permanently relocate." She wouldn't make the same mistake of leaving her father alone again. "I want to be in my dad's life as much as possible."

Levi drew her to him and squeezed her tight. At the party, the crowd seemed to be shifting toward the far end of the pool and a moment later, Kendra knew why. Fireworks exploded in the field beyond them, and streaked the sky with red, gold and purple before fading to black. Applause and cheers sounded just as another explosion of light and sound illuminated the heavens.

"I want you in my life as much as possible," Levi whispered in her ear as he tucked her by his side.

Joy like she'd never imagined filled her as she rested her head on his shoulder, his strength and warmth reminding her she would never be alone again. That she would have this amazing man in her life to count on. To lean on.

To love forever.

"We're going to make each other very happy," she whispered back.

She didn't know if he heard her. But she knew without a doubt that he felt all the same feelings. And right now, that was more than enough.

Epilogue

One month later

"Home sweet home." Levi looped an arm around Kendra's waist as they stood together on the steps in front of the Kingsland Ranch main house. His border collie Gunner sat beside them, tail thumping as all three of them gazed up at the home that had been in Levi's family for generations. The three-story farmhouse much renovated over the years but still true to the original style with deep porches and multiple dormers. The last of Kendra's moving boxes had been delivered an hour ago, and he had a picnic on the back patio planned to celebrate with her. "I want you to be happy here, so please do whatever you wish to make it your own."

After they'd completed the publicity tour, they'd returned to Silent Spring, seeing each other every single day. Levi had travelled to Denver with her to help her tie up her business there, and then he'd assisted with making her father's home more comfortable for both of them. Seth Davies had finished his rehabilitation program and was back in residence in town, committed to his sobriety and excited to have Kendra back in town. Kendra had spent the last two weeks under the same roof as her dad, but she'd seemed intrigued when Levi brought up the idea of moving in with him at Kingsland.

So of course, he'd brought it up early and often to convince her to take the leap. And, to his absolute delight, she'd agreed two days ago. Unwilling to waste another minute apart, he'd hired movers the following day.

"I can't believe I'm really doing this." She turned serious eyes toward him, her fingers coming to rest on his cheek while Gunner ran circles around them before sprinting off in chase of something in the bushes. "You're certain you're ready for me to be here, in your life, day in and day out for the foreseeable future?"

Levi couldn't tell her that even now an engagement ring was being custom made for her by a jeweler in New York. Or that he planned to take her back to the Plaza for her birthday in three weeks, where he would propose to her on a sunset cruise aboard the private yacht he'd rented for the occasion.

Instead, he settled for cupping her face in his hand and gazing into the eyes he wanted to see every day for the rest of his life. "I've never been more sure of anything than wanting you with me forever."

Her smile lit up his insides. He'd never get tired of putting a happy expression on the face that he loved most in the world.

"In that case, I suppose we ought to go inside and enjoy our first evening together as a co-habitating couple."

Unable to resist her or the lusciousness of her lips, Levi was about to lean in for a kiss when the sound of tires crunching on gravel made them turn around.

His brother Quinton's truck kicked up dust as it headed toward them from the main road. Surprised to see him when his sibling preferred to avoid time at Kingsland Ranch after bad memories associated with Quint's youth, Levi lifted a hand in greeting while Gunner ran toward the truck to say hello.

"We should invite your brother for dinner," Kendra suggested as they walked together toward the truck to greet him.

Levi knew Quinton would never agree.

"You're welcome to try," he encouraged her without much hope.

Not that he minded having Kendra all to himself tonight.

The driver's side window on the silver pickup

lowered as Quinton slowed the vehicle to a stop near them.

"Hey Kendra. Levi." Taking off his Stetson, Quinton tossed it on the passenger seat before leaning out the window to pet Gunner's head. "I'm not staying, I just wanted to stop by to let you know the first phase of cleanup on the coal ash site is complete. I just came from a meeting with the foreman on the job, and he said they'll bring out someone from the Environmental Protection Agency next week for their approval."

A two-ton weight slid off his shoulders at the disclosure while Kendra squeezed his hand.

"That's fantastic news. We should put out a press release and let the public know we've made it to the next phase."

Levi kissed the top of her head, amazed and grateful that he would have this incredible woman in his corner from now on.

"First thing tomorrow," he agreed, unwilling to compromise the picnic tonight when she deserved the down time. Then, turning back to Quinton, he gave a nod. "Thanks for stopping by to let us know."

"Sure thing." Quinton drummed his thumbs against the steering wheel while Gunner barked at him in an effort to get another scratch behind the ear. Quinton leaned out the window again to oblige. "I also wanted to see if you'd watch Rocco for a couple of weeks while I head up to Alaska."

"To look for Clayton?" Levi wasn't surprised

that Quinton was determined to find their missing brother, He knew Quint was eager to right the wrongs of their father's will with regard to Clayton and Gavin, whom Duke hadn't acknowledged. "You don't need to go yourself. We can hire another PI. Someone better—."

"No. I'll go." Quinton's quiet determination was clear in his expression. "This is something I need to do for myself."

"Of course I'll watch Rocco," Levi agreed. "Gunner will be glad for the company and so will we." He squeezed Kendra closer to him, enjoying the way she fit against him.

"Quinton, will you join us for dinner?" Kendra asked, smoothing a few strands of hair away from her forehead.

Levi wasn't surprised when his brother thanked her politely and made his excuses. As they watched him drive away, Levi hoped the Alaska trip would point him in the right direction to find Clay.

But right now, he only had one thing on his mind.

"Are you ready for me to carry you across our threshold for the first time?" he asked Kendra as he drew her back up the lush lawn toward the farmhouse.

Their home.

"I'm pretty sure that's a tradition for new brides and not just for random women you're shacking up with," she teased, pausing to plant a kiss on his jaw.

Halting in his tracks, Levi wrapped both arms

around her, pulling her against him so he could kiss her properly. Slowly.

Until they were both a little breathless.

"It may be a tradition for new brides," he said finally, glancing from her pretty face to the old house and then back again. "But I have the feeling it will be a good omen for our future if I can have the privilege of carrying you inside the first time we enter together."

From beside the front door, Gunner barked twice, as if hurrying them along.

"See?" Levi urged. "Even Gunner agrees."

Kendra grinned. "I think Gunner's just in a hurry to get to the picnic. But since I'm just as much of a closet romantic as you are, Levi Kingsley, I'll say yes to this wildly sweet gesture."

Not giving her a moment to change her mind, Levi swept her off her feet, savoring the sound of her laughter as he carried her into their future.

* * * * *

Stacey Kennedy is a *USA TODAY* bestselling author who writes romances full of heat, heart and happily-ever-afters.

Stacey lives with her husband and two children in southwestern Ontario. Most days, you'll find her enjoying the outdoors or venturing into the forest with her horse, Clementine. Stacey's just as happy curled up indoors, where she writes surrounded by her lazy dogs. She believes that sexy books about hot cowboys can fix any bad day. But wine and chocolate help, too.

Books by Stacey Kennedy

Devil's Bluffs

Most Eligible Cowboy
Stranded with a Cowboy

Visit the Author Profile page
at Harlequin.com for more titles.

You can also find Stacey Kennedy on Facebook,
along with other Harlequin Desire authors,
at Facebook.com/HarlequinDesireAuthors!

Dear Reader,

If you love fast-paced stories, laugh-out-loud moments, heart-squeezing emotion and sizzling chemistry, then you've come to the right place!

Stranded with a Cowboy, the second novel in the Devil's Bluffs series, features freelance researcher Nora Keller, who's a romantic at heart, but after two terrible breakups, she's giving up on love—maybe permanently. Until a gorgeous cowboy begins filling her dreams.

Single dad Beau Ward's quiet life has turned upside down since he and his brother went viral as Texas's Sexiest Bachelors. To avoid the reporters who want the private, painful details of the passing of his late wife, Beau leaves town to draw the attention away and hides in his remote cabin. Until, in the middle of a tropical storm, Nora arrives on his doorstep. Beau knows a good thing when he sees it, and Nora is certainly a sexy good thing.

Before long, one sizzling kiss turns into hot nights as they ride out the storm together, tangled up in the bedsheets. But Nora is not a woman you let go. And when Beau goes back for more, he discovers things won't be so easy. Only Nora can decide if Beau's as capable with her heart as he is with her body.

Beau and Nora stole my heart, and I hope they steal yours, too!

To stay up-to-date on upcoming releases and sales, subscribe to my mailing list at www.staceykennedy.com. To stay in touch, follow me on Instagram and TikTok @staceykennedybooks and on Facebook at authorstaceykennedy. I love new friends!

Happy reading!

Stacey

STRANDED WITH
A COWBOY

Stacey Kennedy

For Mom,
who rose through the ashes of grief
with strength, courage and love.

Prologue

Beau Ward sat behind the wheel of his blue Dodge Ram contemplating violence. He'd never considered himself a man who acted out of anger. Most times, he knew to fight with wit over his fists, but as he watched a reporter standing on the grave of his late wife, Annie, who passed away nearly six years ago of a brain aneurysm, his knuckles went white against the steering wheel.

For a couple days now, he'd been dodging the few reporters who had descended on the small town, Devil's Bluffs, like vultures, all because he and his older brother, Colter, had been named Texas's Sexiest Bachelor in a gossip blog out of New York City. He, and his brother had saved a calf from the rapids, and a photograph of the rescue had been published in the blog's fifty-state bachelor roundup piece. The article went viral.

They'd first focused on Colter as "Texas's Sexiest Bachelor." At the time, Colter had wanted the women in town who suddenly realized there was a sexy mega-rich bachelor in the running off his back. A reporter for the gossip blog who'd run the piece, Adeline had needed her story and an exclusive with Colter, since she'd been up for a promotion. Only problem was, instead of just getting Colter's story, they fell in love.

In the end, Beau gave out details of his life so that Colter and Adeline's relationship could blossom, and he took over the role as "Texas's Sexiest Bachelor". Therefore, Adeline could still get a story and not hurt her relationship with Colter by sharing private details told in confidence.

Colter had found love with Adeline as a result of the piece. Beau only found a massive headache. The reporters were hungrier for more of a story than simply a hot bachelor out of Texas. When social media got ahold of his widower status, they wanted the tragic details of his heartbreak of losing his wife and his life as a single dad.

Beau wanted none of it.

"He's been taking pictures," a gravelly voice said.

Beau looked to his left, and through the open window spotted the groundskeeper, Fred, who'd worked at the cemetery for as long as Beau could remember.

"Thanks for me letting me know." He'd called twenty minutes ago to give Beau the heads-up.

"It ain't right, man," Fred said, with a disapproving shake of his head.

"No, it's not." Heat flushed through Beau as he opened the truck's door and stepped out into the sunny day. "I'll deal with him," he told Fred, offering his hand.

Fred's handshake was tight and firm, much like the man himself. "Your father wouldn't stand for the treatment you've been getting."

"You're right, he wouldn't have," Beau agreed.

His father, Grant Ward, had been laid to rest not far from Beau's late wife just over a month ago after a long, cruel battle with Parkinson's disease. Not quite having the right words to say, Beau gave a final nod of thanks to Fred and then approached the reporter.

The scent of fresh cut grass rushed over him, among the floral scents from flowers left for loved ones desperately missed.

"Can I help you?" Beau asked when he reached the reporter, crossing his quivering arms over his chest to ensure he didn't grab the man.

The reporter, maybe in his midtwenties, turned to Beau, his eyes widening with recognition. "Ah…"

"Yes, I'm Beau Ward," he said sternly. "No, I won't give you an interview, and if you do not get off the grave of my late wife, I will remove you."

The man rushed off the grave in a second flat.

"Erase the pictures of the gravesite," Beau demanded, his jaw tightening with every word.

With shaking hands, the man did as asked, finally saying, "All right, they're gone."

Beau took a step forward. The man retreated a step, making Beau wonder just how murderous his expression looked. "Whatever story you're looking for," he said, likely failing at controlling his rage. "Whatever tale you want to write. It has nothing to do with my dead wife. Got it?"

A deep swallow. "Yeah, I got it."

"Don't come back here." The ashen-faced man stared at Beau with bright eyes, and Beau was surprised he wasn't pissing himself. "Go."

Beau watched as the reporter all but ran to his car, got in and was gone a moment later.

With a sigh, Beau looked to the grave. "I won't let them turn our story into some spectacle," he said to Annie. Then he tore himself away from the one place he only came to visit once a year.

He couldn't take more of this, concerned that they were getting closer to his pain and that pain would soon touch his young son, Austin. He slammed the truck's door behind him, thrusting his hands in his hair and cursed. Every minute, every day, they messed with his head more and more. He wouldn't allow the darkness of his grief to reach Austin.

After turning on his truck, he hit the road and thought over his next steps on the drive to his brother's house in the heart of Ward land.

The moment he got out of the truck, he jogged up the porch steps and entered the house without knocking, slamming the door behind him. "You owe me," he growled, causing Adeline to jump at his sudden arrival. Her long strawberry blond hair was pulled up, her kind, honey-colored eyes as warm as ever. His brother had found himself a good woman, and Beau was genuinely happy for them.

He leaned against the door, breathless. "You owe me so bad."

Being two years older than Beau, Colter looked a lot like the father they'd lost. A father they all missed with an unbearable ache. Beau knew if his dad was still alive, he'd know how to manage this viral story and the reporters.

Colter's chestnut brown hair framed wise blue eyes and a strong jawline. He chuckled, hanging the drying cloth onto the stove. "I told you that you never should have gone viral on purpose."

"I had no idea it would be this bad." Beau glared. He loved them both. He'd also make the same decision to protect Colter and Adeline in a heartbeat, but…"You *both* owe me. This is crazy." He'd wanted to find a good woman after a string of terrible dates. He wanted a woman who was real and honest. Instead, he'd found women playing games and fake people who he'd never bring into his son's life.

Even worse, reporters had become ravenous for the personal details of his marriage to Annie and his life as a single dad. From what he'd learned, his name had been trending for two days now. People he didn't know were speaking about his life like they had a front row seat to it.

Suddenly, a loud snort came from the phone in Adeline's hand.

"I'm actually really glad you're here, Beau," Adeline said, her voice chipper. "Since you're Colter's best man for the wedding, and Nora's my maid of honor, you two should probably meet." She turned her phone around. "Nora Keller meet Beau Ward."

Beau narrowed his eyes, closed the distance and snatched the phone away. His breath hitched as he got a look at her.

He'd begun dating when he'd felt ready after Annie passed away, but every woman he'd met had him walking away. Some agreed to a casual sexual relationship that fed his needs well enough, but none had stopped him in his tracks. *This* woman made him freeze. Her hazel eyes locked him in. "What was that laugh about?" he asked this gorgeous stranger.

"My snort laugh, you mean?" Nora countered.

"Yeah, *that*." His chest heaved.

Nora didn't hesitate for a single moment. "Because I find what you said hilarious. Seriously, you have available women chasing after you and you're unhappy about this? What is wrong with you?"

Beau lifted his brows at her boldness. The last woman he took out ordered the same thing he had, said she enjoyed the same things he did and laughed annoyingly at everything he said, hanging off his arm. He didn't like it. He happened to appreciate the challenge in Nora's eyes. The fire in their depths. "What would you do if you were in my position?"

"I'd enjoy the ride," Nora said. "Free dinners. Coffee dates. Fun nights out. Oh, what torture you must be enduring."

Beau's nostrils flared again. "Then *you* make a photograph of yourself go viral."

"I can't," Nora said dryly. "I'm not nearly as hot as you."

He slowly lifted a suggestive eyebrow at her, saw the responding flush in her cheeks. He'd only made one other woman in his life blush like that with a look alone. He loved and lost her. But he knew this chemistry—a rare type that was based on one thing alone: *hunger.* A passion that wasn't based on logic, but on something that connected people on a physical level. Need that didn't make sense but wanted to be fed regardless. "The problem here is it's not only women hunting me down, it's reporters," he told her, handing the cell phone to Adeline. To Colter, he said, "I want to get out of town for a while."

"It's that bad?" Colter asked.

Beau nodded. "Can Austin stay with you two for a couple weeks? You'll have to take him to school and handle lunches and his baseball games, but I can't allow him to deal with this nonsense. He can't understand why there's people always following us."

Colter sidled next to Adeline, leaning against the island. "Yeah, of course he can stay. Where are you going?"

Beau gestured at Adeline's cell phone. "I'll let you know later."

"Just being a voice of reason," Nora said through the speaker of the phone. "But reporters never back down unless given a reason to."

"They won't have a choice," Beau spat. "I'm leaving tonight."

"I wouldn't recommend it," Nora offered.

"Why is that?" Beau glared at the phone.

"Because they'll hunt you down wherever you go," Nora said dryly. "At least that's what I'd do."

Beau closed the distance again and held out his hand for the phone. Once Adeline handed it to him, he said to Nora, "They will never find me."

Nora flashed a smile that sparked fire in his gut. "They will, believe me. You should rethink your strategy."

He made a noise in the back of his throat.

"Are you always this grumpy?" she asked.

Beau frowned at the phone. With curiosity brimming over Adeline's best friend, and locked in her passion-filled stare, he harrumphed at her, reeling in her sassy smile.

Who the hell was this sexy, fiery woman?

Having nothing more to add, he handed the phone back to Adeline and headed for the door. As he wrapped his hand around the door handle and whisked it open, he did one thing that he didn't expect to do; he smiled.

One

"I miss you, Dad."

The strands of Beau's heart snapped at the pain in his son's expression through his tablet on FaceTime. Beau had left Devil's Bluffs four days ago, and every day that passed seemed longer than the last. "I miss you too, buddy." As he'd done a million times before now, Beau searched for any sign of his late wife, Annie, in their son. But like always, he only saw a Ward. Brown slightly curly hair sat atop a round face, with sharp blue eyes and a smile that held all of his son's mischievous spirit. Since day one, Austin had never looked anything like his mother.

Beau missed Annie. He missed being loved by

a good woman, feeling her wrap her arms and legs around him, chasing the chill away in the night.

Sitting on the couch, with his tablet pulled up close to his face, Austin pouted. "When will you be home?"

"Sorry, bud, it'll be a little longer," Beau explained gently, his gut twisting with the uncertainty of his life.

Austin's chin quivered. "Why?"

Beau tore his gaze off his son and stared out the window at the torrential downpour from the incoming tropical storm at the remote cabin, with the loft bedroom above the tiny living room and kitchen, that he built after he lost Annie. Once it was finished, he'd brought Austin there, and they'd stayed for a couple months, just the two of them, trying to find a new way forward. He'd found it in the end.

When he knew his voice wouldn't break, he said to Austin, "A tropical storm is on the way. I couldn't come home now even if I wanted to." He didn't explain everything about the reporters to Austin, only that a story had been written about him and there were people who wanted to know more about him. "Our life is ours, right? We don't need to share it with people we don't know," Beau had told Austin, and he seemed to understand the situation, enough that a six-year-old could. "How's school going?" he asked, shifting the subject to ease Austin's worries before bed.

"Boring," said Austin, the tablet's screen shaking

with his fidgety movements. "Uncle Colter said the rain is gonna be bad."

"Yup, it'll come down hard." Beau leaned his shoulder against the window, staring out into the dark, angry night. It had been a few years since a tropical storm of this size hit Devil's Bluffs, but Beau was holding out hope the forecasted winds quieted, and the rainfall amounts lessened. "You're safe at home with Uncle Colter and Auntie Adeline, and I'm safe here. Plus you get a couple days off school so that's fun, right?"

"Yeah, I guess so," Austin grumbled. His eyes shifted up away from the screen. "Gotta go now, Dad, it's bath time."

Such a mundane part of Austin's routine, and yet Beau craved that normalcy. Out in the wilderness all there was him and his thoughts. "Sweet dreams, bud. Love you."

"Love you too, Dad."

The screen on Beau's tablet shook before Colter's face appeared. "Doing all right up there?" his brother asked.

Beau sighed, moving to the chair set next to the stone fireplace in the tiny living room of the cabin. "You were right, this is hell," he said.

Colter chuckled, though the amusement never reached his eyes. "I told you. Going viral is not all that it's cracked up to be."

"I wanted to meet a woman," Beau admitted. A woman to experience life with and to help raise his son. A woman to help him forget how damn lonely he was. A good woman just like his brother found in Adeline. "They never dug into your story like this," he told Colter.

"They want to capitalize off your grief," Colter grumbled. "It's disgusting."

Beau grunted in agreement. "Are they still slinking their way around town?"

Adeline suddenly appeared over Colter's shoulder, her hair disheveled, a telling sign Austin was keeping her on her toes. "I saw them in town earlier," she explained, her nose scrunched in distaste. "The same three. They were talking to people around town, doing what they do." Adeline should know. She was a reporter until she gave up reporting in New York City to move to Devil's Bluffs and become editor of the local newspaper. "As far as I know, no one has sold you out."

Beau restrained a curse. He'd hoped by now they'd realize the story was dead with his absence, but reports from his brother and mother indicated they were still relentlessly pursuing townsfolk. No one would divulge anything too personal; Beau believed that to his bones. Devil's Bluffs was a tight-knit community, and the Wards, a prominent, wealthy family in the community, had a long history of helping the town, both financially and lending a hand whenever needed.

His eyes began to ache, and he rubbed at the tiredness. The last place he wanted to be was away from his family. They needed him now more than ever. "How's Mom doing?" he asked, dropping his hand.

"Mom is doing fine," his mother called from somewhere in Colter's living room.

Warmth flooded Beau's chest at his mother's sweet voice, which could make any day better. Colter angled the screen to show his mother sitting on the couch and knitting a baby blanket that she made for the animals at the shelter. Her shiny gray curls were as perfect as ever atop her head, but her clear blues were drenched in heartache from the loss of her beloved husband. Life was carrying on, but the pain was ever so vivid. For all of them. "Hey, Mom, it's good to see you," he said.

"Hi, honey," Mom said, a sweet smile warming her features. "You need to stop worrying about all of us. We're all fine. Stay there, let his die down, and then come home to us."

"That's the plan," Beau agreed.

Mom acknowledged his hope with a quick nod.

"So, listen," said Adeline, the screen returning to her over Colter's shoulder. "We've got a bit of a situation that you should know about."

Beau frowned. "What type of situation?" He wasn't sure how much more he could handle.

"Nora is driving up to see you."

Nora was the *very* woman that Beau hadn't been able to stop thinking about. "You told her where I was?" he asked, trying to hide the irritation in his voice.

Adeline's wince indicated he didn't hide it enough. "Of course not. I didn't say a word to her," she implored, "Nora is wicked smart. She's the best researcher I know. If there is something or someone to find, she'll find it."

Beau shook his head in disagreement. "The only people who know about this cabin are family. How would she even find it?"

Adeline shrugged, smiling with obvious pride. "Because Nora is an information ninja."

If he wasn't so annoyed, he might be impressed.

He rubbed his eyebrow, working at the throbbing that wouldn't quit. "Why is she coming to see me?"

"She's taking her role of maid of honor very seriously," Adeline said, nibbling on her lip, as if she was holding back. "She says there are things you two need to discuss, but wouldn't tell us what those things are. She wants us to be surprised."

Beau grunted and rose, moving back to the window. Heavy rain poured from the unforgiving skies. "She's driving to talk about our wedding party duties with a tropical storm heading our way?"

"She lives in New York City, remember?" Adeline countered, her cheeks turning pink. "When she left, it didn't look bad. It just looked like normal rain."

"She didn't listen to the forecast?" Beau asked.

"Or me," Colter stated with a heavy sigh.

"Oh, hush." Adeline flicked Colter's ear, causing his brother to laugh, as she said, "Okay, we should have listened to you, but when are the forecasters ever right?"

Colter and Beau said in unison, "When there's a tropical storm."

Adeline huffed, placing her chin atop Colter's head, staring at Beau with pleading eyes.

Beau smiled at his brother before he said to Adeline, "What do you need me to do?"

"When Nora called, she said she'd pulled over on the side of the road to wait out the storm. Can you go find her?"

Adeline's puppy dog eyes had him pushing away from the window. "Yeah, I'll find her."

"Thank you, Beau," Adeline said.

"Thanks for watching Austin," he said. "I'll reach out when I've got her." They said their goodbyes and then Beau slid his cell into his pocket, aware of the adrenaline rushing through him at the thought of meeting Nora. It didn't make sense. He didn't even know her except for what he'd heard of her from Adeline, and from meeting her once over FaceTime, but that one meeting, and her take-no-shit attitude matched with brutal honesty, had snagged something inside of him that wouldn't let go.

He'd pleasured himself with her on his mind. Repeatedly.

On his way out the door, he scooped up his keys off the kitchen counter and then ran outside, soaked solid by the time he made it behind the wheel of his truck. There was only one road in and one road out of the cabin, but the thin, dirt road eventually opened to a windy two-lane highway that weaved its way around Ward land.

For six generations, the Ward family had worked

cattle and bred American Quarter Horses at their farm, The Devil's Bluffs Ranch. The ranch consisted of five hundred and sixty thousand acres of gorgeous Texas countryside. Six lakes provided water to the Hereford and Angus cattle, and the American Quarter Horses they bred.

Beau had stepped happily into the role of heading up the horse division of the ranch. Most of the fillies and colts were sold after weaning. The horses that showed promise and talent, Beau personally trained before shipping them off to a professional reiner to show for bragging and breeding rights. While Colter had recently stepped away from running the cattle side for the business to return to flying helicopters, hiring a COO and staff to head up the business, Beau was proud of his part in the ranch. Even if he had to give up his dream of competing as a professional reiner himself, which judged the training and athletic ability of a ranch horse in a show arena, when Annie passed away, he regretted nothing. Austin needed a stable home. His only priority was to his son.

Driving slowly down the road, his windshield wipers barely able to clear the windshield, the rain hammering his truck. As the road shifted to the right, Beau squinted, spotting a car in the distance. The closer he got, the more he shook his head.

Next to the Honda Civic parked at the side of the road was Nora, changing a tire. Adeline hadn't mentioned a flat tire, making Beau assume Nora hadn't wanted her best friend to worry about her. He pulled up, facing the car with his headlights shining the light on her. "Changing a tire in the middle of a tropical storm," he said to himself, snorting, throwing his truck into park. "Jesus."

Merciless rain fell from the sky as he hopped out of his truck and jogged toward her. "Nora," he yelled.

She glanced up, her hood covering her face. "Yeah?" Her voice was just as he remembered, bright, with a slight edge of snark.

"It's Beau." He shielded his eyes from the barrage of rain. "Come on, get in my truck. I'll take you back to my cabin. It's not safe out here. We can get the tire changed once the storm is over."

She tilted her head back a little farther, and yet he still couldn't see those pretty hazel eyes and full, pouty lips he couldn't get out of his head. "How do I know you're Beau and not a serial killer?"

"You cannot be serious," he yelled over the pelting rain.

"Just kidding." Nora laughed, hoisting the tire and tossing it then the tools back in the trunk. She grabbed a bag before slamming the lid and heading for his truck.

Like a damn fool, he could only stare after her. Who was this strange creature of a woman, who changed a tire in a tropical storm, who laughed even when soaking wet, who took off running to his truck with all the confidence in the world?

When thunder rumbled then lightening cracked across the sky, he was reminded of the danger and ran after her. A loud honk of her car indicated she'd locked her doors. Again, he shook his head, laughing. She was insane enough to get stuck in a tropical storm but worried about someone stealing her car.

Though the moment he got behind the wheel again, inhaled her fresh, lavender perfume, and she flipped her hood down, he stopped laughing.

Damn.

Long, golden brown hair, currently soaking and dripping water, curtained her round face. Her hazel eyes were something special when he saw them through a screen. In real life, they were so sunny he swore she warmed him just by looking at him. Her features were delicate, nose thin, cheekbones only slightly defined. She was five foot nothing, and she was also *wet.* Heat enveloped him so swiftly he bit back a groan, the all-consuming yearning to tangle his fingers in the strands of her hair battering him.

"So," he said, getting his mind into proper places that didn't involve those perfectly shaped lips, because what in the hell was wrong with him? He never lusted after any woman, not like this, not without reason. He didn't even know this woman, but he'd been counting down the days until she flew to Devil's Bluffs, so he could meet her in person. "You came all this way to talk about our duties in the wedding?"

"Mmm-hmm," she said.

There seemed to be more that she wasn't saying, but he didn't push on that front. Not yet anyway. He reached for his seat belt and fastened it. His brother's wedding was in two weeks from now. Everyone was hoping that the damage from the tropical storm wasn't going to hinder the upcoming nuptials. Being Colter's best man, Beau was determined to ensure nothing went wrong. "You do realize we could have talked on the phone."

"It's too hard to plan things over the phone," she said on a rush, wiping at the water dripping down her face. Giving a big smile, she added, "Besides, this wedding is important. Everything must be perfect. Flawless. Nothing can go wrong."

Shaking his head at her set jaw, he said, "Neither my brother nor Adeline is this intense about *their* wedding. Why are you?"

She wiggled out of her soaked sweater, leaving herself in a clinging T-shirt he had no business looking at. "Because I'm thinking about moving to Paris." Like she hadn't meant to say that aloud, she jerked her gaze to him, eyes wide with desperation. "Please don't tell Adeline. I'm going to tell her, just not until after she's back from her honeymoon. I want all the focus right now to be on her, not me, and I haven't received a job offer yet from Paris anyway. A half dozen interviews—" frustration laced her voice "—but no job offers."

"Let me get this straight," he said, utterly baffled. "You hunted me down when I told you specifically I didn't want to be found, but want me to keep this secret for you?"

"Yes."

The gall of her sent him back against his seat. "Why would I do that, Nora?"

"Because of the other reason I wanted to see you face-to-face."

His brow lifted. "Which is?"

Her grin was pure sass. "I'm going to get your life back for you."

"And just how will you do that?" he asked, doubtful.

The rain dinged off the truck as she reached into her purse, pulling out a folder. "You've got three reporters here in Devil's Bluffs trying to get your story. And it just so happens you now have one of the best researchers at your disposal."

He cocked his head. "What exactly are you suggesting?"

"That we work together," she explained. "You help make this wedding extra special, and I help you get these reporters out of town and make your story go away. All it takes is learning people's darkest secrets, and we'll send them running."

He studied her, searching for any signs of deceit. He found none, only the willingness to help him. Which came as a breath of fresh air. Every woman he'd dated since returning to the scene had an agenda. Some were outright dishonest. Others fake. And some simply had no idea who they were and hung on his every word. "Tell me this—how did you find out about my cabin?"

"You had wood delivered to this location when you were building it," she said, placing the file back into her purse. "You weren't really all that hard to find. I knew you'd go somewhere remote. It was just finding the location of where you were." When she hit him with her sharp, clever eyes, she said, "Next time, pick a friend's place. That would have been harder to find."

He could only stare at her in amazement. *Again.* "You know something, Nora," he said, taking in the way her lush mouth made him want things he shouldn't want with his soon to be sister-in-law's best friend. "I'm starting to like you."

"Great," she said, smiling in return. "Does that mean I'm forgiven for finding you, then?"

"If you get these reporters off my back, then yes, you're forgiven." He shifted the truck into drive, easing off the brake, the headlights bathing the narrow road in light. "Which, in your case, is a good thing since you're stuck with me for the next few days."

She blinked. "How am I stuck with you?"

"Forecasters anticipate the storm will last a few days, and my cabin only has one bed."

Her voice squeaked. "What about the couch?"

"It's a cabin," he said with a laugh, taking the bend in the road easy. "There is no couch."

A long pause. "So, we'll be…"

He grinned, leveling her with all the unexplainable heat simmering between them in this truck. "Riding out this storm together."

Two

The cabin came as a complete surprise. Nora pictured a little woodshed tucked away in the forest. Instead, Beau's cabin was a two-story, A-framed log cottage, surrounded by evergreens and other large trees that seemed to go on and on.

"Yup, they'll kill ya," Beau said dryly.

Seated beside him in the truck, Nora glanced sidelong, instantly captivated by Beau's face. And oh, what a handsome face he had—shaggy brown hair peeked out beneath his black cowboy hat that led to piercing blue eyes and a sharp jawline that could cut stone, but his sculpted lips were what made her heart skip a beat. Perfectly plump, with a grin always seeming etched there, curving the sides slightly, the arrogance in those lips declared he knew what to do with them on a woman's body. And wasn't that exactly why she'd driven there tonight—to meet him face-to-face, and to see if that spark of interest on the FaceTime call was as real as she'd hoped. "What will kill me?" she asked.

Beau gestured to the evergreens dancing in the wind. "Those trees you can't stop staring at." He cut the engine and grabbed the door handle. "The cabin is reinforced to withstand falling trees. The truck isn't."

"Say no more," Nora quipped. She snatched up her bag and was out of the truck a second later, overwhelmed by the earthy scents of pine and sweet cedar. She ran for the door, the spongy crunch of layers of dead pine needles beneath her running shoes, and was soaked by the time she got there.

Beau made it to the front door first and threw it open, charging into the cabin. She followed him quickly inside, immediately awestruck by the simplicity of the space and the warmth carried throughout. Wooden beams stretched the length of the ceiling. A galley kitchen with light oak cabinets and a brown marble countertop took up half of the space, while a small living room took up the rest.

"Come on, let's get into something dry," he said, shutting the door behind them.

As he unlaced his boots, she kicked off her runners. He grabbed her bag and they headed up the staircase on the left side of the cabin. The moment they hit the top floor, she stopped dead. To the right, a single bedroom. To the left, a small bathroom. "So, there really is only one bedroom?" she asked.

A nod. He winked. "Ready to snuggle?"

Yes. Only she wasn't really thinking about only snuggling. She wanted to snuggle a little more intimately. All night long.

Nora had had this cowboy on her mind for days. She'd felt attraction to a few guys, all the crappy ex-boyfriends in her past who made her currently hate love, especially her most recent breakup with Scott. The real estate agent she'd given her whole heart too. The one she moved in with. The one she thought she'd love forever. The one who had also up and moved out of *their* condo six months ago, cut off communication completely and moved on with another woman a month later. Or so she'd heard through a mutual friend.

Scott had sent her into therapy for the last six months to understand why and how she could love a man who'd vanished from her life as fast as he'd come into it, leaving her picking up the pieces of her shattered life. But with Beau, she felt something different than she'd felt with anyone before—something purely *physical.* "You have to have something else?" she asked, out of curiosity to see if he was wanting the same thing she did. "Where does your son sleep?"

Leaning a shoulder against the wall, Beau explained, "Austin only came here once as a baby. Now

I only come here to hunt. He's not old enough for that yet."

She glanced over the railing down to the lower level, and her stomach filled with butterflies. No couch in sight, only two brown leather chairs hugging the stone fireplace. "I see our predicament," she said dryly, in an attempt to seem slightly annoyed.

Beau watched her with heady amusement before he said, voice not showing a hint of his enjoyment, "It's either the truck or my bed, and in a tropical storm, you're *safer* in my bed."

A rush of heat slid through her at just how sexy *safer* sounded coming from that gorgeous mouth. Yet she saw the gleam in his gaze—he was trying to rattle her a little.

Lifting her chin, she grinned in challenge. Beau didn't know it yet, but she had plans herself. Ever since she'd first met him over FaceTime, he'd been on her mind every time she slipped a hand between her thighs seeking pleasure. She'd learned from Adeline that Beau often had casual sexual relationships because of his responsibility to Austin, and Nora was looking to get a taste of him. Pronto!

Two weeks she was in Devil's Bluffs. She planned to use those days having hot sex with an even hotter cowboy. Her therapist had told her to do things that brought joy back to her life, and a sexy country boy seemed like a good thing to do. She couldn't walk the same path she'd walked before. Being adventurous with Beau, as long as he was game for it, was her first step forward into her new life and the new *her*. "The bed sounds great, thank you."

"Great." He headed for the bedroom and began placing her bag near the foot bed.

She stepped just inside the room and all her bravery promptly fell. She'd never done anything this bold before. The only men she'd ever slept with in the same bed were boyfriends, but those boyfriends also either cheated, dumped her for no reason, or moved away with little thought of her.

You got this. You've got game too.

One look at the bed made of thick wooden logs—a sturdy bed, a bed made for some rough and tumble—and she hesitated, wondering if she was in over her head. What kind of lover was Beau that he needed such a strong bed? "I've got that," she blurted out, not yet ready to lay down her intentions just yet, rushing forward to take her bag from him. "Is it okay if I use the bathroom?"

"Sure, it's just there." He gestured outside the room.

Faster than she ever moved in her life, she made it into the small bathroom. In the corner of the room, she found an all-glass shower. The rest of the space belonged to the pedestal sink and the toilet. She shut the door behind her, dropping her back against the hardwood and quickly reaching for her cell phone from her bag.

One look at the screen and she sighed. "No freaking service." The storm must have knocked out the lines. She lifted her phone and said to it, like Adeline could hear her, "Adeline, I need you." To kick her in the ass and say: *Get it, girl!* Or talk her out of this totally insane idea.

Beau was a type—the guy every girl knew to stay away from. The man full of charming smiles and ego and just...*trouble.* The guy who had already found the love of his life and lost her. The one with a young son. But all those reasons were why he was perfect. For as long as she could remember, she wanted love, the good guy, the man who was looking for forever.

Until love lied.

Coming from divorced parents, who hated each other, she wanted to prove to them how to love your partner right. But in the end, she discovered they were right. Love was impossible. Love was cruel.

With that realization, she had decided to go for the direct opposite—bring on the hot sex, the sizzling chemistry with a bad boy cowboy, and then, with her body running on a high and her confidence in her body and self back, she'd hopefully hop on a plane for Paris to start a new life.

The life she deserved.

As she began peeling off her soaked clothing, she didn't know what it was about Beau exactly that made her so physically aware of him. Probably didn't help that he exuded sex and had an energy that said: *I will kiss the hell out of you and you'll melt in my hands.*

Determined to get her plan into motion, she hurried and changed into a pair of capri jogging pants and a T-shirt and combed out the rat's nest of her hair. By the time she was presentable again, she felt ready to get things moving along into a more heated direction, but with the wedding fast approaching, she had to get some of the wedding planning out of the way first.

Though when she found him in the kitchen, looking fine as hell in black sport shorts and a T-shirt with the Devil's Bluffs Ranch logo on the back, she began to rethink her idea of dealing with wedding plans.

"All dry?" he asked.

She smiled. "I am, thanks."

"Great." He opened the fridge. "I hope you're a beer drinker because that's all I got."

"Definitely a beer drinker, and I'd love one." She slid onto the stool at the breakfast bar.

He took two bottles from the fridge and cracked them open. As he set hers in front of her, he asked, "All right, fill me in. What about the wedding planning is so important that you had to drive out to find me?"

"Um, everything." She blinked in surprise. "Have you never been in a wedding party before?"

"Besides my own, no." She cringed realizing her error, promptly putting her foot into her mouth. He took in her—likely horrified—expression and chuckled. "Don't feel bad," he said gently. "It's been a very long time since Annie passed away. I honor her, the entire family honors her, by talking about her."

Relief washed through her. "Okay, then, I'll let myself off the hook."

"Good." He raised his bottle to those kissable lips again and took a long sip, never taking his eyes off her.

Holy hell! She'd grown used to men in New York City. Fancy men, with expensive suits and clean-shaven faces. But this cowboy was a *man*. He had calloused fingers, scruff on his face indicating he spent more time living than caring what he looked like. And he smelled like nature, mixed with the spicy hints of his cologne.

The pull to him was strong, unexplainable and *hot*.

Reminding herself it was totally inappropriate to jump him, and she needed to know they were on the same page, she slid off the stool and then headed for her purse on the ground by the door. She fetched her wedding planner before joining him again.

Beau frowned at the planner. "What's that?"

"Everything we need to do before your brother marries my best friend." Turning away, Beau sighed and headed for the fridge. "What are you doing?"

"Getting us some food, since this is going to be a long-ass night," he said.

She grinned. *You have no idea just how long.* "Hope you're up for it."

Looking back over his shoulder, he winked. "I'm always up for it."

* * *

Seated on the leather chair hugging the fireplace an hour later, Nora lifted her phone in the air, desperate for a single bar indicating reception, as Beau watched from the kitchen. Rain continued to pour from the dark skies, not a break in sight. Country rock played through a docking station on the countertop, and scented jar candles were lit spread out around the cabin to provide light after the power went out. He had listened to her list of all the things she was taking care of for the wedding. He suspected others may view Nora as a little strung tight, but the warmth in her eyes told Beau she was planning the dream wedding for her best friend. He liked the way Nora loved someone, with her whole heart.

When she lowered her phone, she cursed.

"Reception still out?" he asked, swiping her empty beer bottle off the small table between the two leather chairs and replacing her drink with a fresh one. Her floral perfume spiraled in the air around him, and he inhaled her scent deeply, wanting to bring it in deep.

"Reception is dead at this point," she said gruffly, sliding her phone back onto the table. "When does service usually come back after a storm like this?"

"No way to tell," he said, returning to his seat next to her. Heavy rain pelted against the windows. The storm hammering northern Texas was relentless, never letting up, and he was only too glad he'd learned Nora was out in the storm before reception had gone out. "Hours, days, weeks."

"Weeks?" Full of suspicion, she examined him closely, obviously trying to read his expression. "You're kidding, right?"

He shook his head, bringing his beer bottle to his lips. "Not kidding." He took a long drink, holding Nora's gaze, spotting the worry there. She had plans to make and things needed to get rolling. For Austin's sake, Beau hoped the cell service was back up and running by morning. Whenever Beau was away for a long period of time, he always talked to his son in the morning and before bed. That call wouldn't happen tonight. The last thing he wanted was Austin to worry. Especially when he knew his kid worried more than most because Beau was the only parent Austin had.

He never forgot that he had to be both parents to Austin. Most times he felt like he got it wrong, but sometimes, he knew he got it right by the way Austin smiled and how much he thrived.

Nora took a swig of her beer. She set the bottle down and began flipping through her planner again. "All right, have you taken Colter to pick out suits yet?"

News to him. "It's my job to pick out the suits?"

"No, it's your job to *help* your brother to pick out the suits. Give him guidance."

Beau couldn't help it; a snort escaped him. "I don't

think my big brother needs—or wants—my help on this."

"He might not know he needs your help, but he does," she countered immediately, chin lifting. "Trust me, the wedding and all the little details can get overwhelming. There are so many choices for him to pick from. His head is going to be spinning. Even if you're there as a sounding board, you're doing him a solid."

Beau had no doubt that Colter would simply ask the tailor, "What suit would you recommend?" And that's the one they'd go with, but he didn't want to make it seem like his brother wasn't putting in effort. Keeping that thought to himself, he said, "All right. I can help with the suits."

She flipped another page. "I'll get you the color scheme so you can let the tailor know for your ties, etcetera."

"Great," he said.

She hesitated to lick her finger before flipping another page, drawing his whole attention to her tongue...her lips... Damn, he fought back a groan. "What else do I *need* to do?" he asked, refocusing his mind on something other than her spectacular mouth and all the things he'd like to do with it.

Keeping her attention on her planner, she said, "Organize the bachelor party, help me with the rehearsal dinner, keep everyone on schedule for the day of the wedding and whatever you do, don't lose the rings."

He laughed. "I can handle all that."

"Excellent," she said, her gaze meeting his, her warm smile snagging him. "I'll be here if you need any help at all too. Especially with your speech."

"Yeah, I'll probably need help with that," he agreed. Public speaking wasn't really his favorite thing to do. More importantly, he wanted to make sure he didn't say the wrong thing or his message wasn't clear.

The warmth in her smile quadrupled. "Putting words together can be so hard, but you're in luck, because I'm really good at it."

He bet she was good at a lot of things. "I appreciate the help." Even he heard his voice lower slightly with the heat rolling through him.

Something she obviously caught on to as her attention flicked back to her planner, and she nibbled her lip. "Well, I was really hoping tonight we could pick out a place for the rehearsal dinner and figure out all that, but…"

"No internet?"

A nod. "No internet."

Her gaze held his again, and he swore her expression was screaming at him: *Any ideas how to fill the time?* He'd been with women since his late wife, but no connection had ever felt this rich and intense, and he barely even knew this woman. He lifted an eyebrow at her. "Anything else on my to-do-list?"

She cleared her throat like she was clearing away

her dirty thoughts. "You'll need to decorate the get-away car."

Unable to take his focus off the pinkish hue of her cheeks, he asked, "What's the getaway car?"

"Just decorate their car with streamers, cans, that kind of thing."

He paused to consider, forcing his mind back onto the wedding, finally shaking his head. "Knowing my brother, I suspect he'll be leaving the ceremony in his helicopter, but I can ask him."

"Oh," she said in surprise. "Okay, well, streamers and decorations might be a problem then." She nibbled on the end of her pen, drawing all his attention back to her pouty lips. Her brows were drawn tight together in thought.

Damn, she was cute too.

Just as that thought consumed him a sudden *bang* had Nora leaping to feet, and Beau followed her at the deafening *crash* that followed. He glanced up at the ceiling and held his breath.

When the cabin held steady, he blew out a slow breath. "It was only a matter of time before one of the falling trees hit the cabin."

Nora gasped, placing a hand against her thundering heart. "That was a tree hitting the cabin?"

He nodded, returning to his seat again. He took a long swig from his crisp beer, calming his racing heart. "Like I said, the cabin is reinforced for this type of damage. We're safe here."

Her doubtful expression told him she didn't believe him. She took her seat anyway, glancing up at the ceiling like any second it was about to crash in around her.

To take her mind off the storm, he offered, "You've put a lot of work into the wedding. Adeline is lucky to have such a good friend."

Her stare met his, and she shrugged one shoulder nonchalantly. "I don't have any siblings, and Adeline and me, we're just…the same, if that makes any sense. Soul sisters through and through."

It hadn't occurred to him until now how hard Adeline's absence from New York City had to have been for Nora. "You must miss her since she moved back here."

"There are not words to explain how much I miss her." She looked to her planner.

Something unreadable flashed across her face. Beau didn't know her well enough, but he'd almost say it looked like guilt.

When her head lifted again, whatever emotion she felt was erased from her face. "It's why I need this wedding to be a smashing success. It's gotta be just right."

"For Adeline?" he asked.

"Mmm-hmm."

Sweet and all, but something in all this didn't add up. "I might be wrong here, Nora, but I didn't take Adeline to be a woman who cared if things went perfect. She seems more the type of person to only care about having her loved ones there."

"Oh, don't get me wrong, she is that type of person, but…" Nora closed her planner with a *thud*. "But like I said, I'm considering moving to Paris."

"Is this a temporary thing?" he asked, even if he knew it was none of his business.

That same heavy emotion flared in her eyes. "I hope to come back and visit her once in a while, but probably not much as I'd like."

"Gotcha." Suddenly it all added up. "You want the wedding to be perfect for Adeline because you're moving away and feel guilty that it might upset her?"

"Not only for that reason, but it's certainly part of it. I need her to have her happiest moment. It's got to be flawless. Special."

"Before you drop the bomb that you're moving so far away?"

She cringed. "Yeah, it'll be—" she nearly choked as she said "—*hard* for the both of us, but I needed to make a change and I've always wanted to live in Paris." Before he could respond to ask more, she jumped up. "That's enough of that talk. I gotta pee before I burst."

Beau chuckled to himself as she headed up the staircase for the bathroom. He couldn't remember ever meeting anyone who was such an open book. *I gotta pee before I burst.* Another chuckle escaped him. Beyond her beautiful features and hot-as-hell body, he got the feeling Nora was a woman who was just herself, not ashamed to voice her thoughts, not hiding behind a fake persona to impress others, and that came as a breath of fresh air. Lately, the women he'd met had been straight up liars—one about her age, the other about her job—which had happened before in his past, coming from a wealthy and prominent family in Devil's Bluffs. The other women he'd met were insincere, loving everything he did and said, until he felt like he was dating himself. And the worst of all, was the last woman he'd been seeing for a month, who began playing games. One day interested. The next day not. Beau wanted a good, strong woman, not a headache.

From that first FaceTime until the face-to-face meeting, Nora was just Nora. Funny, clever, an open book, and he happened to like her.

Probably more than he should.

Three

Standing in front of the mirror in the bathroom, Nora cursed the lack of reception. *Again*. She was about to do something wild, possibly stupid, and totally out of her comfort zone. Adeline would talk some sense into her, but her friend wasn't there. Nora was done with being the boring woman who did everything *right*. Truth was, she was sick of being the good girl. The one with high morals and a big, sappy, romantic heart. The one not running the show of her own life. The one spending her money on therapy instead of living life. When she set foot on the plane to Paris, she needed to start a new life that began on the right track. A different track than the one she'd been living. A life full of possibilities.

The passion simmering with Beau was the first step forward. While she'd never experienced such a physical attraction to anyone like this before, she had wanted to go up and talk to men or ask them out, but she'd always been too shy.

That timid part of her would die tonight.

With her mind focused on all the things she wanted, and everything she didn't, she whisked the bathroom door open. The wind howled outside, branches scratching at the windows as rain hammered the panes, while she made her way back down the stairs.

Seated in one of the two leather chairs, Beau was finishing off a sip of a beer. When she met the landing, he asked, "What's on the agenda now?"

Before she lost her nerve, she headed for him. "I was thinking something like this." Ready to accept his rejection if he moved away to stop her, she grabbed his face and kissed him.

He stiffened in surprise for only a moment. Then a muffled groan rumbled from his chest and his lips softened beneath hers. His hand cupped her face, and while he tangled his fingers into her hair, he deepened the kiss.

Time didn't pause. Time stopped all together. His kiss unraveling her as the seconds ticked by. She'd wondered if he'd felt the same sizzling energy between them as she had, and now she had no doubt. He didn't only feel it. He'd wanted to act on it too, making her moan eagerly against his hot kiss, which soared heat low in her belly.

The kiss lasted a long, *long* time. When she finally broke away, she was breathing deep, and so was he.

She opened her eyes to meet his heated stare. He arched that sexy eyebrow at her. "Was this something you decided to do while going to the bathroom?"

Bursting out laughing, she straightened. "No, I decided this before I got on a plane to come to Devil's Bluffs."

She went to take a step back, but his hand came to her waist, keeping her standing between his legs. "With me specifically?"

She nodded, hating the blush rising to her cheeks. Strong, confident women didn't blush up to their eyeballs.

"I see." He set his beer bottle down on table next to him but didn't make a move to get up. Keeping one hand on her waist, he regarded her. Intently. "Is that the real reason you drove up to the cabin tonight?" he eventually asked.

She nibbled her lip but then stopped herself for hesitating. Why bother lying? "When I discovered you were at the cabin alone, I figured I'd shoot my shot."

Both brows rose, surprise glinted in his eyes. "You figured you'd shoot your shot?"

Refusing to blush any deeper, she lifted her chin. She couldn't go back out now. This was the *new* her—the woman who didn't play it safe but went after what she wanted. Right now, that was this hot as hell cowboy. "We did need to talk about the wedding plans, and I do plan on helping you get the reporters off your back, but I thought it was the perfect opportunity to see if the chemistry was as hot in real in life as it was on the FaceTime call."

His mouth twitched. "Ah, so I wasn't the only one who noticed the chemistry between us."

Relief settled in deep that she wasn't misreading things. He'd definitely welcomed a kiss. "It was a bit hard not to notice the connection." Hell, she'd never been so attracted to anyone in her life on such a physical level. She wanted *him*, no ifs, ands or buts about it.

And it made absolutely no sense.

But neither did Scott walking out on her like she didn't matter to him at all.

Leaning forward, Beau tucked his finger into her jean shorts and tugged her closer. His voice lowered. "What exactly are you proposing here?"

She shivered against the heat simmering between them. "Well, the way I see it, I have something you need—to get the reporters out of town. And you have something I need."

His voice lowered seductively. "What do you need, Nora?"

She leaned closer. "The pleasure those eyes promised me the second I got into the truck with you."

A long moment passed. Then a deep, sexy chuckle

crossed his lips as he sat back against his chair, intensity darkening his features. She sure had his full attention now, and damn did she *love* it. "What happens after I give you the pleasure you're looking for?"

"I go home to move out of my condo, find myself another job to somehow save enough to go to Paris."

Cocking his head, he examined her, carefully, his eyes searching hers for a long moment. "So, you want a fling?"

She gave a firm nod. "I want to forget all the heartbreak from a recent breakup. I want to be with a man where it doesn't end in disaster. I want to feel good. Nothing more. Nothing less."

His stare roamed down to her lips. "Why?"

Giving the question the time and attention it deserved, she drew in a long breath, exhaling slowly before answering. "Because I've always been a woman who needed a relationship. The romantic at heart who wanted forever. I want to feel a man's touch where it doesn't end with me brokenhearted. I want to feel powerful."

That same single brow arched again, which always seemed a mix of curiosity and arrogance. "Who says I won't break your heart?"

"Because you're not looking for love," she answered immediately. "You've already found the love of your life and your focus is on your son." She hesitated, desperate to get this all right. "Besides, I know for a fact you want what I'm offering."

No surprise hit his expression, or annoyance that

she knew personal information about him. "Did Adeline tell you that?"

"In a roundabout way," Nora explained with a shrug. "She told me that you haven't been in a serious relationship since Annie. After that, I put two and two together." Wondering if she possibly misread things, she added, "If a relationship is what you're looking for, then obviously, this can't happen."

His mouth curved slightly at one corner. "I can handle just sex, Nora."

"Well, good," she said, exhaling the breath she'd been holding. Afraid to ask, but pushing her reservations aside, she pressed on. "So, that's a yes, then?"

Another long pause that seemed to go on and on followed as branches scraped on the window outside as he watched her oh-so-carefully. "I can't do complicated," he finally answered her. "Like you said, I've got Austin. I can't get wrapped up in anything that could hurt him. He's my *only* priority in my life. So, yeah, I'm on board with having some fun, but if this gets complicated, it ends."

"I totally understand and agree," she said with a nod, butterflies fluttering in her belly. "Keeping this uncomplicated is the only way to go."

The seriousness in his expression began to fade with his slow-building smile. "Before I commit to this agreement you're offering, come here and kiss me again."

She shivered against the desire seeping into the air. "Why?"

His voice dropped an octave. "Because I have to see if this connection is really as good as we think it is."

Her legs felt wobbly as she leaned down to him again. One hand stayed on her waist, the other traveled to her cheek, his fingers tangling in her hair. Just as his fingers closed, tugging her into him, his mouth sealed against hers. And she ceased to exist.

It occurred to her then that Beau had been holding back that first kiss, because this kiss stirred her nerve endings, awakening every inch of her body.

Beau didn't simply kiss, he devoured.

Every swipe of his tongue brought more heat and yearning desire until Nora was pressing her thighs together for the friction. She wanted his skilled mouth all over her, bringing pleasure to places currently burning for him.

When he broke the kiss a few minutes later, he nipped her bottom lip. "Yeah, darlin', this will work just fine for me."

He finally rose. She stayed put, which meant he slid his gorgeous, *hard* body against hers. She felt every bit of the man he was as he tugged her hand to follow him to the staircase.

Before he ascended the stairs, he glanced over his shoulder. "Coming?"

Only then did she realize she wasn't moving with him. "Is that a promise?" she rasped.

His gaze positively brimmed with intention. "I dare you to find out."

Four

Beau entered the bedroom, lighting a few more candles, creating a soft glow in the room. The scent of apple cinnamon tickled his nose as he grinned to himself, the rain continuing to batter the windows. Nora didn't need to talk Beau into the idea of a friends-with-benefits understanding while she was in town. He was 100 percent thinking the same thing since he picked her up off the side of the road. Though she wasn't correct about him not wanting to find love again. He did want forever with a woman, and he knew Annie would want that for him. She wouldn't want him spending his nights alone and to never again experience how it felt for a woman to smile at him with love in her eyes. But he needed an uncomplicated situation. The last thing he wanted was Austin to grow attached to a woman and for that woman to leave him.

He couldn't risk that. Not after Austin had already lost so much.

But this thing with Nora was anything but complicated. She was in town for the wedding, and then she was potentially moving to the other side of the world. Truth was, he wanted her—badly. He had from the moment he met her during the FaceTime call. She was a stunner, but more importantly, the spark in her eyes captured him in a way no woman had captured him in a long time.

He couldn't explain it, certainly not to himself, but he wanted to feel that fire burning all around him, if only for a couple weeks. He wanted to taste an honest woman, something he'd been longing for. He wanted to remember how passion used to drive him crazy with need. He wanted to enjoy making Nora blush again and again, and then kiss her until they both couldn't breathe, all to let himself enjoy.

Heading for the bed, he yanked his T-shirt over his head, tossing it on the wooden chair in the corner his father had built. When he turned back around, Nora stood in the doorway, looking shell-shocked. A chuckle escaped him. Damn, he loved the way her gaze hungrily roamed over his chest down to his abdomen. A few times over. "Like what you see?" he asked.

"Yes," she breathed. "You're gorgeous."

Every raspy word passing through her lips twitched

his cock. While he had to hold back from pouncing on her, he waited by the bed, letting her take control for now.

"So, what's exactly the plan here?" she asked, blinking at him.

He arched an eyebrow at her. "To rock your fucking world."

Her eyes widen slightly before she visibly swallowed. "I... I don't know how to do this."

Before he was married, he had never had a friends-with-benefits relationship. But he'd become familiar with a physical relationship in the years that followed. Only recently had he begun to want something more past the physical release. "I've seen the way you look at me, Nora," he murmured, closing the distance. "I have no doubt you know exactly what you're doing." He slid his hand across her cheek, and she lifted her chin as he dropped his, sealing his mouth across hers.

The kiss started out soft and sweet. Though her moan changed that entirely. She offered him everything with her mouth. Need tightened his groin as he tangled his fingers in her hair, tilting her head to deepen the kiss.

Nora tasted of sweet, *sweet* desire, and something much more addictive he couldn't quite place a finger on.

Backing away from her mouth, he trailed kisses along her jawline to her neck, where she shivered as he took a handful of ass into his hand. Groaning, he grabbed her bottom with both hands, bringing her closer, shifting her against his hardening cock. "Damn, Nora, you feel so good."

"Beau," she rasped, rubbing her breasts against him.

He'd tasted women. He touched them. None felt like *this*. She melted in his touch.

He met her heated gaze and grunted against the need glistening on her face. It'd been a long time since a woman looked at him like *that*. So aroused, she looked to him with unspoken hunger.

Urgent to feel all of her, he reached for the hem of her shirt and dropped it to the floor a moment later, leaving her in a pretty lace, light pink bra. He spotted her rosy taut nipples through the fabric, calling out to his mouth. He bent and licked one over the top of the fabric, releasing her moan. He pulled the bra beneath her breasts, which were a perfect handful, and licked a nipple with the flat of his tongue. Her gasp and the shiver that followed was the hottest thing he'd ever seen. Intending to see her do that again, he swirled his tongue around the other nipple before taking the bud into his mouth and sucking deep.

She threaded her fingers into his hair, holding him there, so he sucked deeper.

Her heady moan had him reaching around and unhooking her bra. He licked her other nipple, swirling the bud, as he unbuttoned her jean shorts, pulling those down along with her panties.

When she stepped out of them, he placed a final soft kiss on her breast and backed away, taking his wallet from his pocket. He retrieved a condom, his hands suddenly freezing as she reached for the button of his jeans and undid his pants, then slowly lowered the zipper. He dropped the wallet, leaving the condom wrapper in his hand as she pushed his jeans and boxer briefs over his hips, freeing his cock.

She reached for him and stroked him twice before looking into his face. "Every bit of you is impressive, huh?"

He didn't have words. He couldn't speak as she stroked him, nibbling on her bottom lip like she was starving for him.

When she twirled her hand around him, he thrust his hips forward and groaned. "Oh, you like that?" she asked playfully.

"Fuck, Nora. Jesus," he growled.

She twirled her hand again. And again. Until he thought he might blow from her doing just that.

Desperate for her now, she squealed as he gathered her into his arms. He laid her out on the mattress, covering her body with his, and he had every intention of trailing kisses down her body and tasting her sweetness between her thighs. Until he looked into her face again, trapped into the darkness of her dilated pupils, the sexy part of her lips. He slid his hand down her lush body, moving closer and closer to her sex. The moment his fingers stroked over drenched heated flesh, he only needed one thing— her legs wrapped around him while they both broke apart.

Removing his fingers, he hurriedly sheathed himself in the condom. Then he primed himself at her entrance. "Next time I'll go slower." He kissed the top of her breast, her neck, just below her ear. "I can't wait."

"Don't wait." She grasped his buttocks, lifted her bottom and welcomed him inside her.

Believing the words that escape her mouth in a breathy moan, he groaned, as his eyes shut at the pleasure rocking through him. He shifted his weight onto one arm, lifting his head. Staring into her sweet eyes, he rocked his hips, slowly entering her, and withdrawing just as slowly. He gripped her hip, thrusting up into her as she stroked his biceps like she couldn't get enough of his body.

Fuck, he loved that. "Keep touching me," he growled. "Don't stop."

She didn't, and he thrust once hard in response. Her gasp and widening eyes, told him all he needed to know about her.

With a grin, he slid one of her legs onto his shoulders and then the other. Kneeling, he grabbed hold of her hips and gave them what they both wanted.

As he thrust hard and fast, her eyes widened with the pleasure. Her moans shivered *more* against him, so more he gave her. Building in speed with each thrust until they found a rhythm, moving together, moaning together, losing themselves in a connection taking them higher and higher.

And as Nora's chin tipped back, her back arching off the mattress with the rise of her climax, Beau growled with the heat building in his groin.

Harder.

Faster.

He didn't quit, gritting his teeth as her inner walls began convulsing, her gorgeous body trembling beneath him.

Until the tension broke and her screams of satisfaction shattered his control. With a roar, he bucked and jerked against her, claiming his release.

Many minutes later, her soft laughter drew him to her. He realized he was crushing her. Slowly, he rolled off to the side, trying to catch his breath. "I hope that's good laughter," he commented.

Chest heavily rising and falling with her heavy breaths, she turned her head against the pillow. "For as long as I can remember, I thought love made sex better, but now I know I was dead wrong." She drew in a long deep breath and blew it out slowly, her hooded eyes dancing with satisfaction. "Because if this is what casual sex is, I'm here for it."

He burst out laughing, pulling her into his arms. "You and me both."

Though as she snuggled into him, a sense of wanting to keep her close washed across him, and he knew one thing for certain—he'd had casual sex before.

This, with Nora, didn't feel like that.

Nora had regrets in her life. So many regrets.

Beau wasn't one.

She hadn't expected the cuddling after they'd been intimate, but Beau felt good and warm and strong. He also kept tugging her back whenever she tried to move, so she eventually settled into the comfort of his arms. The rain didn't seem like it was ever going to let up, or the wind.

The bedroom was cute, with a double, wood bed in the middle of the room, a wooden chair in the corner that she suspected was probably used as a place to toss clothes and a small closet was on the far side of the room. The space was tiny, with only one window across from her, but there was something perfect about the space's quaintness, as was being in Beau's strong arms, which seemed to hold her just right. "This is nice," she said, putting a voice to her thoughts.

"It is *very* nice," he agreed, his voice sleepy, as his fingers trailed over her hip.

She laughed softly at his suggestive tone. "I don't mean just *this*. I mean, not having to worry about you."

Eyes remaining shut, he chuckled. "I'm not sure if that's a good thing."

She lifted up, resting on his chest. "I just mean that every time after I've been with an ex, something always goes wrong and I start thinking."

He peaked open one eye. "If you can think that much after sex, something is very wrong and you're not having very good sex."

She paused at that. Finally, she shook her head. "I actually never thought about it like that, but you're right." Compared to what she experienced with Beau, sex with her ex-boyfriends seemed bland in comparison. The heat with Beau, the sparks that she felt off his mouth and touch were nothing she'd ever experienced before in her life. "It's nice, you know, not feeling anything right now but pure satisfaction."

He gave her bottom a hard squeeze. "That's a damn good thing, darlin'."

She laughed softly but wiggled her butt into his hand. "It sure is."

Smiling, Beau shut his eyes again, a long, quiet moment passing between them, and she relished those moments. Minutes that she wasn't thinking about her flaws, about what she could have done better, and what he was thinking about her.

The comfortable silence continued until he asked a few minutes later, "I am curious though—what exactly did you have to worry about with your ex-boyfriends?"

She nearly cringed, hating to admit her faults. Though she figured with no emotions on the line she had nothing to lose by being honest. "Oh, if I was good enough, if I kept them happy, if they liked what they saw, if they liked what I did to them, you know all that kind of stuff."

His eyes snapped open halfway during her admission. Shifting onto his side, leaning up on one arm, he gave a bewildered expression. "*You* doubted if you were enough for them?"

Now she outright cringed. "Doesn't every girl wonder that?" She hoped so. Or she was going to look insecure, and that's not a look she was going for.

Beau held her stare and said dead seriously, "If any woman thinks that, then the man in their life is failing them." He paused like he wanted that to sink into her head before he added, "Besides, it's not your job to make sure someone is happy. That's all on them."

Of course, he thought that. "You think that because you had a happy, healthy relationship. Not everyone has that. It's not always as easy as you make it seem."

"No, you're right, everyone doesn't have that," he said, his voice softening. "But the men in your past sound like idiots if you ever had to wonder if you were enough for them." His gaze raked over her mouth, down to her bare breasts. When he met her eyes again, his expression had heated all over again. "One look at you, and I was nearly knocked to my knees."

Her heart surged with his sweet words. She quickly told her heart to stuff it. Words were easier to say when there were no strings attached to them. "Thanks, I appreciate that."

He gave her a small smile and slowly tucked her hair behind her ear, his gaze following the movement. "All right, now I'm even more curious, why this arrangement with me?"

"Why not this arrangement?" she countered with a laugh.

A roll of thunder cracked across the sky as his eyes sparkled at her. "I'm not saying I'm not thrilled about it, but there must be a reason, more than you just wanting to have some fun."

She considered not telling him. Sharing things

must cross some emotional line that they weren't supposed to cross, but she refused to change who she was. She'd always promised herself to stay honest. "It's not all that interesting really," she admitted. "I'm just done doing things the way I've always done them. You know, be the good girl, date seriously. I've done that. It's failed miserably. I need a redo, and with my move to Paris, I decided this was my time to start over."

"Ah," he said, like suddenly everything made sense to him. "This is a confidence boost."

"You could call it that." She slid her hand under her cheek against the soft pillow. "It's about me not thinking about all the consequences and just doing something because I wanted to."

He grinned. "Doing *someone* you mean?"

She burst out laughing. "Exactly, and that someone being a hot as hell cowboy."

His warm chuckle brushed across her as he laid back down and took her into his arms again, as if he'd done it a thousand times before now. "I like the sound of that. It sure beats riding the storm out reading."

"Just a little bit better than reading."

He tsked, pinching her hip.

She chuckled against his chest. "Okay, okay, a lot better."

"Sounds about right," he said, mouth twitching. Another long, comfortable moment passed as his fingers continued their dance along her hip, tickling across her flesh. "About these reporters," he eventually said. "Do you truly have enough to get them out of town for good?"

"Yeah, I do," she said. "That whole thing has been a big headache for you, huh?"

"For me it's been annoying," he explained. "For Austin, it's been confusing."

"I bet," she said, having heard from Adeline that when Beau turned them down for an interview, the reporters began visiting downtown Devil's Bluffs, asking around, finding locals who would give up details on Beau's personal life. She'd also heard they didn't want to know about his present life, being a horse trainer and owning a multimillion-dollar ranch with his family. They wanted to know about his past. His loss of Annie. His heartbreak. How he reacted after she died, and how their son managed through the aftermath. Painful things that no one would want to share. "Reporters can be persistent when they want their story."

Beau chuckled. "Persistent enough to fake an engagement."

Exactly what had happened to Colter and Adeline after the gossip blog had first published the photograph of Colter and Beau saving the calf from the rapids.

Beau was a good brother for taking all the heat from the story, and Nora really liked that about him. Hell, a good person. Those seemed few and far between lately.

She watched him a moment, stumped on one

thing. "Can I ask why you'd willingly put yourself out in the media like that?"

He huffed and glanced up at the ceiling. "Because Adeline needed a story, and I knew my brother needed her."

"So, you'd just throw yourself out there? Do you not understand how horrible gossip magazines truly are?"

A slow nod. "Family matters above all else."

Her heart did that weird somersault thing again. She wished her family had been close like that. Though she did understand being selfless—she would have done the same thing for Adeline in a heartbeat.

"But the truth is," he continued, "Colter had women chasing after him, and well, I figured the same type of thing would happen."

She laughed, liking his honesty. The trait was rare in the men she'd known. "Guess that didn't work out in your favor, huh?"

"Not exactly." He sighed, tucking an arm behind his head. "The last thing I thought was reporters would descend on the town like vultures and want to hear about my dead wife and all the hell I went through with her passing."

Her heart reached out to him. "People feed on stuff like that. It's really terrible."

Again, he sighed, heavier this time. "My family and I have done well, I think, with Austin. To help him remember Annie's memory in a way that fills him with joy instead of pain. He was only a baby when she passed." His gaze met hers then, and her heart squeezed even tighter at the heaviness on his face. "Having all this brought up again, after surviving it, it's not a place mentally I want to go back to."

Suddenly, something made a whole lot of sense. "That's what you came to the cabin, isn't it? It wasn't to draw the reporters away from you?"

His eyes tightened. "Of course, I hoped that with me being gone from town, they'd leave, but I didn't want Austin to see the way they rattle me. He's never been exposed to that...side of me. The day I left, I was called to the cemetery because someone was taking a picture of Annie's grave."

Knowing she was crossing a line she shouldn't, but not able to stop herself, she slid her hand in his. He tightened his fingers with hers, as she said, "I'm going to help you get rid of them, Beau. I promise you that."

"Thank you." He smiled, but the smile never reached his eyes. Like he realized the mood had shifted, his chuckle simmered across her as he gathered her underneath him. He locked his arms on either side of her. Penetrating gaze boring into hers, he murmured, "Better keep up my end of the bargain then."

Before she had a chance to reply, his mouth sealed across hers in a wicked kiss, and she realized this agreement between them wasn't only something she didn't regret but was the best decision she'd ever made.

Five

Three days later, Nora couldn't get a smile off her face. She and Beau were knocking off the wedding to-do list like champs, even booking the rehearsal dinner location at Devil's Bluffs golf course once the internet came back on yesterday in the early evening. More than getting stuff done, her body was lit up after being treated to Beau's particular brand of pleasure day and night. The man knew a woman's buttons, and she'd never experienced the current high she was riding with any boyfriend. If this was what casual sex was all about, she'd been missing out. Big time.

She thought nothing could touch her happiness.

She'd been dead wrong.

Before they got on the road to return to Devil's Bluffs, she checked her email for any job offers from Paris. Her inbox had been empty. She'd never regretted moving in with Scott more. The lease on their apartment had been a year long. She'd had to endure his share of the apartment and the bills, and she'd gone broke in the process. She had used the remainder of her savings for her flight to Devil's Bluffs and on her maid-of-honor dress. When she returned home after the wedding, she'd have three days to pack up her life and move out. She'd put all her attention into a job offer in Paris, all of which had offered travel and an apartment stipend as part of the employment.

She needed Paris to come through. The thought of going back to New York City alone, without a plan was near suffocating.

If that wasn't bad enough, her mood took a nosedive on the drive back to Devil's Bluffs the moment she spotted her rental car. Trees were uprooted, branches scattered everywhere along the road. They were large enough that Beau had to get out of his truck a few times to deal with them so they could get by, even having to get his chain saw from the cab of the truck and cut their way out on several occasions. She'd seen bad storms in New York City, but she'd never seen anything like this. Truth was, she'd already been anticipating the worst. Nothing, though, could have prepared her for what she saw when Beau slowed his truck next to her rental car.

"It's safe to say a flat tire is the least of your worries," Beau stated dryly.

"This is going to be hard to explain," Nora grumbled in agreement. The car was crushed beneath a huge tree trunk, looking like a hot dog surrounded by a metal bun, glass shattered along the road.

Beau glanced sidelong. His eyebrows raised in disbelief. "Just be thankful you weren't fixing the tire when that tree came down."

"Yeah, no kidding." Still, her gut twisted. "Will the rental car company give me a hard time about this?"

"Not if you got insurance." He hesitated, frowning. "Please tell me you got insurance."

"I got insurance."

"Good. That's damn good." He reached for his cell phone from the cup holder and then placed a call. "Hey, it's Beau Ward," he said a moment later. "There's a car out on road 45 that's been crushed by a tree. It's a rental, belonging to Adeline's friend, Nora Keller. Could you possibly come get it and bring it back to the rental company?" A long pause. "Great. Thanks, Eric." Beau ended the call, setting his cell back into the holder before driving off. "That was Adeline's father. He's got a tow truck and will come with a chain saw and get the car towed for you."

"Thank you so much," Nora said, reaching for her cell phone. She found the contact number for the rental company, and frustratingly for the next hour on the way back to town, she was stuck on the phone first with the rental company and then with the insurance to get the claim started.

By the time she ended the call, Beau had stopped at a coffee shop and grabbed them each a coffee; he knew by now, she liked hers with cream.

As he got back on the road, she opened the lid of her coffee. "When should we approach the reporters?" she asked.

Resting his hand on the steering wheel, the other holding his paper coffee cup, he replied, "Tomorrow."

She wasn't sure how a man could make driving look hot, but somehow Beau achieved just that. She licked her lips that had nothing to do with the coffee, and everything to do with pulling the truck over and putting those hands to a better use.

"I need to look at the damage to the ranch and my place before we start with the reporters," he said, drawing her attention back to appropriate matters. "We've got less than two weeks until the wedding. Fixing the damage at the ranch has to be our first priority."

Nora agreed with a nod. Before her sip of coffee, she said, "I can help with any of the repairs."

"You're good with a hammer?"

"Hammer. Drill. Paint brush. I'm good with it all." Probably the only good thing her father taught her. "My dad is a carpenter. I grew up learning things from him."

"That'll come in handy then." He gave her a quick

look, with an unreadable expression, before setting his focus back onto the road. "Are you close to your family?"

"As much as you can be with divorced parents who hate each other," she explained. "Everything with them feels like a competition, including their time with me."

The moment the words left her mouth she wanted to erase the word *parents*. She quickly added, "I was really sorry to hear about your father's passing recently."

"Thank you," he said somberly. "It's a difficult time for sure, but we honor Dad by carrying on and working the ranch."

"That's a wonderful way to honor him. Adeline told me your dad was an incredible man."

"There was no one better," Beau said. "My mom is pretty great too."

Nora just smiled, but her heart reached for him as she glanced out her window. Streaks of clouds filled the blue sky as they passed a tractor throwing up a plume of dust in its wake. She'd never lost anyone close to her. Beau had lost two people so dear to him.

She tried to come up with something to say to comfort him but failed miserably as the truck suddenly slowed and then he drove up a gravel driveway.

Atop a hill, next to a large lake, was a rustic, ranch-style limestone house with distressed wood accents. They didn't even make it up the driveway before Colter and Adeline were already outside, com-

ing down the front porch, and Nora's heart nearly
exploded. Adeline, with long waves of strawberry
blond hair curtaining her face, freckled nose and
gentle honey eyes, always looked stunning beautiful without even trying. Her long summer dress with
a flower pattern clung to her delicate curves. Next
to her, Colter had a harder edge with sharp lines to
his face but had what seemed to be a Ward trait of
brown hair beneath his cowboy hat and blue eyes.

After the truck rolled to a stop and Beau cut the
ignition, Nora hopped out and Beau followed.

"You're back!" Adeline exclaimed, wrapping Nora
in one of her fantastic hugs.

"I'm back." She returned the tight squeeze, inhaling Adeline's sugary body spray, relishing having her best friend back in her arms. "Which is good
because we've got so much to do for the wedding."

"You're not the only one," Beau said. He gestured
toward his truck. "Want to show me the damage
from the storm?"

"Sure." Colter gave Adeline a kiss that was short
but didn't look all that sweet. There was heat in the
way he took her chin and held her for those few seconds.

Heat that made Nora envious. Though when she
caught Beau's gaze and spotted his grin, she forced
her expression to neutral. *No emotion. Love sucks.
Be strong.*

Luckily for her, Beau didn't comment on her reaction. Instead, he asked, "I'll pick you up tomorrow morning at nine?"

She forced herself not to fidget under his knowing stare. "Sounds good."

Feeling all sets of eyes on her, she noticed Colter and Adeline were watching with equal confusion tightening their brows. "I've got dirt on the reporters to get them out of town," she explained, clearing the bewilderment from their eyes. "We're going to have a little chat with them tomorrow."

"Ah," Colter said, but still looked between her and Beau.

Not paying attention to the stares, Beau grabbed her bag from his truck then brought it into the house before trotting back down the steps. As he passed, he winked at her. "See you tomorrow, Nora."

Her belly turned to mush. No man had the right to sound that sexy saying her name. Keeping a poker face, she gave the politest smile she could muster. "See you then."

Colter looked between her and Beau. *Again.* He eventually smiled at Adeline, following his brother into his truck.

The moment they were on their way, Adeline scooped up Nora's hand, tugging her up the porch steps and into the house, slamming the door behind them. "Tell. Me. Everything," she gasped.

Nora blinked. "How do you know there is anything to tell?"

"Because the only time you and Beau talked you

both looked ready to battle it out. Neither of you looks like that now. And I've never seen Beau smile like *that* to anyone."

Nora considered how to explain but then ripped off the Band-Aid. "I might have slept with him."

Adeline's eyes went huge. She held up a finger to wait. "Hold on. I'm processing."

Nora laughed, not surprised. Nora never had casual sex, which made Adeline's next question expected.

"Are you moving here?" her best friend asked, hope glistening in her expression.

Nora squeezed Adeline's hands, guilt riding her hard as she led Adeline to the couch in the living room. "No, I'm not moving here. I...okay, listen, I just felt this sexual chemistry to Beau on that call." As she sat, with Adeline joining her, she added, "I've never felt that before, and to be honest, I'm done with love. To prove I was, I made a pass at him, and well, he accepted it."

Adeline blinked. "Who are you and what have you done with my best friend, Nora?"

Nora threw her head back and barked a loud laugh. "I know it's out of character."

"Out of character?" Adeline gasped, with raised brows. "You wouldn't even kiss someone until after a month of dating."

God, that was so her she could barf. "I didn't want to rush things before and I wanted to do everything right. Be friends first." Like every self-help book on love had ever told her to do. She'd followed all the rules to make sure she wouldn't end up like her parents. She'd done everything right. And that got her nowhere but hurt. Repeatedly. "But love and me just don't get along. Besides, you know Beau. You've said great things about him. And the best part of all, he's already been madly in love. I don't have to worry about an emotional entanglement."

Adeline cocked her head. "So, you guys are…"

"Having fun while I'm here," Nora said. "That's it. That's all."

Adeline's eyes narrowed thoughtfully until she broke out laughing, shaking her head. "Colter was so right. I thought you and Beau were going to be at each other's throats while you were here, but Colter said he thought Beau liked you."

"I don't think it's as much like as it is lust." Nora hesitated to shrug. "I mean, he doesn't even *know* me."

"I'd say he knows you pretty well now," Adeline said, snickering.

"He knows my body *very* well." Nora smiled.

Again, Adeline paused to watch Nora, searching her eyes. "All right, so this is a healing type of thing for you?"

Nora gave a firm nod. "Exactly. I'm in a rut. I feel stuck. Like I can't go forward. I can't keep doing the same thing. I needed something new."

"And that's Beau?"

"Precisely."

Adeline tucked her legs underneath her on the couch. "Okay, I get all that, but what if you catch feelings for him?"

Nora raised a finger. "One, that's an impossible thing since I'm not looking for that." She raised another finger. "Two, I don't live here, and you know I need more life in my city than what's in Devil's Bluffs." She raised one last finger. "Three, it's hard to catch feelings for someone who's heart belongs to another woman."

"But not impossible," Adeline offered.

"It is when I won't let it be anything but fun," Nora said, waving her off.

When Adeline looked like she planned to say something more, Nora added, "Seriously, don't worry. This is good for me. Everything is spectacular."

"Okay," Adeline said, finally relenting. Then with a quizzical expression, she asked, "Now that we're past that, you can tell me what else you're hiding from me."

Nora forced herself not to squirm. "Who said I'm hiding something else?"

"Your face has been telling me for a week now." Adeline took Nora's hands, squeezing tight, and asked softly, "Nora, what are you keeping from me?"

Guilt nearly swallowed Nora whole, but the stronger part of her heart knew she couldn't tell Adeline about Paris. Not yet. Not until the wedding was over. Adeline deserved this happy moment. Every single bit of it. And Nora would not put a damper on her happiness.

Solidified in her choice to keep this to herself for now, smiled. "Adeline, stop worrying about me. I am fine. This time is about you."

Obviously disbelieving her, Adeline nibbled her lip. "You sure nothing else is going on?"

"Seriously, Addie, stop." Nora jumped off the couch, yanking Adeline to her feet. "I'm riding a serious high from the best sex of my life. You're getting married. Things are so good I should have heart eye emojis as my eyes." To put this matter to bed, Nora threaded her arm through Adeline's. "How about we do something much more important."

"What's that?" Adeline asked, visibly relaxing.

Nora grinned. "Let me see you in your dress."

The sunbaked two-lane highway was a smooth drive through Ward land, as Beau took the roads easy toward his horse ranch. Austin was still at school, and Beau needed to check out the damage to his farm before picking his son up. The days ahead were going to be long and hard, but he didn't want Austin to see that stress on him. Besides, he appreciated the time to get his head straight about Nora. He wasn't expecting her. Not how much she made him laugh. Not how she made him hunger for her. Not how much he liked having her in his arms. The past few days with Nora were damn good.

After he stopped at a four-way intersection and

drove off again, Colter asked, "Are you gonna tell me what's going on between you and Nora?"

Beau chuckled, giving his brother a quick look. "That obvious?"

Colter removed his cowboy hat, resting it on his lap, and ran a hand through his tousled hair. "Been a long time since I saw you looking at a woman like that."

Beau set his attention back onto the road. "Been a long time since I felt like looking at a woman like that." If Nora was a local, Beau would declare he saw the beginning of something great, but Nora wasn't looking for love.

Every day spent in his cabin had been better than the last. He felt attraction to women since Annie passed away. He'd never felt that spark though—a spark that told him something about Nora was special. She was the fresh air he hadn't known he needed, and he was glad he got a couple weeks with her. "It's nothing more serious than having some fun while she's here."

Colter snorted. "Adeline moved back here. Who's to say you couldn't convince Nora to move as well."

Because Nora wants to move to Paris. The secret wasn't Beau's to tell, so he kept it to himself. "That's a big ask for a woman I *just* met." He paused, letting that sink into his brother's head. "Besides, that's a whole lot of serious, and I can't do that right now, not with Austin. Whatever I do has to make sense, and getting wrapped up in a woman who isn't looking for what I'm offering spells trouble."

"Austin has to come first," Colter agreed gently. "You're a good dad, Beau."

"Thanks, brother." Beau never doubted he was a good dad. He had his father for a role model, and a mother who showered him with love. The only thing he doubted was that he gave Austin enough of what he needed, since he lacked having a mother. Though he did have the best grandma looking out for him.

"But you also deserve to be happy," his brother added.

Austin.

His son was still young, only six years old. He needed Beau to remain solid, not wrapped up in his emotions with a woman, or in his own emotions. The last thing Beau wanted was to cause his son more pain than he'd already been through with losing his mother. "I am happy."

Colter lifted an eyebrow. "With a woman, I mean."

"And I'll find that," Beau stated. "Just something a little less complicated than getting involved with a woman who lives in an entirely different state."

Colter chuckled. "Sometimes complicated is where the fun is at."

"No, thanks," Beau scoffed, shaking his head at his brother and kept on driving. "But I like her. She's—"

"Brutally honest," Colter interjected. "Strong. Smart."

Beau laughed. "Yeah, all that."

"I knew you took notice of her when you met her on FaceTime," Colter said smugly. "Adeline didn't believe me."

"It's hard not to notice her." The rumble of an approaching truck made Beau pause as he took in the sweet Dodge Ram driving past. To his brother, he added, "She's gorgeous."

Colter agreed with a nod. "A bit too much fire for me, but she's a very good friend to Adeline. They're like sisters." It came as no surprise Colter's voice firmed a little. "Be careful there. You hurt Nora and Adeline won't forgive you."

Beau scoffed. "How can I hurt a woman who has no emotional stakes in this game and is running the show?"

Obviously satisfied with Beau's answer, Colter set his focus back on the road. "Just a little fun then while she's here?"

Beau grinned from ear to ear. "Just *a lot* of fun while she's here."

Colter's rumbly laughter filled the cab of the truck, and Beau laughed along with his brother.

After the road curved to the right, he took his foot off the gas pedal, slowing down to get a good look at the new construction on a flat piece of land along the road. The recently built two-story office building with timber-framed porch and limestone accents fit right into the landscape—where modern met the old west. "How're things coming along?" Beau asked, gesturing to the new Devils Bluffs Ranch office building.

"Good," Colter confirmed, pride evident in his voice. "Everyone's moved in. Things are going well."

By *everyone* Colter meant the new CFO and staff that had been hired to replace Colter at the helm of the cattle division of the Devils Bluffs Ranch. When their father, who built the ranch from the ground up retired, due to Parkinson's disease, Colter stepped into their father's big shoes. When Dad passed away from the cruel disease, Colter decided to return to his love of being a helicopter pilot. His plan went better than expected. The new staff were great at their jobs, and the ranch was thriving under the guidance of a CFO who flourished in business. A longtime cowboy working the ranch was promoted to manager to run the show at the ranch, and things were running smoothly. "Glad to hear it," Beau said.

He knew his dad would be proud. Not only for Colter choosing his own path in life, but that both Beau and Colter were not only keeping the ranch running but seeing it grow even further. "I've got some fillies being sent out this week," he told his brother. He always had at least five young horses in training at once, sometimes more. His stable manager, and right-hand man, Lee, was tasked with working all the young ones and getting them used to being handled. Beau did all the groundwork and training before they were sold.

When he reached the wrought-iron gates along

the side of the road, he turned up the driveway to his two-story sandstone house, with double cherry-wood front doors. On the left side of the property was a twenty-horse barn with a black roof. Warmth filled him...*home*. He couldn't imagine living anywhere else than right here, surrounded by his side of the business that he made thrive.

As he drove up the driveway, he cursed at the damage to his property. Dozens of trees were either uprooted, hanging or crashed into something. Next to the barn, Lee was fixing broken fences with a couple of the cowboys who worked at the horse ranch. The moment Lee caught sight of Beau's truck, he began heading toward the vehicle, a frown marring his scruffy face.

Lee had boxed his way through high school and had the broken nose to prove it. His face was rough, his attitude, at times, even rougher, but no one worked harder for Beau.

Beau threw the truck into park, cut the ignition and was out a moment later. "I had no idea things were this bad," he said to Lee.

The ranch manager finally reached them. He removed his tanned Stetson and ran a hand through his sweat-soaked, dark hair. "I didn't want to worry you over the phone. I hoped we'd have most of this done by the time you got back." His frown deepened as his dark eyes scanned the fence line. When he met Beau's gaze again, he shoved his hat back onto his head. "The arborists are all helping the town get cleaned up. Won't come our way for another couple weeks or so."

"Dammit," Beau grumbled, surveying his property. The house held up well during the storm, but the barn got the worst off it. Part of the roof was damaged by a fallen tree, and more massive trees were down everywhere. More than fifteen that he could count, crashed down on broken fences, and one of the farm trucks had been thoroughly smashed in, the tree still resting atop the truck.

"Insurance is coming tomorrow," Lee continued, shoving his hands into his pockets. "Figured I better leave the tree on the truck so they could see what caused the trouble." Sighing, he gestured behind him at the fence line. "As you can see, we had bigger problems than the truck."

"Yeah, I see." Beau scanned his property once more, a sour taste filling his mouth, before saying to Lee, "None of the horses were hurt?" The horses at the ranch were prized quarter horses, who all came with a hefty price tag. Any horses that showed potential were broken by Beau and then sent to professional reiners to show for bragging and breeding rights. The big money came in from the ranch's prized stallions. Every year Beau increased profits, but more than the money, he was proud of the quality of the horses. Devil's Bluffs Ranch created a good name in the horse industry, and Beau was satisfied with that.

"Not a single one injured," Lee assured him. "We

found the herd in the west pasture atop the high ground and beneath the forest of big oaks."

"A blessing for sure," Beau said with relief, but stared out at the trees with a frown, aware of the difficult work ahead of them. "This is fucking bad."

Next to him, Colter snorted. "You think this is bad." Beau glanced sidelong at him, and his brother's eyes were tight as he added, "Wait until you get to the ranch."

"It's worse than this?" Beau asked, astonished.

Colter nodded with a sigh. "Yeah."

Beau lifted an eyebrow at his brother. "You do realize you're getting married there in less than two weeks?"

Another long, heavy, *heavy* sigh. "That is our problem, brother."

Six

Seated at Adeline's kitchen table the following morning, Nora took a bite of the quiche Florentine on her plate and looked seriously at her friend. "What happened to you? You leave New York City and you become Martha Stewart."

"Ha!" Adeline exclaimed with a booming laugh, facing the coffee maker. She spun around with her full coffee mug and leaned against the counter. "This is all Colter's mom's doing. She gave me her recipe."

Nora hummed in happiness, unable to stop her moans. "This is so good. Seriously, you'd find something like this in a five star in Soho."

"Right," Adeline agreed with a nod. She took a

sip of her coffee before asking, "So, what's on the agenda for today?"

Nora scooped up her phone next to her, scanning her schedule. "I've got my dress fitting this afternoon, but this morning, Beau's coming to get me so we can start hunting down those reporters."

Adeline slowly grinned. "Is that all you'll be hunting down?" She waggled her eyebrows. "Or maybe you'll be hunting down some alone time?"

"Hilarious." Nora finished off the rest of her quiche, moaning with each bite. Instead of licking the plate clean like she wanted to, she slid off the stool and placed her dishes in the dishwasher. "We had our fun, but who's got time for *that* now. We've got so much to do with the wedding."

"Please," Adeline quipped. "There is always time for *that*. Especially with a hot cowboy."

Put that way... "Okay, maybe, it would be in my best interest to make some time for a little cowboy lovin'."

Adeline laughed, and Nora leaned in to kiss her cheek. It didn't matter how long they were apart, being with Adeline always felt easy, comfortable. Like...*home*. "Message if you need me. If not, I'll see you at the fitting?"

Adeline nodded. "I'll be there."

The crunch of gravel had Nora moving to the window. She tucked the curtain to the side and spotted Beau's truck. She gave her cell a quick look, hoping, *praying*, she'd find a message in her inbox.

When her inbox remained empty, she pushed

the dread aside and slid into her runners. "Wish me luck," she called to Adeline, quickly tying the laces. This morning, she'd put on jean shorts and a tank top, hoping she fit in a little more than her fancier dresses she'd wear walking the streets of Green Village.

"Good luck," Adeline replied.

On her way out the door, Nora blew Adeline a kiss then shut the door behind her. The second she caught sight of Beau in truck, she began to think Adeline was on to something. She should make time for *that*.

Seated behind the wheel, Beau wore a black cowboy hat and a gray T-shirt that hugged his muscular biceps. Through the open window, she spotted the indents and grooves of his forearms, the way he rubbed his finger over his thumb as his arm was slung over the steering wheel. The feeling of his touch stormed through her mind, bringing all the heat that a single kiss from him brought.

When she reached the door, she knew her pinkish cheeks likely revealed her desire. "Hi," she said.

His gaze roamed from her lips to her cleavage then back to her eyes. "Hi," he murmured. "Ready to get some reporters out of town?"

She held up the folders. "You bet I am." She hopped into the passenger seat of the truck, and with country music playing from the truck's speakers, she'd never felt so country on the drive into downtown. A far cry from the Uber and taxis in New York City.

The road was quiet, peaceful even. The wildness went on and on, untouched land, home to nature and animals as far as the eye could see.

Until those sprawling meadows faded away to a town, and downtown Devil's Bluffs came as an absolute shock. Adeline had said the town's core had some great shopping. Though she never said the downtown had charm and old-time elegance. The stores were a mirror image to anything she'd find in New York City. Sure, the men all wore cowboy hats, but they weren't dirty or worn, as she expected. It became clear that the people who lived in Devils Bluffs had money. And a lot of it.

Beau pulled into a parking spot at the curb and cut the engine. "How do we go about finding our first target?" he asked.

She unbuckled her seat belt. "Where was the last place you went and always saw one of them?"

"The coffee shop," he stated, removing his cowboy hat off his dash and sliding it onto his head. "Always."

She reached for her tote bag and opened the truck's door. "Then let's go there."

Quickly, they crossed the road, and she stepped in next to him as they strode down the street. "It's really kinda cute here."

"It's a beautiful place to live," he agreed with a soft nod.

"Pretty, yeah, but *little*."

His hat shadowed his face against the sun as he glanced down at her, curiosity filling his gaze. "You couldn't live here?"

"Lord, no." She burst out laughing. "I need night-life, excitement, history, architecture."

"You'd be surprised," he countered with a slight shrug. "This place might grow on you."

"I'm sorry, but I highly doubt that." She was a big city girl through and through.

He watched her closely for a moment then glanced away like whatever he was about to say died on his tongue.

Though as they entered the coffee shop, she scented the most delicious coffee she'd ever smelled, and she wondered if maybe he was on to something. The coffee would grow on her.

She settled in next to him in the line waiting to order and scanned the coffee shop. The place was adorable, cut right out of a magazine sharing trendy, hot spot coffee shops. Until her gaze stopped at one man sitting in the corner. "Oh, there," she said, squinting her eyes, ensuring she saw him right. "Yeah, that's one of them, I'm sure of it." She searched through her folders and took out a folder. "This guy."

Beau accepted the folder she offered and flipped it open, finding a photograph. He spied the man. "Yeah, that's the guy that was taking pictures at the cemetery."

"Hmm," she grumbled. "He's the one that stole the credit from his intern that earned him a promotion." Fury stole over her logical mind. "All right, let's kick one reporter out of town."

Beau arched an eyebrow. "You've got a plan here?"

"Of course, I do," she said and aimed for the guy, who was in is midtwenties. Handsome guy. All fancy with his Rolex and casual wear that looked like it had never seen a wrinkle.

"Stephen," she called, as he sat at his table, typing away on his laptop. "Stephen, is that you?"

The reporter lifted his head, pushing his black rimmed glasses farther up on his nose. He blinked. "Ah, yeah, do we know each other?"

"No, we don't know each other." She gave her best sweet as sugar smile, sliding into the booth across from Stephen. "But I know you—" she gestured to Beau as he slid in next to her "—and you certainly know Beau."

Recognition flashed across Stephen's face. "Beau, ah, yeah."

"We met at the cemetery if you remember," was Beau's grumbly response. His arms folded across his chest, a deep frown marring his face.

Again, Stephen blinked at Nora.

She smiled, placing the file on the table. New York City was a big city, but sometimes it felt small and certainly connected. Adeline had worked for one of the top gossip blogs in New York City. She had friends still in the business. All Nora had to do was make some calls, find out some watercooler gossip and then confirm her leads. After she opened the file, she spun it around, showing Stephen the intern's hard work and their email conversations. Funny when someone feels burned by their manager, how much they'll easily give up.

The moment Stephen's eyes hit the page, they widened. "What…how…?"

"I don't want to talk about how horrible it is that you stole the credit from your brilliant intern to further your career," Nora spat. "I also don't want to use this against you. What *we* want you to do is leave town. Tell your editor whatever bullshit story you need to tell them to get Beau out of the headlines and to kill his story but do *that*." His lips parted, and she added, "Today, if that wasn't clear."

Stephen blinked rapidly, his skin turning ashen as the seconds ticked on.

Nora hastily added, "Any story that comes out about Beau and has your name on it, and this story comes out." She pointed to the folder. "Got it?" Why the intern hadn't told the editor what Stephen had done was beyond Nora, but she was only glad the intern was willing to provide this proof. Nora had explained that she was helping a friend, and that had been all the intern had needed. Nora kept wondering if maybe she felt like she was getting revenge for the way she had been burned.

Stephen looked up from the file and gave a slow nod. "Yeah, I got it."

"Good," Nora said with a bite to her voice. "You can leave now."

Stephen slowly rose like it was hard for him to stand. Then he gathered his things and was out the door a second later.

"Wow, I don't think I've ever seen anyone move that fast," Beau said with a laugh.

Nora nodded. "No kidding. One down."

Beau slid out of the booth and offered his hand.

Nora brushed her fingers against his, feeling all the heat simmering between them as his low voice brushed over her. "Let's find the others."

What seemed like a great, easy idea turned into the exact opposite. For two hours, they'd walked up and down the street, visiting shops, the local inn, the library, going anywhere a reporter might go. The other two reporters were nowhere in sight.

"Maybe they're gone," Nora finally said, pain shooting through the arches of her feet regardless she was wearing runners.

"Could be." Beau removed his hat to carve a hand through his hair before siding it back into place. "I've been gone to the cabin. Maybe they realized the story was dead."

"Let's hope so," Nora said, lifting her nose and inhaling deep, catching the delicious aroma of Texas BBQ.

Obviously reading her mind, he said, "Come on, let's go get lunch."

Nora froze on the sidewalk, catching the sparkle in his eyes. She adamantly shook her head. "Um, no, thank you."

He moved out of the way of a pedestrian walking by, his brows shooting up. "We've been at this all morning. You've got to be hungry."

"I am hungry," she said with a firm nod. "I just don't do *that* anymore."

Frowning, he looked at her like she had two heads. "What don't you do?" he finally asked.

"Dates. I gave those up."

The seriousness in his expression faded to warm laughter that spilled over like a fine wine. "You gave up going on dates?"

"Yup. Done and done." She wiped her hands like she washed all the pain away from crappy ex-boyfriends.

His eyes flicked to the sky a moment before returning to her. "What about the BBQ from the food truck? Pulled pork isn't a date. We'll be outside, sitting on a bench. That's gotta be considered 'just eating.'"

She laughed, shaking her head at him. Though her empty stomach screamed, *yes!* "Finding loopholes, huh?"

His sly smile was his only reply.

The food truck, Texan's Smokehouse, was a beloved hotspot downtown. The lineup proved that, and it took half an hour to get their pulled pork sandwiches with coleslaw and cheese grits, along with a frosty glass of beer. Instead of leading Nora to a table and making her feel uncomfortable, Beau led her to one of the benches in the small park that overlooked the street.

"Who's Sally Anne Walker?" Nora asked, taking a seat on the bench.

"How do you know that name?" Beau asked, sitting in the spot next to her. She gestured to the metal tag on the bench behind him that had a beautiful memorial to Sally Anne Walker. "Ah, I see." Setting his beer on the ground next to the bench, he explained,

"Sally was the local librarian in Devil's Bluffs for as long as I can remember. Her son owns the food truck. She'd always come here every day and eat lunch to support him. He got this for her after she passed."

"That's really sweet," she said, then took a long drink from her beer. When she set the glass down by her feet, she said, "I bet there are things like this all over the town, right?"

He agreed with a nod, opening his napkin and placing it next to him. "The people who live here are what make Devil's Bluffs what is. Their lives leave imprints here."

"Gotta love that about small towns. We have things like that in New York City too, just on a larger scale. Foundations. Charities. Things like that."

Beau scooped up cheesy grits with his spoon. "We've got that here too. There's old, generous money here in town." Including the money his family donated every year, which now included as much as they could give for Parkinson's research in honor of their father.

Like Nora knew that, and maybe Adeline told her, she smiled then she turned her whole attention onto her lunch and dove in. Every so often, she'd reach down and grab her drink and swallow it back, but mostly, she ate, moaning in happiness, and so did he, trying to keep this feeling casual, even if he didn't mind one bit spending more time with her.

Eventually, she broke the silence. "This is legit the most delicious thing I have ever tasted."

He sucked the sauce of his fingers and agreed

with a nod. "They don't have anything like this in New York City?"

"They have some BBQ places, but nothing that tastes this good." She picked up a fallen piece of pulled pork. "Or at least nowhere that I've been to."

Wanting to get to know her better, but not wanting to come on strong, he thought back to what she'd said about needing nightlife. "Do you go out a lot in the city?"

"When Adeline lived in the city with me, we went out all the time." Her mouth twitched. "Probably too much if I'm being honest. I spent more on eating out than I probably did on my rent."

"Nothing wrong with eating out," he said. "I wish we had more restaurant choices here. At least the ones we've got are great." He scooped up more grits. "What's your place like out there?" He pictured her in a warm space, full of plants.

"I've got a tiny condo in Soho, but the view of the city is out of this world."

"Nice."

A jogger ran by them, his dog trailing behind, tongue wagging out. "Have you ever been to any big cities?"

He nodded. "I've been to a few, but it's not my style. Too busy. Too loud. Too many people."

She scanned the area before looking back at him. "After being here, I can totally see how a big city would get to you." A quick shrug. "I love being around people. The noise. The excitement. The energy."

He processed what she'd told him. So far, he'd

learned she was outgoing, so *alive*. He couldn't imagine any day with Nora would get boring. He'd only just met her, and he could already see that. It made him curious about her past. "Can I ask you a personal question as a friend and not into 'dating territory'?"

She eyed him suspiciously. Then, "Sure, why not."

He set his sandwich down and reached for his beer. "I don't take you to be the scared-of-a-relationship type. What's the story there?"

"Oh, I'm not scared of relationships, I just got smart."

He regarded her a moment. This woman was a confusing creature. Sexy as hell, but utterly confusing. "Mind explaining that?"

Laughter drifted over from another bench as she took a bite of her pulled pork sandwich, the sauce spilling out. He had a moment of regret wondering if he was asking something that was none of his business.

Once she finished chewing, she let him off the hook. "I don't know how it was for you growing up," she explained, her voice sounding oddly…detached, "but for me, I watched movie after movie showing me what true love looked like. As a kid, I bought into the fairy tale hook, line and sinker. You know, the happily-ever-after."

He read between the lines. "When did you stop believing in happily-ever-after then?"

She drew in a big deep breath, lifting her shoulders, like she was preparing herself for the blow. "The day my parents sat me down and told me they were getting a divorce."

"You weren't expecting it?"

"Not all," she said, wiping her mouth with her napkin. "It wasn't until I was older that I realized they simply hid their unhappiness because they thought they were protecting me."

"They never fought in front of you?"

"Never fought. Never got annoyed. Never anything." She sipped her beer, like she needed some help getting the words out. "Looking back at it, I see all the things that I missed as a child. How they never really looked at each other. How they slept in different rooms. How they lived two different lives except where it came to me."

"It's hard to see those things as a kid."

She agreed with a nod. "It is incredibly hard. I was blind to it all."

He processed what she'd told him and what she hadn't. "All right, there's the history, but you've had some bad boyfriends since their divorce?"

She side-eyed him. "How do you know I've had some bad boyfriends?"

"I overheard Adeline talking about the last guy to Colter. Sounded like a real ass."

She barked a laugh. "Oh, Scott was the biggest ass of them all."

"What happened with him?"

She began picking at her pork. "Long story short, I thought I'd marry him. I felt like we had something great, but one day, I went to work and came home to find he'd moved out. I'd spent hours trying to get ahold of him, calling everyone he knew, but it was like he just vanished off the earth."

"Did you eventually get ahold of him?" Beau said, unable to even imagine someone doing that to a person they had lived with.

"I didn't," she said slowly. "The cops did."

To lighten the mood, Beau asked, "Did you kill him?"

She barked a laugh. "I probably might have had I found him, but no, I had called the cops because I actually thought something happened to him." She blinked rapidly, shaking her head. "I remember thinking maybe he had a manic episode or a mental breakdown or something."

"That's not what happened?"

"No," she said with a frown. "He just decided that he hated his life with me, and he wanted a new one. A month later, he was dating someone else. That was six months ago."

"Ouch," Beau said, pressing his thigh against hers, offering the only comfort he could think of. "I'm starting to understand your feelings about relationships."

"Yeah." She laughed softly, without any amusement in it. Then her smile fell, and the darkness crossing her face felt all wrong. "To be honest, for a long time, I was out to prove my parents wrong. I wanted to show them that they simply messed up love and it was all their fault."

"Then you met the ass?" he guessed.

A humorless laugh escaped her. "I think I'm an

asshole magnet. They seem to gravitate toward me, I swear." She hesitated, picking at her pulled pork again, her appetite obviously fading under the painful subject. When she met his gaze again, she gave a small smile. "It didn't take long to realize that everything I once believed in was based on a lie. Look at the divorce rate in our country. Marriages don't last. Love is a giant sham."

"All love?"

"Well, no, I can't say all love. My love with Adeline is stronger than anything I've ever known." She hesitated to give a little shrug. "That's about it though."

As he took a long swig from his beer, he pondered what she'd told him. Considering how she felt about marriage and love, a thought occurred to him. "Do you believe Adeline and my brother are bound to fail?"

"Gosh, I hope not," she said immediately, a hand flying to her chest. "Adeline really knows how to love a person, and Colter seems like he's smitten with her. If anyone is going to make it, it's going to be them, so I'm crossing my fingers that all will work out."

He glanced out, gazing over the line of people at the food truck to the couples walking hand-in-hand, to the life going on around them. His gaze fell back onto Nora, seemingly going there so naturally, nearly pulled in that direction. He'd grown up around deep love. His parents were more in love than anyone he'd ever known. Family was everything to them. He couldn't imagine a world where that wasn't the case. His chest squeezed. A woman like Nora should have love in her life. He wouldn't mind a round or two with any man who made her believe that love was a sham and not life's greatest blessing.

"Don't do that."

He suddenly blinked into focus, realizing he'd been starting at her. "Pardon?"

She held his stare firmly. "Don't pity me. Life is full of lessons, most of them hard."

He knew all about hard lessons. All too well. Terrible lessons no one should have to learn. And yet... *and yet* an odd sense to protect Nora from the hardships of life seeped into his bones. "I don't pity you, trust me. I know how it feels to be pitied. I'd never do that to you."

"Then why are you looking at me like that?"

"Just thinking you're too good a woman to have crossed so many assholes."

Her eyes searched his for a long time before she gave a quick smile that lacked warmth and looked away.

Beau knew two things all at once—Nora didn't believe she could trust what had come from his mouth, because in her world, men lied. And that got right under his skin.

Seven

In the dress shop on the corner of the street, with high price tag designer dresses lining the storefront, Nora turned from side to side looking at herself in the long mirror. Until she poked herself with one of the pins the seamstress had used to pin the waistline. Careful not to turn herself into a pincushion, she ran her hands over the soft material. The eucalyptus-colored dress had a beautiful back keyhole, V-neck and sexy as hell side slit. "You couldn't have picked out a better dress," she said to Adeline via the mirror.

Beaming from her seat, Adeline said, "I knew you'd love it."

Nora scanned over the gorgeous chiffon dress. "Though I should have skipped the pulled pork sandwich," she said with a laugh, rubbing her hand over her bloated belly. "Next time remind me to not eat a huge meal before I have to put on this dress."

"Nora, it's you," Adeline said, dead serious. "You wouldn't listen to me even if I told you that you told me to say that."

"You're right." She laughed, tapping her stomach. "I do love food." And that BBQ was to die for.

"We're all set here, ladies," the seamstress said, coming into the back room. To Nora, she added, "Just remember to wear these same heels the day of the wedding. The dress is fitted to their height."

"Will do." Nora took one more look at herself in the mirror and sighed. "Do I have to really take it off?"

"Yes." Adeline rose and tugged Nora toward the changing rooms. "I told Bev we'd be at the ranch a little after four. We're going to be late if we don't get moving."

That snapped Nora into gear. Tonight, they had to go over the plans for the rehearsal dinner to get that knocked off the to-do list, and to make sure everyone who needed to be there got an invite. Once she had that behind her, she could move on to the bachelorette party—and at the moment she had a few ideas but needed advice from the best man too.

In a whirl of avoiding pins, Nora was back into her flowy summer baby doll dress, and they were soon in Adeline's Jeep Cherokee and on their way to Beau's mom's ranch.

While Nora had found the downtown was an un-expected surprise, when they arrived twenty minutes later, the Devil's Bluffs Ranch was exactly how she pictured it whenever Adeline had spoken about the cattle ranch.

An old, two-story stone farmhouse rested next to a barn with a red metal roof. Beside that, another building had a few cowboys walking through the door. She'd never seen so many cowboys in one place so far on her trip. Some were atop horses riding through the ranch, others pushing wheel barrels or carrying buckets, and others were fixing the storm damage to the property.

Everything was picture perfect, until— "That smell," she grumbled, covering her nose.

"Welcome to a cattle ranch," Adeline laughed, slowing her SUV to a stop when they reached the farmhouse. "Trust me, you'll get used to it."

Nora doubted that. Though that smell soon became a second priority as she surveyed the damage more closely. "Please tell me this isn't where you're getting married," she said.

Adeline cringed. "I know, it's bad."

Nora glanced at all the fallen trees. The porch that was missing half. The fences everywhere that were shattered into pieces. The debris, the mess, the *disaster*. She nearly had a mini breakdown, but one look into Adeline's worried eyes, and Nora faked a smile. "Don't you worry one bit. We've got time to get this all cleaned up." She took Adeline's hand and squeezed tight. "Your wedding is going to be perfect. I'm on it. Just trust me, okay?"

The tension slowly faded from Adeline's face. "You know, I trust you. It's just a lot of work." She dropped Nora's hand to open the door and exit the car.

Nora followed, meeting her at the hood. "Oh, please, we've got this."

Adeline gave a more honest smile.

Behind Nora, tires suddenly crunched against gravel. A quick look over her shoulder revealed Beau driving toward the farmhouse. The closer they got, the more she realized he wasn't alone.

Seated in the passenger side was Colter. Behind them was another little someone.

In most circumstances, this was when Nora would clam up and get the hell out of there. Meeting the mother and the son of someone she was sleeping with was serious stuff. She hastily reminded herself she wasn't serious with Beau. *Cool your jets, Nora. Friends only!*

Any nerves she had immediately washed away when Austin got out of the truck. A spitting image of his father, Austin ran up, passing Beau and Colter and threw himself at Adeline. His hat was a little too big for him. His boots making him a little clumsy. But the whole look and kid himself equaled up to such cuteness, Nora's breath became trapped in her throat.

Adeline caught Austin, wrapping him in a tight hug. "Hi, buddy. How was school?"

"Boring," Austin grumbled.

"Oh, I'm sure it wasn't so bad," Adeline said, stepping back.

"It was," Austin said. Then he set his clear blue eyes on Nora and stuck out his hand like a perfect gentleman. "Austin Ward, ma'am."

"Nora Keller, sir." She smiled and shook his hand, about ready to die from cuteness.

"Ah, so this is Nora," a sweet voice said.

Spinning around, Nora found that voice full of affection belonged to an even warmer woman. Her clear blue eyes exuded kindness, and she had the prettiest shiny gray curls, matched with an adorable rose-patterned apron. "And you must be Beverly." Beau's mom.

"I sure am, dear."

Adeline headed up the porch steps, so Nora followed, offering her hand.

"We hug around here, honey," Beverly said, opening her arms. "Hope that's okay with you."

"I love hugs, so yes." She stepped into Beverly's embrace, and she promptly fell into the warmest hug she'd ever felt in her life.

A hug that came from a good mother.

She hesitated to let go, and as if Beverly knew that, she hugged her just a bit tighter before stepping away.

"I left you some iced teas on the table there." Leaning in closer to Nora again, she grinned. "The Long Island kind."

"Oooh, my favorite kind." Nora smiled.

She winked. "Mine too." To Austin, Beverly added, "Come on kiddo, help me set the table."

"Yes, ma'am." Like his heels were on fire, he ran after her.

When the front screen door shut, Beau said behind her, "One of the reporters was at the school."

Turning around, Nora caught Beau looking as fine as ever. One foot on the porch step, his arm resting along the railing. *How can a man look that good doing nothing?* She was beginning to think Beau had a secret aphrodisiac cologne. Ignoring the heat ping-ponging in her body, she sighed. "So, they all haven't left town?"

"No," Beau said, obvious frustration tightening his strong mouth. "I asked for a meeting tomorrow at the diner. Figured we could get breakfast once we send her on her way."

Nora nodded, grinning. "Now that's just smart thinking."

The conversation soon shifted as she told Beau the unfolding of the rest of her afternoon at the dress shop, and then Colter and Beau talked about the damage to the ranch and all the work that needed to get done.

It wasn't until Austin came back out that Beau put his focus onto his son. He held up a package. "It's time," he said.

"Time for what?" Austin asked.

"To learn how to change spark plugs."

"No, Dad," Austin grumbled.

"Yes, son." Beau headed for the truck, and Austin followed along, dragging his feet through the gravel driveway, kicking up dust. But nearly instantly after Austin climbed up on the bumper, peering into the truck, his mood was piqued with interest.

"Let me go see how dinner is coming along," Colter said, dropping a kiss on Adeline's cheek before heading inside.

Nora leaned against the railing. The roar of a chain saw came from the other side of the barn as the cowboys obviously tried to make a dent in the damage from the storm. Her gaze skipped over the cows grazing off in the distance by the lake before returning to Beau, watching how much he and Austin were similar. They moved the same. Each tilted their head a little while concentrating. "He's a really good dad, isn't he?" she said, more of statement than a question.

"He's incredible with Austin." Adeline grabbed the iced teas from the table, offering Nora one. "Especially considering all they've been through. I know a lot of people that would've broke and fallen apart, not totally stepped up. After Annie passed away, Beau gave up his dreams of being a professional horse reiner to raise Austin and doesn't even seem to hold a grudge about that."

Nora's heart clenched tight. "This whole family has seen sadness, and yet they are the warmest people I think I've ever met." She glanced at Adeline, quickly adding, "Besides you, of course."

"Thanks." Adeline gave Nora a sweet smile. "And you're right—they're good people. Kinda explains why I decided to stay here, huh?"

Nora hated to admit that she'd been hurt that Adeline hadn't come back to New York City, but she had. It'd been the two of them for so long. New York City hadn't been the same after Adeline left. "Yeah, I totally get it."

"Dinner is on," Beverly called, then rang the bell just outside the front door.

Adeline pushed away from the railing. "Get ready, my food loving bestie, you are in for a treat. Bev's cooking is out of this world delicious."

"I am ready to be wowed," Nora declared. She took a step forward to follow Adeline, but then glanced over her shoulder and took it all in.

With Beau and Austin at the truck, Adeline leading the way to a kitchen smelling of heaven, and as peace engulfed the ranch in abundance, she began to see how Adeline fell back in love with Devil's Bluffs and these people.

Nora was secretly falling in love too. And that simply wasn't part of the plan. It *couldn't* be the plan. Because she'd felt these feelings of interest and excitement before—along with the butterflies in her belly—but that always led her down a path of heartbreak.

Doing what she knew was the only way forward, no matter what, she walked away from Beau and told her softening heart to get a grip.

* * *

Stuffed full from Mom's chicken, gravy and biscuits dinner, Beau sat on the swing on the back porch with the ground level stonework beneath his boots and the pergola with climbing vines overhead, and sighed. Austin and Nora were playing baseball in the middle of the backyard between two large shade trees, with the farm's horses grazing in their field behind them.

"You look dumbfounded," Colter noted, taking a seat next to Beau, offering him a cold beer.

"Thanks," Beau said, accepting the beer. He took a long swig, the cool, crisp hoppy taste rushing down his throat. "She confuses me." For the last half an hour, Nora had been playing baseball with Austin, while Adeline and Mom cheered them on. She hit every ball thrown and caught them all too.

"Looks like she's great with kids," Colter said, leaning back against the cushion. "What's so confusing about that?"

Beau pondered his statement as the sun began setting, painting the sky in pink and purple hues. Figuring his brother was the perfect sounding board, he explained, "In one breath, she'll say she couldn't imagine not living in the city. That country life is boring. Then in the next, she fits right in like any local." He rubbed at his eyebrow and the growing tension there. "Like I said, confusing." And *interesting*, he couldn't deny that.

Colter smiled. "Smitten already brother?"

Beau snorted and drank his beer instead of giving an answer. He expected Nora to clam up when meeting Austin. Which was why he figured he'd just rip off the Band-Aid and introduce them, keeping things casual and light. But she did the opposite and was as warm and affectionate as she was with everyone.

She was a standout, a one-of-kind woman with heart, humor and kindness shining in everything she did. And yeah, he *was* smitten. Which was the problem. He shouldn't be smitten. He should keep his guard up. He shouldn't be feeling confusion or anything but desire. And yet he couldn't turn his head off.

"Smitten or not," Beau finally said to his brother, "doesn't change the fact that being here is a vacation to her and nothing more."

"Sounds like a pretty fine excuse to keep your distance."

Beau scoffed. He didn't need Colter to tell him that being with Nora was different. He'd taken lovers after Annie had passed away, mostly as a way to ease his grief, and he'd had his fair share of terrible dates. While he sensed a familiar warning telling him to be wary of Nora, who said one thing and did another, she was more than a fling. He felt that down to his bones.

At his brother's dig, Beau shot Colter a sly smile. "I don't believe I asked for your opinion."

Colter cupped Beau's shoulder and fiercely grinned. "Doesn't mean I won't give it to you anyway."

Beau snorted a laugh. He'd never tell Colter, but he appreciated that most about him, just as he appreciated Nora's honesty and openness in the last few days. Even if her actions didn't always line up.

The sun began to set lower, calling it a day, as his mother and Adeline returned to their chairs under the pergola. Beau stuck his fingers into his mouth and whistled, garnering Austin's attention at the sound he'd heard a thousand times playing out in the fields at the ranch. He rose and called, "Come on, buddy, it's bedtime."

Austin and Nora exchanged a conversation and then came running over.

"You play ball?" Colter asked Nora the moment she reached them, red-faced and out of breath.

She nodded, setting her baseball glove and the ball on the deck. "I play in a recreational league back home."

Colter accepted Beau's half-empty beer and rose. "We should get a friendly game going before the wedding."

"Count me in." Nora grinned. "But be prepared to have your ass handed to you."

Beau barked laugh. "My money's on her."

"We'll see about that," Colter said with a grin, striding past them and heading toward Adeline and Mom.

Nora smirked in challenge.

Austin jumped into his grandmother's arms and hugged her goodbye.

When his son stepped away, Beau leaned in and kissed Mom's cheek. "Thank you for dinner," he told her."

"You're so welcome, honey."

Beau went to hug Adeline goodbye when Austin froze him in his tracks.

His son tugged on Nora's T-shirt. "Can you come read to me tonight?"

All eyes went to Nora, but Nora's gaze flicked to Beau's.

His lips parted to interject, until he reminded himself, for Nora, they weren't anything more than a vacation fling. She wouldn't get attached to Austin because she'd never allow herself to.

Besides, as he saw her eyes soften, as well as Adeline's gentle smile, he knew Austin would always see Nora as Adeline's best friend—a family friend. Adeline needed her old family to know her new family.

For that reason, Beau smiled. "Austin loves when family reads to him." He cupped his son's shoulder. "And that includes his aunt's best friend."

Adeline pointed at Beau. "Don't go making me cry."

Nora laughed. "I'd love to you read to you, but only if I can read you Harry Potter."

Austin's nose scrunched. "What's Harry Potter?"

Nora gasped, placing a hand on her chest. "What's Harry Potter?" She narrowed her eyes at Beau like he'd broken an unspoken rule. "How have you not introduced your son to Harry Potter?"

Beau frowned. "What's Harry Potter."

Nora gasped louder.

Adeline burst out laughing. "Only the best kids' books and movies out there."

"Kids books?" Nora gasped again, shaking her head like nothing was right with the world. "If I didn't know better, I'd think you were all trying to kill me." She placed her hand on Austin's shoulder and turned him around, walking away from the porch. "It's a good thing I have a copy on my phone. I'll get you the paperbacks tomorrow."

Austin looked up at her. "What's Harry Potter?"

Nora's voice sounded like a song. "It's a magical world of witches and wizards and mystical creatures."

"Cool," Austin drawled.

"Exactly," Nora agreed. "So cool."

As they reached the edge of the house, Colter called, "Nora, let me know if you need a ride later."

She didn't turn around, just waved, keeping her attention on Austin.

Beau said his goodbyes to his family and then followed Nora and Austin to the truck, finding them already there. Talk about magic filled the cab of the truck the entire drive back home. When they'd finally arrived, the cowboys had gone home for the night, but the fences were now fixed. A job well done, and family time mattered—his father taught him that—so Beau was glad to see them gone.

The moment he parked next to the porch, Austin

jumped out and took off running into the house. "Go brush your teeth, buddy," Beau called after him. "I'll be in shortly to run your bath."

Austin didn't reply, the front door slamming behind him.

At the silence next to him, Beau turned to Nora, and she wore a soft expression, scanning the area.

"You know," she finally said, her gentle gaze meeting his. "Besides all the trees down and the damage, your property is my favorite."

"Thanks. I'm pretty partial to it," he said, getting out of the truck.

When he met her at her side of the vehicle, she asked, "How long have you lived here?"

Shoving his hands into his pockets, he leaned against his truck. "My dad always said when we had the money to build a house, he'd give us our pick of land. I liked it here. The meadows. The creek running behind the house. It's just a beautiful bit of the property. It took a while to save up enough for the down payment for the construction loan, but I ended up getting it when I proposed to Annie."

"Oh," she said, glancing around again, reassessing. "You proposed here, then?"

He nodded, wondering what she'd say to that.

It came as no surprise when she gave a tender smile and kept things very friendly. "That's a sweet way to propose to someone. You were offering her a home, a life together?"

"Yeah, exactly."

She watched him closely a moment, finally scanning over the property with a long deep breath. "Now you're giving that home and life to Austin."

He didn't feel the need to respond, and just followed her gaze around the property that was all his. Sure, he'd given up his dream of professional reiner career when Annie passed away, but he didn't hold a grudge about that. His son, his life, his work and his ranch were all things that brought him immense pride.

"Come on let's go in," he said, gesturing to the house. "I need to get Austin in the bath and get his lunch made for school tomorrow."

"I'll make his lunch, if you show me where everything is," she said, matching his stride as they headed for the house.

He waited at the porch steps, letting her climb them first. "You sure?"

She nodded. "I'm an expert lunch maker."

She was a whole lot of something special, minus the part where she lived in an entire other state. He followed her inside, quickly showed her where all the food was stashed, indicating Austin's favorite was a ham sandwich, along with a fruit and something snacky. While she busied herself with that, Beau headed up stairs and ran Austin's bath, and soon, his kid was in his pajamas and tucked into bed.

Beau had left Nora seated next to Austin on his bed, reading to him, and visited the barn to check on the couple of horses that were stabled for the night.

One had a hoof abscess that was being treated. The other had lameness they hadn't gotten to the bottom of yet. The remainder of his herd was out living in the wilderness, enjoying being a horse. The ones currently in training were in the pastures next to the barn. But training was on hold until after the wedding. Especially given all the damage that needed to be fixed at his family's ranch.

Fifteen minutes later, when he came back into the house and went upstairs, he stopped just outside the door.

"Chapter two," Nora said, excitement brightening her voice.

Beau chuckled, then quietly entered the room and slid a hand onto Nora's shoulder. "He's sleeping," he told her.

She snapped her gaze up away from her phone. "Oh," she whispered. She gently rose and followed Beau out into the hallway. He left the door ajar and followed Nora back down to the living room. She laughed when she turned around to face him. "Sorry," she said. "I always get sucked into Harry Potter. I had no idea he'd passed out."

"Don't be sorry," he told her. "He falls asleep fast, always has."

"Okay, good," she said, cringing. "Hopefully I didn't bore him."

At the slight worry on her face, he gathered her in his arms, something he'd wanted to do all damn day. He drew in her perfume, smelling of a summer meadow. His groin flooded with heat as she pressed all her soft curves against him. "You could never bore anyone." He tugged her close against him, loving how her eyes simmered in his hold. "I've got a surprise for you." Something he'd put together after he'd checked in on the horses.

"A surprise, hmm?" she asked, curiosity dancing across her expression.

"Mmm-hmm," he murmured, dropping his chin and brushing his lips across hers. "Want to see it?"

She grinned against his mouth. "I want to see all of it."

Eight

Curiosity filled Nora, teasing her mind, as Beau held her hand tightly, leading her through the barn and up a set of stairs to the hayloft. Wooden beams stretched across the ceiling with hay bales filling the rectangular space, but in the center, a keyhole space had been cleared. The air was dusty and held an earthy scent from the hay bales, but her breath became trapped in her throat for a whole other reason than the air quality.

In that keyhole, hay had been spread out to create a bed, where a blanket and pillows rested, with twinkle lights hanging from the wooden beams. "Is it always like this?" she asked, her stomach sinking.

Beau stuffed his hands into his front pockets and

grinned. "Nah, I did this while you were reading to Austin."

She focused back on the makeshift bed, the care that went into how the pillows were positioned and the twinkling lights casting a warm glow in the space. Her heart promptly somersaulted. She'd expected a quicky in the barn or outside. Not *this*.

No ex-boyfriends in her past had done anything like this for her before. They'd never planned out something ahead of time, other than taking her out for dinner. None of them had ever spent time doing something that he truly thought would *wow* her. Except a card on her birthday, attached slippers, perfume, or lingerie. Heat began to slide through her body, and she wasn't entirely comfortable with it. "Do you always do stuff like this for the woman you are sleeping with?"

Cocking his head, he must have read her hesitation since his expression softened. "Have you never had someone do something like this for you?"

"No," she replied immediately, making her suddenly feel foolish. "Nothing this like." And she wondered why that never truly bothered her before. But in this moment, she realized, she should have expected some kind of effort every time she slept with someone. It occurred to her that she never expected this treatment because coming from divorced parents who hated each other, and a long list of crappy ex-boyfriends, she didn't think this type of treatment was possible.

"That's a shame," he said, taking a step toward her.

She raised a hand, stopping him in his tracks. "This isn't a date, you know that, right?"

He chuckled. "I'm aware, but trust me, you'll appreciate the sheets. No matter what anyone tells you, having sex on hay is awful."

He took another step forward and she felt the pulse of desire simmering between them. Her heart raced and heat overwhelmed her. This felt personal—too personal.

She took a full step back, again stopping him. "There is no romance with friends with benefits."

"There should be." One brow slowly lifted. "You deserve that, Nora."

She gulped, feeling for these last minutes that she wasn't the one holding all the cards, and Beau was taking this somewhere they said they wouldn't go. "What about Austin?" she blurted out.

Again, he froze, a smile playing on the corners of his mouth. "He always knows if he needs me to come to the barn. This is where I'd be if I'm not in the house."

"Okay, well," she said, suddenly breathless under the weight of his burning stare, "what if he walks up here?"

"He won't," Beau said, heat edging his voice. "He'd call out for me the moment he walks in. We'd have time to get dressed." That brow lifted higher, his head cocking a little bit more. "Any other concerns?"

She swallowed deeply, fully running out of reasons why she should let this moment happen. "No, no other concerns."

"Good." Then his mouth met hers, and his kiss shattered her.

Full of his usual confidence, with an added swell of emotion, his tongue was sweet fire against hers. His kiss glided against her in a sensual embrace, and she fell gladly into his hold, wanting to give him all of herself. But with each hot swirl of his tongue across hers, she realized she needed to give him *more* to remind him this thing between them was, and would stay, just about sex.

Breaking the kiss, she led him onto the soft blanket overtop a bed of hay and grabbed the hem of his T-shirt, pushing the thin fabric over the deep groves of his six-pack. He yanked the shirt over his head a second later, and she got to work unbuckling his jeans and shoved those, along with his boxer briefs, down to his knees.

As if he knew exactly what she had planned, he slid his hand across her cheek, kissing her like he'd hungered for her all day. Until he leaned away, staring at her with need she felt down to her toes. She lowered to her knees.

Staring down at her intently, he groaned as she took his thick cock in her hand and stroked velvet over steel. Knowing how he liked his pleasure by now, she pressed the length of him against his stomach and she tickled her tongue across his sac, before taking one testicle in her mouth, sucking deeply.

When she moved onto the other testicle, he shuddered and grunted, tipping his head back and groaning. "Goddammit, Nora."

Feeling powerful and fully in control, she took his pleasure as her cue and licked up the length of him, feeling the pulsing veins on his shaft. When she reached the tip, she swirled her tongue around him before taking him deep into her mouth. He grunted, lowering his head, threading his fingers into her hair. She met his red-hot stare as she worked her mouth over him, using her hand to stroke him deeper into pleasure.

With every glide of her mouth, he became a little louder, his movements rougher. Until he was no longer looking at her, and she was no longer looking at him, and he was thrusting his hips with her movements.

She moved harder, faster, lost in the moment.

Until she snapped into awareness at his loud growl. Only then did she realize he was trembling.

She sat back on her legs as he pulled away, giving a low chuckle. "You've already finished me once like that and it was a blow to my ego. That's not happening again."

"Not a blow to your ego," she teased.

"I prefer my ego intact, as well as my pride." Leaning down, he took her chin and kissed her deeply. Intently. Intimately. A kiss that was meant to stir and tease and promise her so much. "Besides," he murmured when he backed away, "you're not the only one that gets a taste tonight."

Her clothes were gone in quick work, and a condom was placed on the bed of hay. He laid down against the pillow and curled a finger at her. "Come here, darlin'." His voice had lowered, a wicked glint glistening in his eyes, and her nipples puckered against the promise in his gaze.

Heat flooded her as she knelt next to him. He grasped her arms and gave her a little tug, until she was straddling his head. She'd done naughty things before. She wasn't a saint. But nothing felt as erotic as Beau grinning up at her from between in thighs. Going into full sensory overload, she shivered as he slid his hands on her bottom and pulled her against him. The moment tongue met her wet, tender flesh, she unraveled. But not nearly as much as when he groaned, a sound of pure masculine hunger, and she melted against him completely.

Pressing her hands against the rough, scratch hay bales, she sank into the pleasure of his mouth. Hot, intense pleasure sending her on wave after wave of bliss while he held her thighs tight and licked, tickled, sucked and swirled her with a skill she'd never experienced, until she was brazenly panting, grinding herself against his face.

And yet she needed *more*.

She reached for her breast and squeezed, tweaking her sensitive nipple, moaning without restraint. She felt the trembling in her limbs before she sensed her insecurities wash away, her *need* becoming the only thing on her mind.

Heat and urgency began to fill her as she dropped her other hand to hold his head. Keeping him where she wanted him, right—*there*, she began riding his mouth, circling her hips, owning the pleasure he offered.

More...

More...

More...

"Yes! I'm—" Her climax hit, stealing the remaining words out of her mouth, replacing them with a scream of satisfaction.

It wasn't until she felt the tip of his cock at her drenched heat that she realized he'd shifted her off his face and onto his waist. Sometime while she'd come down from the high, he'd sheathed himself in a condom, because suddenly, he was holding her waist, primed and ready to take them even higher.

"This is going to be fast and hard," he told her, a sexy intensity filling his features. "*That* was the hottest damn thing I've ever seen."

Before she could respond, drowsy with the pleasure, he sealed his mouth against hers, his tongue thrusting deep. She scented herself, his masculine, woodsy aroma, and the combination was an aphrodisiac made just for her.

Breaking the kiss, he stared deeply into her eyes, and she felt something inside her shift, a guard desperately wanting to fall under the safety in his stare.

Then his fingers tightened on her hips, and he entered her in one swift stroke, stretching her...filling her...her toes curling against the pleasure.

He proved his words true as he thrust upward and she dug in her fingernails into his chest, lost in the depths of his eyes. His groans echoed her moans as he moved faster, harder, rougher. Until she lost sight of him, falling into the sweet darkness that belonged only to them. A place of total surrender where nothing painful could touch her.

A place she suddenly never wanted to wake up from.

Lying against the bed of hay, Nora was snuggled into Beau's side, her head resting against his chest, the heat from her body a welcome warmth. He traced his fingers up and down her spine, and each gentle stroke deepened her breathing. The quiet between them was only interrupted by mouse scurrying around the hayloft, and the horses below chomping on their hay. His mind should stay silent, but thoughts rattled inside his head. Thoughts of this confusing woman so settled in his arms. He knew she had a hard time trusting. He also knew that she had given up on love all together. But he secretly hoped when she was in his arms, she felt...*safe*. He thought it a damn shame a woman like Nora had never experienced a love so real it brought a man to his knees.

"You surprise me, you know," he eventually said, breaking the silence.

She leaned back, resting her head on his arm to see his face. "How?"

"You're the only woman I've ever met that hasn't asked about Annie." Every single woman—even the one night stands—always wanted to know all about his late wife. Who she was, what she was like, and if they had a good marriage. Then came the questions about her death.

Nora's eyes turned guarded as she leaned her chin on her hands resting on his chest. "That really isn't my business to ask about her."

Beau glanced up at the rafters above them. It occurred to him that's what he liked about Nora most. She didn't fuss into someone's life. She seemed to simply make the lives of those around her happier, and that was her sole focus in life. For a person who said she didn't want love in her life, she sure knew how to love a person well. "It's fair to inquire about someone's past," he offered.

"Yes, if you're dating each other, but we're not, so it really *is* none of my business."

He met her gaze again, his jaw muscles clenching at the reminder that she was determined to keep emotionally distant. While he knew that was the right thing, for them, for Austin, her insistence to push him away grated his nerves. "Right."

Obviously reading his irritation on his expression, she nibbled her bottom lip. "Besides, what's fun about talking about all the painful things that happen in life?" she offered lightheartedly. "There's nothing good about it."

"There is nothing good about it, but to truly know someone you've got to know their past."

Suspicion rested heavy in her eyes. "You're telling me you like to talk about that painful part of your life?"

He shrugged. "I didn't talk about Annie for a very long time. Until I saw the effect it had on Austin. Now it's not hard to talk about."

She sat up then, pulling the sheet with her, covering her chest. Her hair fell gently over her bare shoulder, a piece of hay sticking out. "What happened with Austin?"

He blew out the breath that naturally wanted to stay deep in his lungs and plucked the hay out of her hair. "When Annie passed away, it was so sudden. One minute I was kissing her goodbye and leaving the kitchen. The next, she dropped to the floor."

"You lost her that fast?"

"So fast," Beau said. "At first, I thought she passed out. Maybe she hadn't had breakfast or something. But the second I rolled her over, I knew she wasn't breathing. I immediately called the paramedics and then started CPR."

"Did that help at all?"

Beau shook his head, refusing to let his mind drift back to her empty eyes. "I'm not even sure how long I was doing CPR." He swallowed the thick emotion rising to his throat and pushed on. "But I knew her ribs were broken by the time anyone arrived. I could feel them snap beneath my compressions."

"Beau," Nora said, tears suddenly welling in her eyes. She scooted closer, reaching for his hand.

He laced his fingers with hers. "Nothing I did, or even the paramedics could do, would bring Annie back. She was gone. And for a long time, I went with her."

"Emotionally, you mean?"

He nodded, reaching up to tuck a fallen strand of hair behind her ear. "To be honest, for the first year, I was on autopilot. Austin was just a baby, and I had no idea what I was doing. Annie was such a natural mom. It all came easy for her. I felt lost without her, and that wasn't only because I lost my wife. I had no idea how to raise a baby on my own."

Nora leaned into his touch before he lowered his arm and rested it behind his head. "Your mother must have helped you a lot."

"God, did she ever," Beau said with a quick nod. He wasn't sure where he'd be without the help of his mother during the first year of raising Austin alone. "She moved in for a couple months to help me in the beginning. But really, my whole family helped. They rallied around me. I would not be here without their support."

Nora's sweet smile chipped at the coldness in his chest. "It's good you had them. Going through all that alone couldn't have been easy." Then her smile fell, and her brows drew together tightly, creasing her forehead. "So, what happened with Austin that made you start talking about Annie more?"

"It wasn't until he was older and talking," Beau explained, remembering how life changed for the better back then. "My mom always talked about Annie to Austin. At first, I thought she did so to remember Annie and to help with her grief. Later, I realized it was more about keeping Annie's spirt alive for him. You've met my mom. She's good with all that stuff."

Nora agreed with a nod. "She is really easy to talk to."

"Exactly. She's a mother through and through," he said, releasing her hand to run his fingers along hers. "But one night, Austin came home after she watched him while I worked, and he asked me if I didn't like Annie anymore." Nora's eyes widened, so he continued quickly to explain, "He asked if that was why I never talked about her. After that talk, everything changed. His love of Annie and wanting to know his mother was the tool to helping my grief. Sharing the wonderful memories of her reminded me of the incredible woman I'd known instead of all that I lost."

A tear slid down Nora's cheek before she wiped it away. "Gosh, Beau, that's the sweetest thing. You two had each other through that."

"That's right, we did, and somehow came out of it all right." He paused, collecting his thoughts, desperate for her to understand. "Maybe it's a normal reaction, or maybe not, but as years went on, the pain shifted. Now it's hard to even remember the man I was when I was with Annie. I'm different. My life is different. I had big dreams about riding professionally. I worked more than I was home. And loss like that does something to you, changes your whole makeup—what makes *you*. If Annie met me now, she wouldn't even recognize me."

Nora's finger brushed across his, a tender touch he didn't know he needed, as she said, "And that's what helps you move on? Because you're a different man. You're not the man that Annie loved."

"Exactly," he said, unsurprised she got him. Her heart spoke a similar language—he didn't doubt that. "Annie and I shared a deep love. But the love I want to offer now will belong to someone else, and that's okay."

Nora watched him for a long moment then blew out an even longer breath. "I really don't know how you do it. I haven't gone through anything that painful, and I want to stay far, far away from love."

He laced his fingers with hers again and held on tight. "Once you've tasted true, healthy love, the kind that fills you up so entirely, you'd never not want that again."

Her brows knit, her eyes searching his, as if she was searching for a hundred answers in his gaze. "You really believe that?"

Reaching up, he tugged her back into his arms and pressed a kiss to her forehead. She snuggled into him like she belonged right there, molding against him. "Yeah, I really do."

The silence dragged on, and it was comfortable. Happy, even.

Which was why when Nora shifted as if she realized that it had become a little too comfortable, he was unsurprised. She never did seem to let him forget this thing between them was temporary. And that was probably a good thing.

"I was thinking about the bachelor and bachelorette party and wanted to run something by you," she said, leaning up and resting on his chest.

He brushed the fallen strands of hair behind her ear, trapped in stunning eyes. "Got an idea?"

"Maybe." She pulled back slightly, her forehead wrinkling. "What would you think about having a joint bachelor/bachelorette party in New York City for the weekend?"

His fingers froze on her face. "I'm not sure what to comment on first."

She laughed, a sweet, sleepy sound. "I know it's not the usual way of doing the parties together, but…" She shrugged. "I just think it'd be neat to include Adeline's life in New York City into the wedding, and I'm sure she'd like to experience that with Colter."

"It's not a bad idea," he said, brushing knuckles across her jawline.

"Really." She tilted her head and pursed her lips. "You don't think he'll be upset not to have a drunken night with strippers or something?'

Beau took in her tight expression and barked a laugh. "No matter if it's a joint party or not, there will be a drunken night, and there won't be strippers."

"Why?" she countered. "Men like that for bachelor parties?"

He took her chin, giving her a leveled look. "If we want to look at a naked woman, we don't need to pay for it."

Her eyes flared. "I'm sure you have no problem in that department."

To prove his point, he dropped his arm and slapped her butt. "Not presently."

She wiggled against him, sliding her thigh over his. "I know the trip will be pricey. I mean, you, Colter and Adeline can stay at my place, but anyone else that comes will have to get a hotel. They aren't cheap in New York City, and that's not including flights."

"It's not a problem. I'm covering the bachelor party," he said, watching the widening of her eyes, as if she only just remembered his wealth.

"I can't even imagine Colter's buddies in the big city," he said. "It could prove to be amusing."

"It'll be fun." She leaned closer, sliding her thigh higher up his legs. "So whatcha think?"

"I think if you keep rubbing yourself on me like that," he said lightly, "there isn't a chance in hell I'd refuse you anything."

"Oh," she purred, pressing her heat against his thigh and rolling her hips. "I guess I'm getting my way then."

He groaned, grabbing a fistful of her bottom. "You might regret your choices. I don't think you're taking into consideration the task you're taking on by bringing a bunch of cowboys to the big city."

She tsked. "Looks like I'm handling one cowboy pretty well right now." A growl vibrated in his chest as her hand went lower…and lower…until she grasped his cock. "Wouldn't you say?"

He brushed his mouth across hers. "I'll say whatever you damn well want as long as you don't stop *that*."

She squeezed his shaft harder, and her wicked, hot kiss sealed the deal.

Nine

A few hours after sunrise the following morning, dust followed Adeline's car as Nora drove toward Devil's Bluffs Ranch after dropping Adeline off downtown. As editor for the local newspaper, Adeline couldn't help with repairs at the ranch, but Nora could, and she had no intention of sitting around doing nothing instead of helping make sure her best friend had the most magical wedding.

She slowed the car as she rounded a corner and yawned loudly, exhaustion weighing her down to her bones.

Last night, Colter had picked her up from Beau's a little after ten o'clock at night. She was sore in all the right places from the hours she'd spent with Beau in the hayloft. They'd both been tired and beat, but Beau didn't want Austin waking up with Nora there, and she respected him for it. Austin knew her as Adeline's best friend, and Nora wouldn't mess with that.

The tire hit a bump in the gravel road, but nothing could distract her from the vast beauty of Ward land. Beau didn't act like he came from money or flaunt it like those in New York City sometimes did, but the Ward wealth wasn't in possessions but in rich Texas land that was beautiful enough to take Nora's breath away. Adeline had once said it was easy to forget Beau and Colter came from old money, which had been the reasons they were targeted by the blog as well as their viral photograph, but even last night with Beau's offer to pay the way for the trip to New York City, Nora still had a hard time wrapping her head around how rich they really were.

The Wards were good people, and she wished the blog had written about that.

As she passed a lake where birds flew overhead, her cell phone beeped, indicating an email had arrived. She didn't even have to look to know it was from the insurance company with the rental. She'd been on the phone with them for the last hour as she sat behind a desk at the newspaper, while Adeline got to work. A big weight lifted off her shoulders when the insurance company confirmed they were covering the damage to her rental car, and the event would stay a story she could tell others over drinks. Instead of putting her further into debt than she already was.

When the GPS indicated she finally reached the ranch, she slowed the car then headed up the driveway. A cowboy was riding a brown horse, who leaped up and spun in the air, kicking out its legs, looking a moment away from killing the man on his back. "Jesus," she murmured to herself.

Until that shock turned into fear, as she realized that wasn't any cowboy. *Beau.*

Worried now, she parked next to the house and opened the door, quietly stepping out, not wanting to do something to make the horse do anything worse. Not that she knew anything about horses, but she figured making sudden movements was probably not a great idea.

The horse continued to buck and run off, doing all types of spins. Beau being thrust around but staying atop the horse.

Suddenly, the horse stopped, breathing heavily. Beau clicked his tongue and the horse walked off around the pen.

Nora stayed rooted in place, barely breathing, her cell in her hand in case she needed to call paramedics to his aid.

Long minutes later, Beau pulled on the reins, stopping the horse in the middle of the ring and brushing a gentle hand along the horse's neck. As if he sensed her staring—probably gawking at this point—he looked her way. He gave her a smile that lit up his face. A smile that made her heart skip a full beat, and not only in relief that he wasn't about to die by horse.

He swung one leg over the saddle, landing on the ground. "He's done," he called.

A lanky cowboy with a dark brown cowboy hat entered the ring and took the reins from Beau. "Can you fix him up?" he asked in a thick Texan drawl.

"Shouldn't be a problem," Beau said with a slight nod. "I'll work with him over the next few days."

"Good man," the cowboy said, before leading the horse away.

Beau's gaze met hers then, and she tried hard not to squirm under the power in that stare and the confidence that he wholly deserved to hold. He took his cowboy hat off and used his arm to clear the sweat from his forehead before sliding it back into place.

She nearly fanned herself as he began walking toward her. No, walking wasn't quite right. He surged forward, with strength, and the whole vibe of Beau screamed *man*. From the cowboy boots to his worn jeans and light-colored chaps, all the way up to his dirty gray T-shirt and the scruff on his face. Warmth touched very naughty places that demanded his touch.

"Hey," he said when he reached her. A playful smile pulling on his lips as if he knew exactly what she was thinking about.

"Hi." She studied his flexed muscles after a hard workout, with veins protruding and seemingly harder, *bigger*, than normal. She cleared her throat and asked, "Are you hurt at all?"

His brows rose. "Why would I be hurt?"

"Because that horse nearly tossed you into the dirt."

"Nah, he wasn't even close to getting me off," Beau said. He leaned in, smelling of delicious, hard-working man, and he winked. "He was harmless. Just scared and lacking confidence. It won't take long to correct the behavior."

She eyed the sun making the sweat on his arms glisten as he crossed them over his chest, before she looked at him with suspicion. "You're telling me that horse wasn't dangerous?"

"Any scared horse is dangerous." He tilted his head toward the horse walking back to the barn, "but that horse wasn't trying to hurt me. He just didn't understand I wanted him to go forward. It looks worse than it was, trust me."

Nora didn't believe that for one second. "If you say so," she muttered.

His mouth twitched. "Did you come by to see my mom?"

"Oh, sorry, guess you're wondering why I'm here." She returned the smile, suspecting hers looked sheepish. "I wasn't expecting you to be here, but since you are, I wanted you to know that I got that other reporter to leave this morning."

His brows rose. "Did you?"

She nodded. "I saw her in town while I went with Adeline to work. All I had to do was hand her the file I had on her. One look at its contents and she left."

Beau chuckled. "That easy, huh?"

Nora nodded. "It's amazing how good research always goes a long way."

"It is," Beau said. "And I'm grateful for it."

She smiled and believed him too. She couldn't even imagine having reporters digging into the painful parts of her past. And now that she knew Beau and Austin, she felt even more protective to keep their grief private.

"What about the other reporter?" Beau asked. "Any word on her?"

"I actually think she left on her own," she explained, moving to Adeline's car and leaning against the hood. "I asked around when I was getting my coffee for Adeline and I. No one has seen her around. To double-check, I went to the inn, but she's checked out."

"Good." He removed his cowboy hat again and carved a hand through his sweaty hair. "That's good."

"So good," she agreed. "But that's not why I came by. I'm here to help with the damages."

His brows rose. "You really weren't kidding you wanted to help with that?"

"Kidding? Hell no!" She gasped, placing her hands on her hips. "We've got just over a week and a half to get the ranch in tiptop shape for the wedding. I'm not doing anything. So, use me any way you want."

Those raised brows lifted higher. His grin smug. "Any way I want?"

"Not like that," she said, nudging her foot into him. "I meant to fix things."

His grin widened. "What if I need fixing?"

"With a hammer," she sputtered, heat slowly spiraling into her core.

His eyes flared. "I could use a good banging."

"Oh, my God, stop." She pushed off the car, smacking him in the arm. Though the idea wasn't far from her mind either.

He chuckled. "All right then, if you're not up for *that*, let's put you to work."

And two hours later, she was still laughing, not only with Beau, but with all the cowboys on the ranch. A few she learned were friends of Colter's and would come to New York City. Neither Cotler nor Adeline knew yet, and Nora hoped no one spoiled the surprise.

Next to the barn, Beau finished cutting a large branch off a fallen tree before using a chain saw to cut the little branches. Nora grabbed the branch and dragged it along the ground until she reached the big pile that'd burn long into the night once lit.

Just as she dropped the branch, Beverly rang the bell on the porch and called, "Lunch is up. Come get it."

Dripping with sweat, covered in dust, with evergreen needles in her hair, Nora blew the hair out of her face and headed toward the house as all the cowboys aimed there too. Beau, though, was heading her way.

He met her at the porch steps. "After lunch, want to come for a ride?"

She lifted her eyebrows at him. "Back to this, are we?"

He threw his head back and barked a loud laugh. "I meant on a horse, but I'm not opposed to you riding me."

She'd never seen this smile before, and she promptly melted a little, before she elbowed him. "Shh, your mother is right *there*."

Unbothered, he kept laughing.

Trying to look as innocent as possible, she admitted, "I've also never ridden a horse."

"That's all right," Beau said, his laughter finally quieting. "Come on, Nora, give me a little trust. I'll keep ya safe."

She bit the inside of her cheek, but it occurred to her how much she did trust Beau. He had to be one of the steadiest people she'd ever met. A surprising revelation that made her head spin a little. The old her wouldn't have dared to get on a horse, especially after watching the crazy one nearly toss him into the dirt. She also wouldn't have spent any more time with Beau than she already had. Because comfortable was starting to get a little too comfortable. But she wanted a fresh start and that only happened with new adventures, and the truth was, she liked spending time with him. Probably more than she should. "Sure, I'd love to go for a ride." Closing the distance, she played along and said quietly, "As long as I ride you after the horse."

His eyes burned and grin turned wicked. "That's a promise, darlin'."

Beau had forgotten the peace that came from a quiet moment with a woman. The sweetness of riding along the vast Ward land and just existing, breathing, taking it all in.

Atop a thick dun quarter horse, he settled into the saddle, staring at the land his father had cared for as well as he had his family. The rolling hills, the cattle grazing off in the distance near the lake, the wildlife all around them. His father loved this land, respected it, and Beau missed him deeply. His wisdom, jokes and take-no-shit attitude. Most of all, he felt desperate to fill the hole of his father's absence.

Death was not kind.

Beau had tasted death's cruel touch with Annie. He'd never stop missing her, especially for Austin, but as he gazed at Nora, who looked stiff atop the small bay horse, who was old and lazy and a perfect horse to keep her safe, he was only looking at her. Christ, how she stirred him up. He'd wondered what his father would have thought about Nora. He bet he would've loved her.

"Let your hips relax," he instructed gently. She held the reins just fine, resting her hand on the horn of the saddle, but she was ramrod straight. "Feel the horse's movement."

She snorted, rolling her eyes at him. "News flash, cowboy. I don't even know what you're talking about."

"Lies," he said with a grin. "You've ridden me just fine."

She burst out laughing. "That is not the same."

His gaze fell to her hips as they rocked back and forth better now with the horse's movement as she relaxed. "Believe me, darlin', I've seen you move just like that. It's not something I can forget it."

She glanced away, cheeks flaming in color. "Well, I must be doing something right now then."

"I'd say so," he said, shifting against the saddle and the growing heat in his groin.

A comfortable silence fell between them as the grass swished between the horses' legs as they walked through the meadow. The beauty around him was impressive, but nothing compared to Nora. He tried to take his eyes off her, and failed miserably.

The afternoon sun made her glow, her tanned skin tempting him to taste her in all the places that made her squirm. Though the longer he looked, the more softness he saw on her face. "You like this?" he asked.

Her tender gaze met his, and she gave a slow nod. "You know what, I actually do." A long sigh escaped her that visibly relaxed her shoulders. "The quiet moments you get here and the family you have is very special."

"It is," he agreed, resting his hand on the pommel of the saddle.

"I actually could get used to this."

He couldn't hide the surprise slamming into his chest.

"What's with that look?" She laughed.

He stared at her, dumbfounded. "I never thought those words would come out of your big city mouth."

Her shoulders shook with her laughter, her eyes beautifully dancing. "Before I came here, I never would have said that, but I totally get why Adeline stayed here after she came back. In the big city, there's such a rush to do more, to be better, to exceed in every aspect of your life, but here..."

"But here?" he prompted.

A long sigh escaped her. "Here, it feels like I can breathe."

"Funny you should say that," he said in agreement. "I had been thinking the same thing a moment ago."

A quick smile rose to her face before she looked ahead of her, and there was a certain type of peace he hadn't seen on Nora's face before. He got that, the need for quiet. For a moment to just *think*, without the distraction of noise. And horses were the best therapy out there—the rhythmic movement, the gentleness of a horse, it gave something to a person. Something they would carry with them forever.

The comfortable silence continued. The horses' hooves stomping against the grassy ground until she surprised him again by asking, "Is it hard raising Austin alone?"

She'd been so careful not to cross too many emotional lines, and he was careful not to complicate this. But right now didn't feel complicated at all. It felt...*easy*. "Only when he was a baby, but now, he's a smaller version of myself. I'm just relieved he wasn't a girl. I would have been lost."

Her eyes crinkled at the corners. "He's a great kid. I'm sure that helps."

Beau nodded in agreement.

She watched him intently, her eyes searching his. Until that smile faded, and she surprised him for the third time in a matter of minutes. "Obviously, I didn't know Annie, but I'd think she'd be so proud of you and how you've raised Austin. You're an incredible father. I haven't been here long, and even I can see that."

His chest squeezed tight at the sudden swell of emotions. "Thank you for that, Nora."

"Just saying what's true," she said with a slight shrug, relaxing deeper into the saddle, like she'd ridden a horse a hundred times before now. The city girl didn't look so big city now. "It's amazing, really, being here, seeing what you've lost and how you all have handled all that with such grace. It makes me feel ridiculous for complaining about my crappy exboyfriend who broke my heart."

"Heartbreak is heartbreak," he countered firmly. "Don't undervalue yours. There is a big difference in our situations. Mine was full of love. Yours was full of a man who mishandled your heart. That's an entirely different heartbreak. He meant to break you."

She held his gaze, and he couldn't look away for all the same reasons he suspected she was staring at him. Something was there between them. Something that extended the burning heat between them. Something that was growing stronger as each day passed, no matter that both of them were trying to avoid it.

That same feeling held strong on the remainder of their ride and all the way back to the ranch. She kept sneaking him glances with sexy smiles, and he couldn't keep his damn eyes off her.

Until a few hours later, sitting on a hallowed-out tree trunk next to Beau at the bonfire, Colter asked, "Not a good idea, huh?"

Beau looked at his brother. He arched an eyebrow. "What's not a good idea?"

Colter flicked his chin at Nora, who was heading into the house with Adeline for the bathroom.

Beau snorted, glancing back at the fire. He liked Nora. A lot. And he wasn't exactly sure what to do with that. He'd promised himself not to get involved in a complicated relationship because of Austin, but he wondered…*what if?* What if Nora changed her mind and moved to Devil's Bluffs instead of Paris. Her best friend was there. He was there. "Apparently, I'm full of shit."

"Wouldn't be the first time." Colter grinned.

"Probably not the last either," Beau said dryly.

Colter nodded, lifting his brows in agreement.

Around the glowing fire, one of the cowboys played his guitar, strumming a classic country song while his girlfriend sang quietly. Whenever they had wood to burn, they always got together with the cowboys and their partners, who were all longtime friends now, and enjoyed beers, music and laughs.

Austin was in the house with his grandmother, and Beau could hear his son's laughter minutes before Nora exited the house with Adeline walking in stride with her.

Adeline returned to her spot between Colter's legs, while Nora sat next to Beau and said, "Austin's watching *Madagascar* in there. I don't think I've ever heard a kid laugh so hard."

"It was the part where the old lady beats up the lion, right?" Beau asked, brushing his thigh against hers.

Nora smiled. "How did you know?"

"He loves that part. Laughs like that every time."

Her smile warmed. "That's somehow cute and horrible all at once."

Beau agreed with a nod, as the fire crackled, sending embers high in the sky.

"So, Nora," Colter said. "I hear you're a cowboy now."

"Hardly," Nora replied with a snort. She picked up a long stick and poked at the fire. "I'm most certainly a city girl dressing up in cowboy boots." Boots she had borrowed from his mother.

Beau couldn't help himself. "And lookin' fine as

hell in them too." He waited for Nora's reaction to him openly flirting with her in public. He expected her to shut him down, but she surprised him once again when she gave him a sexy smile for all to see.

Her gaze held his, and he didn't look away, letting the sweet moment fall between them. A moment that neither of them was stopping. A moment that told everyone around them that something was brewing between them. A statement that Beau was damn glad was being made, but a statement he wondered how long would last.

So far, Nora seemed to be a woman to take one step forward and then a couple steps back. But he hoped, as her soft eyes held his, that this would last longer than tonight. That maybe he wasn't the only one wondering...*what if?*

Unknowingly breaking up the moment, Adeline yawned loudly.

"There's our cue to hit the hay," Colter said, hopping to his feet and pulling Adeline up to hers.

Beau rose only after Nora had, and he stayed next to her as they followed Adeline and Colter to his truck. Beau had made good on his promise, and Nora had ridden him in the meadow beneath the sun and sky before he'd rode her hard to satisfaction. But he only wanted more, and his gut tightened at the thought of her leaving tonight.

The strumming of the guitar slowly faded away as they strode by the barn. Just as they reached the shadows, he snatched Nora's wrist and tugged her into the shadows against him. "I haven't had enough," he growled against her mouth.

"What took you so long to take more, then?" She melted against him, her lips instantly parting for his tongue. The kiss was hot, urgent and left them both panting for more.

When he breathlessly broke away, he brushed his lips across hers. "What are you thinking?"

Her chest rose and fell with her heavy breaths as she laughed. "I was thinking that I planned on going back to Adeline's."

He arched an eyebrow at her. "Not thinking that anymore?"

She fisted his shirt, pulling him close. "No, now I'm thinking I want to stay right *here*."

"Good," he murmured, nipping her bottom lip. Tonight, he couldn't care about complications, about crossing emotional lines; he only wanted her to know the truth. "Because that's exactly where I want you to be."

Ten

A week and a half went by in a rush of repairs to the ranch, but the ranch wasn't the only thing changing. With every repair, Nora's heart felt lighter than it had in a very long time with unexpected healing. She found surprising joy in the horses, in spending time with Beau and exploring the gorgeous Texas countryside. Even Austin. She found herself loving her time with Beau's kid, reading to him at night, making him laugh, even family games night. And she loved being with Adeline again. Things felt like they were back in New York City before Adeline left.

She felt...*happy.*

Until the night of the bachelor/bachelorette, and everyone, including Colter's good friend, Riggs, along with a half dozen cowboys from the ranch, flew into New York City. Suddenly, the city she once loved felt colder, louder, busier and emptier than she could ever imagine.

She couldn't shake that feeling when they checked all the cowboys into the hotel across from her building. Or after they'd arrived at her place, and she left them all in the living room drinking beers.

Seated at the small desk in the bedroom she had shared with Scott, she felt the cruel, icy reminder of all that had gone wrong in her life. That she was broke, and that the home she thought had once been full of love had been nothing but a lie. She glanced out the window to the shops and restaurants below, glowing in the dark night. The street was busy, people ready for the excitement of the weekend and to put the weekday behind them.

"Is this where you work?" Beau suddenly asked.

She started and glanced over her shoulder, finding Beau was leaning his shoulder against the doorjamb. He wasn't cruel. He had never lied. It occurred to her now that hollowness, the deep-rooted sadness that had vanished while she was in Devils Bluffs had returned with a vengeance. "Only when I'm working from home," she explained. "There's a cute coffee shop I go to a lot around the corner."

He looked over the room, nearly taking up all the space. "I'm not sure I could ever get used to the tightness of everything here."

She couldn't really blame him there. If New York City had one thing negative about it, lacking space topped the list. "I never minded the coziness of the space before, but there is something freeing about the countryside."

He nodded in agreement. Looking even too tall for the area, he moved into her bedroom, taking a seat on her double bed, the only size she could fit in the room. She didn't have a dresser or anything else beyond the small desk, just the bed and a small table for her reading light. "I like the space. It's got you written all over it."

"Me. How?" she asked.

His voice lightened. "The whole space is full of warmth and life."

He *nearly* cracked through the ice in her veins. "You think I'm warm and full of life?"

An eyebrow slowly arched. "You wouldn't describe yourself that way?"

She restrained her sigh. She wasn't sure how she'd describe herself anymore, and being back in New York City only made everything all the more confusing.

Beau's brows drew together. "Wanna talk about what's upsetting you?"

Nora snorted. "That obvious?"

He gave a lopsided grin. "Just a little." He reached for her hand, held it in his strong grip. "What's up?"

She rose and moved to the door, spotting Adeline in the living room still with the guys, their laughter filtering down the hallway. Needing privacy, she shut the door and returned to sit next to Beau. "I didn't tell you the whole truth about Paris." At his frown, she hurried to explain. "Scott and I rented this place together. Ever since he left me, I've been carrying the rent and bills for the last six months, but I'm officially broke." She swallowed the worry nearly suffocating her and forced herself to continue, needing guidance more than ever. "I legit used the last of my savings to buy my flight to Devil's Bluffs and for my maid-of-honor dress." Whatever he heard in her voice had his fingers reaching for hers, squeezing tight. "I was really, *really* counting on one of my interviews from Paris coming through with a job that provided a stipend for an apartment and travel."

"You haven't heard anything?" he asked.

She shook her head. "I keep checking my email, but there's just nothing." She swallowed hard. "I have no idea what I'm going to do."

"What about your current job—"

"My salary isn't enough to pay for my life here," she interjected. "I've been eating into my savings ever since Scott left." She paused and suspected her expression revealed her past pain by his softening eyes. "If Paris doesn't come through, I'm going to have to move back with my mom."

He cringed. "That's a bad alternative, I take it?"

"That will be hell on earth," she retorted. "It's better when I don't live in driving range of my parents or the competition between them starts up again." She paused to sigh, picking at her thumbnail. "I need that job offer from Paris or I need to win the lottery."

His mouth parted when a soft knock sounded at the door.

Refusing to let her mood touch the celebration tonight, Nora forced her expression into netural. "Come in."

The door flew open, and Adeline strode in smiling, her cheeks already rosy from the two glasses of wine. "Sorry to interrupt," Adeline said, "but we've got girly things to do." She looked at Beau and pointed to the door. "Out you go."

"Yes, ma'am," Beau said. He winked at Nora before leaving the room.

She tried to ignore how her stomach flipped at that wink but failed miserably. Rising, she asked Adeline, "Makeup or clothes first?"

"Makeup," Adeline said.

"Okay, let me set something out." Instead of dwelling on all the things she couldn't change, she headed for her closet and got out clothing suitable for a night out in a country western bar.

When she came back out, Adeline had already gone into the adjourning bathroom. Nora left her clothes on the bed, and then joined Adeline in the bathroom.

"Are you going to tell me what's got you all emotional?" Adeline asked, applying foundation to her face.

Nora slid a headband over her hair to hold it back. She glanced over her shoulder, hearing all the guys laughing in the living room. Feeling safe that Beau wouldn't hear, and not wanting to go into the *real* reason, but needing to talk about something else entirely with her best friend, she took the foundation from Adeline and began dotting it on her face. "I'm okay. Honestly, it just feels a bit weird coming home."

Adeline's knowing eyes met Nora's in the mirror. "Beau got something to do with that?"

Nora laughed, rubbing the foundation in with a brush. "He's most definitely an unexpected surprise."

Adeline smiled, moving on to dusting blush on her cheeks. "The whole family is pretty spectacular."

Exactly! "I just didn't expect this to be so…"

"Wonderful?" Adeline offered. At Nora's nod, she added, "The Wards do have a way of getting into your heart."

Nora smiled. "I couldn't have said it better myself."

Adeline slid her arm around Nora, tilting her head to rest against her friend's. "I'm sorry that it's a bit weird being back here, but it's been really nice seeing you so happy."

"Thanks, Addie," Nora said. "Love you."

"Love you too." Adeline kissed Nora on the cheek and then reached for her eye shadow. "Now let's get beautified."

Nora laughed. "Yes, let's!" She pushed away the worry, the swirling, conflicting emotions and focused on making this the best night for Adeline and Colter.

By the time they left the bathroom, Adeline wore jean shorts and a black cami with black cowboy boots, dark, shadowy makeup on her eyes, looking as sexy as Nora had ever seen her. Nora opted for a short jean skirt and a tight red shirt that showed just the right amount of cleavage and belly, and red cowboy boots she borrowed from Adeline.

When they entered the living room, hearing a roar of laughter and rowdy cowboys, Nora was one step behind Adeline when suddenly everyone went quiet.

She entered the living room and discovered why. All eyes were on them. Every single set of them.

"Jesus Christ, Adeline," Colter breathed, rising and coming to her side immediately. He took her hand and spun her around. "I am one lucky, *lucky* man."

Adeline blushed, slapping his arm playfully. "All right, all right, enough of that. Let's get out of here."

The cowboys began filing out of Nora's condo, with Adeline and Colter following, leaving Beau the only one sitting on the couch.

His heated stare slowly raked over Nora before he met her gaze again, the sides of his mouth curving. He finally rose, every powerful step toward her seemingly removing the air around her. By the time he reached her, his gaze was on fire. When he stopped in front of her, he cupped her face, and she could barely breath. "Trying to kill me tonight?" he asked, dead serious.

She laughed. "What?"

"Looking like that." He dropped his chin, his heated gaze falling to her cleavage. "Is a sure way to kill me."

"Nah, it wouldn't benefit me to kill you just yet," she said. "I'm not quite done with you." She reached up, kissed him like she meant it and heard Beau groan behind her when she headed for the door.

She looked back. "Coming?"

"I want to be." He grunted, begrudgingly following her out of the door.

Beau had seen some things in his life, but nothing quite like the female bartenders, wearing corsets and skintight leather pants dancing atop the bar. Women and men sat on the stools beneath, their mouths wide open as the bartenders' poured shots of alcohol from the bottle into their mouths. A live band, with a male singer, was at the back of the room, in front of a dance floor, playing all the latest hits. But what drew the eye were the scantily clad women who made the men at the bar offer up their money easily.

"You look amused."

Beau glanced sidelong at Nora and chuckled, feeling the heat of the alcohol warming his stomach. She'd been out on the dance floor with Adeline for a dozen songs, while he'd been drinking with Colter at the circular high table. His brother was half in the bag, as were a good chunk of their group, so Beau slowed down on drinking to keep an eye on everyone. Even though they'd gone for a spectacular dinner at a rooftop restaurant with fine food and fancy drinks, the booze was hitting him too. "I am amused. This place—" he glanced to the partygoers on the dance floor, feeling the lust reverberating in the space "—it's a lot to take in."

Her eyes crinkled at the corners. "Exactly why I picked it. It's country, but with a little of New York City's flavor." She looked to the dance floor where a few of the cowboys were dancing with ladies nearly wagging their tongues out at them. "I thought you'd all fit in here the most, and it appears I was right."

"I'm not sure you could've picked a better place," Beau said, watching his brother spin Adeline in the dance before drawing her back in close. "They're both having a blast."

"As they should," Nora said, smiling sweetly.

Loving the warmth on her face, Beau stuck a finger into the rim of her jean skirt and tugged her between his legs. "I am curious, though, off all places, why *this* place?"

"Well, because Adeline and I have done the whole New York City dance club thing," Nora said, her gaze landing on her best friend again, sincere affection in her expression. "We've even done some wild things—"

"I'd like to hear about those wild things," he interjected. Especially in that tight, little skirt and revealing shirt she wore.

She pinched his arm. "Maybe some time." Her smile began to fall, seriousness stealing some of the playfulness from her eyes. "But Adeline isn't the same girl I partied hard with. She's got a little country in her now, so I thought this would be the best fit for her."

Beau leaned in and brushed his lips against hers. "You want to get a little country inside you too?"

Her eyes darkened, lust shimmering in their depths. "Always, cowboy."

He pressed his lips to hers but pulled back before

anything heated up. He took a quick look to ensure Adeline and Colter were still on the dance floor before he addressed Nora again. "Are you going to miss it here when you move to Paris?"

"I'm having conflicted feelings about New York City right now," she said. "On one hand, it's just so *alive* here—" she stepped closer to him "—but Paris is romantic and rich with history. It's a whole new experience, and I'm excited for that too. But that can only happen if one of the interviews I had pans out, and I actually get a job."

He ran his hands across her hips, loving how she felt in his touch. "They'll email."

"Not sure how you can be so sure about that."

"Because I'd hire you in a second. Smart, clever and resourceful, what else does an employer need?" He stroked her back. "You found out enough to get the reporters out of my town. You're a fine researcher. They'll figured that out soon enough."

She leaned into him, wrapping her arms around his neck. "Thanks."

Before she could kiss him, like he knew she was about to, hooting and hollering came from behind them. Beau glanced in that direction and burst out laughing. The cowboys, all of Colter's close friends, were spinning their dance partners in true Texas style. The place was interesting, but Beau could tell there were very few born and raised cowboys in the bar tonight. A cowboy had a way about him, and the only ones Beau saw that did were the ones there with them.

The ladies present were eating them up.

Beau glanced back at Nora, who laughed as she watched them showing these ladies how cowboys danced in Texas. He became trapped by her warm smile. There was no making sense out of it, but he felt a peace with her he hadn't felt since Annie left him. With Nora, the relationship was different, something new, something to fit the man he was now, not the younger man he was with Annie.

He watched her closely, remembering that she wanted an adventure, and now understanding that she picked this bar to match who she and Adeline were now. Nora didn't want the good girl image anymore, and Beau suddenly had an idea.

Obviously feeling his gaze, she looked at him. "Want to dance?" she asked, gesturing to the others.

Beau grinned. "Nah, I've got a better idea." Before she could object, he took her hand and pulled her toward the bar.

"Where are we going?" she called over the music.

When he reached the bar, the bartender gave him a sultry smile. He asked, "I'll take a tequila body shot." Her smile grew, but he turned back to Nora and grabbed her hips, hoisting her onto the bar.

"This is not happening," Nora gasped, her cheeks flaming bright red.

"But on *this* body," he said, holding Nora's gaze.

Sudden cheering erupted behind him, telling him that the Devil's Bluffs crew were all watching.

He moved the stool in his way aside then stepped between Nora's thighs, widening them.

"Oh, my God," she said again.

"Come on, wild girl," he said, winking at her. "Isn't this exactly what you wanted? You did plan the night here after all, and weren't you the one who said you wanted an adventure?"

She cursed and buried her face in her hands.

He chuckled as the bartender placed the tequila shot with lemon on top and salt next to Nora. Keeping his gaze fixated on her, he ran his hands up her thighs, nudging her skirt just a little higher.

He thought she might stop him, but as her face burned deeper in color, her eyes darkened with lust, and she gripped the edge of the bar tight. Damn, he liked this woman. Sweet but adventurous, things he didn't know were his type until this very moment.

Keeping his gaze on her, he grinned, slowly pushing her skirt higher and higher, enjoying the hitch of her breath as his thumbs slid across her inner thighs.

With enough skin exposed, he reached for the salt and then lowered his head, loving the surprise in Nora's eyes seconds before he licked from her knee, only stopping when he'd met her skirt. Her harsh shiver battered against his control.

Glancing up into her heated stare, he grinned at the way she nibbled her bottom lip. That mouth suddenly becoming his whole focus, the music and cheering behind him dulling as he sprinkled the salt along her thigh. He reached for the lemon and brushed it across her lips. "Open up, darlin'," he murmured.

Her sexy smile nearly undid him as she parted

her lips, and he placed the lemon inside her mouth. "Suck on that," he told her.

"Is that an order cowboy?" she asked playfully.

"Yes, ma'am, it is."

Her soft laugh brushed over him before her nose scrunched at the sour taste.

His slid his finger against her bottom lip and she opened enough for him to take out the lemon. Not waiting, he leaned down again and licked the salt gingerly off her leg feeling each and every shiver. When he reached her skirt, he rose and slid a hand across her cheek until he fisted his fingers into her hair, knowing how much she liked that.

With her lips parted, awaiting him, he threw back the shot, swallowing the bitter alcohol. Feeling her melt into his touch, he tightened his fingers, and then sealed his mouth across hers, tasting the lemon off her tongue, and devouring the rich moan she gave.

The kiss turned hot fast. Too fast.

She clung to him, moving closer, wanting so much more. He was inclined to give it to her, until he heard the clapping and roaring bringing him back into the present. He broke away chuckling, finding her lips swollen from his kiss.

Though instead of blushing, Nora wrapped her arms around his neck, drawing him closer. "Don't stop now cowboy. Let me taste that again."

So, he let her.

Again.

And again.

And again.

Eleven

The following days were a rush of finishing repairs at the ranch, ticking off the last of the wedding to-do list, with everyone slowly recovering from the wicked hangover from the New York City trip. Things were finally settling down when the final nail that went into the now fixed barn and the event planning company descended on the property. They brought flowers in abundance, a wedding canopy for the reception and dance floor, and truck after truck of tables, chairs and decorations. On the back deck at the house, Nora watched them work tirelessly to pull the wedding together for tomorrow.

Adeline would have her dream day, and Nora breathed a sigh of relief.

She really wasn't sure how things could feel so perfect and so messy all at the same time, but that's exactly how she'd been feeling. On one hand, blissful happiness soared through her. Every day with Beau only got better. She'd never felt so comfortable with any man. He didn't weigh her down, he lifted her up. She laughed more. She *felt* more. She was so damn satisfied, she felt that down to her bones.

But this wasn't the life she wanted. The plan never was to stay in Devil's Bluffs. She couldn't stay even if she wanted to—she had no money, and her job was in New York City. She kept checking, every day, every hour, for a response from Paris.

Still nothing.

The weight of that wanted so desperately to hit her, but she kept pushing it aside. *Adeline.* That's the only person who mattered now. Her best friend who deserved the best wedding, and as the event planner began unfolding the white chairs for the ceremony, Nora breathed a sigh of relief. The wedding would happen and would be what dreams were made of, and not even a tropical storm could have stopped that.

Movement in the distance caught her attention. She squinted, shielding her eyes against the bright sun, finally spotting Austin sitting on the tree swing, but not swinging. His head was down as he kicked at the dirt with his cowboy boots.

Even from this distance, she could tell he was upset. His little shoulders curved inward. She looked around for Beau or any of the family, but only found busy workers. Her heart ached for the little guy. She'd grown close to Austin since she'd arrived, spending more time with him than she had any kid before.

Austin was an easy kid to like. He was fun, full of life and made her laugh more often than not.

She stepped off the deck and hurried to him. The closer she got, the more she realized he looked even sadder than she realized. "You okay, buddy?" she asked gently.

Head remaining bowed, he shrugged his little shoulders.

Not sure if she was overstepping, but not willing to leave him, she took the swing next to him, wrapping her fingers around the metal chain. She lifted her feet and let the breeze swing her a little. "Do you want to talk about it?" she asked.

A long moment passed. Nora thought he planned to shut her out, but he surprised her, finally looking her way. "Today's my mom's birthday."

Nora tried to hide the surprise on her face. She probably failed miserably. "Is it really?"

Austin slowly nodded. "We're going to the cemetery soon. We always go on her birthday."

"That's a nice thing to do," Nora said, desperately wanting to reach for his little hand. "It's good to remember the people who aren't with us anymore."

"I hate going," Austin said sharply.

Nora stopped her swing then, digging her flip-flops into the sand. "Why?"

"Because my mom isn't there," he said, kicking at the dirt. "It's just a stone with her name on it."

Nora looked out, hoping to see Beau or another family member who would know exactly what to say. When she found no one, she swallowed the emotion creeping up her throat, trying to think of the right thing to say.

Before she could come up something, Austin continued, "My grandpa told me when you die you go to heaven. That's where my mom is. With my grandpa."

"I'm sure that's exactly where she is," Nora said, reaching for Austin's hand, unable to stop herself. Talking about his mother wasn't her place, but she couldn't watch him suffer without saying *something*. She squeezed tight. "Sometimes people need a place to visit, so that's why they visit gravesites."

"But she knows where we are," he said, voice trembling, tears welling in his eyes. "She can come home."

"You're right, she absolutely can." Nora squeezed harder. "I'm sure she comes and sees you all the time."

His eyes brightened a little. "Do you think so?"

"I know so." She smiled. "My grandma passed away a few years ago. She really loved butterflies, so whenever I see one, I always feel like she's dropping by to check in on me. I bet your mom does the same thing."

The warm smile Austin gave her in return touched on something very cold in Nora's chest. Something that gave her a feeling she'd never had before, leaving her utterly breathless. A feeling she couldn't quite put her finger on.

"Austin."

At Beau's voice, she snapped her head up, finding Beau heading her way. He was freshly showered, wearing jeans and a white T-shirt, along with his black cowboy hat, a bouquet of flowers in his hand. Her heart squeezed in joy. Until he got closer, and she saw his desolate expression.

Those flowers weren't meant for her.

"We need to go," Beau called to his son.

Austin jumped off the swing and then shocking Nora, he threw his arms around her neck and squeezed as hard as he could muster. "See ya later, Nora."

Nora's teary eyes shut. She hugged him back even tighter before she let go. This kid was wreaking havoc on her heart. "See you at the rehearsal dinner."

In Austin's classic way, he rushed off toward his dad, who was still approaching. Beau stopped when Austin reached him, handing him the flowers. "Take those to the truck. I'll meet you there in a minute."

"Okay," Austin said, taking the flowers from his dad and running toward the vehicle.

Nora couldn't look away from Beau as he approached. The haunted sadness she'd never seen before in his eyes. He was baring his pain, and it shattered her heart for him. For Austin.

When Beau finally reached her, he tucked his hands into his pockets. "Hey."

"Hi," she said, giving a smile that felt a little forced.

Holding her stare, he exhaled slowly before he dropped his chin, looking to his boots, kicking up dirt just like Austin had. "Did Austin tell you what today was?" he asked.

"Yeah."

His eyes met hers. "I'm sorry. I should have told you. I wasn't thinking—"

"Don't apologize. It's totally fine," she interjected, pushing her feet against the dirt to swing a little. The afternoon sun was hot, warming her skin. "I can only imagine how hard talking about Annie can be sometimes. You don't owe me anything."

A single brow lifted. "I don't owe you anything?"

Firmly reminded that Beau was only meant to be fantasy, a hot adventure, a cowboy who couldn't feel anything for her because his heart belonged to Annie, and she wasn't meant to feel anything for him back, she nodded. "Of course not, it's totally okay."

His eyes searched hers for a moment. Then he frowned. He stared for a long, *long* moment before he blinked. "Was Austin upset?"

"A little," she admitted.

Beau's head cocked. "Did you talk to him about it?"

"I did," she said, suddenly realizing that was a terrible move. "I hope that's okay. I didn't mean to overstep—"

"It's fine," he said gently. "I'm glad he felt like he could talk to you. What did he say to you?"

Nora drew in a long deep breath before answering. "I think it's better if you ask him. I feel like…" She paused, but then pushed on. "Our talk was ours. It doesn't feel right to share what he said to me. I hope that's okay."

Beau watched her again with an intensity she'd never seen before. He finally gave a soft nod. "Yeah, it's all right."

Desperation twitched at her to get off the swing, do *something,* say *something* meaningful, but all that came out was, "I'll see you later at the rehearsal dinner, then?"

A firm nod. "You will."

For how easy things had been between them, suddenly the space that separated them seemed taut with tension.

"I'm sorry," he said grimly.

"I already told you, don't be sorry," she said, forcing that smile again. "Everything is just fine." Needing to get away from the tension, the awkwardness humming between them, she jumped off the swing. "I'll see you later."

She turned before he could, and she headed for the house, knowing full well he was staring after her.

As he'd done every year since Annie passed away, Beau placed the flowers on her gravesite at the Devil's Bluffs cemetery. The land was beautiful, peaceful even. Full of mature trees and flowers in abundance. Farther down the row his father was laid to rest.

Emotion after emotion rushed through Beau as he read: Cherished wife and mother. Annie was that, and so much more. Her family still kept in touch, and Austin went to visit them out in Montana at least twice a year, but whenever Beau came to the gravesite, he always felt as if he should be doing more to keep Annie's memory alive. Then came the guilt that he was carrying on with his life without her. Battered sensations slammed into him. Until, like every time, resolve followed, and forgiveness came after that.

Annie would want him living a life filled with love and happiness.

He turned to Austin, whose head was bowed as he kicked at the dirt. A move he always did when something bothered him. "Nora wouldn't tell me what you two talked about. She's good friend to you, huh?"

Austin glanced up. He nodded. "I like her."

"Me, too." Beau smiled down at his son. He let that moment pass between them before he continued, "I can tell you're upset about something. Can you tell me what you two were talking about?"

Austin kicked at the dirt, harder than before. "I don't want you to get mad."

Beau placed a hand on his son's shoulder, feeling the tension running through Austin's little body. "I won't get mad."

"Promise?"

Beau nodded. "Of course."

A long pause. Then Austin looked back at the dirt he was kicking. "I don't want to come here anymore."

Beau felt like the words hit him hard in the chest. He locked his knees, fighting against the blow. Keeping the emotion out of his voice, he asked gently, "Why is that?"

Austin shrugged, indicating Beau hadn't hidden his feelings at all.

He exhaled slowly, nudging Austin's shoulder. "Don't hold back, bud, speak your mind."

Austin's sad eyes met Beau's, his chin quivering. "Can't we do something different than coming here and bringing Mom flowers?" Again, he shrugged, curling his shoulders. "Before Grandpa got real sick and couldn't remember things, he told me not to be sad for him that he was dying."

Beau could barely breath, barely move. The loss of the head of the family had hit everyone hard. Austin had seemed more centered about the death of his grandpa. Beau had wondered if that came from losing his mother, but now he wondered different. "I didn't know he talked to you."

Beneath his black cowboy hat, Austin peeked up at him. "He told me not to tell you. That it was just between me and him."

"It's good you have so many people to talk to," Beau said, squeezing Austin's shoulder tight. "We all need that, and Grandpa would have wanted you to be happy. What did he tell you?"

"He told me I didn't need to worry because he'd be with Mom after he died," Austin said. His son looked at him then, big tears in his eyes. "Do you think he's with Mom?"

"Yeah, I do." Beau couldn't fight the overwhelming feelings tightening his throat. Or the tears welling in his eyes. He went down to one knee, holding Austin's shoulders. "I bet they're together, watching over us, keeping us safe." He forced the sadness down to get his voice out. "What do you think we should do to remember Mom?"

"Grilling and games?" Austin finally offered after a moment to think about it. "She liked doing that stuff."

The only reason his son knew that was from the photographs he'd seen in Annie's album, and that nearly made Beau clench his chest at the pain of it. Through those photographs, Austin learned who his mother truly was. "Yeah, she did love fun get-togethers."

"We should do that then," Austin said, smiling.

Beau rose and glanced down at the grave with the flowers he'd set on the stone. He looked to his son. Damn, Annie would have been so proud of their kid. How good of a heart he had. How smart he was. How strong he was to voice his thoughts. "You're right, Mom and Grandpa would love to watch us have fun."

Austin's hat was knocked off as he threw himself at his father, and Beau hugged him back tight for all the reasons Austin needed the embrace. "Hey, Dad?" the boy asked, leaning away.

Beau smoothed back Austin's hair. "Yeah, bud?"

"Nora is nice."

He kissed the top of his head. "She sure is."

When they'd left the cemetery, Beau had felt lighter than he had when they arrived, but the conversation with Austin had stayed heavy on his mind all day, until the rehearsal dinner when Nora had barely looked at him. He'd messed up. It wasn't until he saw Austin sitting on the swing with Nora that he realized he hadn't told her about Annie's birthday and the tradition of visiting the grave. He'd seen her look at the flowers and her cringe that followed.

A damn idiot.

She'd been stiff next to him when they ran through the wedding ceremony, and he'd walked her down the aisle after the ceremony concluded. She'd immediately let him go and went straight to Adeline, without turning to say a single word to him.

All through the rehearsal dinner, she'd only talked to Adeline. She hadn't looked his way once.

Not after the salad, or the main course, or the dessert.

When she went to get herself another drink, he was ready to crawl out of his skin. Seated at their table in the golf course's restaurant, he leaped to his feet, his chair skidding behind him. He headed straight for the bar, and when he reached her, he said, "Stop ignoring me."

His voice came out harder than intended.

Nora spun with raised eyebrows. She took a quick look around, her gaze falling on Adeline and Colter before relief washed over her face. She took him by the arm and led him out the front door and turned the corner into the hallway. "What are you doing?" she asked.

He folded his arms over his chest. "Why are you ignoring me?"

"I'm not ignoring you," she said firmly. "So, there is no reason you need to be making a scene."

"I didn't make a scene," he said. "I made a statement."

She mirrored his stance, crossing her arms. "You sound grumpy."

"I am grumpy," he shot back. "You're ignoring me."

"I'm not ignoring you," she countered, but her guarded eyes told him a whole other story. "I'm just focusing on Adeline and Colter."

Leaning down, he brought his eyes to her level. "Liar."

She huffed, staring him down.

He stared right back. Until he realized how damn cute she looked with her face all scrunched, her eyes burning hell's fire at him. "Listen, I know I got today wrong."

"You didn't get anything wrong." She looked away. "I already told you that."

He tucked a finger under her chin, drawing her gaze back to him. "I did. I got things horribly wrong.

I should have considered how today would have made you feel. I shouldn't have brought the flowers out of my truck to give to Austin. I should have done a few things different, and I'm sorry for that."

"You don't need to be sorry," she said softly.

Her cautious eyes told him he did. "I clearly hurt your feelings."

"You didn't hurt my feelings as much as just reminded me of our original arrangement," she said, the hurt fading from her eyes. "I just got wrapped up in all this and felt emotional for some reason, and that was my mistake."

Like hell would he let her take a step back from him. He gathered her in his arms, wanting to get back what they had yesterday. Every day with her had been better than the one before. He was...*happy*. Happier than he'd been in a long time. Relief hit him as she didn't pull away. "I'm as wrapped up as you. I'm just terrible at all this now."

A pause. "You are?"

"Yes, I am." He slid one arm around her back, while he raised his free hand and caressed her cheek. "Please forgive me."

She leaned into his touch. "There's nothing to forgive."

"Are you sure?"

She gave him an honest smile and nodded. "I'm sure. It's just been an emotional day for everyone, and weddings only increase that." But there was a tightness in her expression that told him the damage had been done. She was only thinking that she'd be leaving soon. That barrier had slid back up, strong as a brick wall.

The thought of her leaving gutted him. He cupped her face and kissed her, desperate to keep her right there with him. He wasn't ready for this to end between them, and suddenly things didn't feel so casual anymore. He liked Nora. He liked how he felt around her. He loved how she treated Austin, and that Austin liked her too. She fit so seamlessly into his life that he couldn't fathom that this wouldn't work out.

His kiss grew more and more heated, as she angled her head and he deepened the kiss, pulling her tight against him.

Someone cleared their throat next to them.

Then, Colter said, voice amused, "If you two are done eating each other's faces, it's time for me to say a speech."

Beau broke away, breathless. Though Nora broke away laughing, Beau wasn't. He felt like the one great thing that had happened to him in a long time was slipping through his fingers.

Twelve

The next morning, Nora had awakened to a sunny sky in Beau's childhood bedroom after spending the night with Adeline and Beverly before the wedding. Everything should have been perfect. They were right on time for the wedding. Hair and makeup all went well. Adeline was in her dress and looked every bit the stunning bride, and they were just about to leave the bedroom and go out to the ceremony where all of Adeline's and Colter's family and friends were gathered.

Right before Adeline stepped into the hallway, she turned back to Nora and shut the door. "Before I walk down that aisle, tell me what you're not telling me."

Nora parted her lips, shocked by the sudden interrogation. "Um...*what*?"

At whatever crossed Nora's face, Adeline sighed, shaking her head. Her hair was pulled up in a romantic updo, a veil pulled down over her face, covering the heart-shaped neckline of her vintage lace wedding dress. "I can tell you're keeping something from me, so please, just tell me. Do you think I'm making a mistake marrying Colter?"

"God, no," Nora gasped, suddenly becoming aware of exactly what Adeline was talking about. They didn't hide secrets. Of course, Adeline would eventually feel something was up. "No, it's nothing like that."

"Then what is it?" Adeline said firmly. "What has been going on with you? I cannot walk down the aisle without knowing what you're not sharing."

Nora's heart clenched at the worry etched on Adeline's face. Ever since they'd gone to New York City, it had seemed impossible to hide the emotions that had been drowning Nora not only since Scott left, but Adeline too.

At Nora's silence, Adeline took her friend's hands, squeezing tight. "Please just tell me. You know me better than anyone. I can tell you've been keeping something from me. I don't want to make a mistake."

Nora shut her eyes, hoping to hell this didn't backfire. "You and Colter are perfect together," she said, opening her eyes, knowing there were tears in them. "You could not have picked a better partner to experience life with."

Adeline's brows knit. "Is it about Beau then?"

"No, Beau is…well, that's a longer conversation," she admitted, not even sure where she sat with Beau anymore. Annie's birthday shouldn't have bothered her. She wasn't emotionally involved, right? But then, why did she feel excluded? Why had it upset her so much that he hadn't told her about the birthday? Maybe she could have helped Austin make a card.

She knew why. She cared about Beau. A lot, if she was being honest with herself.

Knowing honesty was the only way forward now, she said, "I didn't want to tell you this until after your honeymoon because I didn't want any of this to overshadow your wedding. But I don't want you to worry, so…" She drew in a big deep breath. "I've been applying for jobs in Paris. I want to move there."

Adeline's eyes widened. "Paris, France?"

Nora laughed. "Yes. *That* Paris."

"Oh," Adeline said, her shoulders slumping a little. "When did you decide that?"

"It wasn't a quick decision to be honest," she explained. "But New York City isn't the same without you. I can't stay there anymore. And honestly, it's disappointment after disappointment. After Scott left, I've been struggling financially. Right now, I'm currently broke and I need something new and fresh, and you know how much I've always wanted to live in Paris."

"I do know that," Adeline said, pausing for a long

moment that seemed to go on and on. "I didn't know you were struggling so much with money."

"I didn't want to burden you with it," Nora admitted. "I've been a little stressed because nothing has come from my interviews with employers in Paris, and it looks like when I go home, I'll have to move in with my mom for a bit. I can't afford the condo."

Adeline cringed. "Okay, that sucks, but I wish you told me. I could have helped you."

"There's nothing you could have done," Nora said.

"I could have helped you struggle less," Adeline said. "I could have helped financially. You could have come here."

"My job is back home," Nora said. "But thank you. I know you would have done whatever you could have to help me."

Adeline examined Nora and drew in a deep breath, finally straightening her shoulders. "Well, I'm just glad you didn't see something in Colter that I was blind to."

Nora laughed, wrapping her arms around her best friend. "You should know better. I would never let you marry someone who wasn't perfect for you."

"I do know that." Adeline smiled, but there was sadness in her eyes too. "I know it'd be entirely selfish of me not to be insanely happy for you. Paris is just really far away."

"It is," Nora agreed. "But I can come here for vacations, and you can come to Paris. Besides, we can FaceTime like we always do."

"That's true," Adeline said, a little more sparkle in her eyes. She suddenly began laughing. "I seriously thought you maybe didn't like Colter or something. You never not speak your mind."

"Don't be silly. I love Colter," Nora said. "Especially how he treats you. If anyone is meant to be, it's you two. I just didn't want you to think about me during all this. Your wedding is about *you*. I wanted it to stay that way."

Relief washed across Adeline's face. "I love you for that, but I'm glad you told me." She straightened her shoulders and adjusted her veil again. "I do plan on crying about this later, since you're going to be way too far away from me, and may give you trouble for not sharing your pain and troubles with me, but you're right, now isn't the time to do that."

"It definitely isn't," Nora said with a grin. "How about we go and get you married?"

"That sounds really great to me." Adeline smiled.

Nora followed Adeline out the bedroom door and gathered her best friend's long train, holding it as they descended the staircase to the main floor.

Through the living room window, Nora saw everyone seated in the white chairs in front of the gorgeous arbor surrounded by colorful flowers. But the world seemed to narrow on one person alone.

Standing next to Colter, Beau was smiling at Austin walking down the aisle, carrying the rings on the pillow. Holy Jesus, he was gorgeous. All three of them wore tuxes with brand-new black cowboy hats, but she couldn't look away from Beau. His smile caught the breath in her throat. The happiness in those captivating eyes made her heart skip a full beat.

"Looking at something in particular?" Adeline laughed.

"Oh, just a really hot cowboy," Nora breathed.

Adeline lifted her brows. "You sure you want to go to Paris and not stay here in Devil's Bluffs?"

Nora considered, watching as Beau looked to the window as if he could feel her watching him. She felt the pull to him, to close the distance between them. The crazy part was, she could picture staying there. She could see herself enjoying the quiet life that she'd come to appreciate over the past couple weeks. She could imagine being a part of the Ward family. But that complicated everything, more than it already was.

Luckily before she had to answer, the wedding planner peeked her head through the doorway. "We're ready for you, Nora."

Nora turned back to Adeline and gave her the biggest hug she could muster. "I'm so, so happy for you, Adeline. You look absolutely stunning. I love you so much."

"I love you too." Adeline stepped away, readjusting her veil. "I'll see you down there."

"I'll be the one crying," Nora stated.

Adeline laughed, but there was a sweetness to the sound she'd never heard. Nora had never seen Adeline look so sure, so happy, so *ready* for anything in all the time she'd known her.

Feeling like fate got one thing very right by publishing the photograph of Colter and Beau saving the calf from the rapids, even though the reporters had done their best to monetize Beau's pain, she headed out the back door, hearing the soft music leading her down the flower-lined pathway.

She smiled at Colter, who smiled back, looking like a man who was about to win the lottery. Then her gaze fell to the crowd, some people she knew, some she didn't. She saw Adeline's mom and then her father, Eric, who Adeline had recently reconnected with. Nora couldn't even imagine her parents ever coming together, no matter the reason.

Love filled the air, and a sense of peace washed over her with every step. The closer she got, the more intense the pull she felt. Her gaze flicked to the immense power, and her chest took a hit under the emotion simmering on Beau's face. It didn't feel like she was walking down the aisle to support her best friend getting married.

It felt like she was walking toward her future.

The music filled the night as the guests continued dancing the night away under the white tent.

Most were taking full advantage of the open bar, and Beau was glad for it. No expense was spared on the wedding. Mom called it Dad's final gift to Colter, and Colter didn't put up much fuss after initially insisting on paying for the wedding himself. Neither Beau nor his brother were very good at arguing with their mother.

Beau moved toward Austin on the dance floor. The boy was still dancing with a date of one of the ranch's cowboys, having the time of his life. Adeline and Colter had already left to cheers and applause in the truck Beau had decorated with streamers and cans, with Austin's help. The night was still, twinkling stars blanketing the sky, but the air was hot enough that Beau had ditched his jacket before dinner, as had Colter, rolling his sleeves up.

When he reached his son, who was hopped up on cola and cake, he tugged on the back of Austin's shirt. "Bedtime, bud," he called over the live band that had been strumming classic country hits all night.

Austin spun on his heel. "Do I have to?" he asked with a pout.

"It's after midnight," Beau said firmly. "It's way past your bedtime. Thank the lady for the dance."

Austin turned to his dance partner. "Thanks for the dance, ma'am."

"You're welcome, kid." She tapped Austin's cowboy hat.

Austin grinned from ear to ear before he took off

running toward the house. Beau followed him, spotting his mother waiting with them. With laughter and music fading with his steps, he made it to his mother then offered his arm to her, and they headed down the lit pathway leading the house.

"Today was a good day," he said to Mom.

She gave her classic sweet smile, the exhaustion from the long day weighing on her face. "Very much so. Your father would have loved today."

Beau's chest tightened. His father's absence had never felt as strong as it had today since he passed away. He should have been there. "I hope I did him justice in my speech," Beau said.

Mom patted his arm. "Of course, you did, honey. Funny and sentimental for your brother, and a wonderful tribute to Dad. He'd be very proud of you." Her smiled warmed. "I'm very proud of you."

"Thanks, Mom," Beau said, as they weaved their way toward the house. The wedding planner had done an incredible job. He truly didn't know how they turned a cattle ranch into something so beautiful. Though the abundance of flowers, giving off a rich scent, surely had to help.

As they drew closer to the house, Mom said gently, "Nora is good one. I really like her."

Beau chuckled, glancing down at his mother. "I was wondering when you were going to say something about her."

Mom's laughter cut through the silence. "Impossible for me not to say something when you looked at her like she was walking down that aisle to you."

Not wanting to get into any of that with his mother, or how complicated all this was between them, he stopped at the back deck, leaned down and kissed her cheeks. "Thank you for watching Austin tonight."

Mom lifted her brows. "You're not going to comment on what I said?"

Oh, how she'd love that he was sure, but even he didn't have it all figured out yet. He dipped his chin, bringing his gaze to her level. "No, Mother, I'm not."

She shook her head at him in her motherly way. Blessedly, she let the matter go. "I don't mind watching my baby, honey. Go, enjoy yourself."

Austin ran over then and plowed into Beau. He gave his kid a tight hug. "Behave yourself at grandma's," he told his son.

"I will." Austin yawned.

Mom laughed. "I think he's too tired to do anything but behave."

"Probably right." He pointed at Austin. "Still behave. I'll see you tomorrow."

"Bye, Dad," Austin said, taking his grandmother's hand and heading up toward the back door of the house.

The moment they went inside, Beau turned back to the party, shoving his hands into his pockets. Even he couldn't stop thinking about *that* moment. When he'd seen Nora start walking down the aisle, he couldn't take his eyes off her. More than beautiful, Nora stunned him stupid. He couldn't think. He couldn't move. All he could do was watch her—all damn day. The way she cried happy tears for Adeline during the ceremony. The way she spoke proudly and laughed during her speech at her long, beautiful friendship with Adeline. The way her stunning stare met his whenever he looked at her.

Feeling like she was all he needed to see now, he went looking for her. She'd gone to the bathroom after they'd dance, and Beau thought it a good time for Austin to go to bed. Now on the hunt for her, she was nowhere in sight. Not on the dance floor. Not at the bar. Though as he looked out at the lake behind the band, he saw her walking down the lit pathway to the water.

He hurried his steps, urgency driving his steps.

When he reached her, he moved next to her. She stared out at the glistening black water, the reflection of the moon shining against the ripples. He noted the sadness in her gaze. Guessing what was on her mind, as much as it was on his, he asked, "When is your flight tomorrow night?"

Nora visibly swallowed, glancing his way. "Eight o'clock."

"I can take you to the airport," he offered.

"That would be really great." She smiled. It looked forced.

A thousand things suddenly weighed on his mind. A million things to say to her. And yet the words he sought so desperately to find remained out of reach. A long, heavy moment passed before he said, "Nora."

"Don't," she said, turning to him, her voice raw with emotion. "Please just don't. I don't want to talk about *that*."

"You don't think we need to talk?" he asked.

"We can't talk," she whispered. "It will only complicate this more." Then she was on him and cupped his face, bringing his mouth to hers, and he fully understood, because saying words complicated everything. Declaring what seemed so obvious would irrevocably change both their lives.

Her kiss was full of need, full of passion and full of something that tasted so sweet. He kissed her lips, her neck. He grabbed her bottom, thrusting her up against him, rubbing against his erection.

But it wasn't enough. Not nearly enough.

Needing her, he broke away to pull her farther into the shadows at the end of the railing. Lips pressed against hers, he murmured, "You want me, Nora?"

"Yes, right now, right here," she rasped.

Spinning her around, he lifted her dress and tucked her panties to the side. "Stay right there," he told her, and he didn't only mean for now. He took a condom from his wallet, and she glanced back at him, her eyes hooded, filled with desperation for all the reasons he felt desperate too.

They controlled nothing, but this moment.

He unzipped his pants and exposed his cock,

quickly sheathing himself. Stepping closer to her, his thighs touched her soft, warm legs, his hands sliding over her round, plump ass.

"Look what you do to me, darlin'," he growled, holding the base of his cock while he dipped down and slowly entered her. The soft moan that followed nearly undid him as he slid one hand into the front of her dress, the other arm going around her waist holding her back tight up against him.

"What you do to me too," she breathed, grasping his forearms with her hands, fingernails digging into his skin.

Her touch was fire. Her body was fire. All of her was *fire*.

He wasn't sure if it was her hold that did it, her words, or just *her*, but any control he had to be gentle faded in an instant. Holding her against him, he dropped his head into her neck, breathed in her floral scent and rode her hard. Rapid thrusts that felt oh-so-right made him strain for release. He gritted his teeth, fighting against the groans wanting to shatter the silence.

"Beau," she gasped, a sound beautifully made just for him.

A sound he suddenly wanted to hear every single night of his life.

"I want to keep you here," he told her, damn the consequences. "Right here, safe in my arms."

Holding her tight to him, he rocked his hips into

her, claiming what felt like it belonged to him. With that claim, he felt her soften—her trembling legs, the passion slamming into her. The need overwhelming them both. And he fell into the same sensations, with every thrust into her, her convulsions squeezing him tight.

Even as she fell into her orgasm, and he followed, bucking and jerking against her sweet bottom, he was desperate to hold her right there.

Because tomorrow she would go home.

All he had to do was find a way to stop her.

Thirteen

Seated on the bed the next morning, Nora stared down at her cell phone, disbelieving what her eyes were telling her. She blinked, but the message remained.

We are pleased to offer you the position of Marketing Manager at Monet.

Everything else written in the email blurred after that, but she got the gist of it. Tomorrow, she needed to have a call to talk more about salary, and she was expected in Paris in a few days' time. Her hands shook as she sighed and set down her cell phone, glancing at her packed bag.

She'd waited and wanted this job offer, and yet now she felt torn in ways she never expected.

Beau.

He was a surprise she hadn't seen coming. In the deepest parts of her heart, she knew if Beau lived in New York City, she'd probably not leave for Paris, even if everything inside her told her not to repeat her mistakes. But Beau wasn't like anyone she'd met before. The past two weeks were her happiest with any man.

Bottom line, he didn't take from her life, he gave to it.

"Nora," Beau called from out in the living room. "They're leaving."

She set her phone down on the bed and hurried out of the bedroom, greeted by the warmth of Beau's smile. God, when he looked her like *that*. His whole face brightened, leaving her feeling like her being there somehow made his life better. She honestly had no idea how she was going to leave him. No idea at all.

"Come on," he said, offering his hand.

She happily took it and hurried behind him as they headed out the front door. Waiting next to a SUV that would take them to the airport to their honeymoon in Greece, Adeline and Colter smiled.

"All ready to go?" Nora asked when she reached her best friend.

"God, yes," Adeline said, wrapping Nora in a gigantic hug. "My dream honeymoon is awaiting me, and I want to get there."

"Take so many pictures," Nora said, hugging her back tightly. "I need to live vicariously through you."

"You know I will." She stepped back, giving Beau and Colter a quick look. When they were deep in their own conversation, she looked at Nora again. "Any word on jobs from Paris?"

"No decisions have been made yet," she said, not ready to explain all the things heavy on her mind.

Adeline's eyes brightened. "You know you could stay here. You could live with Colter and I until you get a job and get your finances back in good shape."

"Gosh, do I love you," Nora admitted.

"Well, that's not a no, so I have hope yet." Adeline gave Nora another big, tight hug. When she leaned away, she added, "But I'll be insanely excited for you to go to Paris too. We'll make it all work. No matter what."

"We will," Nora said, her throat tightening. Everything was changing. Adeline was married now. Nora had her eyes set on Paris. For so long it had just been the two of them. But Nora didn't want Adeline to worry about a single thing. "Now go have fun. I'll talk to you when you get back."

"Don't feel like you can't call if you need to talk about anything."

Nora would never, but she just smiled and waved, as Adeline moved to Beau, giving him a hug too before she stepped next to Colter.

"Thanks again for everything you did for the wedding," Colter said, opening his arms to Nora. "We couldn't have done all this without you."

"You're welcome," Nora said, squeezing him back. "I was happy to do it. Take good care of my girl in Greece."

Colter winked. "You know I will."

Nora laughed. Her smile stayed in place as she watched as they got into the back seat of the SUV. They rolled down the window, giving a wave as the driver drove off.

"We did it," Nora said when the SUV vanished.

"Did what?" Beau asked, glancing sidelong.

"We didn't let anything fall apart and now they're on their way to Greece, a happily married couple."

Beau chuckled, wrapping his arm around Nora's neck, tugging her close. He kissed the top of her head. "Yeah, we kicked ass. Was there any doubt?"

"Never," Nora replied. "Not even a tropical storm could have stopped us." She turned a little, looking at his gorgeous smile. Those penetrating eyes staring down at her. All of this—being here in his arms, in Devil's Bluffs, in the country—shouldn't have felt so right, and yet it did. It felt perfect, in fact.

Too perfect.

"I should finish up packing," she said, pulling away, refusing to allow those confusing thoughts to dig deeper into her mind.

His eyes tightened at the corners. "That's all right.

I should go make sure Austin's not getting into any trouble."

"Okay, I'll see you in a bit." Nora strode up the porch steps before she tugged him back into her arms and refused to leave.

Once inside, she headed for the bedroom and sat on the bed, reaching for her phone again to read that job offer, when the phone began ringing. She didn't recognize the number, but the area code was from New York City. Nora answered the call. "Hello."

"Hi, is this Nora Keller?" The woman's voice was strong, firm.

"Yes."

"Hi, Nora, this is, Claire, Adeline's old editor at the gossip blog." The original blog that had posted the photograph of Beau and Colter and made the Ward brothers go viral.

"Um, yes, hi," she said, stumbling over her words. "I'm sorry, Claire, but Adeline has already left for her honeymoon."

"That's not why I'm calling."

Nora froze on the bed, staring out the window to the horses grazing in the meadow. "What can I help you with?"

"I have a proposition for you, actually."

A dozen possibilities rushed through her mind. None of them made any sense. "What proposition?"

A pause. Then, "It has come to my attention that you've been close with Beau Ward."

All Nora's inner alarms were blaring. She rose,

moving to the window, staring out at the young horses playing together. "Would you care to tell me how you know that, and why is that any of your business?"

Claire's voice hinted at amusement, not shame. "I suppose before I present my offer, I should explain myself."

"Yes, I think you should," Nora said gruffly, hugging one arm around herself.

Claire's voice came out as smooth as silk, obviously unperturbed. "A week ago, one of my reporters came back to me, suggesting the story had died."

Nora nearly snorted. Of course, they did. Nora had made sure of that.

"I had a sense that more was going on than he was letting on," Claire continued, "so I sent a private investigator down to Devil's Bluffs."

Nora's teeth ground. "Your point?" How dare this woman?

"My point is that I learned of your closeness with Beau through my PI," Claire explained. "Here is my proposition for you: I want to know more about Beau. I want his story. I realize that you have a personal attachment to him, but I also know that you're flying back to New York City later tonight, so it cannot be that much of an attachment."

"If you think I'm going to tell you details about his life, you are sorely mistaken."

"Oh, I know you won't do it for free." Claire paused. Then, "That's why I'll pay you twenty thousand dollars for the scoop of Beau's life. For the story that my reporter failed to get."

Nora blinked. "You'll pay me twenty thousand dollars to do a tell-all of Beau's story?"

"You're not dating, right?"

She wouldn't give her any fuel. "No, we are not a couple."

"Could you use that money?"

Now Nora snorted. "Ah, yeah, the money would change my life."

Claire's voice lightened. "What is your answer then—yes or no?"

Nora couldn't help but hesitate. She'd never sell anyone out, but the amount of money she offered made Nora worry for Beau. Claire had no intention of letting this story go, and that's when Nora realized, their plan to thwart the blog had failed. "No, I'm not saying no."

"Ah, this is great news then," Claire said. She began to ramble about the plans they needed to make. That she'd send a driver over to pick up Nora once she returned to New York City, and Nora would have to sign a contract and then she'd receive the check.

"You've misunderstood me," Nora said, cutting Claire off. She knew gossip blogs didn't have many morals, but the gall of this woman was unbelievable. "I'm saying *hell no*. I would never take any money to tell Beau's story. You should seriously be ashamed of yourself."

"Business is business, my dear."

Nora restrained the curses that sat on the tip of her tongue. "It's not business you'll get from me."

"A shame," Claire finally said after a long moment. "Please give my congratulations to Adeline."

The line went dead.

"What a bitch," Nora grumbled, staring at her phone. How Adeline had worked for that woman for so long was totally beyond Nora.

Worry began to fill Nora yet again that Beau and Austin would never get out of the blog's grip. She hurried out of the bedroom, running outside until she met a cowboy. "Hey! Have you seen Beau and Austin?"

"They left ma'am," the cowboy said.

"Left? Do you know to where?" she asked, surprised he didn't come to say goodbye.

The cowboy shrugged. "Not too sure, ma'am. I just know he left a few minutes ago."

"Okay, thank you."

Nora returned to the house, heading back into the bedroom, and snatched up her phone. She dialed Beau once. No answer. She wondered if the car taking Adeline and Colter broke down or something, as she searched her contacts, finding Beverly's number.

"Hi, Nora," Beverly said, voice usually tight.

"Hi, Beverly. I don't want to worry you, but have you seen Beau and Austin?"

She expected questions, even ones of concern. What she didn't expect was the bomb Beverly dropped on her.

"I'm sorry, Nora, but he's asked me not to tell you."

The blood drained from her face, her chest heaving as she dropped onto the mattress. "Did he say why?"

"Oh, honey, he heard you talking on the phone."

Emotions hit Nora like a freight train. She recalled what she'd said if he heard only one side of the conversation. *You'll pay me twenty thousand dollars to do a tell-all of Beau's story? No, we are not a couple. No, I'm not saying no.*

He knew she needed money badly, and he obviously hadn't heard her turn down the offer because of Claire's talking. "I…he misunderstood me." No, she realized with a heavy heart, he thought the very worst of her.

"I did tell him that was probably the case," Beverly said. Then a long pause. "Just talk to him, dear."

Nora could barely hold it together as she said a goodbye to Beverly and ended the call. She gripped her phone in her hand, then called Beau again. Once. Twice. Three times. Until the realization dawned on her. He'd had an out, and he'd taken it, and she needed to do the same damn thing.

Tears dripped from her eyes onto her arm as she lifted her phone again and pulled up the email from the company in Paris again.

I am delighted to formally accept the offer, and I'm thrilled to join the team. Would tomorrow at 9:00 a.m. Central European Time work for our call?

Fourteen

One week had gone by, and even during that time, the conversation Beau had heard from Nora still repeated in his mind. It did not matter that he'd gone back to his regular work schedule, or that Austin had returned to school, those words were there on his mind. Every single day. Every single minute.

You'll pay me twenty thousand dollars to do a tell-all of Beau's story? No, we are not a couple. No, I'm not saying no.

He never believed Nora would sell his story, but he'd heard every damning word. He wasn't even thinking when he got Austin into his truck and left, driving through Ward land until he ended up at his mother's, telling her what happened. She'd encouraged him to talk to her, but he, and Austin, took a couple of horses out for a ride instead.

Even now, he still couldn't believe she'd choose the money, and as the days went by, he began to see that quite possibly he'd misunderstood the conversation. Though he realized this was for the best anyway. They could never work, no matter how much he'd wanted it. He'd said he wouldn't do complicated, and things suddenly had gotten complicated.

Instead of taking his mom's advice and calling her, he let her go.

Long after his workday ended, and the weekend finally arrived, Beau grabbed some more firewood from the ATV that he and Austin had used to drive through Ward land to the best camping spot. A longtime tradition for the family was to camp out, surrounded by a lake, forests and a perfect flat spot in the meadow for camping.

When Beau turned back around, Austin was sitting by the campfire, poking the fire with a stick, after they'd gone for a swim in the lake. He looked like he'd lost his favorite toy. The same expression that had been there all week.

"What's up, bud?" Beau asked, taking a seat next to his son on the wooden log.

Austin shrugged.

Beau nudged his shoulder with his arm. "Out with it. Doesn't help anything to keep stuff inside."

Austin glanced up. His blue eyes conflicted. "I miss Nora."

Beau felt the strands of his heart pull tighter. "I

miss her too." Nothing seemed the same in Devil's Bluffs now. The loss yanking him into the darkness he'd fought a long time to crawl out of.

"She didn't even say goodbye," he said, his voice sad.

Beau wrapped an arm around Austin. "Sometimes life gets in the way like that."

"Can we call her?"

Beau barely got breath into his lungs. The hope and dismay on Austin's little face were all the reasons he was careful about letting women in his life. Austin had obviously formed a deep connection with Nora, and he was mourning her absence. "Next time you're with Adeline, you can ask her if you can FaceTime Nora."

Austin poked at the fire again. "She'd want to talk to me, I think."

Beau shut his eyes, reeling at the sureness in Austin's voice. Because he was right—Nora had showered Austin with affection. Beau was torn in a million pieces. He couldn't forget what he heard. He couldn't forget that maybe he'd judged the conversation wrong. He couldn't forget that Nora was adamant about not even talking about the possibility of them being together. He couldn't forget that she didn't want a life in Devil's Bluffs with him. Everything from the moment he woke up to when Austin and him crashed after a day of hiking, exploring, swimming and roasting marshmallows on the campfire, everything felt...*wrong*.

The biggest complication of all. He loved Nora, of that he was sure. Only love would make him feel this upside down without her.

A helicopter sounded off in the distance, getting closer and closer as the minutes drew on. Until the black helicopter began circling around them, finally beginning its descent to land.

"Who's that?" Austin said.

"Uncle Colter," Beau replied, rising. "Stay here." Sure, he expected his brother and Adeline to come home from their honeymoon, but he hadn't expected a visit to the campsite. He hadn't turned his phone off. The only recent phone calls had been the numerous ones from Nora before she'd left Devil's Bluffs.

He jogged toward the helicopter as his brother cut the ignition. By the time Beau reached Colter, he realized he wasn't alone. Adeline was marching toward Beau, glaring daggers at him.

He stopped short. *Shit!*

"What is wrong with you?" Adeline asked when she reached him.

"I'm not sure," Beau said, glancing at his brother. Colter had his arms crossed over his chest, shaking his head in disapproval. Beau winced, setting his attention back onto Adeline's glare. "But you look like you're going to tell me."

"Oh, yeah, I'm going to tell you," Adeline said. "Because I just can't believe you." She paused, blinking rapidly. "Actually, I totally didn't believe what happened. I really couldn't believe any of it."

Beau cocked his head. "I can probably explain if you explain what you're talking about."

Looking more than frazzled, she said, "Beverly told us what happened with Nora."

Good, saved him from explaining. "And this makes you mad at *me*?"

Adeline's eyes widened. "Who else would I be mad at?"

Beau snorted. "It's complicated."

"No, it's anything but complicated," Adeline snapped. "You heard one side of a conversation and didn't hear anything after it. Then instead of manning up and going to talk to her, you just let her leave. What were you thinking?"

Beau frowned. "I gave her an out that she was looking for."

Adeline's nostrils flared. Colter raised his brows at his wife and then interjected, "How do you know she wanted an out?"

Beau sighed, running his hands through his hair. "Because I could tell."

"That's a bullshit answer," Adeline snarled, pointing at him. "You both are scared of being in a relationship where you have to change to be together, at least own that. You weren't expecting to find this beautiful happiness again. And Nora is so damn terrified that what you have can't possibly be real because, for her, love lies."

Beau crossed his arms. "I'm not scared."

"Then why did you not beg her to stay when we all see how much you love her?" Adeline asked, incredulous.

He looked to his brother. Colter shrugged. "Seems like cowardice, Beau."

Beau drew in a long deep breath and blew it out

slowly. To Adeline, he said, "She wouldn't even talk about staying with me the night of the wedding. I tried to talk with her. She wouldn't even discuss it. So, yeah, when I heard the call, I did think the worse. Once I cooled off, I knew I heard things wrong, but it didn't matter. She didn't want to stay here. She didn't want me."

Not letting him off the hook, Adeline threw her arms up in frustration. "Did you ask her?"

Coldness sank into Beau's veins. He locked his knees. "I did not."

"You have no idea how hurt she was by Scott," Adeline said, more gently this time. "He is a horrible person and treated her like she did not matter at all. While Nora is strong, and always looks for the bright side, I saw a piece of her die when that happened. A piece that I saw come back to life when she was here with you."

The world spun a little as Adeline's words sank in deep.

"She needs love, Beau," Adeline continued. "She has terrible parents who treated her like a game they were so desperate to win. She's been failed by every boyfriend, and absolutely crushed by the last one. I know Nora like I know myself. She was looking for a reason to stay. All you had to do was give her one."

Colter smiled and nodded. "She's a keeper, brother."

Beau thought back on all his steps, every action he'd taken, all the things he said and all the things he didn't. "Shit," he finally breathed. "I've fucked up."

"Those are bad words," Austin snapped.

"You're right," said Beau, glancing over his shoulder to Austin standing behind him. He ran a shaking hand through his hair. "Don't ever say those words. I shouldn't have." Turning back to Adeline, she still glared at him. "I didn't think—"

"No, you most certainly did not think," Adeline said, cutting him off.

Beau shifted on his feet, his fingers fisting his hair. "Have you talked to her?"

"Yes, I have."

"Is…is she…"

"No, Beau, she's not okay," Adeline said. "She knows you misunderstood her, but she also knows that instead of answering her calls, you shut her out."

Beau winced, running his hands over his face. He'd thought she wanted an out—and he cowardly gave her one, believing whatever he had to do to make that happen. What had he done? He'd become one of the assholes in her life.

"Nora's sad?"

Beau turned around, dropping to a knee in front of Austin, who stared with pained eyes. "I'm going to make this right. I promise." He rose, turning to his brother. "Borrow a plane and fly me to New York City."

"Wouldn't matter even if I did," Colter said. "She's not there."

The ground dropped out from under him, his lungs crying out for air. "Where is she?"

Adeline said, "Paris."

Fifteen

Quaint cafés, historic architecture, the arts, stunning fashion, the City of Love was everything Nora thought it would be and more. Seated at a table in a café on the corner of a street, she sipped her cappuccino, listening to a woman's heels clicking against the sidewalk that once would have been cobblestone. Beneath a bright sun and blue sky, she sat under a white canopy, pedestrians striding by and cycling down the road. Under the canopy, there were no cell phones, no laptops, no electronics in sight. Only people enjoying reading a newspaper or chatting to someone over coffee.

Paris was magic. Everything should have been perfect, only it wasn't. That same feeling of hollowness in her chest she'd been running from hadn't gone away after leaving New York City and reaching her dream of Paris. The emptiness had gotten bigger. She'd tasted something bigger than a dream of a gorgeous city full of magic, she'd tasted happiness.

And now that was gone.

Nora missed Beau and Austin. She missed Adeline and Colter. Even to her own surprise, she missed Devil's Bluffs. The calmness. The quiet. The scents of nature. She missed it all with an ache in her heart she couldn't push away. She wanted to hate Beau for thinking she'd betray him that way, but she couldn't. He'd thought he heard her agree to sell him out, and instead of her chasing after him to explain, she left too.

Feeling like suddenly she'd gotten everything wrong, she finished her cappuccino and paid her bill then left. She passed a bakery, inhaling the delicious aroma of warmed croissants. Paris had similar smells as New York City. Sometimes the air smelled of pollution. Other times like blooming flowers. But she inhaled the city aroma, even the scents that weren't so pleasing to imprint them into her mind.

She soon reached one of the historic buildings in the heart of Paris that had been renovated from the inside out, and made it into the lobby. She passed women and men dressed in high fashion on her way up the elevator to the fifth floor of the office building.

The doors chimed open, and she entered the office, the sign behind the receptionist read: Monet.

Sure in her steps and ready to fix the emptiness

in her chest Paris couldn't fill, she knocked on her boss's door. Seated behind her desk in the corner office, Gisèle Monet held elegance in everything she did. From her fashion sense to her application of her makeup to her hairstyles, she was as beautiful as any high-paid actress in New York City.

"Come in, Nora," Gisèle called, waving her in. Her English was spot-on, but her accent was gorgeously French.

"Good morning," said Nora, taking a seat in the client chair across from the desk. "How are you?"

"I am well, ma chérie." Gisèle folded her hands on top of her desk, her nails freshly manicured and painted. "What can I do for you?"

Nora drew in a deep breath for strength before she laid it all on the line. "I'm really sorry, Gisèle, but I have to give you my notice."

"Oh, merde!" Gisèle exclaimed. "May I ask why? Is it something we've done to upset you into leaving us?"

"No, of course not," Nora said quickly, feeling heat rising to her cheeks. "I love working for you. I love the company and the people, and I even love Paris, in fact."

Gisèle cocked her head. "What exactly is the problem, then?"

"I miss my friends back home." Nora hesitated, choosing her words carefully, not wanting to pour her heart out to her boss. "I've tried to get past missing them, but I can't." Nothing felt right about Paris, even if she'd miss her mornings at the café and the to die for coffee.

Gisèle's expression pinched as she rose. With long strides, she made her way around her desk, even moving elegantly to take a seat next to Nora. She crossed her slender legs, her posture perfect. "A life is no life at all without friends, so I do understand," she said gently.

Nora nodded in agreement. She'd been running away just like Beau did too. She'd been so dead set on finding this new version of herself that she forgot just how awesome the old version truly was. The one that she'd been with Beau. The real *her*. Somewhere, somehow, everything was so simple. Home wasn't in New York City. It also wasn't in Paris. Home, a revelation even to herself, was in Devil's Bluffs. "I need to go home, and I'm afraid I need to do that right away."

"You must do what you must," Gisèle said with a firm nod. Her head tilted, eyes narrowing in concentration at Nora. "But I must say, Nora, I have grown quite fond of you, and I don't want to see you go." She tapped her finger over her plump, red-painted lips. "Would you perhaps be open to staying on with us, but working remotely?"

"Yes!" Nora agreed quickly. "Are you sure, though? You wanted someone here."

"Ah," Gisèle said. "A company will not last if it is not flexible, and good workers are very hard to find. Your research since you've been here has already helped us grow our social media accounts twenty percent. I'd be foolish to let you go."

"Gisèle," Nora said, her heart in her throat, "I don't even know what to say, but thank you, of course, I'd love to stay on and work remotely for you. This is my dream job."

"Excellent," Gisèle said, slapping her hand against the armrest of the chair. "Your wage would stay the same, but instead of your apartment allowance—" which didn't pay for a full apartment in Paris but most certainly helped with cost "—we'll put that toward travel and hotel. You are open to returning to Paris for quarterly updates and planning, yes?"

"Absolutely," Nora said. She'd already experienced those meetings, and the whole process lasted four days. Basically, the entire staff came together and brainstormed the direction for the months ahead, with Gisèle leading the meeting. From there, everyone branched out into their own departments, and smaller meetings could definitely be held remotely. "There's nothing I'd love more than to return to Paris."

"Excellent." Gisèle smiled and rose, returning to her desk. "I am pleased you're still with us, Nora."

"I am too," Nora said with a laugh, and rose. "I can't thank you enough for being so understanding. I did not expect that when coming in here."

Gisèle tsked, lifting a perfectly sculpted eyebrow. "Know your worth, ma chérie. You do fine work, and we are lucky to have you." The warmth faded to her no-nonsense stare, which Nora had grown to see and respect over the past week of being in Paris. "Take three days to return home and adjust to the time change. I expect you online after, yes?"

"Yes, of course." She leaned over the desk and offered her hand. "Thank you, Gisèle. I'm very excited to stay on with the company."

Gisèle returned the handshake with a gentle touch. "De rien. À bientôt."

Feeling lighter in her steps than she did on the way to work, she walked the same way back down the street she'd walked this morning toward the hotel, where the company had set her up until she found an apartment.

Walking distance to most iconic monuments and museums, the limestone hotel, built in 1908, and with flower boxes on every window, had been whimsically romantic enough, Nora hadn't yearned to leave. She entered through the revolving doors to the lobby, but only got two steps in when she froze, disbelieving her eyes.

"Beau," she barely managed to say. Maybe she was losing it. "Austin."

Standing next to the angelic statue in the middle of the lobby, wearing their Sunday best, they both turned around. Not a wrinkle to be seen in their button-up shirts and not a rip or scuff in their jeans.

When she looked to Austin's hands, her heart nearly leaped out of her chest. "Are those for me?" she asked him, gesturing to the bouquet of flowers.

"From me and Dad." He nodded, offering them to her with a cute smile. "Dad says when you say sorry to a lady you should bring her flowers."

Tears welled in her eyes, and she could do nothing to stop them. "Ladies do like flowers." She leaned down, kissed the top of his sweet head. "But they like apologies more."

"That's what Dad said too." Austin beamed.

She wiped at the dampness on her cheeks when her gaze met Beau's. Intensity and emotion leaked into the air between them. She'd seen him be many things. The strong cowboy. The tough horse trainer. The sweet gentleman. The rough, determined and sometimes gentle lover. *This* man, the vulnerable one, with his tender eyes, was her favorite.

He took her hand, tugging her into him. "The entire flight here I was deciding what I'd say to you. I tried to think of every way that I could say I'm sorry for how I misjudged you. How I could apologize for being stupid enough to believe that you'd choose the money over kindness when that simply isn't who you are. I could call myself a coward and explain that I ran in fear, but none of it truly matters. I realized midflight that there's nothing I can say that will ever make what I did better. It happened. I got things very wrong."

She exhaled the breath she'd been holding. Even she heard the shaking of her voice. "Well, flying all the way to Paris is a pretty good apology, you know."

His mouth twitched, his stare reaching down and

touching a part of her that was so relieved they were there. "It's a good start," he said, his voice thick with emotion, "but I can do better." He took a step back, cupping Austin's shoulder. "Right, bud?"

Austin grinned from ear to ear. "Right, Dad."

The dream of Paris began drifting away as he lowered to one knee. She wasn't even sure how he reached for the black box, but suddenly she was staring at a pear-shaped diamond ring.

"I can promise you I'll never get it wrong again." Staring up intently at her, with Austin there at his side, he said, "I've tasted love before, and I don't need months or years to know what I feel for you. I knew the moment I met you on that FaceTime call there was something uniquely special about you. Then when I looked into your eyes when you got into my truck during the storm, I was done for. When it comes right down to it, I don't want to spend another day without you."

Tears rushed down her cheeks. "Beau…"

Beau's smile was joyous, and her heart rejoiced at the sight of it. "The past weeks with you have filled me with happiness that I never thought I'd feel again. And that's all because of *you*. I know I'm asking a lot to beg you to move to Devil's Bluffs, but I won't be able to live with myself if I don't try. Because you're it, Nora. You're the woman I want to wake up to every morning and to kiss good night."

He glanced over at his son and nodded. Austin stepped up, taking Nora's hand. "We want you to come live with us, and we don't want you to ever leave again."

She choked on a sob, suddenly feeling like whatever she'd done, whatever she'd been through, had led her to this moment. To her happiness. "You do?"

"Ah, yeah, we do," Austin muttered. He leaned closer to his dad. "Why is she crying?"

Beau's mouth twitched. "I think those are happy tears, son."

Nora laughed through the crying and nodded. "Yes, they're happy tears." She got down onto her knees against the cool, marble floor and cupped Austin's adorable face. "I want to come live you, and I'll never leave again."

Austin's eyes went wide. "Really?"

"Yes, of course, really," she said, gathering him in her arms. He hugged her tight. She'd never known Annie, but she hoped that Austin's mother was looking down on them and smiling. Holding Austin with all her might, Nora made a promise to Annie to love, cherish and guide her son through life.

Nora pressed a final kiss to his forehead, and Beau said, "My turn, buddy." Austin left her arms, and Beau eyes brightened. "I love you, Nora. Pretty sure I loved you from day one. You said you wanted an adventure, so let's have it. Marry me."

"I do want an adventure." She cupped his smoothly shaven face. "Yes, Beau, I'll you marry, but I have one condition."

That sexy brow arched slowly. "What's that, darlin'?"

"Ever since I got on the plane for Devil's Bluffs, I've followed my heart not my head like I've always done, and that led me to you two." She wasn't about to change things up now. "So, let's let the adventure continue and do things the unconventional way."

He chuckled. "With you, Nora, I wouldn't expect the adventure will ever stop." He removed the ring from the box.

She smiled as he slid it into place where it would stay forever. "I love you, cowboy."

"And I'm damn glad for it," he said, gathering her in his arms. Then his mouth met hers, and she fell into the kiss that was more than passion now, it was filled with promise of a happy future, of safety, and of what she had never saw coming—so much love.

She yearned to lean into him, let him deepen the kiss, but she slowly backed away to embrace Austin, who looked rightly grossed out by their kissing. "You know what I want to do more than having an adventure right now?" she asked him.

"What?" Austin asked, laughing as she tickled him.

She stared at Beau then at Austin—toward her future. "I want to go home."

Sixteen

Two weeks had passed since they flew to Paris, and even Beau had a hard time catching up with all that happened. They'd stayed in Paris for a couple days to reroute all of Nora's belongings that were on their way to Paris. The trip had been magical, but Nora had been the most magical part of it all.

Standing on his front porch, he looked out to the empty pastures, the full moon lighting up the sky. It'd been nearly a month now that he had horses in training. But a month he didn't regret and knew his father wouldn't scold him for either. He'd made money for the ranch. A lot of money. This past month was all about what was missing in his life, and he'd never felt so...*whole*.

Rustling against grass sounded behind him. He turned and his chest warmed. "Don't you look sharp," he told Austin.

His son ran up the porch steps, wearing a pair of black jeans and a dark navy blue button-up, with his black cowboy hat and black boots. "Grandma told me I can't sit down, or I'll wrinkle."

Beau laughed, squeezing his son's shoulder. "Probably should listen to her. She's usually right."

"About ready to get this done?"

Glancing over his shoulder, he found his brother exiting the front door. Colter was cleaned up, wearing a white button-up with black jeans. "Yeah, give me a couple minutes, all right?"

"Sure."

Beau looked to Austin. "Stay with Uncle Colter."

"Okay," Austin said, moving to his uncle's side.

Beau headed into the house, spotting Adeline dressed in a long, flowing yellow dress, and his mother wearing a light pink one that stopped at her knees. Quietly, Beau sneaked past them and headed up the stairs, hoping he didn't get stopped on the way.

The door to the bedroom was open, and the moment he stepped across the threshold, his breath caught in his throat.

Nora wore a long white dress that had a slit at the thigh, and a V at the neck, where her cleavage drew his eye. Her hair was in waves along her back, with flowers somehow tucked into the intricate twists holding her hair away from her face.

And that face—Beau couldn't look away. Her makeup was light and shimmering, and she shone with beauty.

Suddenly her eyes met his in the long mirror. "Beau! You're not supposed to see me," she gasped, covering herself with her arms. "Out!"

"I can't do that." He stepped forward, shutting the door behind him. When he looked back at Nora, he saw the color draining from her face.

"Do not break my heart, Beau Ward," she barely managed to say.

"No," he said, rushing forward. "No, it's not that at all. I just needed you to see something."

"Something that couldn't wait until after the wedding?" she asked, aghast.

Realizing he was about to make a mess out of everything, he shook his head, reached into his pocket and pulled out the magazine article he'd stashed in there.

She took it from him. Her eyes widened when she read the headline: "Texas's Hottest Bachelor Is a Bachelor No More. Get the Scoop on His Whirlwind Romance!"

"You gave them your story?" she asked in a squeaky voice.

"No," he countered. "I gave them *our* story."

Nora began blinking rapidly, fanning her face. "If you make me cry and ruin my makeup, I'm going to kill you."

He chuckled, drawing her close to him. "I don't

care if your makeup is ruined. You'll still be the most beautiful woman today."

She fanned her face faster. "That's not helping any."

Again, he laughed, but couldn't help but press his lips to hers before backing away. "I really didn't want to make you cry, but I wanted you to see this article. See how proud I am that you will be my wife."

"Beau, I know that," she said, her eyes searching his. "You didn't have to do this."

"I did have to do this." He gestured to the article with a flick of his chin. "Read it."

She watched him a moment and then gave a slow nod. "Okay." She scanned the article, slowly taking her time with every word like each one mattered to her. "You told them everything. All about Annie. About your loss. Your dad." She lifted her head, surprise glinting in them. "You told them about me? About finding love again?"

He slid his hand across her cheek. "I want the world to know I have you."

Tears welled in her eyes as she laughed softly. "Well, they certainly do now." She placed the article on the dresser and then turned to him again. Her brows rose. "There's more?"

He nodded, moving to the bed. He helped her sit and then knelt, eye to eye with her, holding her hands in his. "I realized when I read the article this morning that I have everything I have ever wanted and more. There is nothing I would change. But I also realized this morning that I have been very lucky and blessed to have had so much love in my life." He paused to carefully choose his words. "I know you said you want to do this the unconventional way, but are you sure this is what you want, Nora?"

"To marry you, yes," she said immediately.

"Damn, I love how fast you said that." He smiled. "But what I mean is, are you sure you want to get married today. Here. In the backyard. Have you not dreamed of having a big wedding? With all your family and your friends there. To celebrate you and me. The whole thing—the rehearsal dinner, the bachelorette, all of it."

She dropped his hands to cover his face with hers. "Why are you asking this?"

"Because I don't want you to miss out," he said, finally voicing the thoughts rattling in his head all day. "I want all your dreams to come true. I want you to have the wedding you've always wanted. I want to give you everything…and then I only want to give you more."

A tear slipped down her cheek. "You have given me it all. All the things I wanted, and everything that I didn't know existed." She squeezed her fingers around his face. "I'm happy. Marrying you tonight is exactly what I want."

"What about your family?" he asked. "I've only met them on FaceTime." And both her parents had been shocked to say the least that she was engaged.

Neither of them knew they were getting married, and Nora had said she'd tell them after the ceremony.

"My parents are not like Adeline's," she said, thick emotion in her voice. "They wouldn't come together and get along for my sake. They would fight. There would be drama. I don't want that." She released his face to grab his hands again. "Every person who matters is here, and that's all that matters to me. I need nothing else." A pause, then a warm smile filled her face. "This is the family I want. This closeness. This love. My parents…their anger toward each other affected me for a long time. I told you when I got on the plane to Devil's Bluffs, I was doing things different. And look what it got me—*you*."

"You won't have regrets?"

"Not a single one," she said. "You love me. I love you. What else do I need?"

"Nothing. Just *us*." He leaned in, pressing his lips on hers and giving her a proper kiss. One that he would never give her in front of his mother.

"What—" Adeline suddenly sputtered. "Beau, you are not supposed to be in here."

Beau chuckled, slowly rising. He raised his hands in surrender. "I'm going. I'm going."

"Shoo, shoo," Adeline said, waving him out of the room.

Before she pushed him out the door, he winked at Nora. "I'll see you out there."

She nodded. "Yes, you will."

Adeline pushed him out of the door, but he heard

her curse. Then, "You cried! Great. Now we have to fix your makeup. Men!"

He laughed to himself on his way down the hallway, but stopped when he met his mother at the end of the staircase.

She frowned at him. "You're breaking tradition."

"It's a silly one anyway," he said. Mom narrowed her eyes, heavy concern in their depths. He kissed her cheek. "Everything's all right. Don't worry."

"Good," Mom said, lifting her chin. "I was preparing to give you some harsh words if you made a mess of this."

"No mess made, promise." He went to step by her. "I'll meet you out there."

Mom suddenly took him into her arms, holding him tight. "I am so proud of you, Beau. For all you've been through. For the son and father you are. For how happy you make Nora. I love you so much."

"I love you too," Beau said.

Mom's voice trembled. "This day would make Annie and your dad very happy."

Beau hugged his mother tight. For all the pain he'd been through, she'd been there right next to him. "You're right, Mom, it would." He kissed her cheek again, and then released her to head back outside.

Once out the backdoor, he spotted Austin and Colter by the trees, as well as the cowboys from the ranch and their partners, as well as the cowboys who worked for Beau. The plan tonight was simple. They'd marry under the moonlight. Then they'd party the night away with drinks and country tunes, a bonfire, and catered appetizers already set up on the deck.

Hoots and hollers led Beau's way to stand next to Colter.

"Ready?" his brother asked.

Beau nodded, placing his hand on Austin's back, guiding him toward the officiant. The crowd settled into two sections leaving a wide opening. The music from the speaker on the deck began filling the night sky, and soon, his mother came out, and then Adeline, taking her spot across from Beau.

Then time slowed to a full stop.

Beau had already seen Nora, but nothing compared to seeing her walking down the aisle to become his wife.

As he stared at her, he felt those around him, both there in life and departed, and he knew as he caught her smile glowing just for him that he was the luckiest guy in the world.

Epilogue

"Noelle Annie, let go of that rope right now," Nora yelled, rushing down the porch steps toward her two-year-old daughter, who was leading a horse.

Beau's laughter drifted over, as he walked around the house, obviously watching his daughter with care.

"This isn't funny," Nora snapped, placing her hands on her hips. "It's dangerous."

"Ah, it's not that dangerous," Beau said, scooping up his little girl and kissing her on the top of her head. "Oakey is a good boy."

"With big feet," Nora said in rebuke. She made it to them quickly and took Noelle from Beau, until she wiggled her way out of Nora's hold.

"Down. Down," Noelle said. Then wobbled her way back over to Oakey. "Horsey."

Beau did a terrible job at hiding his chuckle, looking proudly at his daughter. "Can't help it, darlin', she's got horses in her blood." He scooped up Noelle again and then placed her on the saddle.

Noelle laughed, bouncing up and down in the saddle.

Right then, loud hoof steps sounded behind Nora. She glanced over her shoulder and gasped, covering her eyes with her hands.

Beau burst out laughing. "You'd think after three years you'd be used to country life."

"Tell me when it's over," Nora grumbled.

The thundering hooves became quieter and slower and then stopped all together.

"You can look now," Beau said, amusement heavy in his voice.

Nora peaked through her eyes, finding Austin smiling from ear to ear, atop a gray horse. "Why are you smiling?" she asked firmly. "You are in so much trouble. You were going way too fast."

Ten-year-old, Austin smirked. "Going fast is fun, Mom."

Her heart did a full squeeze whenever he called her "Mom." She wasn't sure she'd ever not feel amazed by it. Austin hadn't asked her if it was all right to address her that way, and she hadn't asked him to call her that. One day he'd just called her *mom*. She had hugged him tight, and the rest was history. Loving her family with her whole heart aside, Nora turned to Beau with a frown. "This is all you."

"Yup," he said with a proud smile.

Before Nora could somehow remind them all of the recent injuries she'd bandaged up, the sound of gravel-crunching tires suddenly filled the air. Nora glanced over her shoulder, spotting a taxi driving up the driveway.

"Oh, she's here," Nora quipped.

When the taxi finally pulled to a stop near the porch, a slender, dark-haired woman with a warm complexion exited. "Mom," Nora managed to say.

"Hi, sweetie," Mom called with a wave.

Everything had changed since Nora married Beau. Neither of her parents were upset they weren't at the wedding. Likely because neither of them valued marriage. Both said they just wanted her happy, and glowingly happy she was. Though the biggest change came when they both met Austin, on separate occasions, of course. And that didn't both Nora one bit. Her visits with her parents were wonderful and filled with happiness.

It turned out that while her parents weren't great parents, they were incredible grandparents. Her mother came at least every couple months for weekend visits. Her father called a few times a week and visited as often as his job would allow.

The taxi driver put the bags on the driveway, as Mom made kissing noises, holding out her arms to Noelle on the horse. "Give me that darling girl."

Beau scooped her off the horse and then set her down, so Noelle could wobble her way over to her grandmother's arms.

"Oh, how you've grown, my sweet girl," Mom said. After she attacked Noelle's face with a fit of kisses, sending Noelle laughing hysterically, Mom headed over to Austin, who'd dismounted from his horse. "Your sister isn't the only one who's grown. Good grief. How are you this tall?"

Austin smiled. "Hi, Nan, it's good to see you." Somehow, she held on to both of them, hugging them tight.

Beau smiled with warmth, coming over to Nora, wrapping his arms around her and resting his chin on her shoulder. He'd asked her once if it bothered her that whenever her parents showed up they went straight to her children and not to herself, but she still felt the same. She loved seeing their happiness. Nothing mattered above all else.

The competition for love was no longer a competition.

"Oh," Mom suddenly said as if reading Nora's mind. She put down Noelle, who wobbled over to Beau, and opened her arms to Nora. "I can't leave you two out either."

Nora stepped in her mother's arms, falling into her warm embrace. "It's good to see you, Mom."

"Good to see you too." Mom kissed both cheeks and then took Beau into a hug. Until the taxi door suddenly opened, and Mom stepped away and blushed. "I meant to tell you before, but well... I..."

"You must be Nora." A man in his sixties strode up, offering his hand. "I'm Jacob Grimshaw, your mother's boyfriend."

Nora slowly looked at her mom with raised brows. "Boyfriend?"

"Well, yes, we have been dating for quite some time now," she said sheepishly.

Jacob slid his arm around her mother, drawing her close. "We thought it time we meet each other's children."

Nora blinked rapidly. Her mother never dated. Didn't she hate men?

Beau chuckled, offering his hand. "Good to meet you, Jacob. I'm Beau, Nora's husband."

"Ah," Jacob said, returning the handshake. "Good to meet you, Beau."

The front door opened and Beverly came out first. Happiness radiated on her face. Nora knew how much Beverly lost when her husband died, but she was carrying on with life with grace, with strength, finding a new happiness in her family and her grandchildren, and learning a new joyful way forward.

A heavily pregnant Adeline followed, waddling out of the door. She held on to Colter's hand, looking a second away from giving birth to her and Colter's first child. She waved to Nora's mom and eyed Jacob with curiosity brimming in her eyes.

Nora was right there with her.

"Dinner is up," Beverly called, ringing the bell.

"Come," Nora said to Jacob and her mom. "You haven't had a good meal yet if you haven't tasted Beverly's chicken, biscuits and gravy, and then you can tell me everything about yourself Jacob and just how long you've been dating my mother."

Mom's blush deepened as she scooped Noelle from Beau's arms, talking sweet words to her the whole way up the porch steps.

Austin took their luggage from the taxi driver, heading for the front door, dragging their suitcase behind him.

"You should probably pick your mouth up off the floor," Beau said with a laugh.

Nora turned to him. "Boyfriend," she gasped. "She has a boyfriend."

"Looks like it," Beau agreed with nod.

Nora blinked. "I don't even know what to say."

"Don't say anything, darlin," he said, pressing a light kiss to her mouth. "Look around you. That's what happens with people who come to Devil's Bluffs. They fall in love."

She looked out to her gift of a son, Austin, her mom, pregnant Adeline, Colter hugging her, Beverly watching on with happiness shining her eyes, and then to her sweet Noelle, and finally up to Beau, the man who made her believe in love again. "You're right—they do."

* * * * *

HARLEQUIN
PLUS

Try the best multimedia subscription service for romance readers like you!

Read, Watch and Play.

Experience the easiest way to get the romance content you crave.

Start your **FREE TRIAL** at
www.harlequinplus.com/freetrial.